Praise for the Roxane Weary series:

"Building to a chilling and surprising conclusion, the third book in Lepionka's Shamus Award–winning series is both intricately plotted and character-driven, with a complicated protagonist."
—*Library Journal* on *The Stories You Tell*

"Entertaining. Fans of plucky female detectives will look forward to Roxane's further adventures."
—*Publishers Weekly* on *The Stories You Tell*

"Don't think *I'll read a few pages before I go to sleep*. It won't work. Keeping pace, Lepionka's third Roxane Weary novel will keep you wide-eyed and transfixed."
—*Lavender* magazine on *The Stories You Tell*

"Kristen Lepionka and Roxane Weary are the best things to happen to the genre in years."
—Laura Lippman, *New York Times* bestselling author on *What You Want to See*

"That rare and precious thing—a sequel as good as—or even better than—the outstanding first in the series. It's wise, knowing, propulsive, and perfectly pitched. Lepionka is a major new talent."
—Lee Child, #1 *New York Times* bestselling author on *What You Want to See*

"Lepionka is setting a high standard for crime fiction with the complex Roxane Weary at its heart."
—*Booklist* (starred review) on *What You Want to See*

"Roxane is a wonderfully complex character. . . . This is a remarkably accomplished debut mystery, with sensitive character development and a heart-stopping denouement."

—*Booklist* (starred review) on *The Last Place You Look*

"Introducing a fascinating protagonist who combats her emotional demons with the aid of sugar, booze, and sex, this suspenseful, original, and confident debut will please fans of the hardboiled PI genre."

—*Library Journal* (starred review) on *The Last Place You Look*

"Twisty . . . That Roxane has an alarming habit of diving headfirst into dangerous situations only makes her more fascinating. Fans will no doubt look forward to her next case."

—*Publishers Weekly* on *What You Want to See*

"Action-packed . . . Lepionka has created an appealing, relatable lead."

—*Publishers Weekly* on *The Last Place You Look*

"Lepionka reboots the thriller genre with her troubled hero, Roxane Weary. . . . I have never read a more confident debut."

—James Renner, author of *True Crime Addict* and *The Man From Primrose Lane* on *The Last Place You Look*

"Utterly superb—I can't remember when I last read such an expertly written and perfectly constructed book that gave me so much pure reading pleasure."

—Sophie Hannah, author of *Closed Casket* and *The Monogram Murders* on *The Last Place You Look*

"Just when you think the PI novel is dead, Kristen Lepionka brings it roaring back to life. Roxane Weary is a richly drawn protagonist who proves that 'hardboiled' and 'feminine' aren't mutually exclusive. This book is so good it makes me jealous."

—Rob Hart, author of *New Yorked* and
City of Rose and associate publisher at
Mysterious Press on *The Last Place You Look*

"A beautifully written mystery, one I devoured in a single sitting, late into the night. I'll now follow detective Roxane Weary anywhere: into her hopes and fears, into her past, and—especially—into danger. An extraordinary debut novel."

—Christopher Coake, author of
You Came Back on *The Last Place You Look*

"Kristen Lepionka spins a twisting, turning, enticing tale that keeps the reader guessing and turning pages to find out what happens next. . . . A promising first novel by a remarkable talent and you won't be disappointed if you look here first."

—*The Oklahoman* on *The Last Place You Look*

Also by Kristen Lepionka

The Last Place You Look
What You Want to See

The Stories You Tell

A ROXANE WEARY MYSTERY

Kristen Lepionka

Minotaur Books

New York

Published in the United States by Minotaur Books, an imprint of St. Martin's Publishing Group

THE STORIES YOU TELL. Copyright © 2019 by Kristen Lepionka. All rights reserved. Printed in the United States of America. For information, address St. Martin's Publishing Group, 120 Broadway, New York, NY 10271.

www.minotaurbooks.com

The Library of Congress has cataloged the hardcover edition as follows:

ISBN 978-1-250-30935-8 (hardcover)
ISBN 978-1-250-62145-0 (trade paperback)
ISBN 978-1-250-30936-5 (ebook)

Our books may be purchased in bulk for promotional, educational, or business use. Please contact your local bookseller or the Macmillan Corporate and Premium Sales Department at 1-800-221-7945, extension 5442, or by email at MacmillanSpecialMarkets@macmillan.com.

First Minotaur Books Edition: 2019
First Minotaur Books Paperback Edition: 2020

10 9 8 7 6 5 4 3 2 1

For Joanna,

my guiding star

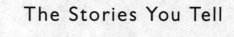

The Stories You Tell

ONE

I could never sleep at Catherine's house, and it made no sense. Everything about her bedroom was engineered to combat insomnia—from the cool French linen sheets to the plush king-size mattress to the blackout curtains—but none of it worked on me. I could never relax there, never quite felt at home somehow. Maybe I missed the nocturnal rustling of people in the alley that ran the length of my own apartment on the edge of downtown, the creaks and sighs of the century-old building, the coppery streetlights that shone straight through my cheap mini blinds. Not even Catherine's soft, even breath beside me was enough to lull me into unconsciousness when I stayed over—she was really miles away, cocooned in a satin eye mask and the chemical white noise of Ambien, and I was alone with the starless ceiling, my thoughts, and the kind of silence that only existed in ritzy neighborhoods and, I assumed, death.

The three o'clock hour was usually when I gave up and went home; we'd known each other long enough for that not to mean anything, and maybe it was even better that way, neither of us exactly being morning people. I kind of liked the streets of Bexley in the middle of the night. The giant houses all dark and silent, the traffic lights flashing yellow. But some nights, like tonight, I just lay there and tried to wait it out. Trading the warm bed for the mid-January temperatures outside was hardly appealing.

But then my phone rang.

The tuneless vibration from the floor startled me. Catherine gave a soft sigh and shifted on her pillow but didn't wake up. I swung my legs out from under the covers, cringing at the chill as I grabbed my jeans and felt for the pocket. I found the phone just as the buzzing stopped and I saw my brother's name lit up on the screen.

It wasn't the first time he'd ever called me in the middle of the night.

The last time had been the night my father died.

I went into the guest bedroom and called Andrew back. He answered halfway through the first ring. "Roxane," he said, his voice tense. "Are you busy?"

"It's the middle of the night," I said, "so no." Through the window, I could see that the street was already blanched white with falling snow.

"Well, I didn't know."

I sat down on the futon next to Catherine's open suitcase, half-full of clothes for her impending trip to Rhode Island. "What's up?"

Andrew cleared his throat. "Something really weird just happened. Maybe bad-weird. I'm not sure."

I leaned forward, elbows on my knees. "What, Andrew?"

"This girl I know—woman—Roxane, shit, I'm getting another call. Can you just come over here? Please?"

"Andrew," I said again, but he'd already hung up.

A few years ago, Andrew bought an apartment on the eastern side of Italian Village, where it was still mostly vacant lots and fixer-upper doubles. Now it was dotted with high-end residential buildings for young professionals who wanted their luxury bath fittings with a side of street crime, or at least uncertainty. My brother could probably sell his place now for twice what he'd paid for it back then, maybe more, but he liked it there. Not least because said young professionals needed to buy weed from somebody, and it might as well be from him. I punched his code into the keypad by the door and went in. It was Thursday morning or Wednesday night, depending on your mood. The lobby was empty and quiet and the elevator doors stood open as if they'd been waiting for me. I rode to the second floor and barely had a chance to knock before Andrew yanked his door open, like he'd been waiting for me too.

I said, "You can't just call like that and not say what's going on—"

But I stopped talking when I got a look at him. At the long, puffy scratch on his jaw and the side of his neck, ragged and pink.

I started over. "Are you okay?"

He nodded, but he didn't say anything—just fumbled with a pack of cigarettes and a lighter. That was how I knew he really wasn't okay. Andrew never smoked in the apartment, only on the balcony. A holdover from growing up with my father's rules: no cigarettes indoors. I studied him. His usual dapper bad-boy aesthetic was not in evidence. His hair, dark like mine and collar-length, was matted and greasy and he wore a faded black T-shirt with sweatpants, all of which told me he'd been asleep somewhat recently. My eyes flicked toward the closed bedroom door, but he shook his head.

"No one else is here."

"What about the *girl* you were talking about?"

"She's gone."

I waited.

"It's not like that. I was sleeping, okay? She rang the buzzer and I let her in."

"Who is she?"

"Addison, I think her name is."

"You think."

"When I worked at the Sheraton, she was on the banquet staff for a hot second. I didn't know her that well. But she'd, you know, been here. Once before."

"How old is this girl?"

"Twenty-five, I guess."

"Christ, Andrew."

"Look, that's not the point. The point is, she came here and rang the buzzer, and she sounded upset. So I let her in. She got up here and she was a wreck. Crying, shaking, no coat. She wanted to use my phone. I asked her what was wrong, but she didn't want to tell me. I even asked her if she needed a doctor, she was shaking so much. But she said no, no ambulance, no police. She just used my phone to make a call, just one call, but whoever it was didn't answer. She left this whispered message. I couldn't really understand what she was saying. So I gave her a sweatshirt and I was fixing her a drink, and it seemed like she was calming down, like maybe she would tell me what was going on. But then something spooked her and she got up and started to run out."

"Was she injured at all?" I asked, thinking maybe a car accident on the slippery streets.

"No."

"Under the influence?"

"No. I don't know. I mean, you can't always tell."

"What spooked her?"

He dragged hard on his cigarette and tapped a grey column of ash into the sink. "Not sure."

"Okay, and the scratch?"

"I grabbed her arm. Which, I know. I shouldn't have."

"When she tried to leave?"

Andrew's face was lined with worry. "Yeah. I just—obviously something was wrong. And it's the middle of the night, plus the weather? It was a reflex. Like, to stop her from leaving, because she shouldn't be wandering around the city like that. So I grabbed her arm. She screamed and we—she—she was shouting for me to let go, so I did."

"And she just left?"

He dropped his cigarette into the sink, the ember sizzling against the wet basin. "I followed her into the hall," he said, "and she jumped into the elevator. By the time I ran down the steps, she was gone." He laughed humorlessly. "I tried looking at the footprints in the snow, like to see where she went. But you know there are drunk assholes wandering around at all hours down here. So that was useless. But something wasn't right. I don't know what, but something was not right."

"Did you call the police?"

"I called you."

"I'm not the police, Andrew."

He leaned his elbows onto the counter and dropped his head between his forearms. "I didn't. She said not to call anyone. She said that. And, you know."

I nodded. He had weed in the apartment, and while most cops wouldn't care about a little bit of weed, Andrew probably had enough to constitute *intent to distribute*. But that didn't exactly matter, not compared to what might be going on with Addison. "We can call Tom," I said. I got out my phone and started scrolling. Tom Heitker was a homicide detective and had been my father's partner before he died. Now I considered him a close friend, though my brothers had never liked him much.

Still facing the counter, Andrew sighed. "Tom. No."

"Either that, or take your chances with whoever gets dispatched here. You need to call the police. You should've called them first."

"And say what?"

"Exactly what you said to me."

"That this girl who may or may not be named Addison showed

up here three years after I slept with her—one time—and she was hysterical and crying and she scratched me and then left?"

My thumb hovered over Tom's name on my phone. "How sure are you that her name's even Addison?"

"It was something like that. Addison, or Madison? Maddy? Rox, I called you because it was strange, and I just want to make sure she's all right. I tried reaching out to a few folks from the Sheraton, but so far no one remembers her. That's why I hung up on you, by the way. A dude from the hotel was calling."

"But he didn't have anything?"

"No."

"What about the number she called?"

"It goes straight to voice mail. The greeting is just that robot voice reading the number."

"So you essentially have zero information about her."

"Exactly. So there's no point in calling the police, even if she *hadn't* told me not to."

I wasn't sold on that yet, but I put my phone down. "What do you expect me to do?"

"If anyone can figure out what's going on with her, it would be you."

I shook my head. "I appreciate the vote of confidence but the best thing to do is probably to call the police and get them on the look-out for her."

But even as I said it, I wondered if that was the right call. The police wouldn't have more information than I did, but they *would* have less time. Other things to do. And if Addison was in some kind of trouble, it might be the sort that she didn't want help from the cops getting out of. My brother wasn't looking at me, though. He was looking down at my phone, the screen of which had gone dark.

I said, "What aren't you telling me?"

He dropped his eyes to the floor.

I folded my arms over my chest. "Andrew, you're my brother, and I love you. But I need to know what happened. Right now."

Finally he said, "I told you what happened. Tonight, everything happened like I said. But here's the thing. She and I . . . it was only twice."

"Twice." I folded my arms over my chest. "You said once."

"It was only once here, and once at the hotel. And here's the thing, it didn't end that great. She got me fired."

Now it was my turn to slump on the counter. "Why?"

"She thought it was a more serious thing, her and me. It wasn't, that was never going to happen. She didn't take it well. She told management that I was selling weed from the bar. And that was that, really. I hadn't seen her or heard from her since then."

"So why'd she come here tonight? If you're just someone she went crazy ex-girlfriend on a few years ago?"

My brother looked at me. His eyes, bluish-grey like mine, were anxious but honest. I saw that he was telling me the whole truth this time. He said, "I have absolutely no idea. It makes me think she's *really* in trouble, if she'd come here after all that."

There was an unspoken ugliness in the air—that the police would listen to his story, take one look at the scratch on his neck, and assume the worst of him.

I nodded. "Fine. I'll try."

TWO

At home, I made a cup of tea while my computer booted up, a strange sense of déjà vu taking hold of me. Andrew, calling with bad news. It had been a cold morning just like this when my father died—in fact, it was almost two years to the day. Last year, to mark the first anniversary, the police department had put together a prayer service and we all knew how to act. But the two-year anniversary loomed up ahead, dark and shapeless and unspoken.

I pushed the thought out of my mind and sat down at my desk with my tea. I started with the phone number she had called from Andrew's phone, but it went directly to the voice mail greeting robot voice announcing the digits of the number I had just dialed. A quick search around the number turned up nothing either. Then I switched gears to see what I could uncover about Maybe Addison Something herself. It should've been harder than it was. But living in the modern world meant latent traces of a person all over the place—social media tags, online petitions, user names, it all told a story that was alarmingly easy to follow if someone wasn't careful. After noodling around on LinkedIn for a while, looking at people who had listed the Sheraton as their employer, there she was: Addison Stowe. She had dark reddish-brown hair, wide brown eyes, generally my brother's type: a small silver stud in her nose and a pair of feathery earrings dangling from her earlobes. Her build was the heavier side of medium, and she smiled like she had a secret.

Her job at the hotel had been "catering associate" and she'd left a year earlier, and either hadn't bothered to update her LinkedIn page since or hadn't gotten another job yet. Her Facebook and Instagram profiles were set to private so there wasn't anything for me to see there beyond the same photo from LinkedIn. But that was fine; all I needed was her name in order to get an address.

It turned out to be a shambling yellow half-double on California Ave., near where it dead-ended into the river. The street, already narrow, was even tighter with cars parked on either side and clogged with snow that hadn't been cleared from the last storm. My boots crunched as I climbed the slippery front steps. The hope was that she'd answer the door, tell me everything was fine, maybe even be a little pissed at the interference, and then we'd all go about our day with the matter squarely behind us. I rang the doorbell and I listened; the house was emptily silent.

I peered through the slats of the mini blinds in the window next to the front door and saw a darkened room with an old, puffy couch and berber carpet and a television atop an entertainment stand packed with the trappings of modern life—DVR, stereo, multiple video game consoles. The other half of the double was similarly quiet, though its blinds were pulled firm.

Stepping off the porch, I looked down the alley between Addison's unit and the apartment building beside it. The snow there was deep—at least eight inches, thanks to Ohio's semiweekly winter storms—and muddled with footprints, lots of them. I added my own to the pattern and moved quietly to the back of the house.

The fenced backyard was long and narrow, like mine. The snow was mostly undisturbed except for a scuffed path from the alley to the back of the duplex. A set of slippery wooden steps led to a tiny screened-in sunporch. Beside them, a dimple in the snow, a length of dirty garden hose, an oscillating sprinkler.

It definitely wasn't sprinkler weather.

I picked it up. Why would someone have gotten this out at this time of year? On closer inspection, the rest of the hose was still under the porch, but someone had been digging at the snow to get to the sprinkler. I flipped it over and saw a flap of duct tape stuck to the side with an outline of a house key on it.

I had to give somebody credit—that was a decent hiding place for a spare key. I wondered if Addison had been here this morning already, or if the sprinkler had been unearthed by someone else.

I looked around, still didn't see anybody nearby, and tried the screen door; it was unlocked. The porch was barely three feet square, a sloping deck with a piece of green Astroturf covering the slats. Three bins stood along one side of it with corresponding signs taped to the wall above them: TRASH, RECYCLE, COMPOST. Next to the back door that led into the house, there was a pair of ankle boots, corduroy, soaked through from bottom to top, and a lump of grey fabric. I picked it up with a gloved finger; an Ohio State hoodie, damp and very cold.

I took out one of my business cards and wrote *Andrew's sister* on the back and underlined it. *Call if you need anything.*

I tucked it between the door and the frame.

I had other things to do. I did. Not necessarily better, but other. For example, I had to go check my new post office boxes—plural—to see if any of the four had received packages in the past few days. It was as thrilling as it sounded. I'd been hired by the owner of Spin-Spo, a viral women's apparel startup whose leggings and sports bras, supposedly unparalleled in their quality and fit, were being knocked off by a competitor and sold in a variety of online stores. Unsuspecting consumers had taken to social media to complain about the sharp decrease in quality, and Gail Spinnaker was sick of it. I was to figure out where the knockoffs were coming from, something that was impossible to tell from simply studying the online listings because it turns out most photographs of black leggings look the same.

Gail Spinnaker was an energetic, rigid blonde, barely thirty but already quite successful, if success was to be measured by people's eagerness to rip you off. A few weeks earlier, I'd gone to the Spin-Spo office by the airport to discuss the drama. She'd made the dingy warehouse space surprisingly cheery with patterned rugs and painted murals on the cinder block walls. One was even in progress when I got there—a young lady with a shaved head and tattoos from her chin on down was inking multicolored flowers over a stark black-and-white typographical piece in the small lobby. O MORE THAN JUST BE was all that was still visible.

"You know how they say necessity is the mother of invention?" Gail was saying in her office, which was just a corner of the warehouse with a curtain separating her desk from the row of floor-to-ceiling bins that contained the brand's styles sorted by color and size. "Well, that's really true. I wasn't happy with the performance apparel on the market, so I dusted off my sewing machine and started making my own."

She paused for effect like she was delivering a PowerPoint presentation. I could almost picture the backdrop behind her fading to the next slide.

"Now I have a team of twenty women who construct each piece for me, here in the warehouse. Could we do it in some factory in China? Sure. But I'm very big on supporting the local economy, supporting the community of working women in central Ohio. The business has grown literally more than a hundred percent in the last year, thanks to some very key partnerships on Instagram, so I definitely couldn't keep up with the demand on my own!"

I knew all of this already. I'd done my homework on Gail and the company before coming here. She was going to pay me for my time regardless, but I wasn't inclined to sit through her keynote address before we got to the good stuff.

"But back to the knockoffs," I said. "Any idea where these are coming from?"

"No. The problem is, we sell direct through our website, but also wholesale through performance apparel and athleisure boutiques. So there are a lot of places where people can get SpinSpo. The real SpinSpo. But the fake stuff is coming from somewhere, and I need to know where."

"Do you sell on Amazon?"

She scoffed. "No."

"Do any of your wholesalers?"

"I don't know."

"I did see a lot of SpinSpo products for sale on—"

"Apparel," Gail said.

"What?"

"I hate the word *product*. We call it apparel."

"Um, okay. SpinSpo apparel is for sale on Amazon for a whole range of prices, starting around twenty bucks, so—"

"I'm not talking about people who are buying knockoffs on purpose. Frankly, I could care less."

I declined to correct her misuse of that phrase the way she'd chastised me about *products*. Instead I just raised my eyebrows.

"I mean," she said, "SpinSpo offers a perfect fit, microsizing, performance fabrics with amazing recovery, and all of that on the cutting edge of fashion. Our leggings retail for ninety dollars, for a *reason*. Ninety-dollar leggings are not going to go for twenty dollars. Anyone with a brain should know that. It's like the people who buy knockoff Louis Vuitton from a street corner in Midtown Manhattan. They don't do it because they think it's real. They do it because they like the bag, they like that for one hot second under not very intense scrutiny, someone might see it and think they're the type of person who owns the real deal. When the straps fall off after three weeks, what are they going to say? *I'm so mad that this obvious knockoff that I paid about ten percent of what it's worth for isn't made well*? No. They chuck it and move on. I'm not worried about that. What really worries me is that someone might be spending ninety dollars expecting to get the quality that we're proud to offer our clients, but getting something worthless instead."

So Gail Spinnaker was not the most sympathetic character I'd ever met, or worked for. But she wasn't the least. She explained her idea to me thus:

She wanted me to order purported SpinSpo merchandise from any store that claimed to sell it, have it shipped to one of a few post office boxes I'd need to open to cover my tracks, such as they were, then catalog the leggings' authenticity or lack thereof, and narrow down the source of the knockoffs that way.

"Why not follow up on the social media posts complaining about the leggings?" I suggested. "Instead, or in addition to. Or did you try that?"

Gail glared at me. "If someone thinks that a brand ripped them off, they'll be too angry to answer honestly. But whatever you think will get to the bottom of it. We're planning a huge event this spring, a major new launch, plus we're a founding sponsor of Columbus's first women's wellness lifestyle expo, and I really want to be out from under this dark cloud by then."

A mystery with a deadline—what could go wrong? But I agreed because the winter had been too shitty for there to be any new puzzles to solve in the city. I wasn't complaining about that—the second a single snowflake melted, people would be raging at each other in full force once again—but it left me with more time on my hands than anyone with an overactive imagination and a tendency toward pessimism should have.

So I'd spent two grand of Gail's money on authentic SpinSpo product in this way, buying from boutique websites, having them shipped to my four new post office boxes; no knockoffs yet. But my client had authorized five times that in expenses, so there I was. My apartment was beginning to look like the wardrobe department of a very basic movie.

I picked up a small box at the post office on Mount Vernon, and two flat padded envelopes from the Mail Boxes Etc. in Whitehall, somehow managing to wait until I got back to my apartment to tear into the packages. Three pairs of leggings in varying shades of black—onyx, ebony, and anthracite—but all with the genuine SpinSpo embroidered squiggle on the back of the left hip.

"The case continues," I said to the apartment. I hung the leggings up on a rolling garment rack I'd purchased at IKEA and entered each style in a spreadsheet—quickly, so that I didn't pass out from boredom before I finished it—while my mind wandered back to Addison Stowe. I was still thinking about the sprinkler, the boots, the sweatshirt.

I called my brother to ask what kind of sweatshirt he'd given her.

"Um, I don't know, I guess it was grey?"

"Ohio State?"

"Like I own an Ohio State sweatshirt."

"Come on. I'm sure Mom's given you at least three Ohio State sweatshirts."

"I don't know. I grabbed one out of the closet. I wasn't really thinking about which one."

"A pullover, or a hoodie?"

"Hoodie."

"But it was definitely grey?"

"Yeah."

"Dark grey, light grey?"

"Roxane, I don't know. Why?"

I sighed. "Do you remember what kind of shoes she was wearing?"

"Boots. Ankle boots. Brown, I think."

"Made of?"

"I didn't ask to see the tag. I don't know. Why are you asking about her clothes? Did you find something out?"

"No."

Just more questions.

I drove back to her place. I wanted another look at the hoodie and the shoes. Maybe these were proof that she'd made it home okay on her own, that there was no reason to be worried.

The backyard was as I'd left it. I went into the enclosed porch and snapped a quick photo of the items in question.

Then I heard someone undoing the dead bolt.

The woman who opened the door a crack and peered out at me was not Addison Stowe.

"Uh, can I help you?" she said.

"Is Addison home?" I said, trying for friendly.

"This isn't the front door, you know."

"Sorry. But is she at home?

She shook her head. She was younger than Addison, barely twenty. She had curly blond hair and wore a preppy green cable-knit sweater. "I don't think so. Hey," she said, calling over her shoulder, "Addy, are you home?" Silence followed. "No."

"Are you her roommate?"

Nod.

"Have you talked to her this morning?"

The young woman shook her head again. "Why?"

"I just wanted to make sure she was okay."

"What do you mean?"

It was a long story, so I summarized: "Just wanted to make sure she got home safe last night."

"Well," the roommate said, seemingly familiar with that type of explanation, "it smells like she got home safe enough to burn her eggs this morning, as usual, so I'm sure she's fine."

Now that she mentioned the burned eggs, I could smell it in the air wafting out of the kitchen. "Well, okay." I glanced down at the doorknob; the business card I'd left a few hours ago was gone. "Maybe she's at work?"

"Maybe?" She looked down at her watch and frowned. "She's never home."

"Do you know where that is?"

"Not really—look, I need to go—"

"Is she still working at the Sheraton?" I tried. I knew she wasn't but I hoped that throwing out a detail like that would make the roommate more inclined to share something useful with me.

"The Sheraton? No, she's, like, a deejay or something now."

"A deejay, like on the radio?"

"No, like at a nightclub."

"Which one?"

"One night here, one night there. But she has a deejay name, it's funny, like a fruit or something? But it's some nickname? Oh—it's *radish*. But with two *d*s."

"DJ Raddish?"

She nodded.

"Does Addison have a car?"

Something hesitant entered her expression. "Who are you, again?"

I told her who I was and produced another card. She took it from me and studied it, her eyes narrowing in a clear WTF expression. "This is super weird. A private investigator now?"

The way she said *now* made me think that I wasn't the first person to come around looking for Addison recently. "Has there been someone else asking for her?"

The roommate sighed. "There was this guy a few days ago. Or a week, I guess. A cop. I told him, just like I told you, she's never home."

"A cop?"

She nodded.

"What did he want?"

"To talk to Addison, but she wasn't here."

"Did he come back?"

"Not while I was here."

"Did he ever talk to her?"

"How would I know that?"

"Okay, do you remember his name?"

Her mouth twisted slightly as she considered that. "No, but I think—hang on." She stepped away from the door and studied the front of the refrigerator and plucked something off. "Here," she said, thrusting the card at me. "This is him. I told her about it but she was like, whatever, okay. That's her usual speed. Now, I really need to go."

"If you see her, can you give me a call?"

The roommate made a noncommittal noise and closed the door in my face.

THREE

The card belonged to one Michael Dillman, a sergeant in the investigative subdivision. A phone number was written on the card in a haphazard scrawl.

I got back in the car and cranked up the heated seats. The car was new, or new-to-me, anyway: a black Range Rover with champagne-colored interior that I'd picked up at a police auction after I'd gotten the bad news about my beloved old blue 300D Mercedes last summer; the car accident I'd been in had bent its frame so severely, there wasn't any hope. It had died a noble death, absorbing most of the impact so that the damage to me was limited to a touch of whiplash and a nasty cut on my neck from the seat belt. But I still wasn't sure how I felt about the Range Rover. Although it was a couple of years old, it was still packed with new-fangled features that seemed wholly unnecessary to someone who'd been driving a car older than I was. But in the dead of winter, the heated leather seats were damn nice.

I studied Michael Dillman's business card and dialed the number written in ink. The line rang three times before kicking over to voice mail. "You've reached Mickey Dillman," a gruff voice said in my ear. "Leave me a message and I just might call you back."

I left my name and number and turned my attention to the information printed on the card.

The direct-dial number under Dillman's name rang and rang and rang, which was weird enough, since city phone lines were generally nestled in a web of voice mail boxes or central receptionists. So it was unusual that one would just ring uninterrupted. Finally, someone picked up, quizzically. "Homicide?"

"Um," I said, not expecting that, "is Sergeant Dillman available?"

"What's this regarding?"

"I'd just like to speak to him—is this his number?"

"This is nobody's number, sweetheart. You called an empty desk."

I frowned. "So Sergeant Dillman is—"

"Hang on."

The phone clunked down.

I waited, definitely curious now.

After a minute, the line beeped in my ear and started ringing again.

"Columbus Division of Police, Professional Standards Bureau," a woman answered.

"Hi, I'm trying to reach Sergeant Michael Dillman—"

"Please hold."

I waited again. Maybe the third time would be a charm?

But no—this time the line delivered me to the voice mail box of "Acting R and D Sergeant Greene."

I hung up, not sure what any of that was supposed to mean but distinctly *not* feeling any better about the situation. Burnt eggs were evidence of nothing. A random visit from a cop was evidence of nothing—maybe Addison had lost an engraved, platinum watch in a Laundromat and he just wanted to return it to her. Unless Sergeant Michael Dillman wasn't a cop anymore.

———

I took a deeper dive into Addison's existence. She drove a maroon Scion coupe, in which she'd been cited for failure to yield nine months ago. I scanned the records for Dillman's name, but didn't see it. That was the extent of the court records on her name. I moved on to her deejaying career; DJ Raddish had a Facebook page with just under a hundred "likes." This one was public, but contained few updates; the last was from the previous October, when she had posted a flyer for a roller-disco fund-raiser at the Skate Zone off of I-71. I clicked on her Events tab; the only thing listed there was a traffic party for the upcoming Valentine's Day at a club called Nightshade. Because what was more romantic than a themed hookup night at a club named for a poisonous plant? In the Past Events section, I saw a few other holiday-themed dance parties, also at Nightshade: Christmas Sucks! and 24 Hours of New Year's Eve. I leaned back in my desk chair. Now that I'd completed my mailbox run, I truly *didn't* have anything better to do. Which meant that the mystery of DJ Raddish was the only thing I had going on at the moment. The name Nightshade was vaguely familiar to me. I remembered hearing about it in the context of a certain type of nightclub with dirt-cheap well drinks and periodic appearances in the news when fights broke out. I opened a new browser tab to find out where it was located.

"Huh," I said out loud.

The club was across the street from my brother's loft.

I called him again. "Do you know anything about the club across the street, Nightshade?"

"Why?"

"Do you?"

"Not exactly my scene," he said. "It got shut down a while back for serving underage kids—they never carded anyone, I guess, so it got a reputation as that kind of place. Self-perpetuating cycle. But that was, I don't know, more than a year ago. I heard it was reopening, or maybe it already did."

"I think Addison deejays there."

"Really."

"Seems that way."

"So it's open again?"

"Unless she's dropping beats for an empty room, yes."

"Dropping beats?"

"Is that not what the kids are saying these days?"

"I don't know any kids. What else did you find out?"

"She always eats burnt eggs for breakfast."

"That definitely seems like a clue."

"I know."

"Anything else?"

"Her roommate said some cop was looking for her a few days ago."

"Why?"

"I don't know. From the roommate's attitude, it seems like it's always something with Addison."

"That sounds about right."

Neither of us said anything for a while.

"Are we being ridiculous here?"

I sighed. "No, this truly seems weird. I might try to check out Nightshade later."

"Good idea."

"What's even *in* Rhode Island?"

Following dinner at Lindy's, Catherine and I were in her bed. Or, rather, I was in her bed, and she was going back and forth between her walk-in closet and her dresser and the open suitcase that had been relocated from the guest room to the corner of Catherine's bed. My sense of uneasiness had been temporarily pushed back by dinner and sex but I could feel it creeping up again. "Catherine."

"I told you," she said. Then she paused, lost in thought over two black dresses.

I cleared my throat.

She looked up and smiled before tossing them both into the suitcase. For a short trip, it was a rather large suitcase, and it was getting rather full. "It's a conference. About art and education. At RISD."

She said it *ris-dee*, like it was all one word.

"Don't go."

"I have to go. They put me on a panel. I'm *expected*."

I snaked an arm out from under the covers for my whiskey. I was drinking it neat tonight—it was too cold out to consider ice cubes. "I still don't think that's a good excuse."

"You've made your objections known."

I watched her as she disappeared into the closet and returned a moment later with an armful of dresses in bold prints. Right now, she was wearing just a T-shirt, white, that barely reached her thighs. She'd gotten her long blond hair styled into a pixie cut last fall once she'd healed up from her head injury and it was shorter than I was used to. But of course she could pull it off. I said, "How many dresses are you taking?"

She dumped the latest armful of garments onto the bed and folded her arms over her chest. "I don't know what I'm going to feel like wearing. So probably all of them."

"Every dress you own."

"Every dress. In fact, tomorrow night, we're going to Saks so I can buy a hundred more dresses. Which one for Saturday night?"

She held up two more black dresses, a shift and a vintage-looking fit-and-flare.

I covered my face with my hand. For months, Tom's girlfriend,

Pam, had been obsessed with getting the four of us together for dinner. I'd managed to get out of it on three separate occasions, but the time had come. It was finally happening.

"I don't know why you hate her," Catherine said. "Which dress?"

"I don't *hate* her."

"Then why the dramatic gesture?"

"I just don't like her that much."

"Isn't that the same thing?"

"Hardly."

"She's nice."

"Yes." I frowned at that word: *nice.* Pam was nice, but I wasn't, and never had been. *You could stand to be a little nicer,* my father told me the last time we talked before he died. *You're a girl. You have to be nice. But not too fucking nice.* "I just don't think she really gets him."

"What is there to get? He's a guy."

I didn't want to talk about the matter anymore. "Come here," I said.

"I'm busy."

"Come here."

The corners of her mouth tipped up. "I already *came* there. As did you." But she flipped the suitcase closed and lay down next to me.

"I'm just going to miss you. Sue me."

"Oh I will." Catherine scooted over until her back was curled against me. I fluffed the duvet over her and slipped an arm over her hip. "I'll take you for every penny you're worth."

I didn't say anything, just breathed in the smell of her.

"It's only four days. Three sleeps."

"I suppose you won't miss me at all."

"Maybe a little." She rolled over and kissed me. Her mouth was full and soft and every time we kissed it felt like the first time. A kiss like that made it easy to forget everything else, at least for a few moments.

FOUR

Later, when she was asleep and I wasn't, I thought about scribbling a note and tucking it into her suitcase: something cute and sweet that would make her want to jump on a plane to come home as soon as she found it. But I didn't really *do* cute, or sweet, and Catherine would never jump on a plane for anybody, except herself. Part of me wanted to ask her to stay. But the rest of me wanted her to *want* to stay, not because I said I needed her, but because she knew I did. If I did. Being with Catherine was like spending money you don't have: a dazzling thrill in the moment, bookended by uneasy weirdness before and after.

I decided not to think about it anymore and got out of bed and put my clothes back on. In Catherine's dark kitchen, I got a glass of water from the sink and gazed out the window above it as I drank; the wide backyard was pristine with undisturbed snow. At my apartment, the fenced-in postage stamp that constituted a yard was always dotted with the footprints of people and animals coming and going. That probably should have unsettled me, but I found it comforting—proof that life continued all around us. Here, the isolation was what left me feeling unsettled.

Then again, when I was at home, I always found something else to unsettle me there too.

I leaned over the counter and closed my eyes for a minute, nearly jumping out of my skin when my phone began vibrating across the counter. Another middle-of-the-night call from my brother.

"Okay," he said when I answered, "this is weird."

I sat down at the kitchen table and slowed my breathing. "So this is one of those calls."

"I came over to Nightshade, and it's closed."

"Closed?"

"Like, unexpectedly closed. The doors are locked. People have been coming up, trying to get in, and leaving."

"No sign?"

"Nothing."

Andrew stood on the sidewalk in front of the place—a hulking warehouse with a neon sign above the door: NIGHTSHADE LOUNGE. The sign cast a sickly yellow glow on the brick façade and the sidewalk below, which gave the impression that it should be open. Then again, the Wonder Bread building a few blocks south had left its sign lit up for years after the factory closed.

The place had no windows, just a black metal door and an empty poster frame mounted beside it. There was moisture trapped behind the pane of Plexiglas in the frame, along with a torn scrap of whatever poster had previously occupied it. WELL DRINKS $2 12AM–

It was pretty uninviting, even for kids looking for a bar that wouldn't check IDs; a giant brick building with no windows seemed sort of like a horror movie waiting to happen. We made a lap around the perimeter but encountered no signs of life, no signs posted that the place would be temporarily closed today, no police seals to indicate that Nightshade had been shut down again for any reason.

"Well, okay," I said.

"Now what?"

I shook my head. "We still have the burnt eggs as an angle."

Andrew yawned and pushed his hands into his pockets. "Remember when we used to come to places like this?"

"I'd like to think we were a little more discerning than this."

"Everyone would like to think that. But we were kids."

He had a point, and I did remember. The days when we just wanted to be somewhere cheap and hot and noisy to drown out the quiet in our heads. Bernie's, Long Street Lounge, Victory's, Little Brothers and the Carlile Club, most of which were gone now, sacrificed to the gods of high-rise apartments. It was a miracle nothing worse than a three-day hangover ever happened to me back in those days.

Whenever I thought about whiskey, I thought about my dad. And whenever I thought about him, I thought about how he was gone and we were all still just as lost, under the surface, like grief was an abscess, walled off but roiling. And that just made me think about whiskey again, repeating the whole cycle. The end result was that I thought about both, constantly. "Do you think we should do something on the eighth?" I said.

Andrew required no explanation to understand that I was talking about the anniversary of Frank's death. "No. I don't know. It's going to be a horrible day. It's never going to be anything other than a horrible day."

"We should go with Mom to Greenlawn."

"Yeah."

"And get flowers and stuff."

"Yeah. So what's your question? You already have it figured out."

Now it was my turn to sigh. "I don't want to be the one to bring it up. Like, *hey, Mom, it's a beautiful day to go to the cemetery, what do you think?*"

"Well," Andrew said, "it's not like she forgot what day it is. I don't think it requires a ruse. Besides, she'll probably bring it up first. Or just go without us."

"Strangely," I said, "that does not make me feel any better."

"You're in a mood."

"No, I'm just—never mind."

"Go home. Get some sleep. Thanks for your help. Sorry for the dramatics," Andrew said.

"Hey, no."

He hugged me quickly around the shoulders and set off across Fourth. When he reached his side of the street, he called out to me, "Go home."

"I'm going, I'm going."

But instead I got back in the car and sat there in the cold for a while, watching Andrew's silhouette blur into nothing. I couldn't quite see his building from back here, thanks to the cars parked along Fourth and a massive drift of snow deposited at the curb by a halfhearted snowplow attempt at some point. But it couldn't have been more than a three-minute walk. I was parked on the left edge of the one-way street, the long brick side of Nightshade hulking up beside me. On the other side of Fourth: a row of porchless brick town houses with three floors that somehow came together to look like an elementary school. I could remember when there was nothing more than a vacant lot from here to the freeway back when Andrew moved in. Now there was a whole community; they'd even named the little alleys that had never been given real names before. Directly across from me, the street was called Neruda, an oddly poetic moniker for a roadway that was still very much a construction zone on Google Maps satellite view. I looked at the cars parked up and down the street. Was Addison's among them?

It was too dark to see.

I used my phone to look at Nightshade's Facebook page again. Three people had "checked in" as recently as last night, posting badly lit, drunken photos full of raised glasses and smeary smiles, meaning that the club had been open twenty-four hours ago. There were no announcements indicating a planned closure here either.

In the past, when I'd been hired to find someone, the person was almost always fine. Just busy, maybe actively avoiding a nosy relative or a shitty boss, but not *missing*. Missing wasn't the same thing as *not here*. Sarah Cook had been the exception, trapped in that nightmare house. But it wasn't like I was going to have another case like that, so why was I so uneasy about Addison? Was this what getting older was like—being reminded by every young person you encounter that it's something of a miracle you're still alive?

I was knee-deep in thoughts like that when I heard the sound of shoes crunching over snow, a split second before ungloved knuckles rapped sharply on my window. I snapped my head to the window, saw only a dark coat over a broad torso and the glint of a handgun. "Roxane Weary," a familiar voice said.

He stepped back and leaned down, one forearm on the roof of my car—tall, buzz cut, with a face I realized I'd last seen eight months earlier, also in darkness, during the shootout in the Capitol Square building. It was Vincent Pomp's bodyguard, Bo.

In the scant moonlight, I could see his eyes narrowing. "What the hell are you doing here?"

"I heard this place has great well drink specials," I said. "What are *you* doing here?" Then I remembered what Andrew had told me about this place. A sleazy dance club would fit quite nicely under the Phoenix Group's umbrella of businesses. "Is he here?"

But the big man shook his head. "It's fuckin' cold out here. Let's talk inside."

The interior of Nightshade seemed to be as uninviting as the outside, just a big black rectangle with a bar on one wall and a damp, murky smell. It wasn't quite as cold as it was on the street, but it also wasn't much better. We felt around in the dark for the light switches and failed at finding them; finally, Bo gave up and just led the way over to the bar using the light from his phone. "What do you drink?" he said.

"Whatever's handy."

He leaned across the bar and grabbed a nearly empty bottle of Old Crow and two glasses.

"So this is the latest Phoenix Group investment, then?" I said.

He poured himself a drink and pushed the bottle to me, and I did the same. Old Crow was worse than I remembered, though that didn't stop me from drinking it.

"Owner took out a loan with Mr. Pomp," Bo said. "A large loan."

"Ah. So not an investment, per se."

"Mr. Pomp just wants his money back. Once that happens, he won't be involved in this shithole any longer." Bo smirked. With his face illuminated from below by his cell phone, his features were stony and intimidating. "So what are you doing here?"

The solidarity during our search for the light switches had made me almost forget that he was a dangerous individual. I took a few steps away, casually. "There's a young woman who I think may have been working here," I said. "I'm just trying to find her."

Bo visibly relaxed. "Who is she?"

"A deejay."

"Well, I don't know the staff so I can't really help with that."

"So why's the place closed?"

"Great question."

"Not supposed to be?"

He finished his drink, frowning at the taste. "Since the place reopened, we've had an arrangement. Every night at two, I come by for Mr. Pomp's take from the register."

"So you're not just a driver anymore."

"No."

"Promotion?"

"I'm glad you're so interested in my career path."

"So what *is* Mr. Pomp's take?"

Bo didn't say anything.

"Okay, so every night at two . . ."

"And tonight, the doors are locked, nobody's home."

"Why?"

He gestured at the dark, empty space. "Like I know? There's no one here, except you and that guy. Who was he?"

"My brother."

Bo shook his head. "Your whole family is like this, then?"

"Who runs this place, day-to-day?"

He frowned, like he was debating whether he wanted to give me any more information.

I said, "I think I proved myself to be a person of my word, last year. I think Mr. Pomp would agree."

Finally, he said, "Look, all I know is I'm supposed to come in and get the cash—it's always in a zippered pouch in the back. I take it. That's it."

"Every night."

"Every night."

"Wednesday night?"

"Every night."

"Anything out of the ordinary that night?"

"It's the same every night."

"Including Wednesday night?"

"Are you deaf?"

"I'm just being thorough," I said. "I'd like to talk to your boss tomorrow."

Bo picked up his phone and motioned toward the back door with it, marking the end of the conversation. "He has a secretary," he said, "and I'm not her."

FIVE

Shelby was working the counter at the Angry Baker when I got there later that morning, patiently waiting while a man talking on his phone listed every variety of muffin to whoever was on the other end. She shot me a smile and tried to get his attention. "Sir, maybe if you could . . . sir . . ." But I shook my head and pointed at the carrot muffin I usually got and handed over a five-dollar bill.

"Keep the change," I whispered so as to not interrupt the Muffin Man's conversation.

Shelby beamed at me. "I'm making chili tonight, you should come by."

I gave her a thumbs-up as I took the paper sack containing my muffin from her hand. She lived upstairs from me now, which was excellent news as far as my prospects for actual dinner food went. With her addition to the building, the queer quotient among tenants was also now three to one, since Alejandro, with whom I shared a wall, was gay as well. But, as I had to remind them, Shelby also brought the average age in the building way, way down.

Muffin and more tea in hand, I headed to Tamarack Circle to visit Vincent Pomp and his secretary at the office of the Phoenix Group. For all the entanglement I'd had with them last summer, I'd never actually been to the office. It was located in an ugly brick building of brutalist inspiration on the northeast quadrant of the massive roundabout. The parking lot hadn't been cleared of ice and snow since winter started so the terrain was jagged and uneven. I picked my way across, grateful for the tread on my warm Sorel boots. I went into the lobby, which was empty in an abandoned sort of way. A bronze plaque on the wall told me that Pomp's office was on the second floor next to a periodontist. I personally would not want to expose my gums to anyone in a building like this, but to each their own. I climbed the steps and found the office and pushed open the door to a narrow waiting area with an unattended receptionist's desk at the front. I looked down the hall past it, saw nothing but closed doors, and heard nothing at all.

A silver bell sat on the counter. I waited a good two minutes before pressing it, not wanting to fill the office with the cheery, out-of-place *ding*. Then, finally, I tapped it with an index finger; even though I was bracing myself for the horror of the sound, it was loud enough to startle me. Almost immediately, a door at the end of the hall snapped open and a woman stuck her head out.

Her hair was disheveled, escaping from her updo, and the large bow on her blouse was askew.

So this must be the secretary.

"Hi there," I said. "I'm hoping to speak with Mr. Pomp. Is he in?"

She patted at her hair and clothing like she was on fire. "Mr. Pomp, ah, no, do you have an appointment?"

"Nope," I said, cheery as the bell on her desk, "but I think he'll want to talk to me. Roxane Weary."

Next I heard the low rumble of a man's voice from the room behind her. She nodded, closed the door, and strode down the hallway toward me, still adjusting her clothing. She wore stilettos that had to be a bitch to walk in on the berber carpet. But she managed it with grace and took a seat behind the counter where I was standing. Only after she stapled a few things together and logged in to her computer did she say, "Mr. Pomp will see you now. Last door on the right."

She still hadn't looked at me.

I went down the same hallway and knocked on Pomp's door.

"Yes?" he said.

I almost laughed. I pushed the door open and stepped in. "So we're just going to pretend you weren't just in here fucking your secretary."

Pomp was seated at his desk, leaning far back in his executive chair, his hands laced over his chest. "I don't see how that's any of your business," he said. "Haven't you heard of calling first?"

I sat down on the other side of his desk. "I did call. Three times, actually. But I don't think you hired Pussy Bow out there because of her telephony skills."

Pomp's mouth twitched. "You're in fine spirits these days. Interestingly, I don't feel the same about whatever your involvement is in my club."

"Bo filled you in."

Pomp nodded.

"So it's not like you're surprised to see me, then."

He smoothed his tie but didn't say anything. Clearly he wasn't going to make anything easy this time around either.

"What's the deal with Nightshade?"

"There's no *deal*. I lent some money. I'm waiting to get it back."

"Who runs it?"

"So you can hassle more of my employees?"

"To be fair, you've never actually seen me in full hassling mode."

Pomp might have been the kingpin of sorts over a seedy financial empire, but that didn't mean he wasn't reasonable. "I shudder to think what that might be like."

Now it was my turn to stay quiet.

"Shane Resznik. He's the owner, in theory."

I wrote it down. "Why in theory?"

"He owes everybody a little something, and some people a whole lot. There's not much left for him to call *his* at this point. I tried to get ahold of him, both last night and this morning."

"Is he the type to avoid his boss's calls?"

"I'm not his boss."

"Okay, his favorite loan shark, then."

"He's a weasely little bastard. So probably."

"What's that mean?"

He said nothing for a few seconds, finally adding, "Just a feeling."

"A feeling you have no intention of acting on?"

Pomp sat up straighter in his chair. "I have no intention of having anything to do with the place long-term," he said. "I'm just trying to recoup what I lost in a bad fucking deal that's none of your business."

"And there was no planned closure or anything?"

"No."

"The club should've been open."

"Yes."

"So now what?"

"About the club?"

"Yeah."

"I guess we wait and see what happens tonight."

I didn't especially like the sound of that. "What about the other employees?"

"What about them?"

"Maybe they can clue you in."

"Shane handles payroll and all that. I don't know who all he has working under him."

I showed him a picture of Addison, but his face revealed nothing. I said, "So that's it? You're just going to wait till you hear from Shane the Weasel?"

"Believe it or not, Nightshade isn't high on my list of priorities."

"I'm going to try to talk to him."

Pomp shrugged. "Go crazy."

"There's literally no one else you can think of to talk to? No employee records or anything?"

"Literally. On your way downstairs, can you ask Nina to come back in here?"

"Is that your way of saying this conversation is over?"

"More polite than 'Get the hell out of here,' isn't it?"

I stood up. He'd given me what I came for. I said, "How's your family?"

He had one son in prison, no thanks to me. "Never better."

"You ever hear anything from our friend Leila?"

"If I did, you wouldn't exactly be the first person I'd tell," he said. It was something of a joke between us, a line we'd thrown back and forth a few times when we first met. I wasn't sure what it said about me, that I had an inside joke with a guy like this. He actually almost smiled. "But no. Wherever she is, I'm sure she's fine. She's like that."

He was probably right. Every few months I put an hour or so into tracking down Leila Hassan. She belonged in prison much more than Pomp's son did. But she'd gotten away last summer, in part because she had fooled me.

Something that was usually reserved for Catherine Walsh and for my own damn self.

"Thanks for the help," I said.

Pomp nodded. "Please let that be the last of it."

SIX

Shane Resznik was, as promised, a weasely-looking guy with bleached hair and a scruffy goatee and the general vibe of someone who always yells "Play 'Free Bird'" at live bands to be funny. He had a full set of social media profiles but didn't seem to use them much, and he also had a conviction on his record from four years earlier—a first-degree misdemeanor theft charge. That didn't tell me a whole lot, but Vincent Pomp had said that Resznik was a bit of a weasel, so it seemed like a good bet that his weaseldom and this conviction were somehow related.

I called Tom and wrote down Resznik's address while the phone rang.

"Please don't say you have to cancel for tomorrow," he said in lieu of a hello. In the background, I could hear the sound of various tense conversations around the small cubicle warren that constituted the detective bureau.

"I'm not. This is work."

"Okay, good."

"You don't even know what it is."

"I don't care. As long as you aren't cancelling. Pam set a New Year's resolution for us to socialize more."

"The *worst*."

I heard a smile in his voice. "So far it's just been with her friends, though."

"That *is* the worst, then," I said.

"No, the worst is that instead of calling it a resolution, she calls it an *intention*."

"Obviously didn't grow up Catholic."

"Exactly. That word will never not remind me of Monsignor Maloney."

The line fell silent. I didn't like making fun of Pam with him, but I also couldn't help it. Tom changed the subject. "Anyway, what did you need?"

I explained about Shane Resznik's record and he said that he'd email the reports right over to me.

"Also," I said, "do you know a guy, Michael Dillman? He was possibly in the homicide division at some point?"

"Mickey? Sure, yeah. Why?"

"What's his deal?"

"His deal? He used to be the second-shift supervisor up here, up till maybe three years ago? He kept having issues with his back though, kept going out on leave, coming back, going out, till finally he took a transfer to something in Administrative."

I thought about that. If Dillman hadn't been in the homicide unit for three years, why was he still using business cards with that phone number? "Is he still with the department?"

"As far as I know."

"What's he do in Administrative?"

"I'm not sure. There are a lot of units under that umbrella."

"Like R and D?"

"As in, research and development?"

"I guess."

"Do we even have that?"

"All I know is, I'm trying to reach him but can't. Or he's avoiding me."

"Drop Frank's name. They were pretty close."

"Humph," I said.

"See you tomorrow," he said before we hung up, "and if you bail now, I'm going to take it as a personal attack."

I called Dillman again and left another voice mail, this one laying it on thick about my father. Then I stood in the kitchen and slathered some peanut butter on a small stack of crackers while I waited for the email from Tom about Resznik, and when I returned to my desk, there it was. I skimmed the Ohio Uniform Offense report for details; the victim was listed as a beverage distribution company off of Fisher Road on the west side, which had been Resznik's employer at the time. The complaint alleged that Resznik had stolen nine hundred bucks over the course of a year on his delivery route, by pocketing a little here and there from cash transactions and pulling funny business with his paperwork to make it look like everything balanced out. I raised my eyebrows as I read. I'd done a few embezzlement cases, always well beyond the misdemeanor cap of a thousand dollars. Small businesses rarely tried to press charges for small amounts, opting instead to fire the asshole and be done with it—restitution often took years and years, which meant signing up for the hassle of a criminal complaint without even getting paid back before they went out of business—so the fact that the beverage distributor had done so either meant they were extremely patient or else holding a massive grudge against Resznik.

If he was trying to embezzle from Vincent Pomp, a criminal complaint would probably be the least of his worries.

He lived in a Goodale Park town house, one of the units facing west toward the hideous fountain. On a day like today, its frozen spray of water looked like a glacial formation. When I knocked on the door, though, he didn't answer. An angry woman did. She had wide blue eyes that were very puffy and very red. "Who the fuck are you?"

I took a small step back. "My name—"

"Like I give a fuck what your *name* is?"

I said, "You literally just asked who—"

"Shut the hell up. Where's Shane?"

"That's why I'm—"

"Where is he?" She practically screamed it, seemingly startling herself. "He's such a piece of shit."

No one who knew Shane Resznik was giving him much of a reco.

"Do you know where he is?" She was about thirty, blond, with tanning-bed skin and long, airbrushed nails. "I've just been waiting, like a fucking *idiot,* and I haven't slept, and I'm just going to go crazy in here."

"What's your name?" I said.

"Lisette."

"I'm Roxane. Can I come in?"

She shook her head. "It's such a mess."

"That's okay."

"It's *not* okay."

"Well, Lisette, how about we go get a cup of coffee or something. Can I buy you a cup of coffee?"

"I look like shit."

"You're beautiful," I said. "And besides, it's winter. Everybody's just trying not to slip and fall on their asses."

Lisette gave me a small smile, calming down some.

A few minutes later we were sitting at a table in the back of One Line Coffee with a mug of single-drip for her and a chai latte for me. Lisette insisted on wearing sunglasses, so I felt like I was interviewing somebody famous.

"So you really didn't sleep with him?"

"Really," I said. "I've never even met him. I just want to talk to him about Nightshade. But he hasn't been home in a few days?"

"The last time I saw him was when he left for work on Wednesday night. He said he'd be home at the regular time. But he wasn't." She paused to sip her coffee. "I know what that place is like. Technically, I'm one of the owners. I gave Shane the money for it, not that he'd ever let anyone know that."

That didn't exactly make her an owner. "Oh?"

She nodded somberly. "Couple years ago, I got in a bad car wreck. You know that guy Kevin Kurgis, with the commercials? *I don't get paid unless YOU get paid?*" She dropped her voice into a decent facsimile.

"Sure."

"Well, it's no joke. I can't work anymore, I can't drive, he got me *paid,* okay? This was when Shane was out of work and he talked me into fronting him most of the money for the stupid bar. Like whose lifelong dream is to own a shitty nightclub?" She cleared her throat. "He said it was a good investment. The place had been in business for years but was struggling under bad management. The way he acted, it would practically be like printing our own money, it was gonna make so much. Fucking idiot. This isn't the first time, you know."

"The first time he didn't come home?"

Another nod. "It's happened lots of times. He's probably in some nasty vagina right now, trying—" She cleared her throat again as several other customers looked up at us. "Shane gets carried away. Too much coke, too many pretty girls. He'll hole up in a motel for a while and then, when he's out of money, he'll be back."

"Any particular motel?" I said, then lowered my voice. "Or a particular, um, nasty vagina?"

Lisette sniffed. "This rathole on East Main, with an old-timey name. East Side Motor Lodge, I think. It's right by a UPS store. He lived there when I met him, if you can believe it."

I said, "The UPS store?"

She smiled a little. "The motel. I *knew* there was something going on with her."

For a second I thought she was about to say *Addison* and I felt my heartbeat speed up. "Who?"

"This goth chick from the bar. Long black hair but a real dummy, you know, with the fake tits and no bra?"

The woman at the next table got up in disgust. It was possible that I could never come back here.

"And she works at Nightshade too?"

"She's a bartender."

"Know her name?"

Lisette shook her head and pushed up her sunglasses to rub her eyes. "So why do you want to talk to him about Nightshade?"

After almost thirty minutes of talking about him, she was finally curious as to why. "Well," I said, "I'm actually trying to find someone else who works there. Addison Stowe? She's a deejay."

Lisette shook her head. "I barely ever go there anymore. I just know that something's going on with this one chick, because we ran into her at the movies and he wouldn't really introduce me. I never heard of any girl deejay. So you just want to ask Shane about that?"

I nodded. "That, and the club was closed last night, and I'm curious about why. Like, if something happened."

"Such as?"

"I don't know. But this woman, Addison, was very upset about something early Thursday morning near Nightshade, and now she's AWOL, the club is unexpectedly closed, and Shane is AWOL too. It's a little strange."

Lisette didn't say anything for a while, just sipped her coffee. Finally she said, "Well, that's a little weird. Maybe they got busted again. For the IDs."

"Is that what you think happened?"

"*I* think that Shane's a piece of shit."

"I gathered that," I said.

SEVEN

My plan had been to talk to Shane and get an answer one way or the other about whether or not something had happened at the club, but I now had even more questions. The database on the Division of Liquor Control's website was very revealing; it cited no fewer than seventeen various violations of Nightshade's liquor license in the past three years. Their misdeeds included: sale and/or furnishing to a person under twenty-one, improper advertising encouraging excessive drinking, illegally advertising price of beer, permit not posted in conspicuous place, fine not paid, suspension in effect, and, most curiously, gambling raffle or drawing. But whatever that was almost certainly had nothing to do with Addison; the most recent offense was six months ago and I could find no evidence of the club being shut down by any authority in the time between Wednesday night and now, and nothing that helped to explain why both Addison and Shane Resznik seemed to have had a bad night.

I found the motel—as promised, next to the UPS store. The place seemed mostly deserted, with just a half a dozen cars spread out around three long, low buildings.

I grabbed a paper bag from my backseat and went into the office. "Hi," I said to the woman behind the counter, "I got a delivery for Shane Resznik, but he didn't put a room number."

She looked at me. She had green and purple hair in tangly

white-girl dreds and she wore a plaid flannel over army-drab cargo pants and Doc Martens eight-eyes. Her feet were propped on the desk, exposing a gun holstered at her ankle. It was impossible to tell how old she was. "We don't collect registration," she said, "and you're not Uber Eats."

"You got me there."

"What's in the bag?"

"Nothing," I said. "I just need to talk to the guy."

"You a cop?"

"Private detective."

"No shit? I'm going to Columbus State part-time, criminal justice."

"Yeah? What do you want to do?"

"Find motherfuckers who skip bail and mess up their women's lives," she said, clearly speaking from experience. "If I can scrape enough money for tuition on what they pay me, anyhow. Your guy, you know what he looks like?"

"Blond, goatee, kind of a weasel?"

The woman nodded. "One-sixteen."

I opened my wallet and pulled out a twenty. "Congrats, you got a partial scholarship."

"Right on."

I went back outside and followed the arrows to the end of the building that ran parallel to Main. There was a rusty old Jag parked next to the door of room one-sixteen. Shane hadn't taken care of it, but it still made me miss my blue tank.

I knocked on the door.

Shane Resznik himself answered—dressed only in velvet Santa Claus boxers and mismatched socks, a handful of one dollar bills outstretched. He was either expecting pizza, or drugs. "Uh," he said when he saw I had neither, and started to close the door.

"Hey buddy, hang on," I said. "I just want to talk."

"Not to me you don't."

"You don't even know why I'm here."

He had the door shut by now, but he stood just inside it and said, "And I don't care. You a cop?"

"Where's Addison?"

He opened the door a crack. "Addison?" His voice went up a little, like this inquiry confused him.

"What did you think I wanted?"

"I told you, I don't care."

"When's the last time you saw her?"

Now he opened the door the whole way and glared at me. "I don't know. The other night."

"Wednesday."

"Sure."

"How come the club was closed the last few nights?"

"Jesus, who the hell are you?"

I gave him a big smile and a business card.

"Someone hired you to find out why the club wasn't open last night? Damn, I kind of love it."

"Babe, who is it?" said a soft female voice.

"Nobody. Go back to bed."

"Is that her? Is that Lisette? Because—"

Resznik slammed the door closed and the rest of the argument was muffled. Finally, the woman seemed to go away and Resznik sighed behind the door.

"I'm still out here," I said.

He opened the door an inch or so. "What the fuck do you want?"

"I want to know what's going on at your club."

Continuing to glare at me, he said, "Plumbing issue. Pipes burst. No running water. This fucking weather, you know?"

"You didn't think to inform your sugar daddy of that?"

"Huh?"

"Vincent Pomp."

He scowled at me. "I, uh, left a message."

"With?"

"His . . . answering machine?"

"Oh, so somebody accidentally deleted it, yeah?"

"Yes."

"You might want to try again. Explain yourself."

"Would that make you get the fuck away from me?"

"Where's Addison?"

"Why don't you ask her that?"

He slammed the door again, and this time, I heard the dead bolt sliding into place.

"Shane, are you familiar with the term *non sequitur*?" I said.

But I only got silence in return.

I was firmly on board with the weaseliness of Shane Resznik. I certainly didn't believe him, but at least the mystery of his whereabouts was resolved. I left a message for Lisette saying that I'd located him, and asked her to call me back if she wanted to know where. I hoped she wouldn't call but figured she probably would.

Some part of me must have enjoyed getting doors slammed in my face, because I found myself heading back to Addison's apartment. All of this weirdness could be put to bed if she was just sitting at home, dropping beats in her living room. I didn't see any signs of a maroon Scion parked on California Avenue. This time I went to the front door, and this time, someone new answered.

The woman in front of me gave me a once-over. She was Addison's age, dressed in a fitted grey pantsuit with neon socks poking out at the ankle. Even without shoes, she towered over me. Her long, dark hair was pulled into a tight, high ponytail at the top of her head but still hung halfway down her back.

I said, "Hi."

The curtains ruffled. "O-M-G," a voice whispered from somewhere else in the apartment, "that's her. That's the lady."

"Um, hi." She leaned one long arm against the doorjamb. "Can I help you?"

"Jordy, that's her, I said." Now Addison's roommate appeared behind the tall woman and they both stared out at me.

I tried to look as unthreatening as possible. "Is Addison at home?"

"No," they said in unison.

I tried, "Are you getting worried about her? Because I am."

The roommate bit her lip, and concern flickered through Jordy's eyes as she said, "Yeah, a little, actually. So could you tell me who the hell you are?"

Her name was Jordana Meyers, and she was a friend of Addison's going back to grade school. The roommate—Carlie—was Jordy's younger stepsister, a current Ohio State student who had moved in with Addison a few months earlier.

"I don't know why Raddish still lives here," Jordy was saying. She had her long legs pulled up to her chest as she sprawled on an armchair, a pose that made her seem much younger than she was. "I mean, all the drunk students around all the time. But I guess it doesn't matter much to her, since she doesn't have to be at work at eight in the morning or anything."

"And she's, like, never here," Carlie added.

"So when's the last time either of you saw her?"

"I heard her come in on Saturday morning, I think," Carlie said from the small dining room table without looking up from a psychology textbook, the publisher of which hadn't even bothered to change its cover from when *I* was in college. "But I haven't, like, *seen*

seen her for a while. We have basically opposite schedules and she's pretty much never awake when I'm here."

"So that's not unusual."

She shook her head, chewing on a pen cap.

Jordy said, "I saw her last week, at one of my games—I coach basketball, at the rec center in Blacklick—that's where we grew up."

"I figured you used to play," I said, and she nodded. "Did she usually come to your games?"

"No, hardly ever. I mean, maybe actually never. Before that I hadn't seen her, oh, since Thanksgiving, I think? She's one of those people, you can go forever without seeing her but when you do, it's like no time at all has passed, she's always the same old Raddish. But that's probably part of the problem."

I waited for her to go on.

"I'm not one to tell somebody to *grow up* or whatever, but come on. Our ten-year reunion is going to be next year and she's still carrying on like she did when we were seventeen."

"Carrying on?"

"Just teenage melodrama," Jordy said after a brief pause. "Except we're not teenagers anymore. There's always some guy crisis, some urgent middle of the night phone call. I can't even tell you how many times I've woken up to my alarm and saw ten missed calls from Addison and spent the rest of the day worrying that she was in the hospital or in jail or whatever. But nothing's ever really wrong, it's never that she actually needed anything. It's just how she is. Honestly," Jordy went on, "in the last year or so, I've kind of tried to take a step back. For my own sanity. I hope that doesn't make me sound awful. But it can be a lot, with her. She's got a lot of problems."

"Problems?"

"Just, self-esteem stuff, really," Jordy said, waving a hand like she suddenly thought better of selling her friend out to a stranger. "I work in real estate at Chase and I'm hoping to be at the AVP level before I'm thirty, so. I just don't have the bandwidth to worry about her like I used to."

"So you have a real job."

Jordy smiled. "A big-girl job. That's what Addison says."

"So the two of you are still close?"

"Well, I wouldn't say that, exactly. Growing up it was me, Raddish, and Elise—always together. Elise and I are still pretty close. Addison is just sort of off doing her own thing. But she can really surprise you, too. Like when she came to the game. It was the sweetest thing, and she cheered so hard for the girls—they were so pumped, I've never seen them play so hard. But anyway, afterwards, we got pizza and she seemed kind of, I don't know, anxious, but in a quiet way. Like she didn't actually want to talk about it, which is weird for her. So since then I've checked in with her a few times."

"Did she ever tell you what was on her mind?"

"No. And I asked. I tried to get her to open up, but she said everything was fine. You can just tell though, you know?"

Carlie looked up from her book. "Maybe something to do with that cop."

"What?"

"There was a cop here, looking for her. A week ago or something. I gave her his business card." She pointed at me.

Jordy said, "And?"

"I left him a message. Well, two messages. I haven't heard back from him."

"Great," Jordy said. "So that's not weird at all. Some cop is looking for her, and now she's randomly not coming home anymore?"

"I told you," Carlie said, "that's pretty much par for the course. She's *never here.*"

It was clear where the roommate stood on whether or not anyone should be worried about Addison. "Do you know what else has been going on in her life, other than deejaying?"

Jordy slid the elastic out of her hair and let it fall over her shoulders. "Well, she told me she was thinking about going back to school. But that's—she dropped out after two semesters at OSU and ever since, she's constantly saying she's thinking about going back. So I doubt it."

"What about a girlfriend or boyfriend?"

Jordy smiled faintly. "There was this guy she was talking to, but I don't think they ever met or anything. On BusPass."

"On what?"

"BusPass. The dating app? Bus, for Colum*bus*. BusPass."

"I've never heard of it."

"Really? Everybody's on it. It's like Tinder, but just for the Columbus area. And it has this feature, called Missed the Bus, that's like on Craigslist, from that Missed Connections section on there, like, 'You: luminous modern hippie at the Dirty Projectors show . . .' Addison has been obsessed with those since high school, but Craigslist is all pervy now."

"So BusPass, that's not pervy?"

"No, it's really cute."

I didn't point out that cuteness and perviness were not mutually exclusive. "So someone wrote one about Addison being a luminous modern hippie?"

Jordy laughed. "No, that's just me spouting some bullshit. But that's the kind of thing she'd like. Under all the drama and mascara, she's a romantic."

Somehow, I had known that about her. "So some guy wrote a Missed Connections post about her on this BusPass app and she saw it."

"Yup. I got her turned on to the app, actually. We were looking for a date for *me*. It's kind of addictive, just flipping through people. But anyway, at some point there was a Missed the Bus post about Raddish. She even said that after reading stuff like that for so long, it was kind of weird to actually find one that was about *her*—she almost didn't write back. But she said it was a great post so she did, and they were chatting back and forth since then."

"Know his name?"

"No."

That would've been too easy. Part of me wondered if Sergeant Dillman could've been the missed connection, and came sniffing around to see what Addison was like. "Know anything about him?"

"He likes tiny houses? You know, little shipping container places and whatnot. Addison's very into those."

"Was it serious?"

"I don't know. Probably not."

"Why?"

"Well, just that when she first wrote to him she said she wasn't even interested in meeting the guy. Look, we're having coffee tomorrow, for Elise's birthday. I'm sure she'll have a whole story about where she's been."

I didn't doubt that.

EIGHT

It was medium-hard to find Dillman's home address—not a surprise, since most cops are more careful than the average citizen about how much personal information they allow online—but I prevailed. He lived in a winding network of identical town houses on the far north side of the city, near a Baptist megachurch and the Lazelle community rec center, which was sad and grey under a heavy blanket of winter. I felt a little weird about showing up at his house. But he still hadn't called me back and I wanted some kind of answer about why he'd been at Addison's apartment with an old business card.

His soon-to-be-ex-wife answered the door instead.

"He doesn't live here anymore," she said, almost gleefully, her hands on her hips. She was barely five feet tall and had the most perfect winged eyeliner I'd ever seen. "Are you with the department?"

"No, I'm a private detective," I said, offering her a card. "I just want to talk to him about a—"

"Weary," she read off my card, something flashing in her eyes. "You're his daughter! Frank's."

I got that feeling in my chest, like something didn't fit quite right. "Yes," I said. Surprised, since it was always other cops who did this. "You knew my father?"

She motioned me inside. "You can come in. I promise I'm not

crazy." The condo was caught in a mid-move nightmare, with boxes stacked halfway to the ceiling. "Sorry," she said, "just ignore all of this."

"Moving day?"

"Hardly. Just getting rid of Mickey's shit." She reached into an open box and pulled out a framed photo. "By which I mean, anything that reminds me of him."

She flashed the image my way—their wedding photo. Diminutive bride in a white sheath, no veil, Mickey in a three-piece suit, charcoal color. He was probably about five-six, built like a fireplug.

"Looking at this," she said, "neither of us even look all that happy." She chucked the frame back into the box. "So Frank, yes, god, what a shame. I'm so sorry."

I nodded.

"I always liked Frank. You know he was in the Navy in Subic Bay, and I grew up in Manila, so we bonded. About food, mostly, like halo-halo. I brought it to a cookout once and he nearly wept with joy. There's not exactly much love lost between me and the department but I had a soft spot for him. Sorry, is this upsetting?"

"Uh, no." I shook my head. It was news to me that my father had ever even been stationed in the Philippines. I didn't know what to say. "I didn't catch your name."

"Sunshine Castro. Call me Sunny, though. You have his eyes, people probably tell you that all the time."

I nodded.

"You do, though. That blue. You know, a copper eye shadow would make the blue really pop. Or a salmon color."

"Excuse me?"

"Sorry," she said again. "Cosmetics. That's my thing. Anyway. Frank. Mickey. What do you need, again?"

"I'm just hoping to talk to Mickey. His name came up in a case I'm working on."

Sunny nodded. "Well, he's only got two speeds. At the hotel or at the bar."

I waited.

"He's been staying in this dump over on Sinclair, right beside Morse Road. He'll send me pictures sometimes. Like I'm supposed to feel bad his hotel bathtub has mildew on the curtain? I had to have my jaw wired shut for two months after what he did to me. I don't care about mildew."

A picture was starting to form here, and it didn't make me feel better about Addison's prospects. I said, "Which speed is he on at work?"

"Work? No. Mickey's not working these days. He's been on leave, five months or so. Back surgery."

For the second time that day, I found myself at a crappy motel. Though the America's Best Value Motel was a cut above the dump Shane Resznik was staying at, it still definitely looked like the sort of place an out-of-work wife-abuser would choose to hole up in and feel sorry for himself. There was no answer at his room. So I tried the bar on the corner, a nameless affair with a sign that just said BAR and another one that said OPEN.

I went inside. It delivered on the promises of the exterior; the place had the grubbiness of a dive bar without the character. Low ceilings, ripped vinyl, a mirror behind the bar that was so grimy I could only see my silhouette, not my reflection. The only patron in the place was barely able to stay on his bar stool, but he was not Mickey Dillman, and the bartender glared at me.

"Hi, I'm looking for somebody," I started.

The drunk man leaned an elbow on the bar and focused in my direction, sort of. "And I'm looking for *you*, toots."

"Trust me, you're not." I looked at the bartender, a grizzled old guy somewhere between fifty and dead in a plaid shirt and a trucker hat that said GUN OWNERS AGAINST CRIME. "His name's Mickey. He's been staying at the hotel over there, he's a cop." The gun owner against crime was still glaring. "Any of this ringing a bell?"

"No."

"Because I think he's here a lot, and you don't exactly appear overwhelmed by customers."

He picked up a dirty rag like he was thinking about throwing it at me. "Well, he ain't here now, is he?"

"That doesn't exactly answer the question."

He shrugged as if to say that wasn't his problem, and I supposed he was right about that.

I wasn't even sure it was mine.

I headed south via 71 with the radio off. Catherine had a Humanities department get-together tonight, something I had not asked her to skip, but still hoped she would have since tomorrow night we had dinner with Tom and his girlfriend, followed by her early flight to Rhode Island the next morning. So I wanted to ease into the silence of my evening rather than face the sudden, jarring quiet that would hit me when I parked on my street and turned the car off and then spent the rest of the night alone. It never used to bother me. I used to love it, in fact, or at least I thought I did. But now I was thirty-five, and I'd spent the last few months getting quite used to having company.

I didn't like how lonely I was without her.

Or the fact that sometimes, I was lonely when I was with her, too.

I hit my post office boxes in Whitehall and headed for home, still contemplating how I'd spend my evening until a pair of too-bright headlights flashed in my rearview mirror to interrupt my wallowing. I reached up to flip the switch on the mirror and change the reflection so it didn't blind me. As I did so, I realized that the same pair of headlights had been right behind me for longer than seemed coincidental.

I changed lanes and so did the headlights. Whoever it was followed too closely for me to see much about the car or the driver other than the shape of the headlights. But it was clear that they sucked at following undetected, or maybe weren't even trying. I slowed; they slowed. I sped up; they sped up. As we climbed the slight hill up the exit ramp onto Broad Street, I got some distance between us easily, enough to tell that whoever it was had a car with an engine that couldn't accelerate on an incline. The car caught up to me as I turned onto Broad. I made a tight lane change to turn right on Parsons and the car had nowhere to go but straight. As it passed me I saw that it was Shane Resznik's beat-up Jag.

There was a note on my door, blue ink in Shelby's bubbly handwriting: *Sweet potato chili! There's chocolate in it!*

I smiled and let myself into my apartment long enough to put my coat and today's leggings haul and my gun inside, and then I climbed the creaky steps to the second floor of the building. I'd met Shelby on a case a little over a year earlier and had sort of fallen into the role of "cool surrogate aunt"—her words, not mine—ever since. She had taken over the lease on an apartment in my building last summer and it was nice to have her nearby. Especially because my refrigerator was chronically empty, and Shelby was an amazing cook. Upstairs it smelled savory and sweet all at once and I heard happy girl voices from behind Shelby's door as I knocked.

"Come in," she called, "it's open."

I turned the doorknob, wincing a little, and pushed into her apartment. It was a mirror image of mine, the hallway on the right instead of on the left, and her walls were a sedate taupe color rather than the craziness of my apartment. And she kept a much neater house than I did. But the similarity was real, and it was always a little odd. "Hi," Shelby said from one end of her couch. "Good, you came, I have literally three gallons of this chili."

"There's a contest at my work. If you win you get a one-hundred-dollar Visa gift card," her friend Miriam said from the other end. They both had plates with bowls of chili and thick hunks of bread.

"And you called in a ringer."

"Naturally."

I closed the door and pointedly locked it, but before I could deliver the corresponding lecture, Shelby said, "I knew it was you, I heard you come in the building. It was totally locked before!"

"It was, it totally was," Miriam said.

I looked at them. "Likely story. You seem very cozy there."

Shelby set her plate on the coffee table. "You're always detecting, aren't you? Sit, I'll get you some."

She went down the hallway and I sat in an overstuffed thrift store arm chair opposite the couch. I said, "Was it actually locked?"

Miriam lifted a solemn hand. "On pain of death, yes."

She and Shelby insisted they were just friends, but Miriam spent an awful lot of time over here. I liked her. She radiated a chillness that seemed to calm down some of Shelby's anxiety. Her hair was a streaky purple color and long on one side, buzzed short on the other. Like Catherine's had been after her skull fracture, except on purpose. She looked edgy and cool and made me feel about a million years old. They both did.

Miriam said, "Shelby was telling me about the leggings. Leggings-gate? If you get any in that anthracite diamond pattern they have in, like, a size zero? I wouldn't hate it."

Shelby came back down the hall with a plate for me and a bottle that turned out to be ginger beer. "It's infuriating how nice they are, stupid overpriced leggings," she said. I saw then that she was wearing a pair I'd given her under a long grey sweater. "I keep getting compliments. They're not even pants! It's like a cult."

"Don't let my client hear you talking like that," I said. I tasted the chili and closed my eyes for a second, reveling in the sweet, spicy, slightly smoky flavor. Shelby had taught herself to cook from the internet, and she was damn good at it, too. "If you ask her, leggings are the only pants."

Miriam broke off a piece of bread and swabbed the bottom of her bowl with it. "What about you, where do you stand on the are-leggings-pants debate? I, personally, am on Team Pants."

"You know," I said, "I don't think I have an opinion. You do you, is what I say about that. I've never worn a pair of leggings in my life."

They both stared at me.

"Never?" Shelby said. "But what about when you exercise?"

I laughed. "I'll let you answer your own question there."

Miriam said, "But you have an apartment full of them! You're not even curious?"

I sipped the ginger beer. It was pretty good, though it was sorely missing the alcohol component. "I kind of figured it was a cult, like you said, and they weren't that great."

"Unfortunately," Shelby said, "they are."

"I don't know, pants that aren't pants are not really my thing. But Miriam, I'll keep an eye out for the diamond ones for you."

"Size zero."

"Yeah yeah, don't rub it in," Shelby said, and they both laughed.

I was glad Shelby had invited me up. It was pretty ridiculous that an almost-nineteen-year-old thought she needed to look out for me just as much as I looked out for her, but she wasn't wrong. After I thanked her for dinner—and waited till she'd locked the door before going downstairs—I returned to the apartment and went straight to my own kitchen. I might not have had any food, but I had liquor. I poured an inch of Crown Royal into a rocks glass and drank it fast, the way whiskey begged you to, and then I regretted it because it was gone. I stood there in the dark, running my tongue along the rim of the empty glass. I wanted another. But I was always going to want another. That didn't mean I had to have one. I thought about my father, about the glass that was always in his hand. He always wanted another, and he always had another, too. That was a good enough argument against it. But maybe, too, it was an overly simplistic way of looking at him. Subic Bay was still on my mind.

I called Andrew. "Did you know Frank was stationed in the Philippines?"

My brother was quiet for a beat. "What?"

"When he was in the Navy. He was stationed in the Philippines."

"No, he wasn't."

"How do you know?"

"Well, he never talked about it."

"Not to us, he didn't, but that doesn't mean anything."

"Where is this coming from?"

I shook my head. "I met someone who knew him today. She told me about him loving Filipino shaved ice. I mean, *Frank?* Mr. Only Vanilla Ice Cream and Not the Kind with the Little Black Dots in It?" I suddenly felt like crying.

Andrew sighed. "I thought you were calling about Addison."

"Oh." I wiped my eyes and poured another whiskey. "Sorry. I'm not. I still don't know. But I can keep at it."

"I guess I should pay you."

"You don't have to pay me. I never pay you, when I drink at the hotel."

"That's different."

"How?"

"Just is."

I drank the whiskey. I still wanted another, just as predicted.

"Well, good night," I said.

"Love you."

I hung up and put the glass in the sink and walked away.

I wandered into the living room and looked out the window at the street. It was dark except for the sharp glow of headlights from down the block. They looked familiar, I realized. I grabbed my coat and gun and went out through the back of the building and up through the alley on the east side of the building so I could approach the Jag from behind. The driver was a grey blob with glasses, not the right build for Shane Resznik. I rapped sharply on his window and he looked up, eyes wide, and stomped on the gas. The engine whined against the parked transmission. Up close, I could see that the driver was a young guy, big, with a neat beard against dark skin.

I said, "Can I help you?"

He frantically grasped at the gearshift, flung the car into drive, and lurched off down the block, leaving me to stand on the sidewalk with my gun at my side, wondering who the hell this guy was and why was he following me—badly, and in a borrowed car—if he was so afraid of me?

NINE

For the third day in a row, my phone woke me up on Saturday, vibrating in the pocket of my jeans, which I was still wearing. I felt vaguely seasick without knowing why. Then I remembered: the third shot of whiskey when I came in from the strange encounter with my friend in the borrowed car, then a fourth, then a fifth because the fourth wasn't a good pour, and I wasn't entirely sure what else.

It had been a while since I'd woken up feeling like this. It was still terrible, and maybe worse.

I answered the phone even though I didn't recognize the number.

"This is Jordy. Meyers."

"Oh," I said, sitting up in bed. I leaned back against the wall and closed my eyes and tried to gather my strength so I could make the room stop spinning. It felt like ages since I'd met Jordy at Addison's apartment, but somehow, it was only yesterday. "Hi there. What's up?"

"Well, I was just wondering. If you would be willing to come out to Blacklick."

I had a hazy memory of Jordy mentioning coffee plans with Addison. "Sure," I said, "what's going on?"

"I feel like I probably gave the impression that I wasn't worried," she said, "but Addison never showed up at Starbucks for Elise's birthday, so now I am."

Elise Hazlett lived in a medium-nice white colonial in a medium-nice Blacklick subdivision with wide sidewalks and zero trees. A massive RV sat in the driveway, and a tall, slouchy guy was standing at its gas tank, looking puzzled as he watched a repair video on his phone.

"Help you?" he said.

"Yeah, I'm looking for Jordy and Elise?"

He pointed me into the open garage. "Yeah, go ahead."

Then he went back to his project.

I knocked on the door before going into the house. "Hi there," I said to the two women standing around a kitchen island—Jordy and a slight blonde in yoga pants and a pink fleece. "The guy in the driveway said to just come in."

Jordy said, "Elise, Roxane, Roxane, Elise. Wait, did I do that wrong? Never mind, I don't actually know how old you are so whatever."

I smiled. "Older than you two, that's for sure." I shook Elise's manicured hand. Her hair was shoulder-length in the front but cut shorter in the back—the classic *can I speak to the manager* 'do. "Roxane Weary. Happy birthday."

"Ha, thanks," she said. "Here's my present." She gestured at the sink, which was completely full of dirty dishes. "My kids 'made' me breakfast."

"Get this," Jordy said, "a peanut butter omelet."

"That's . . . interesting."

"What's interesting is they were being supervised by my husband. Who knows that the boys aren't supposed to eat before their swimming lessons, especially not peanut butter omelets, so the single hour of uninterrupted time I get at the gym every week was interrupted because somebody barfed during the doggie paddle warm-up."

"Elise is living the dream out here," Jordy said.

"Let's go to the basement. Don't let them see you, don't let them hear you," Elise said. I couldn't tell if she was joking. I could hear the bright shrieking of children at play from somewhere else in the house. "They're all suckers for a new face."

"Your kids?"

"Everybody. My kids, my husband—well, I guess you already met him in the driveway—and my parents are both here too."

"The RV," Jordy explained. "How long are they here for?"

"First it was just for a few days, to get some hose fixed on that horrible thing."

"And it's not like Brock's actually going to fix anything. Was he still watching YouTube?"

"He was," I said.

Jordy rolled her eyes. "He is such a boob."

"Well," Elise said, opening an accordion door that divided the basement in half, "my dad's not innocent here either. He could just pay someone to fix it. But no, Brock's in charge which means they may *Never. Leave.*" The doors were concealing what appeared to be Elise's private yoga studio. It had glossy wood floors, low lighting, immaculate decorations, the pleasant smell of white tea in the air. Even the noise from upstairs was muffled.

"This is lovely," I said.

Jordy sprawled out on the love seat, and I perched on the edge of a shiny white desk.

Elise sat down on her yoga mat in lotus pose. "My sanctuary. The only place in the house free of cookie crumbs and the sound of sporting events."

"She was going to do a *she-shed*," Jordy said. "Like in the backyard. Dumb fucking name. But Brock decided he needed the shed more anyway. For his man-tools."

It seemed like Jordy was not a fan of Elise's husband. "Like the whole world isn't already space for somebody's man-tools," I said, and both women laughed. "So what's up?"

Jordy looked at Elise, then at me, then at the floor. "Well, I think we want to hire you."

I waited.

"I looked you up. Online. And you're, like, not just some rando. You're the one who found that woman, the one who'd been missing for fifteen years. And, like, I know Addy's not a prisoner in some creep's murder basement or whatever. But I'm just saying. Something's definitely wrong, for her to bail on coffee without even a text. Maybe it's kismet or something, that I happened to be at her place when you stopped by."

Elise looked a little less convinced about my rando-ness. "Kismet? You sound like Addison now."

"Hey, there are worse things. But there's typical-flaky-Addy behavior, and then there's this. And if not us, like, who's going to look?"

"Fair enough," Elise said.

Jordy flopped her long legs over the armrest of the love seat. "So what do you think?"

I didn't want to take their money. I was already looking for Addison for free. But I could tell Jordy was the type of person who needed to take action; the mere idea of hiring me had changed her whole demeanor. It was dangerous to be like that, dangerous to think that worrying in a certain way was the same thing as making progress. But I nodded. "Sure. I don't have a contract with me or anything, but I'm on your side here."

She gave me a tight little smile. "Thank you. Really. How does it work? Do I write you a check?"

I waved a hand. "We can take care of the paperwork later." I didn't use contracts and never had. "But to get started, I'd want a list of her other friends, family, places she goes, things she likes, stuff like that."

"Well, there's the deejay thing. And anything mythical. Or is it mystical?" Jordy tipped her head back over the armrest to look at her friend.

"Addison's a Libra," Elise said, though that didn't mean anything to me. "She's very into astrology, that kind of stuff."

"Other friends?"

"She never really talks about other friends or anything. But I'm sure she has them."

"So she's secretive, or private?"

"It's not like she's hiding something. It's just how she is."

I didn't respond for a while. Everybody is hiding something, even if it's just how badly they want to be seen. "Do you know anything about the club she was working at?"

"No. She told us we should come by, but like, that's not really my thing."

"Family? Siblings?"

"Only child."

"*Textbook* only child," Elise said.

"Parents?"

"Her mom's gone, oh, since two years ago. Cancer. Her parents were divorced way before that. Her dad's been remarried for ages."

"Is Addison in touch with him?"

Another nod. Jordy said, "To some degree. He's always been very invested in being a cool dad type. He always was. Like in high school, before he moved, he'd let us come over and drink at his apartment. Which is the tiniest bit creepy, looking back." She pulled the elastic out of her hair, shook it out, and redid her ponytail. "But anyway, when Addison decided what she wanted was to be a deejay, he bought her a bunch of equipment. Like a mixer? A sound mixer? I don't even know what that is. I just remember her going, Jason bought me a mixer, and I was like, a KitchenAid? I didn't know what she was talking about."

"She's always, you know, reinventing herself. Or trying to." Elise stretched her legs out on the yoga mat. "I guess that's good. But there's always something she needs before she can really start, you know?"

"Reinvention gear?"

"Yeah. Like, oh, I'm going to be a deejay, I just need all this equipment. Or, oh, I'm going to become an ESL teacher, I just need to save up for this online certification program first."

I said, "So she's the manic pixie dream girl of your friend group."

Elise gave a small laugh, but Jordy's mouth pressed into a thin line. "I don't want to make fun of her, though. So yeah, she's the flaky one or whatever, but she's not a frivolous person, you know? She's very smart—"

"Even if her grades never showed it," Elise interrupted.

"—and sensitive, and artistic. She's a good person. I feel like shit for trying to put some space between us over the last year. It's just that she can be a lot." Jordy shook her head, looking pained. "Till yesterday I had no idea anything was wrong, and now I'm really worried."

"Well," I said, "try to stay optimistic. We don't know that anything is wrong-wrong."

The two women looked at me.

"But I agree, it's troubling that she stood you up on your birthday, without any notice. Is there a chance she would go to her dad if she was in trouble?"

Elise shrugged. "He lives in Georgia now, I think. She'll see him once a year or something. But I guess it depended on what kind of trouble."

I steered the conversation to Addison's potential online paramour.

"Did she ever show you the Missed the Bus post?"

"I remember she sent me a link, when she first saw it. But it was, what, six, seven months ago? It was something about that bar, wasn't it? Where she was working at the time? Skully's, yeah, that was it." Jordy nodded. "And her tattoo! She's got this huge bird on her back, with these big colorful wings. It's cool because when she moves her shoulders, it almost seems like it's flying."

"It had to have cost a fortune," Elise said. "But yeah, it's nice."

"The post though," Jordy said. "It was more than 'Hey, nice ink.' It was, like, a good message. Something like, 'Request for the DJ: I want to hear the story of your tattoo.'"

"Smooth."

"Yeah."

"But you don't know anything else about him?"

Elise said, "She called him BPG, when she talked about him. BusPass Guy. Like the Ohio version of Mr. Big or something."

The odds of me being able to figure out who BusPass Guy was based on that were pretty much nonexistent, but I made a mental note to download the app later and see what I could see.

Upstairs, the door opened and heavy footsteps fell down the stairs. "Elise. Elise?"

Jordy rolled her eyes. "Man-tool incoming."

Elise closed her eyes for a second. "What, Brock?"

Her husband opened the door and looked in at us, a little blearily. He was holding a can of beer. "Oh, you still have friends over. Sorry to interrupt." But he made no move to leave.

"Can you not right now? It's her birthday. Can't she have a little peace?" Jordy said. It was pretty clear that she hated him.

Brock looked at me. "If no one's gonna introduce me, I'll do it. Brock Hazlett." He shook my hand like we were engaged in a grip-strength contest. Without the winter garb, I could see that he was muscular through the shoulders but soft at his middle, his hair dishwater-blond and looking a little thin on top. He gave off the air of a jock who had peaked in high school.

"So what do you want?" Elise said. "Since you did interrupt, and are continuing to do so."

"Oh. Uh, the Wi-Fi isn't working."

Jordy cackled into her palm, and Elise just stared. "Okay, and . . . ?"

"And, could you fix it? It never works when I try to fix it. Please?" He looked around at the three of us and winked. "Pleeeeeeeeease?"

Elise looked annoyed, but he didn't notice or didn't care or both.

After the Hazletts had gone upstairs, Jordy unfolded herself from the love seat and said, disbelieving, "I can't wait for her to get sick of his shit someday."

I brought hot chocolate for Addison's roommate in the hopes that it would make her like me more, but it just seemed to make her more suspicious. "Do you have any idea how much sugar is in these?" she said. She didn't throw it away though, instead carrying it up the steps. She gestured with the cup at the closed door of the first room at the top of the steps. "So Addison's room is here. And the extra bedroom is kind of hers too, it's that one." Now she pointed down the hall, past a small, pink bathroom, to a door that stood partially open. "But the stuff in the closet is mine. Jordy said you're not here to look through my stuff, just Addison's."

I smiled. "I won't look through your stuff. Pinky swear."

Carlie took a small sip of hot chocolate. "Thanks."

The upper level of the apartment was sort of gloomy with the doors closed. "So can I just go in?"

"Yeah, I guess. Call for help if you get trapped."

"Trapped?"

She brushed past me and headed downstairs. "You'll see."

I opened Addison's door. Even though the room had windows, there were light-blocking curtains that prevented any of the outdoor world from coming in and brightening the place up. Still, in the dark, I could see that Addison and I had similar housekeeping styles, which is to say, we didn't exactly do housekeeping. I flipped the overhead light on and took in the extent of the mess: unmade bed with a hump of fleece blankets in the middle in lieu of a proper comforter; a mountain of unfolded laundry in one corner; a desk piled high with odds and ends—a bottle of Aleve, a glass prayer-style candle with an image of Mariah Carey in place of a saint, three Sharpies tangled in a white earbud cord, metallic blue nail polish, a stack of notebooks, a Starbucks gift card, and a dollar twenty-nine in loose change. There was a clear space in the center of the desk where, I assumed, a laptop usually sat. The desk had one drawer, and it was jammed full of more random junk like batteries, lightbulbs, stamps. I flipped through the notebooks—mostly empty except for a smattering of poetry, or maybe song lyrics, written in purple ink.

All the magazines in Barnes and Noble
Look at you all glossy-eyed like you're in trouble
Like you're stuck
Like you're trapped
Like you need a magazine to tell you that

Not bad, though maybe a little melodramatic. I moved on to the nightstand, which had a collection of crystals arranged around the base of a lamp. I picked up a chunk of rose quartz. It was heavier than it looked, with a smooth finish that seemed to indicate Addison had touched it, often. The nightstand drawer contained a clip-on book light, half a dozen different body lotion tubes, a prescription in Addison's name for hydroxyzine—an antihistamine that either treated allergies or anxiety—a dog-eared copy of *The Language of Letting Go,* and a small photo album.

IN MEMORY, the front said.

It was full of pictures of Addison and her mom: in front of a Christmas tree, eating sushi, at the beach, in the shadow of the Golden Gate Bridge. In some of the pictures, Addison was no older than six or seven, while some of them appeared to be shortly before her mother passed away. In the twenty years in between, Addison's look changed a lot. Her hair was black, magenta, bleached blond with dark roots. Her clothes went from punk to preppy to grunge. Her weight fluctuated too; she was a chubby kid, an athletic-looking preteen, heavier in high school, becoming scary-skinny in some of the late teens and early twenties images where the rest of her look was at its most severe, the dyed hair and black, torn clothes. At the end of the album was a dried rose, white, pressed flat.

Her closet was full of jeans and hippie blouses—the present-era Addison a size twelve and a fan of the boho-chic style—and canvas bags adorned with enamel pins. The top shelf had a suitcase-sized gap in the center, which made me turn around and look at the carpet leading toward the door. Although I'd just stepped all over it, I could still make out the marks from suitcase wheels.

Maybe carpet marks were the Midwestern equivalent of tracks in the snow.

I laughed a little at myself. Silly, but still potentially useful: Addison had packed a bag at some point. It wasn't necessarily on Thursday morning, but it wasn't necessarily not.

I kept looking through the room. Under her bed, I found a bag of Taco Bell wrappers, seven socks, a blister tray of NyQuil caplets, a hairbrush, and a Capital One statement; her Visa was maxed out. Behind the door I found a stick vacuum still in its box. And tucked into the frame of the mirror on her dresser, two cards. One was a glossy postcard showing Skógafoss in Iceland; the back of it said *Raddish, Next summer, you and me, here. You'd love it. Fresh air, fresh fish, few people. Karen says hi. Love you, Dad.*

The date stamped in the postmark said 2016. I wondered if her father had really taken his daughter to Iceland the following year and guessed probably not.

The other one was white cardstock printed with DEPRESSION SUCKS in big black type. I flipped it open and read the handwritten inscription:

> *Don't believe anything it tells you. (You still owe me a*
> *new hat though. You better not try to get out of*
> *buying me a new hat.) XO, Wyatt*

That one was a little harder to parse, but it sounded like a joke between friends—or more than friends, considering the XO. No one had mentioned a Wyatt when we talked about people Addison might know. But the card was meaningful enough that she saved it.

I looked in the extra bedroom—avoiding the closet—but it only contained a keyboard, an amplifier, and what appeared to be some recording equipment—the famous mixer her father had gotten for her, I assumed, and a tangle of microphone cords. The chair was occupied by a box of CDs in thin plastic cases, on which Addison had written *DJ RADDISH-Numinosity*. I examined the mixer, which was a flat console with two CD drives and a whole bunch of buttons. I couldn't figure out how to turn it on, let alone how to make it play anything.

I pocketed one of the CDs and went downstairs, where I found Carlie at the dining room table, still poring over the same psychology book. "Do you know who this is from?" I said, showing her the card I'd found.

She took her pen out of her mouth as she looked at the inside of the card. "Wyatt? No." She looked at the front of the card and her expression softened a bit. "Do you think she's okay?"

I had no idea what to think, but there was little value in telling Carlie that.

Addison's father was Jason Stowe, a senior manager in a defense contracting firm based in Texas. I called his work number and left a message with a secretary who called me *dearheart* and advised that Mr. Stowe was currently visiting the UAE and would be stateside again in a day or so. On my way to pick up Catherine for dinner, I popped Addison's CD into the stereo at a red light. The first song was a strange hush of electronic strings over a meandering, trip-hoppy beat that sounded like it came preloaded into Garage-Band, plus snippets of people talking, the sizzle of a match being lit, the cracked warble of Billie Holiday's "Trav'lin' Light."

"Addison," a man's voice said, loud and clear. "You have nothing to lose."

On the contrary, I thought.

TEN

Sometimes you dread something so much that when it actually arrives, it winds up being only a fraction of how bad it could be.

Tonight was not one of those times.

From the second Catherine and I walked into the Whitney House from the frigid Worthington street, it was clear that Tom and Pam had been arguing. The worst kind of argument, too—the one where no one's mad or yelling because both parties know it's already over.

"So what's good here?" Pam said brightly once I'd ordered a whiskey for me and a cabernet for Catherine. "I heard great things about the boozy ice cream floats. Spiced rum and orange soda! Would you judge me if I had ice cream for dinner? It's been one of those days!"

"No judgement from me," I said, trying and failing to read Tom's expression.

Catherine said, "I already had ice cream for dinner, so I'll probably just get steak for dessert."

I laughed a little, but the opposite side of the table was silent.

Pam went on, "Maybe we could start with the duck confit appetizer? To split? Or we could get two orders, or if you guys want something else, or, um, we could just order a bunch of small plates to share? Sometimes for dinner girls just like to nibble on a little bit of everything, right?"

Pam continued reading items off the menu to the table. Her face held the mechanics of a smile but it wasn't fooling anyone. I ran my tongue along the edge of my whiskey glass, racking my brain for something to say to her.

"You know what? I'm getting the salmon *and* the duck. The least you can do is buy me dinner." Pam nudged Tom in the ribs, a playful gesture that he nearly recoiled from.

Under the table, Catherine gripped my hand.

We suffered through two rounds of drinks and a truly delicious spicy shrimp plate before the precise nature of the problem between them revealed itself.

"Look," Pam said as she rolled her wineglass between her palms, "I need you gals to referee this *discussion* we were having before dinner."

"Maybe we could finish the *discussion* later," Tom said. He had a dark beer in front of him, untouched.

Pam laughed. "Oh, we will. Trust me. I just want to get another lady opinion."

Tom propped his chin up in one hand, his eyes on the table. He wore jeans and a black sweater over a blue-and-white-checked shirt, but he still looked like a cop. He always did. But it had been a long time since I had seen him looking quite so miserable.

Pam was saying, "I just wanted to see what the options are. I mean, it's not like we haven't talked about it."

I said, "Talked about what?"

"Because we have. And it's not 1960."

"Talked about what, Pam?"

"A ring! It's common for a couple to pick out a ring together. Right, Catherine?"

I almost choked on my whiskey.

"Well," Catherine said, "I suppose it is—"

"An engagement doesn't have to be a big surprise, a big thing." Pam sipped her wine. Her eyes were bright, lively.

"So you're, um," I said, clearing my throat, "getting engaged? Or *are* engaged?"

"Things are progressing," Pam said, and at the same time, Tom shook his head, his jaw bunching up.

He said, "I really think we can talk about this later."

"All I'm saying," Pam said, "is that I suggested on the drive up here that we stop in at Worthington Jewelers. Just to look. And someone acted like that was just *too much*. Didn't you?" She nudged him playfully again, clearly not able to see that Tom's discomfort was the real deal. "A little forward momentum never hurt anybody. Roxane, did your mom ever tell you the story of when she and Frank got engaged?"

"Excuse me?" I said, setting my glass down a bit too hard. Beside me, Catherine stiffened, and Tom looked away altogether.

"Genevieve said that they'd been dating for almost three years, and every time she tried to talk to him about it, he just shut right down. So finally she said, 'Francis, do what you want, but I'm going to be engaged by Christmas. I hope it's to you, but who knows?' Two weeks later, he bought a ring. And they were together for how long?"

Tom sat back, his arms folded over his chest. "Pam."

"When exactly did my mother tell you this story and in what context?"

"Oh, I don't know, a few weeks ago. We text a lot."

At this, the table fell dead silent. Tom looked like his soul had actually died. I finished my drink and made desperate eye contact with our waiter.

"This has all been very illuminating," I said. I knew that my mother adored Pam—she randomly mentioned how she thought Tom should propose to her almost every time I saw her—but it was news to me that they had entire conversations via text message.

"I need to run to the little girls' room before the food comes," Pam said. She nudged her empty wineglass. "Order me another? Catherine, Roxane, want to join me?"

I shook my head, but Catherine slid out of her chair and followed Pam down the hallway next to the bar. As soon as they were out of earshot, I said, "Jesus Christ, what is happening? You're at the *looking at rings* stage?"

Tom covered his face with both hands. "No. I don't know. No."

"I can still see you."

"Dammit." He dropped his hands and leaned back in his chair. "What was I supposed to do? Wander around the jewelry store with her and say nothing at all? I'm not trying to be an asshole but this kind of came out of the blue. I feel like I missed a crucial conversation, except I'm pretty fucking sure I didn't—" Tom stopped midsentence, as his phone started to ring from his belt. He looked at the screen and frowned. "My sergeant," he said. "I need to take this."

"Yeah, right."

He finally smiled. "No, it is. Word of honor. I'll be right back."

He left me sitting at the table alone. I slurped the melted ice from my glass and I watched Tom step out through the front door and into the cold, his expression hardening as he listened to someone on the other end of his phone call.

He was still out there when they returned from the restroom. Catherine perched on the edge of her chair while Pam dropped into hers somewhat dramatically. "Roxie," she said, further proof that she'd been talking to my mother—no one else called me that. "Did you talk some sense into him?"

Through the front window of the restaurant, I saw Tom turn

around and motion at me, a *come out here* sort of gesture. His expression was still serious as a heart attack. "Um," I said, "I'll be right back."

I went outside without my coat and regretted it. Tom was pacing under a streetlight, hands in his pockets. "What's going on?"

He turned to look at me. "Yesterday morning," he said, "when you asked me about Mickey Dillman."

"Yeah?"

"Why?"

"I told you, my case—"

"I know, but why, specifically?"

"Well," I said, "I'm trying to find this woman, someone Andrew knows. When I went to her apartment, her roommate told me that Dillman had been there a week ago, looking for her."

"That's it?"

"That's it. Why? What's going on?"

He let out a heavy sigh, his breath making a soft white cloud in the night air. "Because they just pulled his body out of the river."

I leaned against the cold brick façade of the building. "Jesus."

"Yeah."

"What happened? And when?"

"They don't know yet. Maybe a while ago. It's been so cold out, so it's hard to, you know, tell." He stopped and looked up at the thick grey sky for a moment. "Do you ever feel like—you know what, never mind. I need to get going down there. Until we know what happened to him, this is going to be all hands on deck. Can you come downtown tomorrow, first thing? To talk about this woman you're looking for."

"Yeah, of course. But, Tom, what were you going to say? Do I ever feel like what?"

He shot me a quick smile and brushed past me into the restaurant.

I followed him and sat down, my hands shaking, and not just from the cold. But Tom remained standing and picked his wool coat up from the back of his chair. "I'm so sorry, but I need to go."

Pam said, "Tom, no, if this is because I was teasing—"

"No, it's—there's been an incident. Downtown. We'll have to do this again," he said gamely, as if we hadn't just endured the most awkward dinner in history.

"But, Tom, I'm—we rode together," Pam said.

"I know. I'm sorry."

"Pam, we'll give you a lift home."

"Thank you," Tom said. He squeezed my shoulder. "Catherine, nice to see you. We'll have to get together again soon. Pam, I'm sorry. This really has nothing to do with earlier. I'll call you tomorrow." He bent down and kissed her cheek.

Then he left.

We sat in silence for a while. Through the window, I saw two police cruisers sail past with their lights swirling, and I could hear sirens somewhere in the distance.

Pam picked up her empty wineglass and rubbed at the pinkish imprint from her lipstick on the rim. "Well, it's just us girls for dinner, I guess," she said.

When the waiter came back, I ordered a strong cup of tea.

Later, after dropping Pam off at her house in Grandview, Catherine and I drove along Neil Avenue in silence, her head on my shoulder. It was only ten o'clock, but it felt like the middle of the night. The Arena District was quiet, everyone in the city hibernating for the winter.

"Your mom really never told you that story before? The ultimatum?" she said after a while.

I'd never felt especially close to either of my parents, but after two revelations in as many days, I was downright confused. "Really.

I mean, she never has a bad thing to say about him, ever. Even though it was hardly a romance for the ages."

"Do you think they're ever having sex again?"

"My mother and my dead father? No."

Catherine sat up and turned to face me, her feet on the armrest between us. "Tom and Pam."

I sighed. "If we're ever that much not on the same page, please just end it. Right in the middle of dinner, I don't even care."

"I don't know if that's true."

"Okay, it probably isn't. But I'm just saying, don't let your manners and good breeding convince you it's better to sit through an experience like that."

She laughed a little on *good breeding*. "I wouldn't have guessed that Tom was a commitment-phobe."

"He's not. But you can't just randomly suggest dropping by a jewelry store to look at rings. Or can you? Is that what straight people are doing now?"

"When Wystan proposed," Catherine said, "he asked my father for permission."

"Ew."

"I didn't know about it until after I'd already said yes. So it's no wonder that the marriage didn't last."

"And you didn't call it off right then and there?"

"Things had already been set in motion. I thought that if I just tried hard enough, I could be the girl he thought I was. But it didn't work."

"Spoiler alert."

She stuck her tongue out at me.

I slowed to a stop at Long Street, my brakes grabbing at the road a little. To our right, the inky black of the river was partly illuminated on its far side, a pulse of blue and red and white. I squinted, trying to bring the scene into focus. At least a dozen squad cars, maybe more; the reflection of the swirling lights bounced off the half-solid river.

I tore myself away from the spectacle across the frozen water and turned left onto Long. Catherine rearranged herself so that her arm was linked through mine on the armrest. "I'm going to miss you too, you know," she said.

I felt myself smile in the dark.

"This has been nice, hasn't it? Behaving like an old married couple, going on double dates where our relationship is definitely the more solid of the two?"

"Yeah."

"Now we just need matching silk menswear pajamas and the transformation will be complete."

"Why does your version of old married coupledom sound like something from *It Happened One Night*?"

"There's nothing I like better than to meet a high-class mama that can snap 'em back at ya," she drawled, her head on my shoulder as I drove. "You'll pick me up from the airport when I get home?"

"Of course."

"Maybe we can get dinner somewhere nice on the way. The Pearl."

"You won't have gotten your fill of oysters in Rhode Island?"

I felt her look up at me. "They have oysters there?" she said, her tone one of mock surprise. "Shit, I might not come back."

"You better."

Catherine tucked her head back at my shoulder. "They might have oysters, but they don't have you."

ELEVEN

I slept a little, possibly a self-defense mechanism after such a tense evening—a tense day, really. But I woke around one, startled and slightly overheated. Beside me, Catherine was at the bottom of the ocean, untouchable. Finally I gave up and went downstairs to charge my phone. While I waited for it to power up, I poured a glass of water and looked out at the snowy backyard, just as I had last night. When the phone finally buzzed back to life, I went to the Dispatch website to see if there were any more details about what had happened to Mickey Dillman.

Police: off-duty officer found dead near Scioto River.

I leaned against the granite countertop on my elbows and read the rest of the article.

> *The body of 43-year old Michael "Mickey" Dillman*
> *was found near the Olentangy River below the Long*
> *Street Bridge on Saturday evening, police said. He*
> *was a veteran officer of the department, serving a*
> *decade in the detective bureau before taking on a*
> *supervisor position in the Administrative bureau in*
> *2014. He was currently on leave following surgery*

and expected to return to active duty in two
weeks . . .

Even though Dillman was no longer in the detective bureau, the people who'd worked with him probably felt this acutely. Not that there was ever such a thing as good timing for someone to die, but this wasn't it: almost two years to the day that my father was killed.

I thought of Tom's face in the streetlights outside the restaurant.

I started to send a text to him but wasn't sure what to say. Anyway, it was the middle of the night. Middle-of-the-night text messages were fraught with meaning, though maybe that wasn't the case if they were in reference to a dead body.

I thought about getting in the car and driving over to Nightshade, but I already knew that this case wasn't going to be as simple as finding the missing—or at least misplaced—employee back at work like nothing had happened. Instead, I pulled up the club's Facebook page and saw half a dozen new posts of varying degrees of politeness, asking why they weren't open, and what was going on.

That was an excellent question.

Catherine was mostly silent on the drive across 670. Her flight was early, six-fifteen, the type that always seems like a good idea until you remember how shitty early flights are. Maybe that was why she was quiet, why her posture was rigid, uneasy. When I pulled up to the United doors at the passenger drop-off area, she turned to me, her eyes impossible, and said, "Do you want to come with me?"

We looked at each other for a long time. The flight left in less than an hour. It wasn't a real invitation, and we both knew it.

"I mean," she went on, "I'll be busy the whole time, but since you're going to miss me so much, why don't you just come?"

I didn't want to argue right before she left. I said, "Catherine."

"So I guess you aren't going to miss me then?"

Something had changed overnight, and I didn't know what. "I can't."

"Why?"

"I have work."

"Work from the hotel."

"How?"

"Um, your crusty MacBook? Can't you Google people from any-where?"

"Well, there's more to what I do than that."

Catherine unbuckled her seat belt and pulled her handbag up from the floor. "Right, you have to run around talking about crimes to what's-his-face, Tom, who's clearly in love with you, by the way—"

"That's not—"

"Just kiss me good-bye, okay?"

"But—"

"Roxane."

I didn't know how to talk to her when she got like this, so I leaned over and kissed her, my eyes squeezed shut. "Can I call you tonight?"

"I'll call you, okay? I'll be in and out of things but I'll call when I can." She got out of the car without saying anything else and went around to the trunk and rapped her knuckles on the back window.

I pulled the release and got out too. "Come on, what kind of a good-bye is this?"

She heaved her rolling suitcase out of the trunk and shoved it toward the curb with one heeled boot. "You're asking me?"

"Catherine, if you really wanted me to come with you, why didn't you ask me last week? Or last night, when we were talking about it?"

Yanking up the handle on the suitcase, she said, "I don't know why I asked at all. I have to go."

"Please don't do this. You always do this."

"It's fine. Everything's fine. I'll see you in a few days."

She dragged the suitcase up over the curb and disappeared through the sliding glass doors that led into the airport.

I stared after her, my heart pounding. The thing of it was, I wasn't even surprised. Catherine had always been this way, picking fights out of nowhere, acting like I was the one being unreasonable. Especially when she was about to leave. She'd done a lot of leaving, both physically and emotionally. I thought something was different this time—we were different, older, more self-aware—but something always seems *different this time*, right up to the moment that it doesn't.

I knew she wouldn't turn around and she didn't.

The officer behind the desk at the police headquarters knew me and clipped a visitor's badge to my collar because my hands were full—coffee for Tom, tea for me. I went up to the third floor, which housed the detective unit. I squeezed in through the door on the heels of someone I didn't recognize and wound my way through the maze of cubicles until I found Tom's. His chair was empty, but his coat was still there. I set the tray of beverages down on the desk and stood around awkwardly for a while, thinking about what Catherine had said. *Clearly in love with you, by the way.* What would she have said if I hadn't interrupted her?

I looked at my phone, pretending to myself that she actually might have called already.

She hadn't.

There wasn't much in the way of personal items in Tom's workspace, but I did notice a photo of him with my father—an actual photograph on glossy paper—tacked to the burlap wall behind his computer monitor. I pulled out the pushpin and squinted at the picture. It was one I'd never seen before, probably from five or more years before Frank died. They were both in jeans, both holding beer bottles, Tom caught in mid-laugh while my father looked right into the camera, his piercing blue eyes crinkling up. They were outside, in front of a picnic shelter or something. I flipped it over; the back bore a few lines of neat cursive handwriting in black ink.

Tom Heitker and Frank Weary, July 4

I sat on the edge of Tom's desk and studied the photo again, wondering who had taken it.

When I heard footsteps on the carpeted hallway outside Tom's cube, I stuck my head out.

"What the hell are you doing in there?" Ed Sanko asked. Then he leaned in and kissed me on the cheek. I guessed he had decided after the Arthur Ungless case last summer that I wasn't just a brunette Veronica Mars, but a detective with some smarts. He added, "He's around here somewhere. You hear what happened last night?"

I nodded. Sanko gestured at the photo I was holding.

"I found that in a box of old pictures this morning. I was looking for ones of Mickey."

"You know what this is from?"

"Some cookout Mickey and Sunny had, years ago."

I wondered if this was when my father had bonded with Sunny over the halo-halo. "Did you know him well?"

Sanko held up a hand and tipped it back and forth. "He left not too long after I moved to homicide, and he was over the later shift anyway. But we all work so close. You know how it is."

"I'm very sorry to hear about him."

"Yeah." He stepped farther into Tom's cube and rested an arm on top of the burlap divider. "Kinda glad to run into you," he said, his voice lower. "You think he's okay?"

"Tom?"

Sanko nodded.

I thought about the conversation I'd had with Tom last night. *Do you ever feel like . . .* It was possible to be okay and not okay at the same time. But I told Sanko what he wanted to hear: "I think so. Why?"

"I just . . . I know you two are close, so he probably confides in you. But it seems like something is going on. Even before we heard about Dillman, it seemed that way."

Before I could respond, Tom rounded the corner, saying to someone over his shoulder, "I'll definitely let you know as soon as you can get it back, okay?" He stopped, looked at me and Sanko and added, "Oh. Hi."

"I was just telling Weary here about this picture," Sanko said, nodding a good-bye to me before disappearing into his own cube.

Tom sat down heavily in his chair. "Please say this is coffee and that it's for me."

I pulled the cup with my tea out of the paper beverage tray. "With real cream and everything."

"Bless you." He peeled back the plastic tab on the lid. "So you're snooping around my desk now."

"What can I say? Nosiness runs in the family." I sat back down on the edge of his desk. He wasn't acting like someone who was in love with me. He was much more interested in the coffee. "I just saw this and had to get a closer look."

Tom took the photo from me and studied it for a while. "It's like a time capsule."

I glanced over his shoulder at the photo. My father looked about the same as he had up to the end, though maybe he eventually got a little greyer at the temples. Tom was thirty pounds heavier in the photo, almost baby-faced, and he looked happy in a way that I'd never seen in person. It wasn't like a time capsule so much as it was an alternate reality.

"Ah, Christ," Tom said. He opened a desk drawer and swept the photo inside. "Thanks for coming in this morning. I'm sorry about ditching you last night like that."

"Well, you should probably be telling Pam that, not me," I said, then wished I hadn't. Something sank in his expression. "I just mean—oh, never mind. It was fine. You know she adores Catherine. It's not lost on me that I keep introducing people in my life to other people in my life and they always wind up liking each other better than they like me."

"That's not true."

"It is. My mother and Pam? Pam and Catherine?"

He finally gave me a small smile. "Your mother and Rafael."

"See, you're getting the gist." I sipped my tea. "But anyway, I know you didn't want me to come in so I could whine about how I'm the least likeable member of my family."

He grabbed a yellow legal pad and a pen. "I could debate you on that point all day, but you're right. Let's go into a conference room."

Conference room was better than interrogation room, though the two felt similar—too small, bad lighting. I told Tom and another detective, Evangeline Clark, about how my path crossed, so to speak, with Mickey Dillman. The story was short on real information: the previous week, Dillman, who wasn't even on active duty, had showed up at Addison's apartment, told her roommate to have Addison call him about an unknown matter, and left an old business card that identified him as holding a job he hadn't actually had in years.

"I suppose if I was out of cards," Clark said, playing devil's advocate, "for my current gig, but I had some old ones laying around— no, I still don't see it." She was new to the detective bureau, about thirty, an athletic black woman in a tailored blue suit. "Because why would he be identifying himself as a police officer at all? He hasn't been working."

I said, "Would he have been required to hand in his badge before he went on medical leave?"

Tom tapped his pen on the legal pad. "Depends. We'll have to find out the exact nature of the leave. And you have no idea what he wanted with this woman you're looking for?"

"None. He didn't say, and the roommate didn't ask."

Tom gave a heavy sigh. "I can see it being nothing. Like he side-swiped her car and was trying to do the right thing, while also trying to get out of doing the right thing."

"Is that like him? I didn't know him," Clark added, the last part to me.

"I don't know. He was a decent guy, maybe a little bit inclined to cut corners sometimes. But who isn't."

The younger detective elbowed him. "You, for example."

Tom gave a half-smile. "I knew you were going to say that. Anyway, I guess Addison's the one who could probably tell us what was going on, if only we knew where she was. You said she took a suitcase?"

I sipped my tea, which was cold and had been for a while. "I said I think she took a suitcase, based on the wheel marks in her carpet."

"Right, I forgot I was talking to the resident carpetologist here," Tom said.

I laughed around a mouthful of tea and almost gagged. Nothing was funny, but everything was. Tom laughed a little bit as well. Clark shook her head, saying, "You two."

After they were done with me, Tom walked me down to the lobby. "Just keep me posted if you figure out where she is."

"So you aren't going to tell me to stay away from it?"

"Not that you'd do it anyway," he said, holding the elevator door open for a pair of patrol cops in bulky uniform jackets and gloves, "but you're trying to give this woman's friends some piece of mind, while this—we—I have no idea what we're dealing with here."

"Any idea what happened?"

Tom lowered his voice a little. "He was pretty banged up from being in the river—from the rocks. It's so cold out, and the water's half-frozen, too, so it's hard to say how long. Or where he went in. No sign of his car yet—he's had the same car forever, this black Thunderbird, from the mid-nineties. His pride and joy. I've been in that car. It's surreal, putting out an alert for a vehicle that I've personally been in." He shook his head. "Not supposed to happen like that. But anyway, no, no idea what happened."

"Did he drown?"

"Don't know yet. There was a big gash, here," he said, touching the back of his head. "But they won't know until the autopsy is finished."

"Could it have been a suicide?"

He winced a little. "I never thought he was depressed. But that doesn't mean anything."

"Right."

"From what Sunny said—his wife, from what she said, he wasn't in a great place. Emotionally."

"Assaulting your spouse will do that."

Tom pressed his mouth into a thin line. "That," he said, "and the back problems, not being able to work. It sounded like a lot. But if you're asking technically, based on the state he was in, the answer is maybe. Please keep that to yourself."

"Of course."

"And will you let Andrew know that we might want to talk to him about Addison?"

"He'll be thrilled."

"I know."

The revolving doors spun open and with them, a burst of

liquid-nitrogen-cold air. Tom looked outside, at the grey sky and the grey street and the grey concrete steps. "Are you guys doing anything on the eighth?"

I felt myself sigh. I was no better equipped to deal with the anniversary of my father's death than I had been days ago. I was possibly less equipped now. "I'm sure we will. But I don't know what yet. I'll let you know." I thought about what Sanko had said upstairs and had no idea what to do about it. "Hey," I said, "are you doing okay?"

He turned away from the window and gave me a look like he had no idea what to do about it either. "I'm fine," he said. "Thanks for the coffee."

I went to Upper Cup for tea and a muffin and wireless internet. I had two of those things at home, but I didn't want to go home. So I holed up at a table as far away from the door and the cold winter air as possible and tried to make sense of the card I'd found in Addison's room yesterday.

Wyatt. There were a lot of people with the name in Columbus. I tried a few different combinations based on what I knew about him—admittedly, very very little—like *Wyatt + Addison, Wyatt + hat,* all of which was useless. Then I went back to Addison's deejaying profile—DJ Raddish—and clicked for a while to make sure Facebook's algorithm wasn't hiding any salient information from me and was rewarded with a brief exchange in the comments on her long-ago post about an event at Skate Zone.

> <u>Wyatt Achebe</u> *Girl. Are you ever going to update this page?*
> Like • Reply 5w

Addison Marie @Wyatt Bitch, be quiet. Facebook is
dried up.
   Like • Reply 5w
Wyatt Achebe @Addison Marie You're dried up.
   Like • Reply 5w
Addison Marie True, true. ;P
   Like • Reply 5w
Wyatt Achebe People of Columbus, forget about
Skate Zone. _DJ Raddish_ is now at Nightshade almost
every damn night! Get on it.
   Like • Reply 5w

I clicked on Wyatt's name to view his profile and almost dropped
my muffin.

This was the guy who'd been driving Shane's Jag from the other
night.

And his profile said that he was a bouncer at Nightshade.

In daylight he was younger than I'd thought, college-age or so,
well-built to the point of vanity, his dark skin stretched tight over
impressive delts, which were on display in sleeveless shirts in the
handful of pictures his privacy settings allowed me to see. He had
a big, easy smile, friendly. But he'd been following me, which wasn't
exactly friendly.

I closed my laptop and focused on my muffin. This was going
to require energy.

In short order I'd learned that Wyatt Achebe was twenty-three
years old and on parole for assault, a charge to which he'd pleaded
no contest a year earlier. He lived in a small blue Cape Cod on Loretta
Avenue in North Linden. It was an area split off from Clintonville
by the freeway, a phenomenon of urban planning that arbitrarily
made a neighborhood get a reputation as less desirable. But the

houses, while inexpensive compared to the ones just on the other side of 71, were mostly neat and well-maintained, their sidewalks clear of snow. When I knocked on Wyatt's door, the curtains fluttered almost instantaneously.

"Yes? What is it?"

She was tall, forty-five or so, dressed in a cotton housecoat with hearts on it; she had the same soft features as Wyatt did and she was clutching a wad of wet tissues.

I told her who I was and why I was there, and she pressed her mouth into a flat line. "I'm afraid something awful's happened," she said, and began to cry.

TWELVE

"I called the police," she said a few minutes later, once we were sitting at a small round table in the kitchen, mugs of tea in front of each of us even though I'd already had enough caffeine to power me for a few days. "On Friday. When I said that he'd replied to a few of my texts, the officer kind of laughed and said Wyatt was probably just out sowing his wild oats. I tried to explain that my son is—he doesn't do that, he doesn't not come home. Ever."

I could see where the police might have been coming from but disagreed—the fact that something unusual had happened with or to both Addison and Wyatt on the same night didn't seem like a good sign. I said, "What did he say in the texts?"

She took her phone out of the pocket of her housecoat and showed me their exchange.

> Honey, where are you?
> Wyatt?
>> *I had to get a ride to Dr. Franco's office with*
>> *Lenny next door.*
> Where are you?
>> *I'm sorry mom*
> When are you coming home?
> I need to get my pills from Kroger

     I don't know

     I'll get you an Uber

   I don't want an Uber, I want you to tell me where you
are

     Taking care of something.

     I'll be back when I can

   What's wrong?

     Nothing

   What are you taking care of?

   Wyatt?

   What on earth is going on?

The last response from Wyatt had been Saturday afternoon.

"I take it that it's unlike him not to respond to you?"

"He's glued to his phone. And he knows that I know he's glued to his phone. He always texts me back. Especially since I've been sick . . ." Wyatt's mother trailed off. Her name was Gwen and Wyatt was her only son. "And you know, I get it. The police probably get calls about all kinds of things that don't amount to much, but when I say my son would not do this, I am absolutely positive."

"You're close?"

"Very." She dabbed at her eyes. "Also, I'm having a procedure in two weeks. So things are stressful lately, which Wyatt knows, of course, so he definitely wouldn't do this, not right now."

"And the last time you saw him was Wednesday."

Gwen nodded. "Around seven. I fixed dinner for us. Then he went to work. When I got up in the morning, his door was closed so at first I thought he was still asleep—he always sleeps late, since he doesn't get home till four a.m. Sometimes a bit later, if he decides to go to the gym after. The yellow and purple one over by North Broadway. But anyway, he's always home in the morning. At about ten, I saw his car wasn't here, and that was when I knew something had to be wrong." She swirled her tea bag idly around her mug. "He shouldn't be working in a place like that. But he's—he's a felon now," she said, shaking her head. "So his options are limited."

"Mind if I ask what happened?"

"Oh, it was a terrible thing. He tried to break up a fight outside a bar on campus—a transgender classmate of his was being harassed. Wyatt stepped in and it—it wasn't a fair fight, of course, it was two against one, but he's very strong, my son. He put these boys in the hospital, one of them had a broken jaw. And of course it turned out that he's the nephew of some bigwig who gives a lot of money to the school. So in one swoop, Wyatt's expelled and charged with assault. All because he was trying to help." She shook her head slowly, disbelieving. "This world is not fair."

"No, it isn't," I said. It was probably a safe bet that the bigwig's nephew was white, and Wyatt was not, which was at the heart of a lot of the unfairness. "So not a lot of places are hiring people with felonies on their records."

"He's still looking for something better. But without his student loans, and with my health . . . he needed to start working right away. So that's where he wound up. A real snake pit, from the sound of it. Rather than a paycheck, he just gets a stack of cash from the register. His boss is always having him run weird errands. I keep telling him, you need to keep records of what you're getting paid, what he's having you do. Don't get wrapped up in whatever funny business this is. And do *not* socialize with those people."

"What kind of weird errands?"

"Well, he told me about going to Microcenter to buy a bunch of techy stuff."

"Techy stuff?"

"Cameras, computer stuff. A couple thousand dollars' worth. And then the next day, they made him return it all."

"Why?"

She shook her head.

That was definitely weird. Laundering cash from the bar, maybe? It was a wildly inefficient way to do that, especially when you were already in cahoots with something of a master of the medium. But maybe Shane was trying to short Vincent Pomp's proceeds and lacked the brainpower to devise a better system?

I said, "Did Wyatt ever mention a young woman named Addison? A deejay?"

Gwen's eyebrows went together. "Yes," she said, an edge in her voice. "He told me about her. He said she had some trouble with someone, in the club. He had to toss some woman out because of it."

"Really."

She nodded.

"When was this?"

"Oh, I don't know. A while back."

"Do you know what the trouble was?"

"It sounded like something to do with a man. Like so much trouble is, you know. But I don't know the specifics. Wyatt just said that Addison is a real nice girl with the worst luck."

There was that word again: nice.

"Do you think they might've been involved?"

"Involved? No. My son is gay. They're just friends."

"Any idea if they hang out together outside of work?"

Gwen said, "Unless she likes to lift weights, I don't think so. But like I said, my son is glued to that phone. I'm sure they message each other and whatnot. I just hope he's been smart enough not to get involved in anything ugly over there." She shook her head. "The past year has been nothing but pain."

There was no answer at Shane Resznik's motel room. That was my first guess as to Wyatt's whereabouts, since he'd been driving

Shane's car just a few days earlier. But the car wasn't here either. I sat in the parking lot for a while just in case one or both of them spontaneously showed up, and I mulled over what Gwen Achebe had to say: trouble at the bar, over a man, which led to Wyatt throwing some woman out.

There was definitely something brewing between Shane Resznik's two lady loves, Lisette and the braless Goth bartender, but it didn't seem like Addison fit into that saga. Resznik had seemed downright surprised when I asked about her.

That left me with BusPass Guy, who could easily have had a wife, along with pictures of Addison on his phone. But who, also, could have been literally anybody.

People, in general, weren't all that mysterious. But when you looked into their lives from the outside—no background, no context—they suddenly looked that way. I was no different; if a detective who didn't know anything about me needed to figure out where I might have gone or who I might have gone with, there weren't many obvious answers.

An interesting thought experiment: my own disappearance, and how I'd investigate it. I'd check my mother's house, my brother's place—Andrew's, not Matt's, because he sucked—and Catherine's place, if anyone pointed me in her direction. I'd already checked Wyatt's mother's place, his sister lived in Michigan and hadn't heard from him, and I didn't know of a love interest or any friends other than Addison, who was, of course, also nowhere to be found.

I spent a bit of time systematically "friending" some of Wyatt's connections in case this would magically release any clues hidden behind his profile privacy settings. According to his mother, he worked, went to the gym, and came home—no exceptions or diversions. I didn't know how likely that was, but the purple and yellow gym by North Broadway could only refer to one place— the Planet Fitness on Indianola. It was beside a large Volunteers of America thrift shop, where I'd once tracked down a porcelain urn containing the remains of someone's beloved pet ferret.

Clients hired me to find lots of things, and I took them all seriously—but people, most of all.

When neither Shane nor Wyatt had resurfaced in close to two hours, I decided to try the gym. There was a perky blond woman in a black-and-purple uniform behind the counter when I went into the gym. I wondered if she owned SpinSpo leggings and assumed she did. Proof that the universe has a sense of humor: two different fitness-related cases at the same time, despite my firm anti-exercise stance other than running my mouth. I showed her a picture of Wyatt on my phone. "I'm looking for my friend," I started, not expecting much.

But then her face lit up. "Wyatt!"

"You know him?"

"Sure. He used to come in here all the time."

"Used to?"

I noticed she had a streak of purple in the lock of hair tucked behind her ear. "Like last year."

"Was he friends with anyone here?"

"Friends? I don't know, probably not. Although, he applied for a job here, had an interview and everything. Then he started going to another gym. I'm not sure why they wouldn't hire him. He's super nice. Great smile."

I figured I knew why—a failed background check—but there was no point in splashing Wyatt's business around. "Do you know what gym he goes to now?"

She tipped her head to the left, the way people so often did when trying to remember a name or to think of a lie. I hoped it was the former in this case. "He told me what it was called but it's just gone, you know? But it was something like—it sounded like a deodorant brand."

"What, like Speed Stick?"

She laughed. "No, *fresh* or something."

"Any idea where it was?"

Purple Streak shook her head. "Sorry."

I went home and spent an hour making a list of gyms in Columbus that also potentially sounded like deodorant brands:

> *Speed Round*
> *Clear Confidence Fitness*
> *Purity*
> *Stride*
> *CleanSweat*
> *Crystal Sweat*
> *X-Treme System*

But by now it was Sunday night and it looked like most of them were closed.

I stood at the front window and looked out at the dark street. There weren't any headlights shining this time—where was my low-key stalker when I actually wanted to speak to him?

A woman in a parka with a fur-lined hood walked by, a husky trotting alongside her. The dog looked happy. The woman looked miserable. I sat down on my sofa and said to the empty room, "I am so fucking frustrated I could scream."

Sometimes saying it out loud helped a little. This time it didn't. All of this runaround might be over nothing, but without knowing what exactly had happened at Nightshade, I'd never figure it out.

I grabbed my keys and left.

THIRTEEN

Shimmy's was over on 161, about where you'd expect: in the long string of condemned motels and nightclubs with names like the Blue Fox and Tart. From the name, I was afraid it was going to be a strip club but when I got there I realized that very little shimmying was going on. One lone dancer in fishnets and a neon-green swimsuit stood on a small parquet stage with an antique pole in the center, talking on the phone. "I know, sweetie, I miss Grandma too," she was saying. When I walked in, she looked up, turned away from the door, and went back to her conversation. There was music playing, but it was an unidentifiable blare of bass and crackling speakers. The place was empty except for the dancer and a bartender, similarly dressed. I sat down on one of the bar stools.

"Um," the bartender said, "can I help you?"

I kept finding myself in bars that didn't want me this week. It was starting to seem like a metaphor for something. "Crown Royal, neat."

"No, I mean, do you need help?"

"Why, because I'm here?"

She bit back a laugh. "This isn't a ladies' night kind of place."

"And yet, here we all are. Is Mr. Pomp here?"

Under the hazy lights, her expression changed. "Nope."

"How about Bo?"

She'd been slowly working the lid off a bottle of Crown, but now she reached for a phone that was underneath the worn bar top.

"Tell him it's Roxane Weary," I said. "He'll be happy to see me."

Bo wasn't that happy to see me. Maybe it was because I'd come to him, at the slightly embarrassing Phoenix Group social club, or maybe it was because I was interrupting his Sunday night with business.

"Why the fuck would I let you see the security cameras at Nightshade?" he was saying.

I had no idea what was up with Wyatt's electronics-return routine, but Gwen had given me an idea. If something had happened at the club, maybe there would be a recording of it. "Because I asked nicely, and because I think something happened there on Wednesday night, two people are suddenly nowhere to be found, and you might want to figure out what's going on before someone other than me starts wondering about it."

"Two people?"

I explained about how two employees had sort of gone AWOL in the past few days.

"I ask again, why would we show you the security footage?" he said, glaring at me a little.

But I could tell that under the tough-guy act, he knew that what I was saying wasn't exactly good news for his boss. I said, "If you could help clear a little smoke, don't you think Mr. Pomp would appreciate that?"

Nightshade looked the same as it had the other night: black, empty, uninviting. Armed with a real flashlight this time, we did a full search for the light switches, finally locating a panel on the wall in the loading dock that required a key to operate.

"Jesus Christ," Bo muttered. He held up a massive ring with at least three dozen keys on it.

"What are all those for?"

"The fuck if I know."

"Here," I said. I squinted in the flashlight beam at the small lock, then picked through the keys until I found five likely contenders.

The third one worked.

"Magic," I said.

Bo just frowned and slid the switches up into the on position; one by one, lights buzzed on and illuminated quadrants of the club.

It looked better with the lights off.

The floor was a scuffed tile in a brownish-black shade and dotted with smears of spilled liquor and fuzzy with dust. A network of amplifiers was arranged above the dance floor, the grille cloth ripped and hanging down like the wings of bats. A trash can near the front door was overflowing with crumpled plastic cups and a pool of murky liquid was slowly leaking out of the bottom, and other cups and beer bottles were scattered around the place—on the floor, on the edge of the stage, on bar stools.

Bo turned off a few of the lights. "What the fuck."

I shined my flashlight around, looking for security cameras: one above the door, two behind the bar, two more in the hallway that led to the restrooms. They looked old and possibly defunct. I pointed at a door at the end of that hallway. "What's that?"

"Basement."

There was another door opposite the restrooms. "And that?"

"Office."

"I assume that's where the security system would be?"

We went down the hall, our shoes sticking to the floor. I supposed that most bars were probably this gross, but you couldn't hear the suction under your feet because of the music. Maybe that was why bars played music in the first place.

The door to the office was locked. Bo consulted his key ring again and got it on the second try this time.

The office was little more than a closet with a desk, a decrepit old computer monitor, and a bank of file cabinets. Bo nudged the computer's mouse; the monitor stayed black. While he felt around for a power switch, I studied a white board on the wall opposite the desk.

MIN 10 FOR SKELETAL, someone had written in messy block letters.

> *ADDISON BAR XCEPT 10–1230*
> *FIND NEW DOOR GUY?*
> *.23*

I took a picture of the list, though I had no idea what it meant. Bo was still rooting around under the desk, so I turned my attention to the file cabinets—thinking maybe they contained personnel records or something useful.

But no: they were empty.

At least the one closest to the door was. The second was jammed full of promotional items like T-shirts and can koozies. The third just had packages and packages of black napkins.

"Goddammit," Bo said behind me. He shoved the computer monitor in disgust. It had booted up but was asking for a password, presumably one that he didn't have. "I don't know how to see the camera footage. They don't even work, for all I know. But can we agree that nothing sinister happened here?"

Things were rarely that simple. I had to agree that the place looked like a crappy nightclub after a regular crappy night. Plus, I assumed, there would have been patrons around on Wednesday night—people who would have seen some kind of incident, if there had been one. So maybe my theory was just plain wrong. Maybe Addison was upset about being told she had to work behind the bar in addition to deejaying, she quit in a huff, and Wyatt and Shane were still off partying together somewhere.

I could almost believe it, but not quite.

I dragged a chair from the office to the security camera in the bathroom hallway and climbed up; the device had a layer of dust on it so thick that it obscured the little light that was supposed to blink in green if the camera was operational; under the grime, the light was off. I sighed in disgust. But while I was up there, I could see a spot above the door to the office, where the painted cinder block was a slightly lighter shade of beige, like something had recently been ripped down.

I moved the chair, Bo watching me with annoyed amusement, or amused annoyance.

Up close, the spot was half-moon shaped and still sticky.

But that didn't tell me anything.

I did one more lap of the place, looking for other sticky half-moon spots on the walls. The exposed brick walls of the bar and dance floor area weren't painted. So unless I went around touching every inch of wall looking for a sticky patch, there was no way to tell.

And there was no guarantee of the composition of any sticky patches I might find. The thought made me shudder.

I turned the basement doorknob but it, too, was locked. "Can you?" I said.

"That's not supposed to be locked. It's one of the exits."

"Well, it's locked. So can you?"

"You're very demanding."

"I prefer *thorough*."

Bo unlocked the door.

A rank, moldy smell wafted up the steps. I covered my mouth with my hand, suddenly afraid of what the basement contained.

But halfway down the steps, I found the problem—standing water, a lot of it, almost the whole floor submerged. Or, rather, the layer of flattened cardboard boxes and trash that covered the floor was almost submerged.

"I guess he was telling the truth about the pipes bursting," I said.

Bo looked down the steps in disgust. "This is a fucking health hazard. I'm going upstairs."

I went down a few more steps and looked at the mess from top to bottom; I could see a segment of pipe near the ceiling with an ominous bulge, and another with a jagged tear in the metal, something brown dripping from it.

I gagged a little and took the steps two at a time back up.

"So we're done here, then?" Bo said, in a way that meant we definitely were.

After Bo left—with a word of advice to leave Vincent Pomp alone now—I stood on the street and stared up at the club. The vinyl sign over the neon one fluttered in the cold night air. I tried to put myself in Addison's shoes: on the sidewalk in front of her job, upset about something, but not the kind of upset that makes you jump in the car and just drive. No, the kind that made her go across the street and ring the doorbell of a guy who was an acquaintance at best and ask to use his phone.

An emergency. An *I have to get off this street immediately* type of emergency.

I presumed her phone call had not been about the sewage in the basement, though I was feeling a fairly urgent need to wash my hands.

But she hadn't gone into Andrew's place to do that.

She needed to make a call.

Where was *her* phone?

Who had she called?

Also, where was her car?

She'd walked home, had to use the spare key to get into her place, so that meant her keys were probably AWOL as well. I thought about the lockers in the hallway back in the club, imagining that her phone and keys were locked in there during her shift. And, what, she left suddenly, without a chance to grab them?

Whatever had happened, it must have been bad.

I looked up and down the street. Most of the cars were shellacked with snow and ice, their colors and makes hidden from view.

I'd never be able to find Addison's maroon Scion this way, even if it was here.

FOURTEEN

I washed my hands more thoroughly than I ever had in my life at Andrew's sink, and he gave me a shot of Crown Royal and a blanket, both of which were necessary to ward off hypothermia from being outside.

Andrew sighed and poured us both another shot. "I just had this feeling. That it was bad. That's why I called you. And you obviously had a feeling too. I was really hoping we'd both be wrong this time."

"Unfortunately, no one is ever wrong at the right time. If they were, no one would ever be wrong—we'd all just be right."

"I can't tell if that's the whiskey talking or if you just said something profound."

I threw back my shot and held the glass out for another. "Maybe both."

Andrew poured. We were on opposite ends of his sectional sofa, grey and soft. It always reminded me that I needed to get a new sofa but I always forgot about it by the time I went home. He said, "So now what?"

"I don't know. I was hoping the club would give me an idea of what to do next, but it didn't."

I yawned.

"You look awfully cozy over there."

"This blanket is the best thing that ever happened to me."

He refilled my glass again and I didn't stop him. "Do you think something bad happened to her?"

I sat up long enough to swallow my shot and then burrowed back under the blanket. "I definitely think something weird happened. I don't want to think about it in terms of good or bad. Not yet."

"Since when is the Weary family the denial type?"

"Since always."

Andrew tipped the whiskey bottle in my direction but this time I shook my head.

All things in moderation.

"And it's always worked out so well," he said.

We went silent again.

Finally, Andrew said, "Maybe February is just cursed. Did anything good ever happen in February?"

"Catherine was born in February."

"I said did anything *good* happen."

I flashed an upright middle finger at him.

"So where is the witch this week? I've seen an awful lot of you."

I sat up and rearranged the blanket over my lap. "You always see a lot of me. And this week, in particular, you're seeing a lot of me because you somehow found yourself in the middle of a fucked-up situation and you asked for my help."

"Fair enough."

"But," I said, "she left this morning for Rhode Island, some kind of conference."

"I knew it."

"You did not. Lucky guess."

"No, I could tell. You think you're the only perceptive member of the family?"

"Hardly, but it was still a lucky guess. And don't call her a witch. I seem to remember you getting bent out of shape that time I told you Trina—or whatever her name was, the one with the dolphin tattoos—when I told you she was an idiot. And, to be clear, she was an idiot."

"And Catherine *is* a witch. Not in a cool, pagan way. A *Macbeth*-style evil manipulator."

I shook my head at him, but I didn't argue. I didn't have the energy, not after the disorienting conversation en route to the airport. Not when I hadn't heard a word from her all day, even though she had said she'd text me later. To Catherine, later could mean not at all.

Andrew added, "Trina just *really* liked dolphins." His phone started ringing from the bedroom. "Jesus, what time is it?"

We both looked at the clock on the wall opposite the sofa. One of those minimalist things with no numbers or even little tick marks. It was sometime between one and three, that was all I could tell.

A bad time for a phone call, either way.

Andrew got up and went out of sight for a moment and I listened as he answered the call.

A note of concern entered his voice. "Who is this?" he said. He put the call on speakerphone and rejoined me on the sofa.

"Put her on the phone, asshole," a man said.

"Who is this?"

"Let me talk to my daughter. I know she's there. She called from this number."

Andrew winced. He covered the mouthpiece of the phone and whispered, "What do I do?"

"I don't know. Tell him—"

"Do I need to call the police?" the man barked.

"No—"

"Then put her on."

"Give me the phone," I said. "Mr. Stowe? My name is Roxane Weary, and I left a message for you on your work line?"

He made a gruff sound of affirmation.

"We're all trying to find Addison, and—"

"Yeah, I bet. Just wait till I'm—"

Abruptly, the call disconnected.

"What the fuck," my brother said. He dropped his phone on the cushion like it was hot to the touch. "What—okay, so that's one mystery solved. She called her dad."

The guy who was off in Dubai for business. Maybe that was why he hadn't answered her call, had taken so long to get worried. "Maybe we should reconsider here," I said. "About the police." Getting Tom involved now seemed like the wrong call—he had enough to worry about. But it was one thing when Addison's friends hadn't heard from her; another if her father hadn't, given that she was the one who used her emergency phone call to get in touch with *him*.

"I don't—but I offered to get her help that night. She said no. She didn't want help."

"If that's really true, and she doesn't want help, then what the hell am I doing?"

Andrew sighed. "Fuck. Maybe you're right."

We just sat there for a while, the only sound the ticking of the useless clock.

Finally he said, "I need to get some things in order, if we're going to do that. Can it wait until the morning?"

"I think so."

"I need to go to sleep."

I nodded. "I'm sleeping here."

"It folds out, into a queen."

I shook my head. "This is fine."

"You'll regret it in the morning."

"Andrew," I said, "that's my personal motto."

I woke up to the smell of fried eggs and espresso. "Good morning," Andrew said as I emerged from my blanket cocoon. My neck was stiff and I regretted not folding out the sofa, as predicted. "Do you still like your eggs over-hard?"

I nodded and stretched my arms above my head, trying to work out the kinks in my spine. The clock on the wall said it was sometime between nine and twelve. "Shit," I said, "I didn't mean to commandeer your sofa for the entire morning."

I pulled myself up to a standing position and folded my blanket into quarters and set it on the ottoman next to a black duffel bag that hadn't been there last night. "Where are you off to?"

"What? Oh—nowhere. I just thought about it, what you said. I need to take that somewhere if I'm going to talk to the police."

"Well, you don't have to talk to them here," I said. I peered into the bag and was greeted by the woodsy tang of weed. "Hello."

"It's not that much."

"How much?"

"Little less than half a pound."

"That seems like a lot."

"Eight hundred bucks' worth, maybe. Why, did you want some?"

"I'm good."

"You know," Andrew said as he brought me a plate of eggs with salsa, "I've been thinking lately. It's only a matter of time before Ohio goes for free-market legalization. The medical marijuana system is just getting up and running, and I'm thinking I might like to give that a try. Get a job at one of the dispensaries, maybe open my own, eventually."

"Really?" I said around a bite of eggs. "Wouldn't that be crazy expensive?"

"Yeah, but it's also going to explode. Have you seen what it's like in Denver? Shops are everywhere, and they're nice places, I mean, it's not like Waterbeds 'N Stuff, they're more like cell phone stores. Clean, and organized. There's nothing sketchy about it."

"And after almost twenty years of sketch, you're over it?"

He shrugged. "A little bit, yeah. I'm over drunk businesspeople and entitled party girls and the special type of asshole who shorts me 'by accident' and then acts like, 'What are you going to do about it? You're just a drug dealer.' That term, I fucking hate it. And there's going to be money coming, at some point. From Dad's stuff."

We ate in silence for a while. My father's death benefit—what a phrase—was root-bound in some kind of trust. Our mother kept the specifics to herself, mostly, but I assumed I'd never see any *money*, if it even existed. "And what better way to honor Frank Weary than opening a head shop? Opening a bar might be more appropriate."

"You know what, Dad would've loved weed, if he'd ever tried it."

"Maybe he did," I said, "in Subic Bay, along with the Filipino ice cream and whatever else he did that we had no idea about."

Andrew sighed. "People never seem mysterious until they're gone."

"Hey, tell me about it."

Andrew promised we'd meet up later and walk into the police head-quarters together, once his pungent duffel bag was squared away. I didn't like thinking about his side-hustle much; what was exciting and convenient when we were teenagers just seemed reckless and a little stupid to me now. Maybe it seemed that way to him too. The idea of getting in on the legal marijuana trade was an interesting one, and I knew my brother was smart enough to make something work if he really wanted to. And who was I to judge—I trafficked in reckless and a little stupid as well.

As I was driving home, my phone rang. "What do you know about my daughter?" Jason Stowe said before I even had a chance to say hello.

"Sir," I tried, "I'm a private investigator and I'm just—"

"Are you related to him or something? This Andrew?"

"Yeah, he's my brother—"

"Where is she?"

"If you'd stop interrupting me," I said, getting a little annoyed, "I could tell you that I don't know where Addison is, but I'm trying to figure that out. She went to Andrew's apartment in the middle of the night, scared about something. She left, and we're not sure where she went after that. But if—"

"I just got in," he interrupted yet again, "so maybe we ought to talk about this in person."

"I'd rather—"

"I'll come to you," Stowe said, rather ominously, before hanging up.

I called my brother next—to warn of a potential angry visitor—but he didn't pick up.

At home I made a cup of tea and sat down at my laptop and pulled up my list of potential gyms where Wyatt Achebe might have been a member. It didn't look like much, but it was all I had to go on for the moment, which made it feel like more. I started making calls—"Hi, I just realized that I grabbed someone else's watch by mistake somewhere—and I think it might have been at your location. It's engraved and everything! Can you tell me if someone named Wyatt is a member there too?"—and went down the list. The first two said no, Purity's phone number was out of service, no one answered at Stride, and CleanSweat didn't appear to have a phone number at all. Or a real website for that matter—just a

Facebook page with a lot of photos, mostly of the owner, a span-dexed, ponytailed man called Boomer K. Wiggins, author of *Sweating Through the Pain: An Addict's Journey Back to Fitness*. But as I clicked around, I glimpsed Wyatt's broad smile in one of the photos.

Bingo.

I was writing down the address when I heard a knock at my door.

FIFTEEN

There are different kinds of knocks. Most people might not have a reason to think about it much, but I did. There was the classic, friendly, shave-and-a-haircut knock. There was the impatient double knock, two sharp raps in quick succession, favored by UPS drivers and solicitors from radon remediation companies who hoped you weren't actually home so they could just leave the flyer in your door frame. Then there was the cop knock, from the side of the hand, not the knuckles. Pound pound pound.

This knock was one of those.

Was Jason Stowe ex-police? With a career in defense contracting, it certainly seemed possible. But when I parted the curtains, the man I saw was clearly someone else. I didn't recognize the guy but if the knock hadn't given it away, his wardrobe made it clear that he was a cop: not-quite-tailored suit, thick-soled black shoes, a telltale bulge under his wool coat where his handgun was holstered.

I opened the door. Frigid air from the unheated lobby pooled around my ankles.

"Roxane Weary?"

"That's me."

"I'm Detective Mizuno, Columbus Police. Do you have a moment to talk?"

I let him in. We sat in my office, me at the desk, him on the couch

I kept meaning to replace. He said, "I'd like to talk about a young lady named Addison Stowe."

I nodded.

Mizuno was taking a notebook and a pen out of his coat, but he looked up at me—scowled, really. He was somewhere in his late forties, with black hair threaded with grey and hard eyes. "Oh, so you admit that you know her?"

"Yeah, when did I say that I didn't?"

"Why don't you tell me how you came to be involved with this?"

I summarized—the call from my brother, the shoes and the hoodie and the burned eggs, the unshakeable feeling that something was wrong, and what had happened since. "I already looped in the detectives from the homicide unit, about Mickey Dillman."

His ears perked up on homicide. "And why would you do that?"

"Loop them in?"

Mizuno nodded.

It was kind of a long story—how I'd asked Tom for the lowdown on Dillman a few days before his body was found, how I was with Tom at dinner when he got the call. I just said, "My father was a homicide detective. So I have contacts."

"Contacts," Mizuno repeated.

I was getting the feeling that he didn't like me.

"So you're trying to locate her because . . . ?"

I repeated what I'd said about Andrew trying to help her that night.

"At what point did you reach out to her friends in an attempt to get yourself hired to locate her?"

I stood up without meaning to and then tried to sit casually on the edge of the desk. But I felt anything but casual. "That's not what happened at all. I spoke to Addison's roommate and the roommate's stepsister, who's one of Addison's close friends. Jordana Meyers. On Saturday morning, Jordy called me and asked me to come out to

Blacklick and talk with her and another of their friends, because Addison hadn't shown up for a coffee date they had planned."

"And why would Miss Meyers call you?"

"I don't know, maybe because when we spoke, she was aware that I was interested in her friend's well-being too."

Mizuno wrote something down.

"Is she saying that she didn't call me?"

"You were up front with them, about how you came to be involved here, is that right? Your brother and everything?"

I was starting to feel a little sick. "I'm not sure exactly what I said, but I told them about how my brother used to work with her at the Sheraton three years ago."

"Do you know why Addison would've been afraid of your brother?"

"What—no. She went there for help."

"For help."

"Yeah, for help."

"Why would she do that? Someone she worked with three years ago?"

"Well, that's what I've been trying to figure out. She works at the nightclub across the street, and I can only assume that something went down, and she—"

"So what you're saying is that something—you don't know what—went down at a nightclub and scared Addison so much that she ran directly to the apartment of a former coworker, with whom she had a sexual relationship that ended badly, asked him for help, then left a few minutes later? Is that what you're telling me?"

I stared at the worn wood floor between my feet, my brain still a few words back. Andrew's relationship, such as it was, with Addison—how had anyone else known about that? Then I realized how big of a mistake I'd made with Addison's roommate and friends. "Yeah," I said. My voice was small.

"I just want to find the young lady," Mizuno said. "That's it. If you can help me do that, I'd really appreciate it."

"I want to find her too," I said, "but—"

"You need to be truthful with me, Miss Weary."

"I'm being truthful."

"Why did your brother really call you on Thursday?"

"I told you why."

"I just want to find Addison, okay? Let's start over. Why did your brother call you?"

"He was worried about her—"

"Why did he call you?"

"I think this conversation might be over," I said, my chest tight.

Mizuno stood up too and continued, "Because here's the thing. That call Addison made from your brother's phone? She left her father a voice mail, frantic, scared, begging him to come get her."

I gripped the edge of the desk against a jab of worry so sharp it made me a little dizzy.

"I've heard the message, okay? This is a young lady who's absolutely terrified of something. Not of someone who then calmly walks away. So I'll tell you again, I'm only interested in finding her. Help me find her."

"I told you everything I know."

"Help me find her, Miss Weary."

"I'm not saying anything else. This conversation is over."

Mizuno raised an eyebrow. "A cop's kid, you'd think the spirit of cooperation would be a bit stronger. I wonder if your brother will be any more forthcoming. Maybe a search warrant will persuade him to be?"

There were a lot of things I wanted to say to that. But I kept my promise by keeping my mouth shut.

Eventually he set a business card on the coffee table and said, "If you change your mind, give me a call."

———

I punched in Andrew's code at the front door and took the steps up to the second floor and pounded on his door with the heel of my hand. "Andrew. Open the door."

There were no sounds from inside his condo, just like there was no answer when I called him, and no texts back, either.

I banged on the door again. "Andrew, I swear to god."

The unit down the hall opened and a woman peered out. It was two in the afternoon but she'd clearly just woken up. "Can you not," she said.

"Sorry, it's an emergency—"

She went back inside and slammed the door.

As I drove over to the Westin, I called Matt. "Have you heard from Andrew today?"

"Why?"

"Because I need to get ahold of him and he's not answering."

"No," my oldest brother said, "I meant, why would I have heard from him."

I laughed, decidedly without humor. "You're such an asshole," I said.

"I love you too, sis."

I hung up.

The bartender at the Westin hadn't heard from him either. "And it's not really like him, to not let us know if he's going to be late."

"When was he supposed to be here?"

"He usually comes in at three on Mondays."

I calmly walked out into the bright light of the lobby and sat down on a low couch and tried to breathe evenly.

It didn't work.

I went back into the bar and ordered a shot.

"He probably just misplaced his phone," the bartender told me, splashing whiskey into a glass for me, barely even enough to call it a shot.

"Yeah," I said, throwing it back quickly. "I'm sure that's all it is."

I returned to Andrew's building, but he still wasn't answering. Maybe he went to the gym. To the movies. I ran through a list of possible midday diversions, but it was pointless. I knew something was wrong. Why hadn't I pushed? I always pushed. On the street, I looked around for my brother's car, a taupe-colored Escape. Twelve hours earlier, I'd been doing the same thing, except looking for Addison's car instead. I pulled on a pair of gloves and gave it another try. Taupe Escape, maroon Scion. What would either car tell me? *If you don't know what you're looking for, you won't find it,* my first boss in the PI business had once told me. But that was never my experience. On the contrary, you're more likely to miss something if you look too closely for it. I thought about what old Gil Safka would do in this situation—go home and call Detective Mizuno and set up a time to come in for a formal interview—and decided to do the opposite.

With shaking hands, I called Tom. He said, "I was just getting ready to call you."

His voice had a note of warning in it.

"Why?"

Tom said, "Because I just saw your brother going into an interrogation room on the third floor."

The lawyer's office was on City Park Avenue in German Village, a weird little brick structure nestled among the colorful houses that lined the cobblestone streets. The lawyer herself was named Julia Raymund and my brother had given me her magnetic business card years earlier as the person to call if anything ever happened. So I'd called, but she already knew the drill, had already been downtown to sit in on the interrogation, and suggested that I meet her here. Then she left me to wait in a massive conference room that contained an antique set of encyclopedias and a huge map of the world with Yugoslavia still on it, while she heated up a late lunch—a chicken Cup Noodles. I squinted across the room at the map, trying to make out the capital city; I couldn't remember.

"Sorry," she said, gesturing at the room with the hand holding the soup. "I just rent space from the office upstairs. This is their conference room. They have a flair for the old world."

"I really don't care," I said. I was impatient after waiting for the Cup Noodles. "Just explain what's going on."

"Well, some judge signed off on a search warrant, which is, frankly, shocking. Of course there was nothing to find in regards to this missing woman, but your brother did have some marijuana in the apartment."

I closed my eyes.

"Andrew is going to be arraigned on some possession charges," she said. "Tomorrow."

I opened my eyes again. The room was still the same and so was the lawyer—dark blond hair, fortyish, pantsuit and heels that looked like a bad idea in this weather—and so were the circumstances.

She continued, "It was in a duffel bag on the floor. Apparently they first asked if Andrew was planning on leaving town. Now he's probably looking at a third-degree felony. Definitely a fine, possibly a stint in jail. There's a good chance that the warrant shouldn't have covered the bag, which was zipped closed. But honestly, if they were just trying to keep him occupied for a couple days while they continue investigating the woman's disappearance, this would definitely do the trick."

"Great."

Julia stirred her Cup Noodles and the smell of it wafted saltily in my direction. "Mizuno and Blair are very interested in this voice mail from Addison." She paused to take a bite. "I heard it. And, I have to say, it's troubling. She sounds very afraid."

"But we don't know what happened. What she was afraid of."

Julia gave that faint smile again. "Look, Andrew's side of the story is that a woman who got him fired from his job several years ago, showed up in a panic at his apartment in the middle of the night, used his phone, and left. From the outside, what it looks like is that she made a panicked phone call to her father, specifically asking him to come get her, and she hasn't been seen since."

I pushed away from the table and stalked across the room to the map. Belgrade, the current capital of Serbia—that had been the capital of Yugoslavia and it couldn't have mattered less right now. "Her roommate said she'd been home. Even that she burned her eggs that morning, as usual."

"Eggs?"

"She'd been home that morning, is the point. So there's no reason for anyone to think that Andrew did—I don't know, whatever, anything."

She stirred her noodles. "Sure."

"Do you even believe him?"

She smiled that smile again. "It doesn't matter if I believe him. It only matters what they can prove. I'm aware of how this looks. Given that she'd been to his place before, and why."

I studied her. The way she said *why*, a slight flare of the nostrils— something about it gave me the feeling that Addison wasn't the only one who'd gone to bed with my brother.

But there wasn't space in my brain to sort through that one at the moment. "So the only thing you can make out from this voice mail is my brother's address?"

"It's hard to understand. She said something like '*he found me*' and she mentions something about a bus pass."

My ears perked up at that. "BusPass. It's an app, a dating app."

"A dating app?"

"Apparently Addison was talking to some guy she'd met on there."

"Do you have a name?"

"No. What exactly did she say about BusPass?"

Julia shook her head. "Like I said, you can't make out most of what she's saying."

"Why would she be talking about a dating app in this phone call she was frantic to make?" I chewed my lip for a second, stopping when I got the metallic taste of blood. "Maybe she met up with the guy from the dating app and it went badly—"

"Let's not worry about a dating app at the moment."

"So what do I do? Go in to do a formal interview?"

"It might not be the best idea."

"Why?"

"Because talking to the police is like going to Target—you always end up paying for it."

I shook my head. "Can I just say, that's the worst metaphor. I hope my brother didn't hire you for your brilliant metaphors."

She looked mildly offended. "It might be an okay idea if you can corroborate your story in some way, though."

"How?"

"Did you record the conversations with Addison's friends, for example?"

Who did she think I was? "No."

"Well."

"But there's more going on here than just Addison. The night-club, where she works—did my brother tell you about that?"

"Briefly."

"Well, there's another employee who's sort of missing."

"Sort of?"

"The bouncer, his name's Wyatt Achebe—he didn't come home

the same night Addison showed up at my brother's place. Plus the owner is mixed up with a player in the—for lack of a better word, the underworld. He's been hiding out at a motel." I could tell that I was talking faster and faster but I couldn't quite seem to get ahold of myself. "And yesterday, I spent two hours talking to the police about the officer they found dead in the river."

"Wait a minute," Julia interrupted. "What are you talking about?"

She gave me a look that said I was acting as crazy as I felt. "Let's stick to one puzzle at a time."

I stood up to pace the room again. "What exactly do you suggest?"

"We'll know more after your brother's arraignment."

I wondered how long my brother had known her, and how much he was paying her. Was there a law about lawyers not fucking their clients, or was that doctors? Or maybe it was neither. I sat back down. "Sure. Fine. Do I need to get bail money together, or—"

"No need."

"Oh."

"Your brother has a plan in place for just this kind of situation."

"Well, probably not exactly this situation."

Julia said, "Andrew did want me to ask you to give this to your mom."

She passed a white envelope to me.

I probably would've preferred the bail money. "What's this?"

"Part of the plan. He just doesn't want your mom hearing through the grapevine. News can travel in cop circles, and I know she's currently dating one. I'd avoid mentioning Addison to her, though."

"So what do I do in the meantime?"

Julia stood up and pushed her chair in. "Other than talk to your mother? Nothing. Whatever you normally do."

"That's—no. That isn't how I'm wired. I need to do something."

"Right, the old *how I'm wired* defense. I get that you want to help, but you really can't. The immediate issue is the drug charge. That's always been a risk your brother chose to take—it's just compounded now by the fact that Addison made this phone call from his number. Now, I'll give you a call when I know a bit more about what's going to happen next. Okay?"

It wasn't okay, not by a long shot, but saying so wouldn't make any bit of difference.

SIXTEEN

Andrew was my mother's favorite. It was no secret growing up, though of course it would break her heart if she knew how obvious it had been. It was even less of a secret now, what with all of us being adults at this point and above pettiness like favorites—in theory, anyway, as my oldest brother Matt actually wasn't. I typically stayed out of the ongoing battle for favorite son. But I knew that being the bearer of bad news in this case wasn't going to improve my standings.

My mother wasn't alone when I walked into my childhood home; Matt was there, along with Rafael Vega, a detective from the property crimes unit she'd started seeing last summer. He was the opposite of my father in almost every way: he was warm, almost silly sometimes, an outspoken liberal, lover of red wine and spicy food. Even physically, he was my father's inverse—tall and heavy-set where Frank had been average height and wired with muscle, a mustache where Frank had declared facial hair to be a sign of weak character, and friendly, light brown eyes where Frank's had been icy blue and critical. It was strange, the thought of my mother dating someone. But at the same time I was rooting for them. Happiness was something she never quite experienced while being married to my father. Not real happiness. If you'd asked her, she would have said she was happy, that she was madly in love with

Frank. But it was the kind of happiness you feel when you get the thing you thought you wanted, not the kind of joy that bubbles up when you're with someone on the same page as you.

Rafe was cooking when I walked in. "Roxane, we're having patacones, hope you're hungry!" he called over his shoulder. He was wearing an apron, my mother's—pink-and-brown polka dots. I had to smile. "Smells incredible," I said.

My mother and Matt were doing a jigsaw puzzle at the dining room table, one of those photos of a sleeping baby in a ladybug costume. The scene was so idyllic that I almost just turned around and went back to the car.

"Sit, honey, you can help. You were always so good at these."

Matt glared at me from under his beard.

"Actually, Mom, I need to talk to you."

"Okay!"

"Like, privately."

My mother patted the place at the table next to her. "You can say anything you need to in front of Rafe."

I nodded at Matt. "What about him? I'm not going to talk about tampons in front of Matt."

That did the trick. Matt stood up and said, "I'll go switch out my laundry."

"I can't believe you still bring your laundry here."

"At least I do laundry." He hipchecked me out of the way as he squeezed by to go into the basement.

"Fuck off," I said warmly.

"Roxie, language."

I sat down in Matt's seat. "Mom," I said. "I have to tell you something. It's not about tampons."

"I figured that was just code for *girl talk*."

"Uh, yes."

"Is it Catherine? Because, honey, I know you love her but—"

"No, it's not Catherine. It's about Andrew."

My mother fiddled with one of the edge pieces of the puzzle and didn't say anything. I could tell she knew already, even just subconsciously.

I placed the envelope on the table and slid it over to her.

"He got arrested today. He wanted me to give you this."

From the kitchen, I saw Rafe glance over his shoulder at me.

I continued, "He wanted me to let you know, so you didn't hear it from anyone else first."

My mother was still messing with the puzzle. "Is it because of—" She stopped there.

"Yeah."

"Andrew Joseph Weary," she murmured. "Is it going to be like the last time?"

She meant over a decade ago, when Andrew needed bail money and my father wouldn't help. "No," I said.

"Do you think he's going to learn his lesson now?"

Telling people what they'd wanted to hear lately hadn't gone so great for me. But that didn't keep me from doing it again. "I do, actually."

My mother stood up and smoothed down her sweater with one hand. The other was clutching Andrew's envelope so hard it had crumpled in the middle like a bow tie. "Thanks, honey. I'll be right back."

She went down the hall and disappeared into the bedroom, closing the door behind her. I knew she went in there to read the note and cry.

I didn't follow her.

When we were growing up, she always kept her emotions in check. Probably because my father got angrier the more emotional anyone became in front of him.

Even with him gone for two years now, some things never changed.

I went into the kitchen and said, "I can't stay, but that truly smells amazing."

"You want me to wrap some up for you to take home?"

"No, that's okay. Listen, Rafe—"

"I know, sweetheart. I'll take good care of her tonight."

"Thanks."

"What are the charges?"

"Felony three possession."

He pushed a spatula around in the skillet for a moment. "So drug court's out."

"Yeah. And it's worse than that, too. The way it went down, sort of in the middle of an interrogation about something else. Something he didn't do. You know Blair or Mizuno from missing persons?"

He shook his head. "Sorry. Missing persons?"

"You know what, never mind. I don't want to burden you with this."

"Hey, no, no burden. You know I love this weird little family."

I felt myself smile in what seemed like the first time in ages. Rafe waggled the spatula in my direction. "Are you sure about this?"

"Not at all."

"That's right." He winked at me and opened the cabinet for a takeout container.

Shelby was standing on my doorstep when I got home, her youthful face stiff with worry. "Shel, what's wrong?"

"Oh, well, I guess it's nothing. Um," she said, "it's just that there was this guy down here, banging on your door and yelling. I texted you."

"Oh," I said. "Sorry, I was driving. When was this?"

"Just now. I thought he left so I came down to make sure."

"What kind of yelling?"

"Like, 'Open up, I know you're in there.'"

"Young? Old?"

"I don't know."

Well, that didn't exactly matter. I assumed the angry man had been Addison's father—true to his word, he'd come to me.

"Sorry," Shelby added.

"It's okay. I'm sorry if he freaked you out."

"Who was it?"

"Oh, just someone who's worried about someone," I said, which probably applied to everyone in the world.

I left Jordy another message. She hadn't called me back after the first one, but I was still hoping she could help smooth things over with Jason Stowe.

He didn't seem like a good person to be on the wrong side of.

SEVENTEEN

I dressed up for my police interview—black trousers and an argyle cardigan over a silk blouse, plus a little copper eye shadow like Sunny Castro had recommended for my blue-grey eyes—in the hopes that looking the part of a calm, collected professional would somehow assuage my nerves. I'd gone downtown to talk to cops about a million times, but only because a case of mine overlapped with a police matter, never because they thought I'd done something. I wasn't sure exactly what they thought I'd done, though. Helped my brother dispose of a body? When Julia Raymund had called me last night, she advised against talking to them.

"Blair said he wants to talk to you, but of course he's going to say that. Remember, talking to the police is like—"

"Yeah, the shitty metaphor, I remember." I'd been heating up the patacones and the kitchen was filled with the smell of fried plantain. I couldn't remember when I'd eaten last and I was that kind of hungry that mostly just feels nauseous. "But I'm the one who's been asking around about Addison, not my brother. So I can probably give them more information than he can, and if I can help his situation, I'm going to do that. Even if it's like a trip to Target."

Julia had sighed. "You might not help, though. That's what I'm saying."

"But can it hurt? How could it hurt?"

"It may not hurt him, but it could hurt you."

I still had the feeling that she didn't entirely believe my story of what happened, and it pissed me off. "It's fine," I said. "I want to talk to them, set the record straight."

"Are you sure?"

"Yes."

In the morning, though, I was less sure. A lot less. I'd eaten the last bit of rice and plantain for breakfast right before I left—cold, straight from the fridge, still just as good that way—and it now sat in my esophagus like I'd swallowed a golf ball as I walked up the front steps of the police headquarters. Julia Raymund was waiting inside with a massive briefcase and a general look of irritation. "Now," she half-whispered as we signed in at the desk, "this is very important. You need to listen to me. If I tell you not to answer something, don't answer it. I know you think you know everything, but you didn't go to law school, okay?"

I actually laughed. "Trust me, I don't think I know everything."

She gave me that thin-lipped smile of hers and didn't respond.

Detective Mizuno was waiting for us at the third-floor elevators and led us down a narrow hallway and into an interrogation room—small and clinical looking, with white walls and beige carpet and a table, empty except for a single, facedown piece of paper, around which only three chairs were arranged. The other detective, Blair, a big guy in a small suit with sandy, thinning hair, made a big show of getting another chair. Julia shot me a look and said, "I'll stand."

I sat on one side of the table and Mizuno and Blair sat on the other. Mizuno fiddled with a recording app on an iPhone. I felt like I was about to be interviewed for some job I didn't really want. I squeezed my hands into fists in my lap.

"Thanks a lot for coming down, Roxane. It's real good to just get a few things cleared up. Maybe you got off on the wrong foot with Detective Mizuno here yesterday, but we just want to talk, make sure we have all the info we need to find this young lady. That's all we want. I'm sure you want that too."

I nodded.

Mizuno said, "You'll have to give a verbal answer, for the tape."

His partner said, "Isn't it funny, how we still call it a tape?" He shook his head at the mystery of life. "Gives me a real good chuckle every time."

So he was the good cop to Mizuno's bad cop. I restrained the urge to comment on this knee-slapper of an observation and just said, "Yeah."

"So let's talk about when your brother called you. In the middle of the night. Was that unusual?" Mizuno said.

"A little," I said, "but we're close. We're both night owls."

"So what happened when you got there?"

I told the story again, for what felt like the hundredth time. I could kind of see how people wound up confessing to crimes they didn't commit—the conversation was circuitous and confusing, à la "What you're saying is . . ." when that wasn't what I'd been saying at all. I also could see why Julia had warned me against sitting down with them. But in the end, it was worth it, because I learned something: after an hour of talking in circles about everything I'd learned so far, Mizuno pulled out a photo.

"You know who this is?"

"No," I said. I didn't. The picture was a grainy computer printout of a guy who looked like his wardrobe was comprised solely of Affliction T-shirts, with floppy, chin-length hair, a colorful dragon tattoo curling up his forearm, and an expression that could only be considered *smoldering*. "Who is he?"

"Looks kind of like Andrew, don't you think?" Blair said.

"No."

"No?"

"He has a tattoo and longish hair, but that's it. This guy looks like a douchebag."

Behind me, Julia cleared her throat.

I'd promised to watch my language during the conversation; apparently nice, law-abiding citizens didn't say *douchebag*.

I added, "Who is this?"

Mizuno flipped the image back over, but not before I glimpsed a familiar icon in the bottom right corner—the BusPass logo.

This was a profile picture from the dating app.

It took every bit of self-control I possessed not to blurt that out and demand more information—which they obviously wouldn't give me—and I just sat there, quietly, law-abidingly, until they'd asked all their questions.

While Julia and I waited for the elevator, she said, "See?"

"See what?"

"That wasn't exactly the silver bullet you thought it would be, was it?"

"I don't know. The picture was interesting."

Now her expression turned suspicious. "Do you know that guy?"

"No, of course not, but did you notice the logo in the corner? It's from BusPass, the dating app. That's probably the guy she's been talking to on there."

"I really don't see how some dating app has anything to do with your brother."

"It doesn't. That's why it's good news. Now we just have to figure out who he is."

"We?" Julia said as the elevator dinged open. "You're a witness here, maybe even a potential suspect. You can't go digging around anymore." She held the elevator for me, her hand spinning a *hurry up* gesture.

"Think I'll take the stairs," I said.

I paused in the stairwell to leave another message for Jordy Meyers, my second in as many days.

"Jordy, this is Roxane Weary. Um, again. I'd love to talk to you to clear things up—"

A few lines into it I realized this probably wasn't helping my cause. I hit the pound sign, hoping to activate the menu that let you listen to your voice mails and then delete them, but it told me invalid entry so I ended the call.

Tom was at his desk when I got down to the second floor, watching a YouTube video with one white earbud in. "Planning to become a vlogger?" I said.

He stabbed the space bar to pause the video. The girl on the screen was frozen in time, her mouth in a perfectly round O. Tom said, "Someday, we won't even need to interrogate suspects. We can just pull up their social media and listen to them confess."

"What'd she do?"

"Asked her four thousand followers if anyone would be willing to assault her ex-boyfriend for her."

"Seriously?"

"Yes, and spoiler alert, someone wound up dead, and it isn't the ex-boyfriend."

"The poor schmuck who offered to do it?"

He nodded. "What's up? You're looking very fly today."

I felt myself smile. "This is my *polite citizen who never says 'douchebag'* look. I was just upstairs talking to Blair and Mizuno."

"And how'd that go?"

"About how you'd expect. Why does this keep happening? Me, at odds with the police."

"Well, to hear you tell it, that's been happening your whole life."

"What, so this is just carrying on the tradition I had with my father?"

"Maybe so."

I leaned my head back against the burlap wall of his cube and closed my eyes. "I should've called you the night this happened. I thought about it. But now here we are. What would you have done?"

"If you'd called me the night Addison was at your brother's? Probably exactly what you did—go to her apartment and see if she was there. And if it looked like she'd been there and left again?" He shrugged. "That would've seemed like the end of that."

"But Andrew wouldn't be in jail right now because some missing persons' detectives think he knows way more than he's saying."

"Your brother's in jail because he had drugs in his house, Roxane. That could have happened any time in the last however long he's been doing that."

"Since we were in high school."

"Then it's a small miracle it hasn't happened before now. It sounds like he was prepared for it, even."

"But the circumstances."

"I know. I wonder who signed off on that search warrant, based on nothing but a voice mail."

"My brother's lawyer seems to hate me and I'm pretty sure she's sleeping with him. So that's awkward."

"Never a dull moment with the Weary family."

"Unfortunately," I said.

We looked at each other. I had the sudden desire to bury my face in his collarbone and weep, but I didn't. Instead I said, "I should go."

I squeezed his shoulder and walked out of the cubicle maze, blinking fast.

As I crossed the lobby, I almost ran smack into a woman who was coming down the steps. "Jesus Christ, watch it," she said, her voice thick with tears.

I recognized the voice. "Sunny," I said.

The woman paused and looked at me. "Oh, it's you," Dillman's ex said. "I didn't—the copper shadow. See?"

"You were right."

"I'm always right about eye shadow. Can you believe this?" She seemed stunned. Grief, in its many incarnations, had a way of doing that. Then she grabbed me in a tight hug.

Because she looked like she needed a friend about as much as I did at the moment, I hugged back.

EIGHTEEN

We went up the block to the Leveque Tower and got a table at the Keep. Near the window, where the views were usually good, but the midwinter city just looked like grey on grey. Thin light slanted in on us and cast Sunny's face half in shadow.

"We used to come here a lot," she was saying. "Any time we had something to celebrate, or we just wanted a nice meal. Not that I'm celebrating right now."

"No, of course not."

"I just don't know what I'm supposed to do. I'm responsible for making all these decisions now—he left me responsible for making decisions about what happens. And I can't just say, 'Do whatever you want.' No one gets to say that. His family has no idea we were splitting up. So I have people expecting me to be the grieving widow. But I'm not. I'm also not *not*, if that makes sense. I don't know what I'm supposed to be doing and it feels terrible. You wouldn't even believe how many decisions have to be made. Actually, I guess you know that already."

Our server brought us drinks—whiskey for me, gin and tonic for Sunny. I said, "When my dad died, I kind of felt the same way. We had a pretty rocky relationship, to be honest. And when he died, it was like I was grieving for the end of something that didn't exist, or grieving for the end of the chance that it might exist at some point, rather than for a person. You know?"

"Yes! That's exactly it. I'm surprised to hear you weren't close. He bragged about you a lot."

I sipped my drink, or maybe it wasn't exactly a sip. "See, even now, hearing something like that? It makes me feel like shit. Just because it's pretty clear now that he and I just misunderstood each other to some extent. I'm not saying that what Mickey did to you was a misunderstanding, but you know what I mean."

Sunny nodded. "I do, yeah. It's like getting credit for something you didn't do. But it's also infuriating, because of what happened between us. Four or five times, the neighbors called the cops on us, we were arguing so bad. They'd come, talk to me, talk to him, talk to me again and convince me to let it go. He'd go, 'Sun, baby, I'm so sorry, I'm ashamed, I can't believe I raised a hand to you, I'll never hurt you again.' Crying these big crocodile tears. A man crying, that just does something to you."

"Yeah."

"I always forgave him. And it always happened again. Till the last time, when I was just done. I drove myself to St. Ann's and a nurse there got me a lawyer. But you know what? Even when I tried to press charges, it wasn't happening. I didn't have any *evidence*. You hear about the thin blue line on cop shows and you figure that's Hollywood, but no. There really is a line. Or a wall. Whatever it is."

"So he was never charged?"

"Never. But to be honest, after that, I was clear with him that we were over. I think he knew he was lucky to get out of the situation with his career intact. I knew *I* was lucky. Plenty of women in my situation would have been worried for their lives. But in the end, it wasn't like that. The air went out of our relationship after that night. The pressure valve got released, if that makes sense. It was just done with. I was going to file for divorce once he went back to work."

"That's magnanimous of you."

Sunny shrugged. "Not really. I was mostly just thinking about how the alimony would work."

"So you weren't trying to spare his dignity?"

"Not particularly. It's like how after his surgery, I let him stay at the house for a few weeks while he recovered. I think I did it so I could feel smug about how magnanimous I was being. It wound up being fine. As soon as he was able to get around on his own, back he went to the motel. But now, even though I know I did what I had to do, I'm doubting myself. Was I too harsh with him, or something? You know, they told me they aren't sure what happened, if it was some accident, or he took his own life, or what. And how can I ever be sure what they tell me is the truth anyhow?"

"You really think that?"

She crunched on an ice cube from her glass. "I don't know. You never felt like that? About your dad?"

"Well," I said, "they knew what happened to my dad—there were witnesses, lots of them. So it's different. But I guess you're right, that they wouldn't necessarily tell us everything. Not about his death, but about his life." I was thinking about the halo-halo again, still impossible for me to reconcile with the Frank Weary I knew.

"Like if he killed himself, because of something I did? Are they going to tell me that?"

"Sunny—"

"No, I don't think they would. They might say, 'Oh, we don't know what happened, it's undetermined.' To spare me."

I said, gently, "The police aren't in the business of doing things to spare anyone."

"Not even to spare him? To spare Mickey from being the cop

who couldn't handle it?" She stopped, rubbed her eyes. "I'm sorry. You must think I'm a lunatic."

"Hey, it's okay. You're just feeling feelings."

Sunny smiled. "Feeling feelings."

"That's the clinical term."

She opened her mouth, closed it, then said, "Could I hire you? To make sure I have the whole story about what happened?"

The last time someone had asked me that—Jordy Meyers— things hadn't gone so great. I said, "I know one of the detectives working the case. Tom Heitker. He'll give you the whole story."

Sunny shook her head. "There was this guy Mickey told me about once. I don't think he knew him, but he'd heard this story. The guy was a narcotics cop, and everybody knew he had a problem. Problems. Pills, gambling. But he was good at getting people to open up and confess, so people looked the other way. He had a wife at home, three little girls, good at his job. Anyway, then the guy died. Where? In the middle of a whorehouse. He had a massive heart attack, there's Oxy and cocaine everywhere, no fewer than three hookers servicing him all at once. This could have called into question a couple hundred possession cases, not to mention what it would have done to the guy's family. So his squad covered it up. Got him dressed, put him in his police vehicle, said he must have had a heart attack right there. The man got to die a hero."

This story sounded like squad-room lore rather than an actual event. "And that's what you're afraid of?"

"Oh, the story isn't over yet. Three years later, the guy's wife, who's been celibate since her husband died, gets the stomach flu and she can't get rid of it. Finally she goes to the doctor and finds out she's HIV-positive, has been for years, and it's progressed to AIDS-defining symptoms. And she hadn't been tested before her last pregnancy, so it turns out her daughter's HIV-positive too. And no one

knew, all because this guy's buddies chose to cover up the circumstances of his death."

"Sunny," I said.

"I know. I know that isn't what happened to Mickey, I know the
story probably isn't true. But what do you think the context was,
when he told me that? We were talking about family, and how you
stick with your family for better or for worse, no questions asked."

From what I knew of Mickey Dillman so far, he did seem like
the type to use a bullshit anecdote to try to make a point that it
didn't even come close to making. But Sunny's point was an easier
sell. Even if Mickey's story wasn't true, Sunny had experienced first-
hand how some cops could trample other people in the efforts to
protect their own.

"I can try to keep an eye on things for you," I said, "if that would
give you some peace of mind."

"It would."

"Okay."

"Thank you, Roxane."

"Is it okay if I take notes?"

She smiled. "You are definitely your father's daughter."

"Tell me about the last time you saw Mickey."

Sunny finished her drink and signaled for another. "He seemed
like Mickey. I don't know. He came over to pick up some boxes from
the basement."

"What was in the boxes?"

She shook her head. "I don't know. He'd texted me the night before, I told him I wasn't going to be home, but then the weather was
bad and my salon was opening later in the day than usual. So I was
there. He showed up with Rick—his cousin, pretty much his only
non-cop friend, or maybe his only friend these days. I was there,
Mickey asked me if he should come back another time and I said
no, it was fine. He got his boxes, he told me again how sorry he was

and how pathetic life was living in the shittiest motel in America. I was kind of like, well, you get what you get, and that was that."

"His cousin, Rick . . . ?"

"Dillman. Mickey and Ricky, they called them growing up."

"And are they still close?"

Another nod. "I mean, what's 'close' when you're talking about someone who is so invested in being a 'tough guy'? But yeah, I'd say so. Mickey has a heck of a temper. But I never saw him lose it at Rick. The whole time we were together, they went bowling once a week. Even when Mickey couldn't bowl, because of his back, he still went to the Columbus Bowling Palace every Wednesday. Rick's some kind of bowling genius, I don't know, perfect game after perfect game." She studied her cuticles and said, "I have no idea how this could possibly be helpful to you."

"You'd be surprised," I said. It had been late Wednesday—or early Thursday—when Addison had showed up at my brother's apartment. "I've solved cases based on less than a bowling score. Did you tell the police about bowling night?"

"Oh, sure. But like they're going to listen to me, about anything? I'm just the woman who lied about him getting violent. See, this is why I feel like I can't trust what they say to me."

After lunch we stood just inside the doors to the restaurant and finished our conversation. It had been so long since I'd just shared a meal with a friend, and even though the circumstances were hardly ideal, it was nice to make a connection with a person who wasn't related to one of my cases, or related to me. In the past six months, I'd barely spent time with anyone other than Catherine.

Sunny said, "Roxane, thank you, really, for this. I don't think I realized how not okay I was today."

This seemed to be a bit of a theme around people I knew lately.

The thing about funerals is every last detail needs to be decided by someone. Although I'd been to my share, I'd never thought about it until my father died. A family liaison officer and a chaplain from the department came over with forms and papers and a bleak little pamphlet called "Continue the Journey: Planning the Catholic Funeral Mass." My mother put Andrew and me in charge of selecting the readings while she and Matt were picking out a casket, and we sat side by side on the couch simultaneously paging through the pamphlet and a Precious Moments bible that one of us had gotten as a first communion gift years ago. It was the only one we could find in the house.

"These are terrible," Andrew said. "Isaiah, twenty-five: 'On this mountain he will destroy the veil that veils all peoples, the web that is woven over all nations. He will destroy death forever.' Is this supposed to be comforting?"

I rubbed my eyes. "Yes?" I said. "No?"

"He wouldn't want any of these. He'd want us to get drunk and go to the goddamn movies."

"The funeral is for the living," I said, something someone had told me or I'd read somewhere in the last few days and I felt stupid even saying it, because it sure as hell wasn't for me. "We just need to pick. You know she wants this done by the time they get back."

I was worried about my mother. She was eerily calm, muted, artificial. There had been people around constantly—my brothers and me, Tom, the chaplain, the liaison officer. But eventually there would be no one, and I was afraid of what would happen then.

"Lamentations, three: 'My soul is deprived of peace, I have forgotten what happiness is.' Seriously, what the fuck," Andrew said. He stood up and went to the liquor cabinet in the corner of the dining room, returning a minute later with a bottle of whiskey and two shot glasses.

I shook my head but I took what he poured.

"Are you worried," he asked, "about, you know, who is going to show up?"

I downed the shot. "Yeah," I said. There had been other women. Four that we knew of, probably more. Once, when I was nine, I picked up the phone to call a friend and I heard my father on the line, talking to one of them. Her voice was breathy and she was crying. My father's voice was just his voice, rough and flat. Later, he came into my room and said, "Sometimes when you're a little kid you hear things that you don't understand, because you don't know the whole story," and then he said he would get me my own phone line, but he didn't. When I was twelve, he moved out for six months and was staying in a shambling duplex in Groveport with a woman named Sylvie. I visited once and got head lice and wasn't allowed to go back.

"Maybe we can have a guest list," Andrew said. He refilled our shot glasses. "Bouncers. The whole deal."

I fanned the pages of the "Continue the Journey" pamphlet.

"I don't see anything in here about bouncers."

Andrew swallowed his second shot. "I'll tell you right now," he said. "I want the same exact funeral as Dad. Minus the cop stuff. I don't want anybody having to plan it."

"Don't even say that," I said. I flopped backward and balanced my glass on my stomach. "I want to be cremated and shot into outer space as fireworks. I heard they can do that. No funeral."

"I like it."

"Or make me into a diamond."

"Who gets the diamond?"

"Throw it in the river," I said.

We sat in silence for a long time.

"Let's just use these ones," Andrew said finally, pointing to the suggestions in the pamphlet. "It's going to be over in five minutes anyway."

"Yeah, okay," I said. But I was afraid it was going to be unfolding forever.

The funeral was on a Sunday. The sky was the color of a dead fish and it was raining, the kind of steady downpour that seemed to be a judgment. There was a full agenda: private prayer service at the funeral home. Procession to St. Joseph's downtown for the Mass. Procession to Greenlawn for the burial. My mother had selected the "last radio call" tribute instead of the three-volley salute, not wanting to hear gunfire. The chaplain warned us that there would be a lot of tears at the cemetery. The last radio call made everyone tear up, he said. Even the members of the honor guard, who probably had never met my father, but hearing his badge number broadcast over the radio for the last time did something to everybody. It made no sense to me, this litany of obligations, of separate opportunities to fall apart. After the burial, we were to retire to Rita's house for light refreshments. Rita Andosca, my mother's neighbor, a dead cop's wife too. Her husband had died of an aneurysm many years earlier. She knew the drill.

I didn't want to go to any of it. I woke up shaky and nervous and the feeling didn't go away as I dressed in black and drove to my mother's house. We were meeting there, would ride to the funeral home in a limousine like we were rich kids going to prom. When I arrived, Genevieve looked at me and, despite her unsettling calm all week, she freaked out.

"You're late," she said, throwing the door open. "And what are you wearing? No."

I was wearing a suit, a fitted black jacket and trousers that I'd bought at Express the day before because I didn't want to contaminate any of my actual clothes with this horrible time. My mother had asked me what I was going to wear and I said a suit and flats and she said fine.

"What is wrong with you?" she barked as she gripped my arm

and pulled me into the house. "You can't wear pants to your father's funeral."

"Mom—"

"No. Go home and change."

"But we're already late—"

"And whose fault is that, Roxane? I can't believe you."

It was five days' worth of grief pouring out all at once. My father wouldn't give a shit about what I wore to his funeral. I pressed my lips together and let her go. Finally Rita intervened, said that her daughter was about my size and might have a black skirt I could wear. My mother locked herself in the bedroom while Rita went back to her house to see. I asked Andrew if he had any Xanax on him.

"She didn't want it," he said. He'd gotten a haircut, was wearing a black suit of his own with a white shirt and a tie with somber black-and-grey stripes. It was pretty bad, I realized, if Andrew had done better in the wardrobe department than I had.

"I meant for me," I said.

"Oh," Andrew said. "Yeah, of course."

Rita brought back a grocery bag full of garments. "You can just get this back to me whenever, no hurry, hon. Here, this would be so pretty on you, Roxie, so ladylike," she said. A black wool fit-and-flare dress and a cardigan with thread-woven buttons. An unopened pair of nude pantyhose in that cheap plastic egg from the eighties. There were shoes, too: black patent heels.

"No," I said.

"I took a guess that you were a nine," she said as she removed the shoes from the bag.

She was right, and the Xanax had gone to work already, so I took the clothes. I didn't feel better but I also didn't feel like fighting. I went to the bathroom and thrashed around with the hose before just stuffing them in the trash and I pulled the stupid dress on and sat on the lid of the toilet and stared at the wallpaper, a striped pattern with seashells thrown into the mix, like this eighty-year-old house was situated on a beach somewhere, which it definitely was not.

Someone knocked on the door, lightly. "We need to go in five minutes," Andrew said.

"I'm not going," I said.

"Yes you are. Five minutes," he said. "Can I come in?"

"No. Yes. I don't know."

My brother opened the door.

"I can't do this," I said.

"I know."

"How are we supposed to do this?"

Andrew took me by the arm and pulled me gently into a standing position. "The same way we do everything else."

NINETEEN

Before everything had gone to shit yesterday, I'd been about to follow up on CleanSweat, the only lead I currently had on Wyatt, the Nightshade bouncer. In addition to sounding like a deodorant brand, CleanSweat was a second-floor storefront on Cleveland Avenue above an optometrist and a sub shop. It was done up in a black and red color scheme, the power suit of interior decorating, and the space had a troubling smell, a sort of low-key gym funk with notes of spray-cleaner and damp carpet. There were exactly zero customers using the assortment of weight and cardio machines on the workout floor, but the sounds of an out-of-sight aerobics class indicated that CleanSweat did have customers, somewhere.

The front counter was attended only by a dog-eared paperback copy of Boomer's book, *Sweating Through the Pain: An Addict's Journey Back to Fitness*, the cover of which featured him standing behind this very desk. The whole enterprise had a homespun quality to it. I called out, "Hello?"

A few beats later, a door along the back wall opened and a man emerged. As promised by his book cover, Boomer K. Wiggins was tallish and muscle-bound, squeezed into shiny black workout pants and a red polo shirt with the gym's logo embroidered on the chest. His ponytail, which was yellow-blond on his book cover, was a frizzy ash color in person and resembled a coonskin cap more than human hair. "Hello!" he exclaimed. "Welcome to CleanSweat! Are you here for a consultation? We're doing the Spring Break Challenge right now, to get you beach-body ready for—"

I cut him off. "Isn't any body at the beach a *beach body*?"

He deflated a little bit. "Well, yes, I didn't mean . . . it's just a marketing saying? Um . . ."

"It's okay. I'm not here about me."

We retired to his office, a cramped closet-sized space jammed with random fitness equipment and paperwork. Boomer balanced on a core-strength ball behind his desk—he'd offered it to me, but I elected to stand.

"Wyatt's a real good kid," he was telling me. "We met at the Habitat for Humanity Re-store over on Westerville Road. Volunteering. His was court-mandated but he was no stranger to community stewardship. He grew up very active in his mother's church, although he's drifted away a bit. We struck up a convo. He was angry— and I don't blame him, not after what happened. But you're not defined by what *happens to you*, rather, by what *you happen to do* about it." His voice took on a rehearsed quality on the last sentence.

"Is that from your book?"

"Yes, ma'am, and it's a lesson I've learned the hard way."

"So you're friends?"

"I think Wyatt would consider me a mentor."

"A mentor that he pays so he can work out here?"

Pain flashed through Boomer's face. "He doesn't pay me. Not a cent. He works out for free in exchange for cleaning the place for me. Wish I could do more for him, but you know how it is. Money's tight for everybody these days."

I frowned. It sounded like Boomer was the one getting something for *free*. "How often does he do that?"

"Clean, or work out?"

"Either. Both."

"Every day, usually."

"When was the last time you saw him?"

"Last Monday, I think it was. He was cleaning when I came in, around seven in the morning."

That was, of course, before whatever had gone down at Night-shade. I said, "And you haven't talked to him since?"

"No."

"Has he been here to clean?"

Boomer bounced up and down slightly. "Well, yeah. I run a tight ship. He has to clean every morning. That's the deal."

"So he was here this morning?"

"Not when I was here, but the place is spotless, so yeah."

Spotless might have been a little strong considering the stink out there, but that was hardly the point. It seemed odd to me that Wyatt hadn't gone home but had managed to keep up his end of the arrangement with Boomer. I realized that CleanSweat would be a good place to hide out if you needed to hide out. "Does he ever confide in you?"

Boomer nodded gravely. "We talk. Mostly about macros."

"Macros?" I was thinking camera lenses.

"Macronutrients. The building blocks of nutrition!"

"Do you talk about anything other than macros? Something not fitness-related," I amended as I sensed a lecture about deadlifting coming on. "Like maybe about the club where he works?"

"No, ma'am. He knows where I stand on that front."

I raised an eyebrow.

"Sobriety turned my life around," he said. "That, and my lord and savior Jesus Christ. I told Wyatt, 'You don't have to do what I do. You don't have to go to church, you don't have to pray, you don't have to live like a monk. But I don't want to hear anything about that place. I don't want people from there coming in here. You don't come here hungover or hopped up on anything.' He's a good kid, but he's a kid."

"Does he respect that rule?"

"'Course he does."

We chatted a while longer, but Boomer didn't have anything else useful for me. As he walked me out, I said, "Well, if you do see Wyatt, would you mind giving me a call? I'm interested in helping him get out of whatever trouble he might be in." Then I noticed a rack of fitness apparel near the door and realized that I was neglecting my only paying client pretty severely at the moment. "Hey, do you carry SpinSpo here?"

Boomer laughed. "Heck no. My customers are here to get right, not play dress-up." He frowned at the young woman staffing the front desk, who seemed suddenly interested in our conversation, and said, "How's that list coming?"

She blushed bright pink. "I'm working through it, Mr. Wiggins."

Boomer disappeared into his office.

I went over to the counter. The woman busily typed away on her keyboard and didn't look up at me. Her name tag said Tara. "Either you're very into SpinSpo, or you know something about Wyatt."

Now she looked up, blinking innocently. "Can I help you?"

"It's okay, either way. I won't tell Boomer. Who, by the way, I can't believe makes you call him Mr. Wiggins."

She gave me a small smile. "He likes things a certain way. And I do wear SpinSpo. Not today," she said, half-turning to check out her own ass, "but some days. He actually told us not to. There's even a policy, it's right here. He's very serious about it." She pointed at the surface of the desk, where a sheet of orange paper with black text was adhered with masking tape.

NON-DRESS CODE
- NO FROWNS
- NO "BELLY" OR "MIDDY" (MIDRIFF-REVEALING) SHIRTS
- NO BRANDED LEGGINS—THAT MEANS LULULEMON, SPINSPO, NIKE, UNDER ARMOUR—ANY AND ALL LOGOS <u>HAVE</u> TO BE <u>COVERED</u> <u>NO EXCEPTIONS</u>

I cracked up that Boomer had actually typed "leggins."

I said, "I could probably hook you up with a few free pairs of SpinSpo, um, pants."

"Really? Do you work there?"

"Something like that, as unlikely as it seems. What's he got against logos?"

"He says it's lustful. To put a logo near your butt."

"That is the dumbest thing I've ever heard. But anyway, Tara, if you can help me with Wyatt, I can help you with lustful athletic wear."

Her expression went back to vaguely uncomfortable. "It's just that," she said, and stopped.

"It's okay," I said, "I'm not looking to jam anyone up."

"Well, it's that—I'm not sure, but I think—I *think* Wyatt has been doing laundry here. And taking food from the kitchen."

"Really."

Tara nodded. "Mr. Wiggins would totally freak out. You can't tell him."

I promised not to tell Boomer. "Why do you think that?"

"Well, we always have a box of clementines in the kitchen. Mr. Wiggins thinks they're just the best. He eats like ten of them a day. But I noticed that the box was getting low really fast. Then I found some of Wyatt's clothes in the laundry the other day." She nodded at a bin of towels behind the front desk. "When I gave the stuff back to him, he acted like he'd spilled some cleaning spray on his shirt and had to wash it. But then when he was putting the clothes into his bag, I saw that he had, like, so many clementines in there. And he got really embarrassed."

"Interesting," I said.

"But you can't tell Mr. Wiggins."

"No, I won't."

"Wyatt's a nice guy."

"So I keep hearing. Hey, if you see him again, don't tell him you talked to me."

Her expression went quizzical.

"Do you like the ebony leggings, or onyx or anthracite? Or all three?"

Now she smiled. "Could I have all three?"

"Size?"

"Two."

"Deal."

That evening, while I waited for Wyatt to show up at the gym, I sat in the Ethiopian restaurant across the street with a plate of sambusas and a bad idea to keep me company: BusPass. I was hoping that enough swiping would show me the Affliction douchebag's picture, and I could leverage that into figuring out who the hell he was. The app was a Tinder rip-off, right down to the "swiping" motion, though of course the app referred to it as "passing." There was no way to search for a specific user; you had to create a profile and the app matched you with potential fuck buddies based on literally nothing but your age, as far as I could tell. I made a profile under the name Rose Warner and assigned the young lady a birth-date close to Addison's—1992; how was that even a real birth year for adults?—and for a profile picture, I snapped a photo of some blonde in an ad for laundry detergent in a magazine that was left on my table. With a couple filters applied, Rose looked sort of artsy and cool. I wrote her a one-sentence bio that read, "Travel, good beer, red meat, let's chill." Essentially meaningless, but it was not lost on me that this app buried the bio under a little "info" icon at the bottom of the picture for a reason—the reason being that whatever Rose had to say wasn't anyone's top priority.

It only allowed her five hundred characters anyway.

The whole thing was pretty silly. Matches were no more significant than "any men between twenty and thirty" within fifty miles of my current location. Everyone's five-hundred-character bio had about as much thought put into it as Rose's. But I could sort of see the appeal, the anonymous act of judging someone based on their picture alone. Yes. No. Right. Left. It was almost the automated diversion of a slot machine, but for people.

My sambusas were gone by the time I'd swiped through a hundred pictures and I unlocked a feature called "Express Bus," which allowed users to only see profiles of people who were looking for a fuckbuddy right now—for the low low price of one token, which equaled two dollars. Or I could pay $7.99 a month for the "Metro Pass," which unlocked all the premium features, including Missed the Bus.

I groaned a little and typed in my credit card.

There was still nothing happening across the street at Clean-Sweat.

The missed-connections feature was about as deep as the rest of the app. A user would post a short, five-hundred-character shout-out with a date, time, and location; if you passed to the right, it meant you thought the post could be about you. Then the app would show both parties each other's profiles the next time you were going through the stack, and if you both passed right, it would announce that you'd made a match. Because it only did so if both the poster and the subject of the post were interested in each other, it ensured that the experience was still based on nothing but looks.

Maybe it was the detective in me, or maybe it was the cynic, but either way, this app sounded like a whole bunch of crimes waiting to happen.

I scrolled through Missed the Bus and wondered how many of these "connections" were actually connections—versus how many were just people preying, maybe subconsciously, on the hopeless romantics of the world, the ones who wanted nothing more than to find meaning in the meaningless.

I imagined Addison seeing a post about her tattoo and passing right on the Affliction douchebag. Why? Out of boredom? Was that her type? Did she look into his brooding eyes and imagine a future with him, a story to tell the grandkids about how they met? "Well, Grandpa thought I was hot, and he posted on the internet about it, and I thought *he* was hot too, and we lived happily ever after."

It appeared that once the "connection" was made, the post disappeared from the app. So even if the content had gone back far enough—which it didn't—the post would've been gone anyway.

Technology: only so useful.

When it got close to eight o'clock, my waiter came over to gently advise they were about to close. He glanced down at my phone and said, "You lonely?"

"No," I said. "No. This is for work."

He laughed. "Do not be ashamed of wanting someone to love you."

Now it was my turn to laugh. "Someone does love me," I said, although that someone still hadn't sent so much as an ironic emoji since she left for her trip. I gave him a twenty and told him to keep the change.

"Thank you, sister," he said. "Maybe I see you on there. You pass right for me, okay?"

"You got it."

I sat in the car and continued my "work" for a while. Aiden, 24. Jared, 28. Milo, 33. Out of curiosity I clicked on the "info" icon under his picture to read the bio: *Just looking for a cool chick to send nude pics. Im married so be cool with that.*

The state of straight people was troubling.

I braved the cold long enough to root through the back of the Range Rover for a blanket; I found two, plus a hat that I didn't think was mine—stuffed with a roll of duct tape and a coil of nylon rope. The previous owner of my vehicle had no doubt been a charming individual. I shook out the creepy items and turned the hat inside out just in case and got back into the driver's seat.

I flipped through the "stack" for another thirty minutes. The hat and blanket kept most of me warm, but my feet were frozen and all the twentysomething men of Columbus were starting to look exactly the same. I switched over to Facebook; a mistake. The first story I saw was a news clip with the headline "Reward for Info on Missing Clintonville Woman."

When I pushed play, Jason Stowe's commanding frame filled the screen.

"My daughter Addison has been missing for four days," he said. "She was last seen going into an apartment on Fourth Street, owned by a local drug dealer. No one has seen her since—"

I relished interrupting him for a change and closed the app and called Peter Novotny. "Are you really retired yet?" I said. I'd met the old private investigator on a case a year or so ago, and he kept threatening to *really* retire but so far hadn't managed it yet, at least not when I asked him if he wanted some work.

"For you? No. What do you need, doll?"

"I need some help. Overnight. If you know any young guns looking for work, that would be fine too."

"No, I got you."

"It isn't fun."

"Is it sitting in a car in the freezing cold?"

"You know me so well," I said, and he laughed. "Feel free to say no, on account of your old bones."

"Eh, I'm Norwegian on my mother's side. How much is this endeavor worth to you?"

I didn't really have a paying client, so that didn't especially matter. "However much," I said. "Feel free to bring in reinforcements if necessary, within reason."

"Oh, so I have to do the work and provide the reinforcements?"

"You know you're my only reinforcement, Petey."

"Well, that's tragic."

I sat with that for a second. I guessed it kind of was. "So do you want to do it or no?"

"Text me the details, honey, you know I can't say no to you."

Once CleanSweat was squared away in Peter Novotny's capable hands, I headed home. I didn't want to go home. But I didn't have anywhere else I wanted to go, either, so home I went.

At least I had whiskey there.

I helped myself to some and curled up in bed with BusPass and a vague sense of determination, which lasted for about an hour before I grew tired of this particular tactic. I wasn't getting anywhere, anyway, and it felt like I had already looked at approximately a million faces. Out of curiosity I pulled up some statistics on the app.

There was no shortage of press about it. Thirty thousand active monthly users, which meant, according to the app's own website, one in six millennials in Columbus was on it. That seemed a little grandiose to me, but at thirty-five I was too old to count myself among them, so what did I know? The app was created by a twenty-one-year-old computer science student at OSU and sold to a software development start-up for forty grand—a decision the creator no doubt came to regret after the app blew up. Most of the press was good press, though a data breach six months earlier had caused a sharp decrease in downloads. But it was only temporary, and since then, the active monthly user numbers were higher than ever. I was deep in the weeds on the provenance of funding for the start-up when I saw a familiar name:

Kenny Brayfield

"Hi buddy," I murmured.

He was a bit old to call himself a millennial too, though he had the money to call himself whatever he wanted. It appeared that in the two years since I'd met him on a case, he had gotten into venture capital funding and had pretty good instincts; his portfolio included a hip Skee-Ball bar that had opened downtown, along with a mixed-use building in the Short North that was getting buzz because, it was rumored, a Shake Shack was coming to town.

I wondered if my acquaintance with Kenny would be enough to get some insider information about BusPass's users.

He did owe me, after all.

TWENTY

I took a tray of vegan blueberry crumb cake by the office of Next Level Promotions in the morning. I was not above purchasing people's affection, or cooperation, with sweets and in fact found it a valuable strategy. The hipsters working for Kenny Brayfield went for it anyway. Kenny himself was a little more wary but I supposed he was entitled to exercise some caution; I'd pointed a gun at him the last time we spoke in person.

But when I advised that I wanted to talk about BusPass and not his decades-old high school indiscretions this time, he relaxed. "You use it, right? Damn, it's cool! Did you know that the average user spends forty minutes a day up in there?"

I did know that, because I'd read it on the app's website last night. "I'm more curious about the group that runs it."

"Transit Tech, yeah." He lifted a bottle of gold-flake vodka out of a box behind his desk. "You want some?"

I was acquainted with the sickly-sweet cinnamon flavor of the liquor, which was produced by Next Level's only client. "You know any of them?"

"Know them? Sure. I got their dream off the ground."

"Great," I said. "Perfect. Because I'm in need of some information that they have."

He leaned back in his chair and studied me. He might've been good looking if he didn't dress like he was going as a hoodrat for Halloween—oversized T-shirt, baggy jeans, flat-billed New Orleans Saints cap, a tangle of fake-looking gold chains around his neck. That he was from the richest, Waspiest family in the southern half of the Columbus metro area was evident only in the fact that he'd been running this business for several years despite having only the one client.

Kenny said, "Information?"

"There's a young lady who matched with someone from Missed the Bus. She's missing."

"Shit."

I nodded, solemnly. I knew it would make Kenny keep talking and it did.

He said, "And you think—the app—you're saying you think she met someone through the app who . . . missing-ed her?"

"Yes."

"Aw, *man.*" He took off his hat and ran his hands over his buzzed hair. "That is not good news."

"No, it isn't."

"So you want, what? You want to know who she matched with?"

I nodded. "It might help me find her."

"Are the police involved?"

"They don't have to be," I said, which didn't answer the question, but he appeared to accept it.

"Okay, because I think it's safe to say that we'd *def* prefer they aren't. You know?"

"Sure."

"I mean, maybe it doesn't have anything to do with the app at all."

"Maybe not. But maybe so, Kenny."

He sighed and put his hat back on, adjusting it in his reflection on the glass surface of his nearly empty desk. "Okay. I'll see what I can find out for you. I just need the email she signed up with. Just, please, keep this on the DL."

"Def," I said.

As I walked back to the car, it started snowing, sloppy, silver-dollar-sized flakes. The sky was grey-white and thick-looking; it was probably going to snow all day, and it was probably going to stick. I got into the driver's seat, brushing snow from my hair, just as my phone rang.

Catherine.

I'd wanted her to call so bad that I almost refused to answer it on principle, but then I answered anyway. "Hi, stranger," I said.

She made an impatient sound. "You know, you can call me whenever you want."

"I seem to remember you making a big deal about how you'd call me—"

"Are we seriously discussing who's supposed to call whom?"

I felt my eyebrows pressing together and I rubbed the spot between them, a prickly headache zinging to life. "Well, you're calling now. What's going on?"

"What's going on," Catherine said, "is my flight's canceled."

I looked at the dashboard clock—it was just after ten. Her flight home wasn't for another several hours. "Already?"

"There's this storm. They're closing the airport. It's that bad."

"It's just starting to snow here, too."

"Great."

Silence vibrated through the connection.

"Have you had a good trip?"

"Yes, it's been very interesting."

More silence.

Finally, she said, "Well, I just wanted to let you know that I won't be making it back today. Hopefully tomorrow, but I don't know."

"Okay, well, keep me posted."

"Roxane?"

"Yeah?"

Catherine sighed. "I'm sorry. I'm just stressed out by the uncertainty."

"It's okay. You'll be home soon. To me."

"Good," she said.

I tossed the phone onto the seat beside me. I still had no idea what the hell had caused her mood to tank on the way to the airport. She'd been herself after dinner, in the car as we drove back to her place. *They might have oysters, but they don't have you*, she'd said, her head on my shoulder. But by morning, something was different. Maybe everything was. I hadn't given myself much space to think about it since, and I realized that some part of me was relieved she wasn't coming home today. I was too caught up in what was going on with my brother to have the emotional bandwidth to figure out what was going on with Catherine. With us.

Did that mean something?

Despite the snow blanketing the roadway, everything was still business as usual at the courthouse, where one of three weekly arraignment sessions was taking place in room 5C of the Franklin County Court of Common Pleas.

Thanks to the luck of the alphabet, my brother came nearly last.

I stood in the back of the courtroom and watched as Julia Raymund stood next to my brother—rumpled and exhausted looking—and argued for him to be released on bail. She'd made it sound like a done deal, but it turned out to be far from it.

The arraignment judge remanded him to the county jail because he was in violation of his probation.

My mouth went dry.

Andrew had failed to mention any ongoing legal trouble to me, and so had Julia for that matter. The entire thing was over almost as soon as it began, and a uniformed bailiff was leading my brother back out of the courtroom before I even had a chance to talk to him.

When Julia saw that I was there, she frowned. For an attorney, she didn't have a very good poker face. That, or she wanted me to know that she hated me.

I guessed it could have been either.

"Julia, what the hell?" I said, steering her by the arm over to the windows when it appeared she was going to make a break for the elevator.

She removed my hand from her sleeve. "I told you he didn't want you to come."

"No, you told me I didn't have to come, but I thought that I did. Why didn't you mention this probation the other day?"

"I'm not in the business of sharing my clients' privileged information."

"This is different."

"Is it? If Andrew wanted you to know about it, perhaps he would have told you. I have to get to a meeting. Excuse me."

This woman was infuriating. "What was the probation even for?"

The elevator doors opened and she escaped.

I leaned my forehead against the cold windowpane. The street below was a snowy parking lot. All I could think of was my mother.

Rather than dealing with the snow, I decided to wait for visitation hours at six on the off-chance that Andrew would be booked in already at the adjacent courthouse and I'd be allowed to see him. One of the benefits of the storm was that the line was shorter than usual, but I'd still only get fifteen minutes.

It seemed like a lot of ground to cover in fifteen minutes.

When he filed into the visitation booth in a khaki-colored prison get-up, I had to blink hard to keep frustrated tears from falling and making everything worse.

"Hey you," I said into the grimy phone.

Andrew sighed. Through the handset, it made a hissing sound. "Are you okay?"

"I need a fucking drink," he said.

I wanted to press my palm against the glass but worried it was too much like a Lifetime movie.

"You've been here for hours," he added.

"Yeah."

"Why?"

"You wouldn't want to see me, if our roles were reversed?"

Andrew was barely looking at me. "Of course I would."

"Why didn't you tell me?"

"I don't know. I didn't want to bother you with it."

"Since when? When did it even happen?"

"Back in July," Andrew said.

"*What* happened?"

"It was just a misdemeanor. I had a baggie of Darvocet in my cup holder when I got pulled over. Speeding."

I rubbed the place between my eyebrows. "I don't get why you wouldn't tell me. If not at the time, then the other day. When we were talking about going to the police."

"I mean, because I didn't want you to know. What if it somehow got you jammed up in this? Jules told me last year, the less anyone knows, the better."

"*Jules*," I said.

Andrew breathed noisily instead of answering.

"How long has *that* been going on?"

"For it's none of your damn business long."

"Come on. I'm not Matt. I'm the one you're supposed to tell this stuff to."

"Like how you told me you're sleeping with Tom Heitker, of all people?"

"I'm not!"

Andrew shook his head.

"Okay, fine. I'm not anymore. But I was."

"I fucking knew it."

"I didn't tell you because I knew you'd be like this."

"Like what?"

"I know you don't like him."

"Just because I personally don't want to spend time with the guy doesn't mean I don't want you to," Andrew said. "I mean, I know you're friends."

"I believe we were talking about you and *Jules* though."

Andrew sighed.

"I'm pretty sure she hates me, so that's going to be a problem."

"She doesn't hate you."

"Oh, maybe what I meant is that I hate her."

"Well, we're even then. You have Catherine, I have Jules, and literally nobody's happy."

Now it was my turn to sigh. We looked at each other through the dirty glass. "Andrew, I'm so sorry about how this went down."

He shook his head. "What went down is half me being a dumbass and half the world not being fair. I don't know where they got this idea that Addison never made it out of my place. I mean, this would all be pretty fucking elaborate. Me calling you to pretend to look for her? They kept showing me this picture, some douche in a skull shirt."

"They showed it to me too."

"Who is it?"

"No idea. But the picture had the icon of that dating app, Bus-Pass, which Addison also used."

"Why are they showing me that?"

"I don't know," I said. Our fifteen minutes was almost up. "But I'm going to find out."

TWENTY-ONE

The phone woke me up around five o'clock. This was getting to be a bit of a habit, and one I didn't like. "Morning, doll," Peter Novotny said. "Good news and bad news."

"Let's hear the bad news first," I said. I dragged myself down the hall and perched on the edge of my desk, nudging my laptop awake. The fruits of my research into Mickey's cousin Rick were still up on the screen, though they didn't amount to much: he'd had the same job at Best Buy for eleven years, lived at the same address his entire life, no record, not even a speeding ticket. I didn't have any emails from Kenny Brayfield, either. I closed the lid.

Novotny said, "Okay, the bad news is your guy must have gone into the gym at some point during the night and I missed it."

"You missed it, or your reinforcement missed it?"

"Something like that," he said, not answering the question. "But that brings me to the good news."

"Okay?"

"I got him leaving this morning, and I'm currently on his tail."

I was already pulling on my jeans. "Where?"

"On 71 now, headed towards downtown."

By the time I got myself out of the house and onto the snow-covered freeway, Wyatt and Novotny had exited onto Main Street, driven east a while, and pulled into a motel.

A familiar motel.

"Right in there is where he went," Novotny said once I had joined him in his car, a plush maroon Caddy that made me miss my old Mercedes, may she rest in peace. He pointed at the door at the end of the building. The room where I'd talked to Shane last week. "He took two grocery bags in. So what's the approach?"

"Approach?" I said. "I figured I'd wait till somebody came out. Wyatt knows what I look like, Shane knows what I look like, so the element of surprise is out. Not to mention I don't know who else is in there."

Novotny clapped his hands together. "I know, isn't it exciting? Here's what we should do."

Ten minutes later, I watched as Novotny shuffled up to the room, hunched over in an exaggerated old-man posture. He knocked tentatively on the door.

Wyatt opened it. "Can I help you?"

"Oh my goodness," Novotny said loudly, "Thank you. I can't find the room, my daughter—it's so cold—can I use your phone, young man?"

Wyatt looked out across the parking lot, saw nothing amiss, and motioned for Novotny to come inside.

A few seconds later, my phone rang. "Dad!" I said. "Where are you?"

We put on a brief teleplay wherein he told me that two nice young men were helping him, and I said I would be right down. Then, with a hat pulled low over my brow, I knocked on the door too.

"Dad, it's me," I called.

Wyatt opened the door and let me in.

Over his shoulder, I saw Shane Resznik fake-sleeping on one of the room's double beds.

I took my hat off. "Hi guys," I said. "Sorry for the trickery."

"What the—" Shane said, jumping out of bed.

Wyatt, meanwhile, sat down heavily on the other bed.

Shane swatted the back of his head. "What the fuck, man?"

"I thought it was some old dude who couldn't find his room."

"Well," Shane continued, "get the fuck out of here. This is trespassing."

I picked up a plastic baggie from the desk, a crumbly white substance inside. "This looks like possession."

"It's not—no, it's just—"

"Right, right, it's just borax," I said.

Shane was apoplectic. "The fuck is borax? What are you trying to pin on me?"

"Nothing. We're just going to have a little chat. We got off on the wrong foot the other day, Shane, and Wyatt, we haven't met personally yet, other than that time you followed me to my house. Your mom sends her regards, though."

Wyatt slumped even further, something I didn't think was possible.

"Sit down," Novotny told Shane.

We all looked at each other for a while.

"So, Shane, you're what, holed up in here getting high and making Wyatt bring you groceries?" I emptied one of the paper sacks onto the desk. Energy drinks, beef jerky, vodka, crackers, a *Maxim* magazine, a bottle of multivitamins.

I picked up the vitamins. "Interesting assortment here."

"You spent my money on vitamins?" Shane snapped.

Wyatt covered his face with his hands. He was wearing a newsboy cap, tweed, and a black V-neck sweater. Of all the people in this room, he looked like he belonged here the least. He said, "You need nutrients, dude."

I almost laughed, thinking of the soulful macro conversations Boomer claimed he'd had with Wyatt. "Let's discuss what happened at the club the other night."

Shane shook his head. "I already told you. The pipes burst."

"And you're hiding out in this shitty motel because . . . ?"

"I just . . . felt like it."

"And that's why you're not going home?" I asked Wyatt.

He nodded unconvincingly.

"Your mother's worried. Why not let her know what's going on so she doesn't worry like that?"

"He told me not to. He's the boss."

"So he's paying you."

Wyatt froze. Shane cleared his throat loudly, until the younger man nodded.

"He's not, for example, holding something over your head to make you do it? Just like he does at the club, with whatever funny business he's trying to pull against Vincent Pomp?"

"You don't know anything about it, you ugly bitch."

"Shane," I said, "I don't think I was talking to you. Wyatt?"

"Yes," Wyatt said.

"Yes what?"

"I mean no, he's not doing that. He's paying me. I need the money."

"What all are you making him do for that money, Shane?"

Shane said, "I'm not a fucking *homo*, if that's what you're saying. He is, but I'm not."

I was sick of him. I backhanded him across the mouth. "Shut up."

His eyes widened and he touched his lip and then looked down at his fingers as if he expected to see blood. There wasn't any. Wyatt sighed miserably.

Beside me, Novotny shot me a glance. I put my hands in my pockets, my right metacarpals throbbing. Wyatt was looking at the bland motel carpet between his boots.

I said, "Wyatt, what happened the other night?"

He didn't reply.

"Why were you following me the other day?"

Wyatt muttered something.

"Say again?"

"I wasn't." With the blinds drawn it was dark in the room, but I could still make out his face winching up in frightened tears.

Slapping Shane across the mouth had felt good, but so far this wasn't proving to be especially useful. I said, "Wyatt, how about you let me take you home to your mother's house. She's crazy worried about you."

Wyatt glanced at Shane, then back at me.

I added, "Shane, if you so much as think about making trouble for Wyatt, I'll tell Vincent Pomp exactly where to find you, okay? I can assure you, he's fonder of me than he is of you."

Shane looked genuinely freaked out by that.

"And my associate Mr. Novotny here is going to keep an eye on you to make sure I'm kept informed about where exactly that is. Got it?"

Shane looked like he was processing something. Finally, he said, "You mean he's not your dad?"

Novotny promised to keep an eye on Shane from the parking lot—no reason to give the man and his *Maxim* magazine an audience—and to update me if he went anywhere. But I sort of doubted that Shane would be leaving his room for a minute. If his face felt anything like my hand did, he'd probably want to lie around with a bag of ice on his mouth for the next week.

Wyatt didn't say anything when we got into my car, just buckled his seat belt and sat there with his hands folded in his lap.

I said, "I did you a favor. Whatever that guy has on you is nothing compared to what Vincent Pomp has on him."

"Thank you," Wyatt murmured.

"You're still scared."

"And?"

"What happened at the club?"

"I already told you."

"I guess I should have specified that by taking care of Shane for you, I wanted your cooperation."

"Did you really talk to my mother?"

"Yes."

"Is she okay?"

"Not really, Wyatt, she's been terrified that something happened to you. Why didn't you call her?"

"Because—there are just some things you don't tell your mother."

"I can help."

"No, you can't."

"How do you know? I mean, aren't you even a little impressed that I was able to find you?"

At this, he gave me a tiny smile. "I'm more impressed that you slapped him."

"Let me guess. You've been wanting to do that for ages."

"Maybe."

The car was quiet as we drove slowly toward downtown with rush-hour traffic. Finally I said, "Tell me about Addison."

"Is she okay?"

"That's what I'd like to know."

Wyatt palmed his beard.

"She's a good friend of yours."

He didn't say anything, just nodded slowly and sadly.

"Do you know anything about the guy she was talking to on BusPass?"

Out of the corner of my eye, I saw Wyatt's head snap toward me. "BusPass?"

"Apparently everybody in the entire city uses it."

"Yeah, I just didn't know she does. It's not—Addison hates that crap. Curated existence, she calls it."

"Profound."

"She's like that. Philosophical."

"And you?"

"I just didn't know she was on BusPass, is all."

"So you don't know anything about who it was?"

"No, she never mentioned it to me."

"What happened at the club that night?"

"Nothing."

"Wyatt."

He kept quiet again.

I tried something else. "How about a couple weeks ago? Some kind of altercation. Whatever it was, you mentioned it to your mom."

Wyatt cleared his throat. "That was nothing."

"Nothing?"

"Nothing to do with—nothing. It was nothing."

"What kind of nothing?"

"Just some drunk chick who freaked out on Addison, like, saying she recognized her from pictures on her husband's phone."

"Really."

"Addison was like, 'No way, I don't fuck with that, sexting randos or whatever.'"

"What happened next?"

"I practically had to drag the lady out by the elbows and pour her into an Uber."

"Addison didn't know who she was?"

"No."

"Or who this husband might've been?"

"It wasn't like we stood there and talked about it after."

"But you talked to your mom about it?"

"It's just because she scratched me, here," Wyatt said, gesturing to a spot under his eye. "So she asked, my mom asked what happened and I told her. But so what, it's just a scratch, I never saw the woman again."

"I just want to find your friend."

But Wyatt remained quiet for the rest of the drive to his mother's house.

It was still early when we got there—just after seven—but Gwen Achebe had clearly been up for a while. She flung the door open when I knocked and exclaimed, "God bless you, you found him. Honey, come here."

She threw her arms around her son, who stiffly accepted her embrace and mumbled, "I need to lie down, Momma."

He brushed past her and into the house. "What—my goodness, what's he been up to?"

"I'm not sure, to be honest. Mind if I come in for a minute?"

"No, of course, come in."

Wyatt had gone into his bedroom and locked the door. Gwen tapped a knuckle gently and said, "Honey, why don't you unlock this door and we can talk about whatever's going on."

"Nothing. It's fine." His voice was thick with tears.

"Miss Weary just wants to help you."

There was no response from inside the bedroom.

I sat with Gwen for twenty minutes or so, but it was clear that Wyatt had no intention of coming out and talking to me. So I put my coat back on and said, "If he wants to talk, or even if he just comes out, give me a call. I think something happened that scared the hell out of him, and I'd love to know what. Because Wyatt doesn't seem like the type to scare easily."

His mother shook her head. "No, he is not. Did he crash his car?"

"What?"

"You brought him home. I just wondered where his car was."

That was a really good question. He'd been driving Shane's car earlier. Since Addison's vehicle was missing too, maybe all of this really had been something as simple as a car accident like I'd first suspected.

"Hopefully we'll talk soon," I said.

I spent the morning poring over incident reports from the police department's website, looking for traffic accidents from that morning. It was harder than usual on account of the weather that day—though it hadn't snowed as much then as it had in the last twenty-four hours, the streets had been slippery, and the cops weren't taking as many reports as usual. There'd been a fatality on the exit ramp from westbound 670 to Fourth Street, but that was some distance away from the nightclub and, anyway, the time on the crash report made it late enough that Addison was already at my brother's condo, or maybe had even left by then. I wasn't sure what kind of incident would cause something to happen to both Wyatt's and Addison's cars, anyway—a collision with each other? That didn't make any sense.

I flipped back to my research about Mickey Dillman's cousin Rick. He was forty-two, taller than Mickey, dressed in a polo shirt and khakis in literally every photo I could find of him. He had light brown hair cut short and bronze-colored wire-rim glasses, rectangular in shape. He looked like a history teacher I'd had in ninth grade, a benevolent nerd.

I wondered what, if anything, he could tell me. So far, no one was being especially forthcoming about Addison.

Rick Dillman was shoveling the sidewalk in front of the Merion Village house where he lived with his parents. From a distance I thought he had on bright red earmuffs, but up close I could see that they were fancy headphones. I'd called around to all the Best Buy stores in the city, trying to figure out which one he might work at; the Reynoldsburg location was kind enough to volunteer that he wouldn't be in until two o'clock, which meant that I didn't have to either wait till the evening to talk to him, or pop in on him at work—something I preferred to avoid whenever possible. Having to be at work was terrible enough without a random interruption from a stranger. So there I was. I said his name but he didn't react on account of the headphones. I looped around the driveway apron and approached from the front.

He stopped mid-shovel and stared at me from behind his glasses. The lower half of the lenses were slightly fogged; he was breathing hard from the exertion of clearing the sidewalk.

I pointed at my ears.

Rick slid the headphones down around his neck.

"Hi," I said. "Rick, right?"

He nodded. He was looking at me but not quite making eye contact; his gaze was around my mouth. He pushed the snow shovel vertically against the frozen mound he'd created in the yard, shoring up the edge.

I told him who I was and why I was there. "I just wanted to ask you about last Wednesday. Did you go bowling with Mickey?"

"Yes." He pressed at the snow with the shovel again.

"How was it?"

"I scored two-oh-eight, then one-eighty-nine, then two-twenty." He said it flatly.

"How was Mickey?"

"He doesn't bowl because of his back."

"How did he seem?"

Rick shored up the snow again. I tried a different approach. "Can you tell me about what happened that night?"

"Yes," Rick said but didn't go on.

To my left, the door of the house opened and a man looked out at us. He was older, with thick white hair and a silver-handled cane. "Ricky-boy, who's that you're talking to?"

Rick said, "Her name is Roxane Weary, she is a private investigator who knows Sunny and she is asking me questions about bowling."

The man, who I assumed was Rick's father, squinted at me. "Come here a second, young lady."

"Dad, stop it." Rick huffed a sigh.

But the man continued motioning at me, so I went over to him.

"You know my son doesn't like being interrupted in the middle of things."

"Excuse me?"

"He's an Aspie. He has Asperger's. Well, that's what they said when he was a boy. Now they call it something else."

I glanced over my shoulder at Rick. He was methodically finishing the sidewalk, his headphones back on. His father continued, "I'm telling you that because he doesn't like to be interrupted. How do you know Sunny?"

"I'm very sorry about your nephew," I said.

He nodded. He was still looking at me with suspicion. "And Sunny," he said. "How'd you know her?"

"She's a friend of my father," I said, "who was a cop, before he died. She wanted me to make sure she was kept informed about what happened. And she mentioned that Mickey went bowling with Rick last Wednesday."

"Rick's very literal, so you have to ask him your questions the right way. But he remembers everything. You might as well wait inside here till he's done."

Though the sidewalk was long and the snow was heavy, Rick was finished in ten minutes. He came into the house and hung up his coat and took off his boots. His father said, "Rick, do you want to talk to this lady?"

"Okay."

Rick sat down in an armchair across from the couch where I was perched. His hair was dripping wet with sweat and his glasses were completely fogged over now.

His father tossed a box of tissues at him. "Wipe your face," he said.

Rick took off his glasses, mopped his forehead, and polished the glasses on the edge of his polo shirt. Once he could see again, he resumed staring at my mouth.

I said, "What happened last Wednesday? When you saw your cousin."

Rick cleared his throat. "He came over at six forty-one and he drove us to the Columbus Bowling Palace. We ate hot dogs and Mickey had a beer and I had a Coke. I bowled one game and my score was two-oh-eight. Then I bowled another game and my score was one-eighty-nine. Then I bowled another game and got two-twenty. Then he drove me back here."

"What time was it?"

"Ten-nineteen."

"Did he say where he was going next?"

"No."

"Was he dating anyone?"

"No."

"Did he ever use the dating app BusPass?"

A slight pause. Then he said, "Yes. He showed it to me."

"Did he ever meet anyone from there?"

"He said it was like a game."

"The dating app was like a game?"

"Like Two Dots. Two Dots has different-colored circles on the screen and you have to connect them, like this." He drew a square in the air between us with an index finger. "The dots don't mean anything."

"Is that what he said about BusPass? That it doesn't mean anything?"

Rick nodded.

"Did he ever mention a woman named Addison?"

"No."

I pulled up a picture of Addison on my phone and held it out. "Do you know who this is?"

Here something flickered through Rick's face. Recognition? I couldn't be sure. But he said, "No."

"You don't recognize her?"

Rick glanced at my phone again, almost wincing. "No."

"Are you sure?"

"He said no," his father chimed in.

"No, I don't know her at all," Rick said.

TWENTY-TWO

It took some doing to convince Jordy Meyers not to just hang up on me, and even more to get her to agree to meeting. But in the end she did, and that night at six I took a whole fried chicken, biscuits, mac and cheese, and collards from the Eagle over to Blacklick.

"You didn't have to do all this," Jordy said as I unloaded my bag onto Elise's kitchen counter. "I mean, this is amazing, but you didn't have to. I'm the one who asked you to come the other day."

"It's okay," I said. "I'm happy to. This is a terrible situation you guys are in and I didn't exactly make it better."

"Say thank you to Miss Roxane," Elise said to her son, a little boy with blond, cowlicky hair and big, round eyes about the size of the paper plate he was holding up. His mother cut up a piece of chicken and set it on the plate. "Come on, honey, you can say it."

The boy mumbled something unintelligible and scampered into the living room with his dinner.

"Thank you, Miss Roxane," Brock Hazlett said in a mock-child's voice. "Are you gonna make a plate for me, too?"

"Brock. No. We're going downstairs. Please parent your children for the next thirty minutes, okay?"

Brock winked at me. I decided that I didn't like him any better than Jordy did.

The three of us filed down the steps. Jordy had a plate piled high with chicken and sides, while Elise only had a small serving of collard greens on her plate. "I'd have to do Pilates for three days straight if I ate like that," she said, nodding at Jordy's plate.

Jordy sat on the velvet love seat and waved a hand at her friend. "I keep telling her," she said, glancing at me, "there's no virtue in being able to wear the same jeans you could wear in tenth grade. 2008 can keep its jeans, Elise."

"Whatever." Elise sat on the floor and ate a tiny bite of greens, looking at me expectantly.

"So listen," I said. I leaned on the edge of the white lacquer desk. "What I told you, about my brother. That was the absolute truth. I guess if I'd mentioned his name, you might have realized who he was, though."

"Uh, yeah," Jordy said around a mouthful of mac. "Andrew from the Sheraton? We sure would have. *That* was a mess and a half, let me tell you."

Elise, still chewing, kept quiet.

"I'm sure it looked like I was trying to pull something on you, but I promise you, I just want to find your friend. I don't want any money. I just want to find her. That's what I wanted since the other day. My brother only wanted to help. I only want to help. Jordy, I don't know if your stepsister spoke to them and told them what she told me, about Addison being home long enough to burn her eggs. But I promise you, everything happened exactly like I said it did, and now finding Addison is as critical for my brother as it is for her. Okay?"

Jordy pointed a fork at me. "It helps that you brought food."

"I thought it might."

"So what else could help you find her?"

"I just wanted to talk some more about BusPass."

"The app you never heard of till you met me," Jordy said.

"You've already broadened my horizons. But let's talk more about BusPass Guy. BPG. Did you ever see a picture?"

Both women shook their heads. Jordy said, "She showed us the post, but that was before she replied to it."

"Did she ever describe him?"

No.

"And she never mentioned a name?"

No.

I described the picture the detectives had showed me. "Does that sound like Addison's type?"

"Well," Elise said, "if you asked her if she had a type, she'd say no. But yeah, that's totally her type."

Jordy was nodding too. "The more tortured, the better."

I showed them a photo of Mickey Dillman. "What about this guy?"

Jordy snorted. "What on earth," she said. "He's, like—who is this?"

"I take that as a no?"

Else shook her head.

"Too old?"

"Not really, I think we already told you about her daddy issues, right? Addison's definitely dated some older guys."

"Real silver-fox types, handsome." Jordy gestured at my phone with her fork. "He looks like a roofer or something."

"Blue collar, you mean?" I said.

She winced a little. "Yeah, I guess, which probably makes me horrible. I'm just saying, everyone has a type, and Addison's tends more towards the, um, handsome. You know?"

Elise set her plate down on the rug beside her. "But I guess you never know, though, right?"

Jordy shrugged in an *okay, okay* gesture. "I guess. I mean, your type is handsome too, and look what you're stuck with."

Elise cracked up, a flush creeping through her face.

Jordy said, "The joke is, Brock was the star of the swim team back in high school, and now he's a glorified janitor at the rec center."

"But he's a good provider," Elise said, with Jordy saying the last two words right along with her.

Next I showed them a picture of Shane Resznik, who fared even worse than Mickey Dillman had.

"Good god, that pervy little goatee? No."

I looked at the picture; there really was something a bit off-putting about the shape of the goatee, too pointy. The back of my hand still throbbed from coming into contact with it and the face it was growing on. "Okay, how about him? They weren't dating, but I wanted to know if you'd ever seen him, or heard about him—Wyatt is his name."

Both women looked down at a picture of Wyatt. "Okay, he's adorable, but no, she never mentioned a Wyatt," Elise said.

Jordy's expression had turned sad. "Are we the worst friends ever? That she didn't tell us anything about anything?"

"I think that's just called getting older."

"Unfortunately, I can report that that's true," I said.

On the way out, I passed Elise's husband making a mess with a snow blower in the driveway. When he saw me, he turned it off. "Hey, that chicken was good. Did you make it?"

"Hell no. It's from the Eagle, in the Short North."

"Well, thanks for bringing it over. Elise was making baked fish, and believe me, I was glad to see that hit the trash can."

I glanced back at the house, though Elise was still in the basement. "She threw away what she was making?"

"Yes, thank god."

I felt like a jerk. "Well, I didn't want her to throw out what she was cooking. I was just trying to be nice."

Brock blinked dumbly at me. "Oh and you were! That was great!"

"Well, have a good night," I said.

"You too, Miss Roxane!"

I refused to look at him, even when he revved the snow blower in my direction as I pulled out of the driveway.

TWENTY-THREE

Kenny Brayfield was very concerned that I was going to embarrass him in front of his business partners. "Just be nice," he had told me in the elevator as we rode up to the suite that housed Transit Tech. "Don't, like, wave a gun around or something."

I almost laughed. "Do you actually think I would do that?"

"Please just don't," he said.

I could have told him that my gun was locked in the glove box of my car, but I didn't.

He introduced me to the officers of the company and gave me a brief tour through the office, a two-story loft with a Ping-Pong table, a rock-climbing wall, and a free vending machine that dispensed beer—all of which existed, no doubt, to trick the employees working seventy hours a week into thinking that they loved their jobs. The sky was blue and clear through the floor-to-ceiling windows that ran the length of the office. There were no cubicles or even actual desks, just a bunch of tables of varying heights where said employees could sit, stand, or sprawl at will.

The person I really needed to talk to had his own office, albeit one with a sliding glass door that probably just made everyone assume he was talking about them whenever it was closed. His name was Ramonte Barnes, and he served as Transit Tech's resident data expert.

"It's not like we want to make a habit of just splashing people's info to whoever," he was saying, "but in this case, I mean, we don't want to sit on something that could help you find the young lady. I heard her name on the radio, on WOSU. So you know it's serious."

I nodded. I liked him; he was probably about Addison's age, dressed like a college kid in jeans and a Black Nerd Problems T-shirt, but he seemed to be handling my request with the gravity of a professional.

"So basically, we have a ton of data. The app is about making human connections, but it's also about data, and using that data to make other types of connections, right?" As he spoke his eyes were on his computer screen, fingers flying across the keys. "We're using the data we collect to develop a really sophisticated advertising platform. Micro-targeting already exists, but we're drilling down into user behavior on a neighborhood level, specific to Columbus—something that has huge potential in the ad space. Does that make sense?"

"Not really."

Ramonte grinned. "Okay. Here's an example. Where do you live?"

"Olde Towne," I said, and he nodded approvingly.

"Okay, so you live in Olde Towne. If you were using the app and you went to, say, New Albany, the app would pay attention to the businesses you checked into, how long you spent there, if you used social media there, if you reviewed on Yelp or Google, and so on, and then, it would integrate that information into future display ads shown, specifically, to other Olde Towne East users who happen to go to New Albany. Obviously that's a massive oversimplification of what it does, but does that make sense?"

"Yes," I said, "and it sounds creepy as hell. So the app keeps track of every place every user goes?"

"It's saved anonymously, but yeah. And before you think it's a little too Big Brother-ish, you have to remember, every app you use is collecting data on you constantly unless you opted out from their terms of service."

"That just makes me want to delete *all* apps, rather than look the other way for this one."

Ramonte shook his head. "It's kind of like, if you can't beat 'em, join 'em. This kind of data collection is happening all the time, so you might as well embrace it and benefit from personalized recommendations."

This was all very troubling. But it probably had nothing to do with Addison's disappearance. "So when you say the data is stored anonymously, does that mean you can't pull up anything on a specific user?"

"No, we definitely can. See, the location data for the purposes of the display ads? That's one thing. It's like how the navigation app Waze can integrate real-time traffic without actually tracking users on an individual level. Location info is not saved to a user profile. But, activity within the app, that's a different story. Here you go."

Ramonte spun his monitor around to show me; it displayed a wall of text, dates, and times of everything Addison's profile had done via BusPass. I said, "Exactly what am I looking at?"

He leaned forward so he could look at the screen too. "This here," he said, tapping at a line of text, "means her user session lasted almost an hour. She passed left on ten profiles, right on twenty-three, and spent most of her time reading Missed the Bus posts."

That seemed about right. "Can I see her profile?"

Ramonte copied a string of characters from the list on his screen, switched applications, and pasted. The profile that popped up said ADDISON s below a picture of a curvy shadow against a graffiti-covered wall.

"This is it?"

"Looks like it."

Addison's short bio was very short indeed:

Least likely to.

That was all it said.

"Does she have any other pictures?"

Ramonte clicked on the arrow next to the shadow. There were two other images: one of a pair of black stilettos discarded on a parquet floor, colored lights shining on them; the other was a close-up of a brown eye with electric-blue mascara.

"It doesn't look like she was seriously trying to use this to meet somebody," Ramonte said. "I mean, I get it, she's artsy and cool, but this app isn't about that."

"I think she did meet someone, though. She connected to someone through a Missed the Bus post."

Ramonte went back to the list of data and scrolled for a while. "Here we go. It looks like she only ever interacted with one post from Missed the Bus." He copied another string of text from the window into the page with Addison's profile, but the screen that came up displayed an error.

"Okay, so that means whoever posted it has since deleted their page."

I sighed in frustration.

"Easy, tiger," Ramonte said. "We can still get to it—just have to go about it a different way."

A few dozen keystrokes later and he'd pulled up a Facebook profile belonging to one Corbin Janney. "This is the profile he used to create his account."

The profile picture wasn't the same one that the police had showed me, but it was clearly the same guy.

I wrote down his name. "Can you tell me anything else about him?"

"Well, he signed up using the Facebook authentication, meaning he didn't have to enter an email address into our system."

Ramonte typed a few lines. "But I don't know if—wait a minute." He tapped the keyboard with a bit more force. "That's weird."

"What's weird?"

"Well, I know that deleted user account data is regularly removed from this system, though it's copied over into our long-term storage—just to keep the data size reasonable. That happens once a week, but it looks like only part of Corbin's old profile actually got moved, which shouldn't have happened. Unless he actually only ever interacted with one user. Your girl Addison."

The data list on Corbin's file was much shorter than Addison's, and only showed him passing right and messaging with the string of characters that represented her user ID.

Ramonte said, "I'm going to have to look into that a bit further."

I asked if he could go back to the page that showed Addison's public profile. "What's this?" I said, pointing at a grey circle under her name.

"Oh, that means she's not online." He moused over the dot and a box that said OFFLINE. "It shows when a person was last active for up to three days—so if she'd last been on yesterday, it would say LAST SEEN YESTERDAY. And if the person is online right now, it's a green light, obviously."

I studied the scant information on the page for a bit and pointed next to a small green arrow with text beside it that read: DOUG J. "How about this?"

"Oh, that just means that a user recently looked at her page."

"It displays that publicly?" I said, immediately feeling embarrassed for Doug J and every other user of this app.

"No, only people you're connected to."

"So Addison's already connected to this person?"

"No, we are." Now he pointed at the log-in bar at the top, where the profile picture was the BusPass logo. "This is basically a master account. It's connected to all the users, but invisibly. So because this account is 'friends' with both Addison and Doug, this shows up. The point being that if two of your friends are checking each other out, that's something you might want to know. It would also display in the main feed, here," he said, switching to a view that listed activity from dozens of users within the last few minutes. "But because this account would get these from every single user in the system, it's probably buried."

That seemed like a treasure trove of information, much more useful than my pathetic attempts to create a fake profile who had zero connections. "I don't suppose there is any way you could give me access to this? Or printouts? Just so I could explore Addison's connections a bit closer."

"You mean without a warrant?" He winked at me. "I guess there's no harm, since none of this is private information that the users submit to the app—it's all public-facing stuff to their connections. You just have to promise not to let anyone else use it. We don't need a paper trail here."

"You got it," I said as it dawned on me that Kenny had told Transit Tech that I was a cop. That would explain why everyone was being so helpful.

I did not exactly tell him otherwise and just let him write a convoluted web address and password on the back of his business card.

In the elevator back to the lobby, I elbowed Kenny in the ribs. "You could have at least *warned* me that you told him I was a cop."

"What? No! I said you were working *with* the police department. Not for."

"Well," I said, "it worked, so I can't be too upset. So thank you, even though I almost blew it there at the end. It just would have been nice to know."

Now Kenny tried to act like this had been his intention all along. "I knew you could handle it," he said, smoothing down the front of his hoodie.

Curated existence, Addison had said. That applied to way more than just a dating app.

It would be helpful of me, I decided, if I got some background information on Corbin Janney before I reported back to the police on my findings. With this in mind, I went home and helpfully sat at my desk with my laptop. But this was not the ace in the hole I had been hoping for. Corbin Janney had a Facebook page and an Instagram feed wherein he posted lots of pictures of his post-workout smart watch, Spotify screenshots, and the occasional wet-haired mirror selfie in what appeared to be a locker room. His captions were emojis, mainly. Nothing especially helpful or unusual there. But other than his social profiles, I didn't find anything. No driver's license, no address. His Facebook page was set to private, so nothing there, either. I was about to close the browser tab when I noticed that we had a mutual friend, and when I clicked on the square, my mouth went dry.

I badgered Julia Raymund into claiming I worked for her as an investigator so that I could visit my brother again before regular visiting hours. Well, we. I thought this, unfortunately, was a matter that required both of us, but I wasn't actually telling Julia anything she didn't know; Mizuno and Blair had been to the jail to talk to Andrew about it that very morning.

"I swear to god, I have no idea who this guy is," Andrew was saying. He leaned back in his chair, hands over his face. He was pale and jittery. "I mean, Facebook isn't real life, right? Do you personally know every single person you're friends with on there?"

"Yes," Julia said.

Andrew parted his fingers long enough to look at me. I said, "No, but I only use it to spy on people."

My brother went back behind his hands.

"And you have no idea why or how you're Facebook friends with this Corbin Janney," I said.

"I have, like, twenty-nine-hundred connections on there. I tend bar, in a hotel; you have no idea how often people are like, 'Hey, let me friend you and I'll send you the whatever video we were talking about.' It's literally all the time."

"So you think you met this guy there?"

"No? I don't know? I get requests and I just accept them. It's not like I have a bunch of personal information on there or anything."

I wasn't so sure about that after what I'd learned from Ramonte that morning. But this was not the time to lecture him on data security.

Julia said, "I think the answer to that one is no. Blair said this Corbin Janney may not even be a real person."

That tracked with my admittedly brief background research. "But what then—" I began, stopping as I realized. "They think *you're* Corbin Janney."

No one spoke for a while.

"So—what—they think you catfished Addison into coming over to your house, a place she's been before? That makes no sense. And besides, wouldn't there be a digital footprint of some kind? On your computer, your phone? There are—"

"Rox, just stop," Andrew said.

I ran my hands into my hair and tugged just enough to make it hurt.

"They said Addison hasn't used her phone or her debit card since last Wednesday." Julia flipped pages in her legal pad somewhat officiously. "The voice mail places her in Andrew's apartment, and that's the last place she was known to be. All of this other stuff is just distraction."

"What about the roommate?" I said. "She mentioned that Addison had burned her eggs that morning, so she'd obviously been home."

Julia's eyes narrowed like she wanted to throw me out of the tiny attorney meeting room. "So what? That doesn't change the facts."

"Okay," I said, my voice going up a little in pitch as I got more and more wound up. "What about security cameras in the lobby of Andrew's building?"

"They're working on it."

"What does that mean?"

"It means they're working on it, Roxane. I don't know the precise steps they're taking to do so."

"Does it exist, or not?"

"I. Don't. Know."

"Did you ask?"

Julia looked at my brother in exasperation.

"Or is this like Schrödinger's Security Footage, which may or may not exist, despite the fact that they are *working on it*? How much work is required? What is it, eight millimeter?"

Silence fell over the room again. I pinched the bridge of my nose as my eyes filled with angry tears.

Finally, Julia said, "The good news is, there's a lot of digital information for them to comb through, and precisely none of it is going to show that Andrew made up this Corbin Janney person. Eventually, they'll have to see that."

I wasn't so sure it worked that way, and Julia obviously knew that. "So now what?"

"Now we just wait. This could take a while."

I wondered if Addison even *had* a while.

Corbin Janney did sound like a made-up name. The only other person called Corbin I'd ever even heard of was the *L.A. Law* actor and for all I knew, his was a made-up name too. That night I sat at my desk and pored over his fake Facebook page, the one I'd been looking at when I reached the terrible conclusion that my brother knew him in a digital sense. He had two-hundred-some Facebook friends, a believable amount, but as I scrolled through them I saw that they were mostly minor local celebrities—tattoo artists, dudes in bands, restaurant managers, artists. People who, like Andrew, would probably just accept any and all requests.

So was this a profile that existed for the sole purpose of being able to set up a BusPass account? I could believe it.

I wasted some time trying to find a cached snapshot of Corbin's Missed the Bus post and found nothing. Had it actually been about Addison—a targeted attempt to ensnare her—or was it about some other woman with a big tattoo, or about no one in particular, a wide net content with the first user who nibbled?

This was a case that existed in the cloud, in the space between people. There were few physical clues to follow, just a smattering of digital footprints that didn't tell the whole story. I preferred hard clues, like suitcase tracks in Addison's bedroom carpet. Like the card Wyatt had given her.

I went back to the dating app and pulled up Wyatt's profile. I wasn't even sure why I was doing it; I had no reason to think he was Corbin Janney, or that he wanted to hurt Addison in any way, but I knew he was involved—somehow—and wasn't sure how to go about getting him to talk to me. Maybe I could figure out some of his other friends this way, other people he socialized with since it creepily captured recent activity if you knew where to look.

Next to the green arrow, it said the person WYATT A had recently messaged with was ADDY MARIE S.

ADDY MARIE S

I stared at the name for a second, at the profile picture that was most definitely Addison Stowe—but this was not the profile I'd looked at yesterday with the blue-mascaraed eye and the cryptic bio and the same email address as Addison's real Facebook page.

I went through the rest of ADDY MARIE S's profile. Dozens of photos, all of the real Addison: her onstage at the nightclub; her trying on a swimsuit in the fitting room at Target, smirking sulkily in the mirror as she took the selfie; her in snow pants and a balaclava, a snowboard under one arm.

Her bio was quite a bit more thorough too:

I don't want to sit across the table from you wishing I could run. Jazz standards, spicy food, good beer, faultless honesty. Please have blue eyes and a job that doesn't start at 8 a.m. because we have some livin' to do.

I recognized the first line as a lyric from a Cake song. Addison would've been a child when that song was popular. Her weird CD had sampled Lady Day, so her tastes ran the time continuum. But anyway, the most interesting part was that she was currently online.

TWENTY-FOUR

I dialed Gwen Achebe's number and asked if Wyatt was talking yet.

"Not to me," she said, "but he's been awfully busy on his phone, and he just left."

"Oh?"

"He said we'll talk when he gets back."

"Where was he going?"

"He said he had to meet a friend. He borrowed my car."

"Did he say where?"

"He said just over on California Avenue. Unless he was just saying that so I'd let him take it—the tires are bald and it's not safe . . ."

I tuned the rest of her explanation out.

That was where Addison lived.

I realized something terrible was underway as soon as I turned right from Weber onto High Street and I saw two cop cars squealing hard left turns onto California Avenue. I sped up and did the same, or tried to—the narrow street was a wall of emergency lights, impassable. I parked and jumped out of the car and squinted in the dark. The sidewalk was full of people, rubberneckers craning for a view of what was going on. Farther down, closer to Addison's apartment, I could make out dark forms in bulletproof vests emblazed with

POLICE in white block letters. A chopper was circling the block with a sweeping searchlight.

"Please, everybody, go back into your houses," a guy in a SWAT vest was saying. "We can't do our jobs properly if you're standing here like this."

I sidled up to a woman holding a small black dog in a puffy dog coat. "Do you know what's going on?" I said.

"Our tax dollars at work," she hissed back.

I jockeyed for position closer to the SWAT guy and asked him the same question.

He glared at me. "You need to keep this area clear."

I searched my notebook for Carlie's phone number and sent her a text asking if she was home.

No, why?

I was relieved—really, I was—but also disappointed. I cut between two houses and over to the alley that ran parallel to California, which was still dark and quiet. Jamming my hands in my pockets, I started down the alley.

The police helicopter was illuminating the block in wide swaths, but I realized its circles were getting smaller. It juddered above me, its blades beating urgently. As it arced away, I could hear snippets of shouting from farther down the block, just a few seconds before the voices were swallowed up by the chopper when it arced back around.

"We all just want—everybody gets home safe."

My eyes were streaming from the cold.

"You don't have—on out. Just come on out. We can—"

The next voice I heard was quavering with fear. It belonged to Wyatt Achebe. "I can't."

Ice seized my heart.

"I can't—" Wyatt said next. "—left alone."

I broke into a run and almost collided with the guy in the vest just as he entered the alley from a narrow gap between two houses. "Listen," I said, "I know this guy. I don't know what's—"

"Lady," he said, "what the hell are you doing back here?"

I wasn't sure if he'd followed me this far, or if he'd simply seen me walking in the gap between houses.

"Please, listen to me. I know him. He's a nice kid."

"A nice kid?"

"Yeah—"

"A nice kid who took some woman hostage. I'm not arguing with you. Go." He pointed back to California Avenue.

"Hostage? No—"

"Yes." He grabbed me by the bicep and shoved. "What else do you call threatening someone with a gun?"

When we were back to the street, he said, "Wait here for a second."

For a moment I thought he was going to get someone else to talk to me, but then it dawned on me that he just wanted me out of his hair. I pressed farther into the melee, my brain somersaulting over possibilities. It didn't make any sense.

Meeting with a friend.

Threatening someone with a gun.

What was I missing?

I flagged down another cop and tried my spiel again. "I know this kid. Can I talk to him or something?"

She frowned at me and told me to move back.

The chopper hovered overhead, its searchlight finally stationary.

I fumbled with my phone.

Tom answered on the third ring.

Over the noise, I shouted, "How quick can you get to Clintonville?"

But it didn't matter. My question was too late.

Before I even heard the trio of gunshots, I saw the muzzle flash from Addison's backyard.

I screamed no, or maybe just in my head.

The cops on the street started moving in toward the house, the all-business posture that told me there was work to be done. Two paramedics hustled a stretcher to the backyard.

I found myself drifting after them. I was on the wrong side of the house to see anything, but I could hear a terse conversation going on back there.

"Where is it? Where the hell is it? It has to be here somewhere. I *saw* it."

"Maybe it's in the house? Maybe *she's* in the house?"

"Open it."

I flattened myself against the porch of Addison's neighbor and listened as someone kicked open the back door.

Footsteps.

Less than a minute later, the cops were back. "It's clear. There's nothing. No woman, no gun."

"Maybe this is what you saw?"

A note of anguish: "Fuck. *Fuck*. A fucking cell phone?"

I dropped my own phone into the snow and realized Tom's voice was still saying my name.

"Roxane, with one *N*," I said to the SWAT commander for at least the third time.

"R-O-X," he said, hulking over me with an incident form on a metal clipboard, "A-N-A?"

He couldn't begin to understand my name or anything about me, including what I'd heard. I pulled my coat tighter around my middle. We were sitting in the front seat of his police-issue vehicle, heat blasting, but I couldn't stop shaking. "Does it matter? Is anyone even going to see this report?"

His features were stony but somehow turned even stonier. "What's that supposed to mean?"

I shook my head. I was recording the conversation on my phone just in case anyone ever tried to deny that it had happened, tried to claim I didn't hear what I'd said I heard.

Maybe Wyatt would make it, I told myself.

Maybe it looked worse than it was when the two paramedics wheeled him on a stretcher up to the ambulance, a Rorschach of blood oozing at his chest.

Things never looked worse than they were.

It was always the other way around.

I was numb. I didn't understand why he came here. Addison wasn't anywhere to be found. The duplex she shared with Carlie was empty. But someone had called 911 to report a black man with a gun, threatening a woman in the backyard.

But there was no woman, no gun.

Just a cell phone in the darkness.

"Is there anything you want to add to this, Miss O'Leary?"

I opened the car door and got out without answering.

I had a headache that rivaled the worst headaches of my life already, but I held out my glass for more.

Tom and I were in my living room and we had already killed off half of an old bottle of Woodford Reserve—his choice from my liquor cabinet. He was more of a beer drinker, usually, but this wasn't a usual situation.

"Swatting," he said.

"What?"

"Swatting. I've seen it in the news a few times, usually some on-line gaming flame war that escalates. Someone calls the police on their enemy, well," he said, adding air-quotes, "'enemy,' and claims so-and-so did such-and-such, some outlandish thing to get them into big trouble. Some departments have a fine, where you have to pay for 'police services' like if the search-and-rescue helicopter goes out."

I thought of the sweeping searchlight, scanning the quiet street. "People do this in Columbus?"

"I'm not sure if we've had anyone do it. But, I mean, probably. Not that I'm saying this is what happened here, but it's a possibility. Another possibility is someone with some very, very wrong information."

I swallowed the rest of my drink and leaned my head back on the cushion behind me and closed my eyes. Wrong information didn't seem to cover it, but at the same time, that was exactly what had happened. There was no gun, and there was no woman, no victim. The house was empty. "So what happens now?" I said.

"Now we hope and pray the kid makes it, right?"

"Hope and pray," I repeated. "Fuck hope and prayers." I was running short on both. "I tried to get three different people to listen to me at the scene, and no one would. I get it—you can't act on everything any random person says at an active scene, and that's fine. But, I mean, come on. They shot him. For doing what? Standing on a porch while black?"

"The information they had—"

"Tom, fuck the information they had. I was trying to give them information. They didn't want it. The situation was always going to go down exactly the way it went down."

"No one's that fatalistic about police work."

My father had been. Or maybe he was just stubborn, his views immutable, new information be damned. I said, "You don't think it's a tragedy?"

"Of course I do. I'm just saying Halliwell isn't a monster. He's a good cop, for what it's worth."

"Is that his name?"

Tom nodded.

"It doesn't matter if he's been a good cop up till now. He wasn't in that moment. And that moment is all that matters."

"It's complicated," he said, and held up a hand as I started to object. "I'm not defending him. I'm not."

"It's not that complicated. A white cop shot an unarmed black man."

"You're right. It's a tragedy. And if Wyatt doesn't make it, Halliwell is going to beat himself up for the rest of his life about it."

"Well, fuck that guy."

We both fell silent.

Then I said, "I don't know what it's like, to be in that situation. I'm not saying I do. But, I mean, if there's a name for this kind of thing? You have to be aware that the information you have might not be accurate, and that's why the information you get from your own two eyes has to be the most important. Did he really think he saw a gun? Or did he *expect* to see a gun?"

He touched my arm. "You're absolutely right. I'm agreeing with you. It's the ultimate responsibility. I don't buy into the *it's him or me* sort of thinking. Because far and away the majority of situations aren't like that."

His expression had gone tight. The majority of situations weren't like that, but Tom had lived through one that was.

I asked, "Do you ever think about him? The kid who shot my father." *The kid you killed two seconds later,* I thought but did not say.

He studied the rim of his glass. "All the time."

That wasn't the answer I was expecting. "Really?"

"I had to go through the evaluations and meetings and

assessments after that, all the stuff Halliwell will be doing, and it was different, because he *was* armed, he'd just shot my partner. A justified use of force. But some of the guys had that attitude about it. Like good for me, taking down the punk who shot Frank. An eye for an eye. But that's not what it was. It was training. I fired at him because I told him to drop the gun and instead, he fired at us. It wasn't revenge, it wasn't justice. When I say I think about it, I think about his family, really. How I made it two tragedies instead of one."

"I didn't know that," I said.

"I told you, it's complicated. Using force. Taking a life. I never even fired my gun on duty before that night. I never needed to, never wanted to. Jesus, this conversation got dark fast."

"Sorry."

He looked at his watch. "I should probably go. Seven o'clock is going to come very soon. I have a task force meeting."

It was after one now. "Are you okay to drive?"

He stood up, rested a palm against the wall, and sat back down. "No."

"Stay."

"Will it be weird?"

I wasn't sure about that. But I said, "You can help me finish this off." I filled my glass again and topped his off too; he didn't protest. We drank in silence for a long time.

"It's been a hell of a week," he said instead.

I nodded. "How are you and Pam?"

Tom sipped his bourbon and looked up at the ceiling. "When are you going to start baring your soul?"

"I'm an open book, Tom," I said, and he gave me half a smile.

"I think Pam and I are over."

"No."

He didn't answer.

"Because of dinner?"

"Because of a lot of things."

"Shit, I'm sorry."

"Dinner was just the latest in a long line of situations."

"I'm sorry."

"You said that already."

"Well, I am."

"Yeah." He sipped his drink and gave a heavy sigh. "I started taking an antidepressant, did I tell you that?"

I turned to look at him. "No. I mean, not that you're obligated to or anything."

"Well, I did. Five, six months ago."

"Is it helping?"

He nodded.

"Then good for you."

"It's not like a switch getting flipped on or anything. It just helps with the feeling of—well, you know what depression is, I don't have to explain it. Anyway, I didn't tell Pam either, not right away. I don't actually know why, or maybe I do. Maybe I knew how she'd react."

I pulled my knees to my chest and waited.

"She saw a statement from my insurance on the dining room table at my place, she read it, she asked me about it. When we talked, I thought she understood what I was saying. That I, you know, can feel stuck in place. That it's hard to make things happen sometimes. Is this making any sense at all?"

"Yeah, yeah, I'm listening," I said.

"The point is, I told her this, and she started acting like, I don't know, a life coach. Which, to be clear, I don't need a life coach. I just need the antidepressant, which I have, so things were fine— the only difference is that she knew about it. And it's like her takeaway from the conversation is that I need external motivation or something. She's like, let's go running, let's go on a couples' retreat, let's go car shopping, let's get engaged—like me having depression is the only reason none of these things have happened already."

"What's wrong with the Taurus?" I said.

He laughed, the kind of laugh that took him by surprise. "Right? It's not like I take the antidepressant because I drive a Taurus. It's more like she wishes I drove something else, like *she* wants to go running and attend a couples' retreat."

"And get married."

He finished his drink and reached for the bottle again. "We did talk about it. A long time ago. That yeah, I wanted to get married, that I wasn't interested in a relationship that wasn't going to go somewhere. But somehow, in all of this, she convinced herself that we would have been married already if it wasn't for my brain chemistry, and Pam's very determined, if you hadn't noticed."

"I have, in fact."

"So at dinner the other night, you got to see the tail end of that. She said, you have problems getting started, but I don't, so let's just do this."

I poured the rest of the bourbon from the bottle into my glass. "Have you talked to her since?"

Tom nodded. "She apologized, but it was for telling you guys about it. Not for doing it. And it's not been a great time to have that going on. I mean"—he gestured at the room around us—"Frank. Plus Mickey Dillman now, and granted, he wasn't a close friend to me. But he was a friend, and I went with the guys who notified his wife, and things had been bad between them—you know all of this. But they're getting divorced, she more or less hates him, and she's still his emergency contact in his personnel file. So at the time I thought, that's really fucking sad. Then I realized my emergency contact's probably my mother, and she's been gone for eleven years. So if anything happened to me, there'd be no one to tell."

"Hey," I said, "don't go there."

"I mean, I'm there already. It's true."

"You can change your emergency contact, Tom."

"To who? Not to Pam, not now."

"Your sister. Me. Anyone. Just because your paperwork, which you filled out almost two decades ago, is outdated, that doesn't mean you're like Mickey Dillman, is my point."

"What if he walked down that boat ramp thinking to himself, 'This is it, but at least someone will know'?"

"Christ, Tom."

"I know. Sorry. This is the bourbon talking now."

"Is that really what happened? He walked into the river and, what, laid down?"

He leaned back and closed his eyes. "I don't know. Maybe. Cause of death is drowning, officially. His BAC was off the charts." He glanced at the bourbon remaining in his glass and set it on the end table. "They found his wallet in the river by the King Avenue. boat launch. Someone at the Tim Hortons across the street said he saw some guy stumbling around in the dark on Wednesday night, under the bridge. But who knows."

I closed my eyes again too, wondering what in the hell had happened to Mickey Dillman in the hours between the Columbus Bowling Palace and the King Avenue bridge. But there was no way to know. There might never be a way to know.

When I opened my eyes again, the clock said it was after four and Tom was curled on his side on the sofa next to me, his face pressed into the crook of one elbow. I turned the other way and went back to sleep.

TWENTY-FIVE

When I woke up for real, morning light was streaming in through the window and an alarm was going off somewhere in the apartment and the sofa beside me was empty.

I sat up, confused. My phone was on the coffee table, so the alarm wasn't mine. "Tom?"

The beeping was coming from down the hall. I dragged myself into a standing position, swallowing hard against a pulse of nausea.

He was in my bedroom, on top of the blankets but with a corner of sheet pulled up and around him. The beeping emanated from his pocket. "Tom," I said again, patting his shoulder.

He made a soft noise, rolled over, and looked at me, just as confused as I was.

"Is the beeping, um, something important?"

He pulled his phone out and stabbed at the screen. "Well," he said, holding the fingertips of one hand to his forehead, "I was supposed to be in a conference room two hours ago, but fortunately the meeting has been postponed. Jesus Christ." He put the phone down on the mattress and covered his eyes with both hands. "I don't know why I came in here—I got up to use the bathroom at one point and I guess—I'm sorry—"

"It's fine," I said. As the surprise wore off, the reality of my hangover set in.

"I'm so sorry."

"No, it's okay, definitely more comfortable in here than in there."
I touched the back of my neck, which felt like it had recently been
folded into a suitcase.

Tom sat up, hands still over his face. "Can there be coffee?"

"Instant, or fancy?"

"I don't know what that means." His voice was muffled under
his palms.

"Catherine got me a fancy one-cup thing," I said. Saying her
name made the throbbing in my head even worse.

"Surprise me," he said.

I went into the kitchen, squinting at the bright light coming in
through my windows. A beat later I heard the bathroom door close,
then the uncomfortable sound of gagging. I leaned out into the hall.
"You okay?"

"Great," he called back.

I rooted through the basket of single-serve coffee cup things
until I found the one that I always thought smelled the best and
stuck it into the machine to do its business while I heated up more
hot water for tea.

The old wooden floor creaked as Tom joined me in the kitchen.
"In addition to taking your bed, I also owe you a toothbrush," he
said. "There was one in the medicine cabinet, still in its package.
So I used it."

"That'll be a dollar seventy-nine," I said. When the coffee was
ready, I added some milk to it and reached for the bottle of whiskey on my counter. "Hair of the dog?"

"Good god, no," he said. He sipped the coffee and nodded.
"It's nice. I'm impressed. Catherine must think you're pretty
special."

I shrugged. "She thinks someone's special. I don't drink coffee."

We looked at each other for a long time. It felt like we could have entire conversations without saying a word sometimes. I pushed back the urge to bury my face in his shirt.

Finally he said, "This is why I don't drink liquor with you."

I waved a hand. "Yeah, yeah."

It was a beautiful day, but the city was raw. I put gas in my car at the BP on Broad Street and overheard two motorists at the next pump talking about what had happened. "This girl they claim he had with him, the one who doesn't exist. What you want to bet she's white?" one said.

The other said, "Practically guaranteed."

I didn't disagree with the sentiments, but no one knew yet what had happened, who had called, what they'd said. I drove over to Grant Hospital, thinking. Maybe it was a case of mistaken identity— some other guy in some other backyard threatening a woman with a gun.

Or maybe it had been swatting, like Tom had said. Maybe general, maybe specific.

There's a man with a gun in a backyard.

There's a man with a gun in my *backyard.*

The irony that my brother was currently enmeshed in this situation because of a potentially similar phone call? Not at all lost on me.

Was all of this Addison's doing somehow?

Wyatt's mother seemed shrunken in her red cardigan, its pockets puffy with balled-up tissues. "He looks so small," she said.

It was true. Wyatt looked shrunken too, his muscular frame hidden under bandages and sheets. He had a plastic mask over his nose and mouth from the ventilator he was on.

"The bullet ricocheted all around in his chest," Gwen added. "They said it's a miracle he even hung on this long, that if he can make it through today, maybe he has a chance. What on earth is my boy mixed up in?"

"I don't know," I said. "I really don't. He didn't say anything to you?"

"Nothing. He spent pretty much all day in bed, buried in his phone. Then he took a shower and got dressed and I asked him when he was going to talk to me, and he said we could talk when he got back. That he just had to go meet with someone." She dabbed at her eyes with a tissue. "My car is probably still at that place. I had to take an Uber here."

I was furious at someone, but I didn't know who. My hands balled up into fists in my pockets.

"A police officer came here. To tell me all about the *very credible threat* that was called in to the dispatcher. He said when they approached the house, Wyatt freaked out. Crying and panicking. Why would an innocent person do that, is what he wanted to know."

"I highly recommend you get yourself a lawyer," I said, "and don't speak to them again until you do. Definitely don't sign anything."

"Wyatt is nothing to them," she whispered. "They might not even care what really happened, as long as they can prove what they did was okay. Can you help me?"

"Yes," I said. "I can help you. There's more to this story, that's for damn sure. Gwen, do you have Wyatt's phone?"

"His phone? Yes, it's in here." She stiffly got to her feet and opened a cabinet on the wall of her son's small room. A paper bag sat on the top shelf. "His clothes, and his shoes—" She stopped speaking abruptly and sat down, hard.

I looked into the bag, saw Wyatt's camo pants and a pair of black-and-red Lebron Soldiers and a watch with a rubbery white band that was misted with blood. His phone was in the pocket of his pants, its battery dead.

"I just want to see if I can figure out who he was trying to meet yesterday," I said, rubbing the specks of blood on his watch with my thumb; his mother didn't need to see that. "I'll bring it back."

"I don't know if I can pay you," Gwen said, her voice quiet.

"Don't worry about it," I told her. "Please. Just focus on your son. I'll get answers for you."

That afternoon, I lay on my bed in the dark and powered up Wyatt's phone after it had charged. My sheets smelled like bourbon and faintly like Tom's cologne and I pressed my face into the pillow for a moment, breathing it in. Then I adjusted the brightness on Wyatt's phone so the screen didn't hurt my hungover eyes and typed in the first of a series of possible access codes his mother had given me; fortunately, her second guess was correct.

I looked at the recent calls first. He'd made fifteen of them to Addison over the past week, but based on the duration of the calls, it didn't look like she'd answered or called back. Shane's number was saved in Wyatt's contact list and they'd talked twice yesterday— once in the afternoon that had lasted for eleven minutes, and once at seven o'clock that was over after twenty-three seconds. He had no saved voice mails. Apparently he was one of those people who listened to and deleted messages instead of just reading the transcription and ignoring it like I did.

His most recent texts with Addison had been ten days ago, a random exchange of GIFs. Since then, he had unanswered texts from his mother and someone named JD and half a dozen from various delivery services alerting him that his food was about to arrive.

None of it told me anything.

I scrolled through his email—marketing messages from indie brands like Dagne Dover and Allbirds, a group thread about JD's birthday in two months, no all-caps admissions of guilt from any-one.

Shocking.

I flipped through the screens of apps, pausing on the familiar icon of a bus with heart-shaped headlights.

Navigating BusPass's interface, I found his private messages.

There was only one thread, and it was from yesterday, and it was with ADDY MARIE S.

I opened the chain and scrolled up to the beginning.

> WYATT A: Girl. Where are you
> WYATT A: I can't decide if I am worried about you or pissed at you
> WYATT A: I can't live like this
> ADDY MARIE S: That's dramatic

This message was sent yesterday at four-thirty.

> WYATT A: Oh so you're not returning calls but still up on this thing? Amazing
> ADDY MARIE S: I had to get a new phone
> WYATT A: I think we should go to the police
> ADDY MARIE S: Can we meet? To talk
> ADDY MARIE S: You know this app is prolly selling our convo to the NSA
> WYATT A: Sure. Fine. At Nightshade?
> ADDY MARIE S: Noooooooo
> WYATT A: You're not being very helpful
> ADDY MARIE S: Just scared. Do you have a gun
> WYATT A: Wtf addison
> WYATT A: This is insane

ADDY MARIE S: I need to be able to protect myself

WYATT A: Well he's obviously not going to hurt you anymore

ADDY MARIE S: I don't want to talk about it on here! Just come to my place. 6:30. Go around to the back

Then, at 6:32:

WYATT A: Yo im here

WYATT A: Where are you

WYATT A: Addison I'm on your back porch

WYATT A: Look I'll stay a few more mins but I'm not waiting around all night

I guessed there was my answer. Addison got him to go to her apartment, then called 911 on him.

"Bitch," I said to the empty apartment.

I was mad that I'd ever been worried about her. Finding her was still just as important, but now for a different reason.

I reread the conversation. It was a strange one, obviously about something serious, though it didn't come right out and say what. I supposed that didn't necessarily mean anything; when you're in a situation with someone, you didn't spell out the details of it in text for a third party to decipher.

But *who* wasn't going to hurt her anymore? What did she need protection from?

I went into the other room and got my computer, along with the business card that Ramonte Barnes had given me to log in to the BusPass master account.

Maybe she'd messaged someone else yesterday too, someone who might not currently be intubated and in intensive care.

I found Addy Marie's profile, scrolled down to the "recently connected" section.

"Holy shit," I said.

Wyatt's name was the most recent one listed, but halfway down the list was MICKEY D.

TWENTY-SIX

Keeping in mind what Rick Dillman's father had told me about him not liking to be interrupted while doing a project, I waited until he came out of Best Buy and walked down the street to BW3 for his dinner break, red headphones over his ears. I stepped up beside him and gave a little wave and he slid the headphones down around his neck, a faint stream of "God Bless the Child" escaping. I said, "Hi Rick, can I pay for your food?"

He spun around and looked at me. "Because you want to ask more questions?"

"Yes, and because I'm generous that way."

His eyes, hazel with flecks of gold, locked on mine for the first time. "Okay."

We ordered plain chicken wings and potato wedges and sodas. The cashier knew Rick's order by heart and appeared surprised when I said to double it and offered up my credit card.

"Yo, is Rick on another date?" she said.

"*No,*" he replied. "If we were on a date, I'd be paying, because I'm a gentleman."

"Yeah you are," the cashier said, winking at me.

As we took a seat in a booth near the back of the restaurant, Rick said, "I sit here every day. Alone. But hey, you might be good for my reputation."

"Happy to help."

He gave a short laugh. "Did you used to be a cop?"

"No, but my dad was a cop. He knew your cousin Mickey, actually."

"You have a cop," he said, pantomiming a circle over the table between us, "visage."

"Thank you?"

"Mickey died, you know."

"Yeah. I'm sorry to hear about him. I wanted to talk to you about someone I think he knew. Remember the other day when I showed you a picture of a woman?"

Darkness edged into his eyes. "Yes."

"And you said you didn't recognize her?"

Rick was quiet.

I showed him the Addy Marie profile on my phone. "What about her?"

Rick's eyes lingered on the picture of Addison onstage at Nightshade. He still didn't say anything.

"Did Mickey show you this?"

"No."

"So you've never seen her before?"

He took a long gulp from his Coke.

"You can trust me, Rick."

"Mickey said not to tell anyone," he said.

"Tell anyone what? About her?"

Rick's posture had stiffened. "He said she was bad."

"Bad?"

Now he shook his head. "I'm not supposed to say that."

A server appeared with our wings and fries. The greasiness of the spread before us appealed to the remnants of my hangover, but Rick pulled a small bottle of bright red sauce out of his bag along with a plastic container with a screw-on lid. When he uncapped the bottle, which featured a strip of masking tape that said *12-15* in lieu of a label, a sharp aroma wafted out and it got me a little worried.

"So you put your own sauce on?"

He nodded. "We made this. Mickey and me. A good hot sauce is complex, more than just hot. Much research has gone into this sauce. It's for connoisseurs. For people who love the experience of hot sauce, not just for dumb jock guys who want to act like they're so tough because they order the spiciest wings but then cry for a week whenever they take a shit."

I almost gagged on my soda. "On a scale of one to ten, how hot is this going to be?"

"Ten. Well, if you don't like spicy, maybe higher for you. Do you?"

"Yes, within reason."

"What you do is, you take small bites, and chew slowly. If you think it's better to eat fast because it's too spicy, you're wrong. That makes it worse. Small bites, and then take a drink of pop after. Not water. That only moves the capsaicin around in your mouth or throat, but sugar helps soothe the flavor. You can spit out the pop if your mouth is still too hot. The spicy goes with it, whether you swallow it or spit it out."

I watched as he moved the wings into the plastic container and dumped his homemade sauce on top, screwed the lid back on, and shook it hard. When he took the lid off, the smell was ten times stronger and stung my sinuses a little.

Rick dug in with gusto, but I nibbled a potato wedge to start. "So what didn't Mickey want you to tell anyone about? That Addison was bad?"

Rick shook his head again. "He said not to tell, so I can't tell."

"Not even to help figure out what happened to him?"

"They said he fell in the river."

"Who said that?"

"My dad and the hosebeast."

"The hosebeast? As in, *Wayne's World*?"

"My dad's girlfriend."

"She's awful, huh?"

"She Talks Like This." He enunciated the words like a Shakespeare community theater actor. "But only to me, of course. 'Richard, It Is Time For Dinner, Will You Be A Good Boy And Set The Table Please?'" He rolled his eyes. "I act like I don't hear her sometimes because it's so annoying but that makes her be even louder."

"Do *you* think Mickey fell in the river that night?"

He wiped his mouth with a napkin but didn't say anything.

"Can you tell me what you talked about with him?"

"He said not to tell anyone. Are you going to try one?" He pointed at the sauce-covered wings.

"I'm a little scared of them, to be honest."

"Try them."

"If I try one, will you tell me what you guys talked about?"

"It's in the vault."

"The vault?"

"It's where you put secrets that can never, ever come out."

I could respect someone's ability to keep a secret, but at the same time, I really wanted to know this one. "What would I have to do, to prove you can trust me?"

Rick shrugged, helpless. "It's in the vault."

I bit into the hot wing and immediately regretted it. "Oh fuck," I said. "This is definitely higher than a ten."

"It's okay, it's okay, power through." He nudged my soda toward me. "Small sip. Another small sip."

My eyes watering, I did as he instructed.

"Now spit it out."

I spit into a napkin. The oh-shit level of spiciness receded from my mouth.

"See? It works."

"It does," I said.

"You're very brave. But I still can't tell you, okay? It's private."

I nodded at the bottle of sauce. "I think you're onto something here. It has a good flavor, underneath the spice. Something a little sweet."

"That was Mickey's idea. He's the one who said we should take it to farmers' markets and whatnot. He said it could be his second act. But the recipe was in his head, and I don't know what it is. So I guess it'll just be for me now, at least until it runs out."

Something had happened at Nightshade or nearby. I knew that much. But it was basically all I knew. The something had involved Addison, Wyatt, and Shane, and possibly Mickey as well, since he'd wound up in the Olentangy River the same night that Addison freaked out and Wyatt and Shane began hiding at the East Side Motor Lodge. In the meantime, both Wyatt's and Addison's vehicles had disappeared. As far as I knew, Mickey's Thunderbird still hadn't turned up either.

But how did Corbin Janney fit into any of this?

What was I supposed to make of Addison's two BusPass profiles?

After Rick had gone back to work, I remained in our booth and made a list of theories that could fit with the facts, such as they were.

1. Mickey Dillman was catfishing Addison using Corbin Janney's profile. After figuring out her identity and going to her apartment to talk to her about ????, he found her at Nightshade, scared the shit out of her, and jumped in the river.

2. Addison was chatting with both the fictitious Corbin Janney *and* Mickey Dillman, regardless of whether her friends thought he could be her type. Mickey wanted to meet, but Addison didn't. So

he employed some light stalking to track her down, scared the shit out of her, crashed his car somewhere, and fell into the river.

3. Addison had invented Corbin Janney for some reason, had lured Mickey to the club somehow, got Wyatt involved in something, then promised to meet him last night but instead called 911 on him with a made-up story.

4. Corbin Janney did exist and was just some home-birth, home-schooled, no-social off-the-grid type who had managed to lead a life entirely off the books, until he felt the burning desire to create a BusPass account one day.

5. Nothing meant anything.

These theories all sucked.

I needed something else to go on here.

Jordy's stepsister was loading two suitcases into the back of a silver CR-V when I parked on California Avenue. Her face was pale, her eyes red. When she saw me, she ducked back into the duplex. A beat after that, Jordy came out. Her long hair was in a messy bun on the top of her head, adding a good four inches to her already-intimidating height.

Her eyes were red too.

"What the fuck is going on?" she said. "Carlie's gonna come stay with me for a while, until this gets figured out. After what happened last night. I mean, thank *God* she wasn't home."

I nodded. "Is she okay?"

"Not really."

"Are *you* okay?"

"Not really."

We stared at each other.

"My dad and I came over this morning, to help her fix the door.

There's apparently some kind of voucher, from the police? For breaking in the door? Like they'll pay to get it fixed, somehow. It's the dead of winter, who has time for a freaking voucher? But the more I thought about it, the more I realized it's just stupid. To stay here. We don't know what happened to Addison. For all we know, someone grabbed her off the street right here."

That was not what had happened. But I had to agree that getting as far away as possible from Addison was a good idea.

Jordy went on, "I'm just so worried and mad all at once. I'm terrified that something awful happened to my friend, and then two minutes later I'm furious at her for being the kind of person who sucks at responding to texts sometimes. And then two minutes after that I feel like shit because I know she's had her struggles, and maybe it's not her fault."

I remembered that she'd sort of pulled back from this topic the first time we met. "What do you mean?"

She bit her lip. "Well, when we were seventeen, eighteen. She kind of had a little bit of a breakdown. She had—she got super skinny, just acting really erratic. She had to go into a treatment center for an eating disorder for a while, get therapy for anxiety. And it, well, it sort of came out of nowhere. She didn't ever want to talk about it. It was so weird, because it's just her nature to act like things are so dramatic when they aren't. But when something really *was* the matter? For a long time, I felt like we let her down. Like why didn't she want to talk about it to her best friends? I know now that's not how mental illness works. I just don't know what to think."

I didn't either.

When I turned onto my street, I saw a pair of taillights idling in a haze of exhaust in front of my building. I drove past for a look; it was Vincent Pomp's Crown Victoria. As I parked I saw him get out of the backseat, dressed in a long black wool coat and brogues that looked both expensive and slippery. "I thought we talked about this," I said, my voice echoing across the dark street, "the whole showing up at my home thing."

"This is a friendly visit."

"Oh?"

"I just wanted to tell you, personally, thank you."

"For?"

"Whatever you said to Shane Resznik."

I stopped on the sidewalk a few feet away from my door. "What are we talking about?"

"You were very persuasive."

I didn't recall being very anything except annoyed at Shane; maybe one slap across the face was all it took. "What happened?"

"Well, after over a week of us trying to get ahold of him, he walked right into my office today and said he wanted to come clean."

My heart started to speed up. "About Nightshade?"

"Yes, about the money he's been stealing from me."

I felt my eyebrows pressing together. "Now why would he do that?"

"He's not cut out for the life, I suppose. But the point is, you can stop poking around in the whole affair."

I didn't respond right away.

"Isn't that good news? That your work here is done?"

"Just because you don't have questions doesn't mean I don't. How do you even know what he told you is true?"

"Why on earth would he lie about stealing from me?"

A fair point.

"Anyway, he was very forthcoming. He told me all about his method, how he'd ring in cash transactions ending in a specific amount so he could find them later and void them. Twenty-three cents."

As he said it, I remembered the note written on the white board in the shitty little Nightshade office.

Then he added, "Bo mentioned what you found on the wall in there."

"That's hardly proof of anything. Something happened that night. I'm absolutely sure of it."

He nodded, the buttons on his coat flashing in the ashy street-light. "Addison, the deejay you were asking about."

"What about her?"

"She found out what he was doing. Confronted him. He yelled at her and she got upset and left."

I waited for the punchline, but one didn't come. "You've got to be kidding me."

"I thought you'd be relieved that misfortune didn't befall her."

"There's not even a chance that all of this is over her getting yelled at. Did you hear about what went down last night? There's a kid on a ventilator in the hospital—he worked there. As a bouncer. At Nightshade. And someone set him up to get killed in a hail of SWAT team bullets. Did Shane tell you about that?"

Pomp's eyes hardened. I took that as a *no.*

"So I'd take his entire story with a grain of salt."

"Okay, what is it that you think he's really covering up?"

"I don't know," I admitted. "But I don't think this is the moment to stop poking around. You don't want to know what actually happened in the club that night?"

"Every day it's closed, I'm losing money."

"Ah, so that's what this is about."

"What do you mean?"

"You want to resume regular operations over there, and you're here to ask me if I'm going to interfere."

Pomp chuckled. "I was thinking of it more like *telling* you that you're *not* going to interfere anymore."

"Where's Shane?"

"You don't need to worry about him anymore."

"Thanks, but I'll be the judge of what I need to worry about."

"Leave Resznik alone, is what I'm saying."

Though Pomp wasn't too much taller than me, his voice could take an edge that was way more intimidating than height.

"So you weren't actually here to thank me," I said.

"I suppose not."

"You really just want to buy whatever bullshit he's selling you, I guess."

"Thanks, but I'll be the judge of who's selling me bullshit. Stay away from him."

"He thinks I'm working for you, doesn't he?"

Pomp's mouth said nothing, but his hard eyes said *yes*.

"So what you're telling me is that he fed you some nonsense story about Addison catching him in the act of stealing, in an attempt to convince you that everything was fine, and hoping you'd get me to stop poking around. A ploy that apparently worked. I thought you were smarter than that."

"Listen—"

"No. Enjoy untangling whatever Shane Resznik got you involved in," I said. "Good night."

Pomp made a sound that might have been a growl. I walked past him, daring him with my eyes to touch me.

He didn't.

Inside, I flung a load of laundry into my washing machine and slammed the lid and kicked over my ironing board, which was really just a place to stack things, and I didn't feel even a little bit better. A minute later, I heard a tentative knock on my front door.

"Roxane, everything okay in here?" Shelby called.

"Fine. Great, even."

But I opened the door and tried not to scowl, which was easier than expected, because she was holding a plastic container of chili. "I thought you might be hangry," she said.

We sat on opposite ends of my office sofa while I ate. "I think this is even better a week later," I said. "How is that possible?"

"Well, I froze it the day after I made it. So it's still fresh, but the flavors had a chance to meld. So do you want to talk about what's going on?"

"No."

She waited for me to go on, but there wasn't anything else to say. "I'm sorry, Shel, I'm just in a shitty mood."

She gave me the side-eye and got up and went over to the rolling wardrobe rack where my leggings stash was stored. "Any progress on these guys?"

"No. None. I haven't checked my mailboxes in days."

"Why not?"

There was no simple answer to that. "A lot on my mind."

"My grandma has this framed embroidery thing on her wall," Shelby said. "It says, *You can't do everything at once, but you can do something at once.* It makes me feel better every time I see it. Because when things are overwhelming, you don't have to figure out the whole thing right this minute—you just have to start."

I thought about that. *An old soul* didn't even begin to describe Shelby, something that probably made life both easier and harder for her. But she was right. I said, "Is that your way of saying you want me to go see if there are any leggings for Miriam just sitting in my boxes?"

"I mean," she said, giving me a sly smile, "if you said you had a reason for me to text her, I wouldn't say no. I mean, I could just say, 'Come eat chocolate with me,' but I feel like that's not very cool."

"Chocolate."

She nodded at the bowl I was holding. "There's chocolate in the chili. It's called Cincinnati style, I think."

I got an idea. "Hey, have you ever made your own hot sauce?"

"Like Sriracha?"

"Yeah, something like that."

"No, I just buy the Kroger brand, it's like a dollar. Why?"

"I'm looking for a recipe for a hot sauce with chocolate in it."

"The Case of the Fancy Flavor Profile?"

"Exactly."

"Do you want me to work on one? I don't think hot sauce is all that involved, it's just throwing some stuff in a blender."

"That sounds incredibly involved to me, but yes, that would be great. Even trade, hot sauce for leggings? I promise I'll go to the post office tomorrow."

"I'll take that deal."

TWENTY-SEVEN

I woke up mad, still thinking about Shane Resznik's weasely little goatee and wondered where the fuck he was hiding now. I didn't believe for one hot second that all of this trouble was over Addison getting yelled at. The bigger question was almost why would Shane lie to Vincent Pomp about it? Shane had actively sought him out. Because he was scared after what happened to Wyatt? Because he was scared of me?

I went back to the list of Addy Marie's BusPass connections. There were ten in all—probably the maximum number the site would display on a profile. All of them were from the last two weeks.

WYATT A
BD E

I recalled a meme I'd seen floating around on social media recently. BDE: Big Dick Energy. Is that what this meant? Straight men were the worst, so probably.

JOSEPH J
BD E
BD E

MICKEY D
RAJIT M
BD E

The Big Dick Energy profile looked a lot like the first Addison profile I found—no selfies, no faces, just random objects and food. Not
a serious profile by any stretch of the imagination, probably using
the app as a game.

Joseph J's profile picture was of a clean-cut thirtyish man in a
suit, nice jaw, razor-part hair. Subsequent pictures showed him in
various Ohio State attire, always with a beer in his hand. His bio
said: *Just looking for a cool girl to spend money on.*

Rajit M was a tall, wiry guy with brown skin and curly black hair
and a stubbly beard and a good smile. One of his pictures showed
him with a sign from a protest: FAMILY SEPARATION IS UNCONSTI-
TUTIONAL. Another featured him in hiking gear in what looked like
Scotland, posing quizzically next to a sign that said FERAL GOATS
FOR 2 MILES.

I shelled out some more cash for additional app tokens so I could
send each of them a message without waiting to match with them
using my "Rose Warner" profile. But what to write? I made a cup of
tea and paced up and down my hallway, trying to compose the perfect message.

Not unlike actual online dating, I realized.

Then I sat back down and looked at BD E's profile. I was clearly
overthinking things and went with a classic hook:

Hey ;)

———

This time when I showed up at Elise Hazlett's house, I only brought coffee, assuming it was safe to do so without anyone feeling like they had to throw an entire meal away out of deference. Elise had forgiven me, though. "God, yes, coffee, please," she said when she answered the door. "The joy of having kids is that they wake you up at six-thirty in the morning every day, even Sundays, and there is not enough coffee in the world to make up for those two hours of sleep that should've been mine." She took the lid off a Starbucks cup and doctored the coffee with almond milk creamer. "Jordy just texted that she'll be here in ten minutes. I guess the ramp to 70 is closed again."

"Typical central Ohio," I said. I had brought tea for myself and it was somehow still too hot to drink.

"Do you mind if I finish folding some laundry before she gets here? My husband took the kids to story time at Barnes & Noble and I only have about a half an hour of peace before they get back."

"No, that's fine."

Elise disappeared down a hallway, leaving me to lean against her kitchen counter and survey the spotlessness of her home. It was a typical suburban house circa the nineties with a kitchen island, neutral flooring, and a ceiling with that pointless meringue texture in the paint. But the furniture was nice, modern enough without looking out of place with the slightly dated warm-wood baseboards. The living room offered a sectional sofa and a huge ottoman with toys trailing out of the storage compartment in the middle and a tangle of blankets on the top. On the fifty-some-inch television, a lady was selling reusable sandwich bags on QVC.

The doorbell rang, two quick bursts, and Jordy came in with a tray of coffees too.

"Coffee for everyone!" she said. "Where is she?"

"Laundry room," Elise called.

Jordy laughed. "And you just left Roxane out here with your

infomercials?" Now she looked at me. "Sorry I'm late. The fucking construction! I got my place by the Commons almost three years ago, and the construction has literally not stopped."

"You must be doing well for yourself," I said, "buying a place at age twenty-three?"

She smiled and sipped her coffee, holding one pinky out. "I'm so fancy. Actually, no, I'm totally not. I'm sort of renting-to-own from my older brother—he moved to California to work for Google. *He's* fancy, what with his new house in Palo Alto—it is unreal. The bathroom has heated floors. I'm like, who even thought of that?"

"Thought of what?" Elise reappeared with a round laundry basket bent against her hip full of onesies and tiny socks.

"The heated floors at my brother's new place."

"Heated floors sound damn good right about now," I said, and Jordy laughed.

"Touché."

I explained to Addison's friends that I wanted to talk about Bus-Pass. "It looks like she has two different profiles. One that she uses to talk to Corbin—BPG—and one that she uses to talk to a lot of people."

Jordy opened the refrigerator door. "BPG has a name? Corbin?"

I nodded.

"And has he heard from her?"

"Well," I said, "it seems like maybe he doesn't actually exist."

Elise, clutching a purple sock, said, "What does that mean? She made him up?"

"No, no, I think she probably has been talking to someone who calls himself Corbin, but that's not his real name. His Facebook page is just a prop, really—no actual engagement, just connections to people around town who have a lot of 'friends.' In the interest of full disclosure, my brother is one of them."

The two women exchanged glances.

"I'm telling you that because I want you to trust me," I said. "Andrew tends bar at the Westin now and he accepts friend requests from anybody who sends him one. So the person behind the Corbin profile could be some random hotel guest that Andrew talked to once."

Jordy closed the fridge, slowly. "Okay. So you came all the way out here to tell us that?"

I shook my head and thumbed my phone screen until I found the Addison profile, the one she connected to Corbin with. "This is the first one I found. She used her real Facebook page to sign up for this."

Elise and Jordy bent over the kitchen counter to study it. "'Least likely to,'" Jordy read. "God, she's so weird. In, like, the best way."

I navigated to the Addy Marie profile.

Jordy flipped through the images, stopping on the one of Addison in a bikini. "Whoa. I mean, that's Addy, obviously, but she's not really the dressing room–selfie type." She looked up at me. "Why did she make two different profiles?"

"I don't know. I was hoping you might."

Elise said, "Didn't she have some issue with her Facebook getting hacked a while ago? Maybe she had to make a new BusPass profile too."

Jordy was still looking through the images of Addison. "This is so strange. It's like, clearly this is her, but also the Addison I know would not put a picture of herself in a bikini online. Or probably even take a picture like this. But here it is, this picture exists, so I guess she's changed a little."

"I'm told getting older does that to a person," I said.

"Yeah, but does it make you more likely to take a picture like this? Or *less*?"

Jordy held up the bikini shot. Addison looked completely relaxed, smiling faintly.

"You know how she's into all that personal development stuff," Elise said. "Her crystals and bullet journals and intentions and whatever. Maybe she's kind of using the app to get more comfortable with herself."

"Bullet journal?" I said.

"It's like a planner, except you draw it all yourself? I don't know. I think she saw it on Pinterest."

Jordy handed my phone back to me. "Good grief, Addy's on Pinterest too?"

Elise pressed a palm onto a stack of neatly folded onesies. "What's wrong with Pinterest?"

"Nothing's wrong with Pinterest. It's just that she's always been so anti. You know? The only reason she even got Facebook is that she wanted to set up a page on there for her deejaying stuff. People were constantly asking her for a website or whatever, and she didn't want to make a website, so she decided to just use Facebook. But obviously you have to have a profile before you can make a page, blah blah blah."

"Yeah, but it's not like her to actually respond to a missed connections post either. But she did that. You don't think people can change?" Elise said.

Jordy leaned onto her elbows on the counter. "I guess they can, and do," she said grudgingly. "But where is she? How are we supposed to know where to look if she's turning into this completely different person?"

The motorized whine of a garage door going up drifted through the kitchen.

"Uh-oh, quiet time's over," Jordy said.

The door swung open and Elise's kids tumbled into the house, shrieking, "Mommy, we had cake for breakfast!"

"You had cake? Where?"

"Chocolate cake with coconuts!"

"Brock," Elise said, her hands on her hips.

A beat later her husband appeared from the garage, arms full of assorted baby gear and a bag from Cabela's, the big hunting store north of the city.

"Hello, ladies," Brock said. "Oooh, you better have brought more of that chicken, that was so good—"

"Brock. Can I speak to you for a moment?"

The happily married couple disappeared down the hall. Jordy held a hand to her throat and drew a slow horizontal line. "Dead meat, Brock is. God. What kind of person takes his kids to the gun store on a Sunday morning and then feeds them cake?"

That was a pretty good question. "Maybe he was shopping for hiking boots?"

"That fat ass? No." She made a face. "I shouldn't say that. Addison hates when people talk like that. Brock is the worst but that has nothing to do with his body and everything to do with his awful personality. She could do so much better. I mean, Elise is the queen of getting what she wants. But sometimes it just seems like she's given up."

Elise and her husband emerged from the hallway. Brock looked deeply chagrined. Elise cleared her throat.

"I apologize for what I said about the chicken," Brock said, making grudging eye contact with me.

I had to restrain a laugh. "No worries. It's good chicken."

"I don't know how exactly you came to be friends with my wife, but I sure do appreciate having another foodie in the house."

"Friends?" Jordy said. "I mean, Roxane, no offense."

Brock looked at her blankly.

"Roxane's the private investigator? Who's looking for Addy?"

"Addy?"

"Jesus Christ, you don't listen to anything your wife says to you."

"What about Addy?" His hands were out to his sides like he was about to link up in prayer.

I couldn't be sure, but I sensed a touch of darkness entering Brock's expression.

Elise placed her hands down on the counter as if she could smooth out the situation with the right amount of pressure. "Brock, I told you all of this. No one has seen Addison for like two weeks and we're really worried."

Brock folded his hands together over the top of his hat and let out a long stream of air.

From elsewhere in the house, the playful shrieking of the kids turned into a mournful wail.

Elise picked up her laundry basket and said, "If you'll excuse me. Thanks for the coffee."

When she was out of earshot, Jordy punched Brock in the bicep, hard. He made a noise that sounded like *oof* and clutched his upper arm in pain. "What was that for? Shit."

"That was for being a dumbass."

"God, you're strong."

"It's not strength, it's strategy," Jordy said. "Shall I demonstrate again?"

Brock picked up his coat and the Cabela's bag, wincing slightly. "That won't be necessary."

TWENTY-EIGHT

Shelby had left a note on my front door—*hot sauce taste test now in progress!* I realized I'd forgotten to check the mailboxes and made a mental note to do it later as I climbed the steps to her apartment. I heard her voice, along with Miriam's, laughing. When I knocked on the door, Shelby called, "It's unlocked."

I went in. "Look, not to nag, but you really need to lock this door."

"No, I know!" Shelby said. "I do! But I heard you coming in and unlocked it just a second ago."

"How'd you know it was me?"

"I can always tell it's you. You have a specific sound."

I waited.

Shelby got up from the sofa and pantomimed opening a door. Then she stepped in, stomped her feet, and sighed like the weight of the world was on her shoulders.

Miriam giggled. "Dude, that's totally what it sounds like."

"I don't want to track snow into my apartment," I said, pointing down at my boots. "Whatever. I was promised hot sauce."

Shelby pointed at the spread on her coffee table. "From mild to hot," she said. "Made with dark chocolate, chipotle, and a touch of orange."

I sat down cross-legged at the table and broke a cracker in half and dipped it in the first cup. The flavor was smoky and sweet, with just a little bit of heat to it. "Shel, this is delicious."

"I think this might be her new calling, actually," Miriam said. "Hot sauce maker."

"Feel free to go into business," I said. I tasted the others; as promised, they got progressively hotter. The fifth and final option made me cough.

After Shelby got a cup of water for me and I had regained my composure well enough to speak, I said, "This is the one. Can I have a jar of this?"

"What, you like coughing like that?"

"It's not for me—for my case. But if you have extra of the first one, I'll take a jar of that."

Miriam dipped a cracker into the mild version. "Is six dollars too expensive for hot sauce?"

"Hey, I thought we had a deal."

"We do," Shelby said, "though I notice you're empty-handed."

"I'm going in a little bit. I promise. So what's this six dollars about?"

"For Shelby's future hot sauce business."

"Six dollars? No. I bet you could even charge eight if you put it in a fancy little bottle."

"I *love* fancy little bottles," Shelby said.

Back in my own apartment, I got more water—my throat was still on fire—and sat down to take a look at Rose Warner's BusPass profile to see if her messages to Addy Marie's connections had gotten a response.

BD E said, *Hey urself ;)*

Joseph J said, *Slut*

Rajit M didn't say anything.

I felt a flash of gratitude that I had a person already—fickle though she might be—instead of having to pursue online dating.

To BD E I wrote, *what's up? ;)*
To Joseph J I wrote, *you say that like it's a bad thing ;)*
BD E responded almost immediately.

> BD E: Nothing, just chilling. U?
> ROSE W: Same
> ROSE W: It's so cold out chilling is all you can really do
> BD E: Lol
> BD E: Not really ALL u can do . . .
> ROSE W: Lol you don't waste any time
> BD E: Life is short
> BD E: Anyway I don't know what ur thinking about, I meant I'm watching the game and working out
> ROSE W: And texting girls on here ;)
> BD E: Hey u wrote to me if I recall
> ROSE W: True
> BD E: So how are u keeping warm
> ROSE W: Day drinking
> BD E: Yeah? What's ur drink
> ROSE W: Rosé all day, of course
> BD E: Lol
> ROSE W: What do you drink?
> ROSE W: Wait, let me guess
> BD E: Ok
> ROSE W: IPAs
> BD E: Lol yes how'd u know that?

I started to type, *because I'm a detective,* then reconsidered.

> ROSE W: Lucky guess
> BD E: So why'd u message me?
> ROSE W: I liked your bio. Why'd you message me back?

BD E: because why not?
BD E: brb

He went offline a beat later. I checked my thread with Joseph J, but he hadn't responded again. Still nothing from Rajit M, either.

It was only five o'clock, but the light was already low on the street outside. My office took on a bluish cast from the screen of my computer. I reread the conversation with BD E. No one had ever solved a case based on a bullshit chat window. I wondered what life would be like if I'd taken the job I was offered around this time last year, at the fancy security firm. I would have had to buy new clothes, for one thing. But I'd also have cases that were straightforward, where I knew exactly what to do and how to do it, where I'd probably avoid going deep into the weeds on a dating app and asking my teenaged neighbor to make hot sauce for me.

Sometimes, I couldn't imagine things not being this way.

Other times, like right now, I was in the mood for a change.

I closed the computer, plunging my apartment into darkness.

TWENTY-NINE

The midwinter evening sky was pitch black, the roads quiet. No one was going anywhere. It was too cold, too slippery, why bother. Even though the weekend still had several hours of life left to it, the cloak of darkness made it feel like the day was over already. But Shelby had come through with her end of the bargain, so I needed to come through with mine. I checked the four post office boxes, starting with the location on Parsons and finishing up on East Main, collecting seven new packages in total.

The errand had taken forty minutes. There was still a lot of night left.

I stood in the Main Street post office, the light sickly yellow and dim, and looked through my reflection and out at the street and called Catherine.

"Are you ever coming home?" I said when she picked up.

"Hello to you too."

"Three sleeps turned into an entire week."

She hesitated before she answered, just a second. But enough for me to notice. "I *am* home."

I watched as my reflection ran a hand through her hair, a sad, tired lady in a shitty post office with a stack of plastic mailing envelopes in front of her. I said, "Really."

"I just got here. I took a cab home from the airport. I didn't want to bother you."

"Catherine, what the fuck?"

"I was trying to be considerate."

"Considerate would have been actually telling me what was going on with your flight or whatever."

"Why are you still trying to fight with me?"

"I'm not."

"Just come over."

"No."

A tense silence filled the line. "No?"

"No, I don't want to come over. I've had a terrible week, and I don't feel like talking about it, and I want you to tell me what's going on instead of just leading me into your bedroom and making me forget anything was wrong in the first place."

Catherine sighed. "Isn't that what I'm supposed to do?"

"Just tell me."

I didn't think she was going to do it. I was about to say forget it and hang up when she shocked me by saying, "I had a job interview. In Rhode Island."

I turned away from the window and focused on the rows and rows of antiqued-gold mailboxes. "You had a job interview."

"Yes—"

"In Rhode Island. This week."

"Yes."

"So the whole thing about the conference was a lie?"

"No, there was a conference. But I also met with the dean at RISD."

"The dean."

"Yes, it's an amazing opp—"

"This wasn't a first interview, then. The dean didn't happen to meet you at the cheese tray."

"Roxane."

"You went to Rhode Island to interview for a job, and you didn't mention it to me?" I felt like throwing up.

"I didn't know if I even wanted the job."

"Again, you didn't mention it to me?"

"There was honestly no point, not when I didn't even know if I would, one, get the job, and two, want to take the job."

"But you do."

"I wish you would just come over."

"So we can have this awful conversation face-to-face? So you can look me in the eye when you tell me you've been considering a job opportunity in another state and I wasn't even worth telling about it?"

"I'm telling you now," she said, and I choked out a strangled laugh. "And, honestly, I tried to tell you. At the airport. But you were so distracted by whatever mystery of the day you just have to solve that—"

"No. No. You don't get to do this. You don't get to rewrite history to make this my fault. You randomly asked me to come with you on your trip, with zero notice. That's not the same thing as telling me you want to move to Rhode Island with me." I paused, pinching the bridge of my nose. "Or maybe you don't. Maybe what you're telling me is that you want to move to Rhode Island, period."

"No, of course that's not what I'm saying. I want to be with you."

I tucked the phone between my ear and shoulder and scooped up my packages. "In Rhode Island. Not here."

Now her voice was going up a bit too. "It's worth discussing, isn't it? Providence is a great city.

"So is Columbus. My entire life is here. My business, my family—"

"You can build a new life, with me."

I pushed out into the cold night air. My breath came in frus-

trated puffs. "Catherine," I said, "you're acting like the lack of discussion here is my fault. You're the one who chose not to tell me."

"Why would I bring it up, if I didn't even know if I wanted it or
not?"

"Because it's a conversation that involves both of us!"

"My career involves both of us?"

"Whether or not we've been building a life together sure as hell
does."

"This is why I wanted to talk to you in person."

"This wouldn't be any different in person! Jesus Christ, how do
you keep finding new ways to do this to me?" I threw the packages
onto the passenger seat; now I was a lady shouting into her phone
in a parking lot.

"I think that's a little bit hysterical."

"Hysterical?" I said. "Hysterical?"

Catherine was still talking in my ear, but I said, "I can't do this
right now."

"You can't *do* this right now? You started it."

"How did I start this? You're the one who didn't think to mention you're considering *moving*—"

"Yeah, and you're the one acting like a lunatic right now, even
though you started this—"

"Good-bye, Catherine," I said.

I was shaking as I stood there with the door of the car open, the
dome light casting jagged shadows across the pale leather interior.

You started this.

The words hung in the air, the way only Catherine could make
them.

I wanted back into Nightshade, but obviously Bo wasn't going to let
me in for a third time. Not after the conversation I'd had with his

boss last night. Shane's Jag was not in evidence at the motel, and when I banged on the door, I heard nothing in response. I was mad enough to kick it in—this was not the kind of place to have a reinforced door—but opted for a more nuanced approach instead: I went down to the office and hoped the green-haired woman was working again.

She was.

Her name was Kez, and she reported that Shane had only paid for a week in the room. He hadn't come in to renew, so as far as she was concerned, he was no longer a guest.

"Has his room been cleaned?"

"Uh, yeah." Her thin face wrinkled up in something like annoyance. "I already told him, gotta stay up on the trash situation here. Otherwise we get roaches the size of hamburger buns."

"You talked to him, afterwards."

She didn't say anything.

"Did he leave something behind?"

"Like I told him, we put the trash in the Dumpster behind the building and he could look through it if he was so inclined, which he was."

"I'll bet that was a sight."

"Oooh, I'll tell you, it was. We got a good laugh."

"Did he find what he was looking for?"

"I don't think he did, no."

"Did he say what it was?"

Her eyes made a split-second flick to something on the desk. "No?"

"Is that a question?" I craned my neck to see what she had looked at—either a grubby desk phone or a box of blue nitrile gloves. I realized that when I asked if Shane had left anything behind, she was the one who mentioned the trash. "What are those for?"

"Just a safety precaution. I know there's hepatitis all through this shithole."

"Yeah, especially in their garbage. You go through it?"

"What's that supposed to mean?"

"Kez," I said, "you know how the other day you told me you want to track down guys who screw over their girlfriends on bail money?"

She gave a curt nod.

"Well, this asshole borrowed a bunch of cash from his girl's car accident settlement, bought a crappy nightclub, had to get a loan from a loan shark just to keep the lights on, and is currently screwing over both of them. So he's not exactly worthy of your protection."

"I'm not protecting him."

"Did you go through the trash?"

"Hey, people throw out so many cans—I'm thinking of Mother Earth here, and definitely not the cans-for-cash place over on Fulton."

"Look, I'm not judging. I just want to know what he was looking for."

She took her feet down off the desk and stood up, arms folded over her chest.

I said, "I don't do skip-tracing for bail bondsmen, but I know a couple guys who do. Maybe I can connect you. If you help me out here."

Kez sighed. "Some sneakers, nice ones. And a bunch of little webcams."

"Little webcams?"

"Yeah, these cute little stick-on things."

"If they weren't in the Dumpster, where are they?"

"Ah, come on."

"Do you still have them?"

She led me into a back room where it appeared the trash sorting happened. Two giant bins of crushed cans stood on one side, while the other side had a wide range of small electronics—smartphones, headphones, tablets, flatirons, handheld Nintendos, digital cameras, e-cigarettes, razors—and approximately one billion charging cables for everything thereof.

"This is the lost and found, I take it?" I said.

"Something like that. Um, let's see . . ." Kez sifted through the stuff.

"So is this all left behind in rooms, or do you steal it?"

"Steal? No. Most of it's just left after people check out. If they call later to ask about it, we'll give it back. Unless they're assholes. Then we might just say we didn't find it and proceed with the plan."

"Which is?"

"Here they are, this is them."

"And they were just in the trash in one-sixteen?"

"Swear to goddess."

Kez held four white plastic items out to me. As far as security cameras went, these looked more like a novelty than something that would actually increase the security of a place; they each had an oval-shaped head attached with a ball joint onto a flat base, the back of which had a small pad of adhesive still attached from where it had been affixed to the wall of Nightshade. I probed one of them, looking for a way to connect it to a computer. Tucked up under its neck, I found a slot that looked about the right size for an SD card, but it was empty. I checked the others and found two that did contain cards.

"You," I said, "are amazing."

THIRTY

I wasn't normally a germaphobe, but given the fact that the cameras had been first at Nightshade and then at the grossest motel in the world, I didn't want to take any chances. I wiped them down with Windex—better than nothing?—before I set about a full inspection. The cameras themselves were lightweight, probably inexpensive. They operated on a nickel-sized watch battery and featured an on/off switch and a button labeled "sync" below the memory card slot, along with a mini-USB port.

I opened my nightmare cord drawer and teased a mini-USB out of the mess, along with a memory card reader. When I inserted one of the cards from the camera, my laptop thought about it for a while, clicking and whirring, but the little icon didn't pop up anywhere.

I took it out and switched them.

Same deal.

I tried hooking up the camera itself via the mini-USB, which worked—except there was nothing stored on the camera.

I googled the model number and read about what it was meant to be used for: *Wi-Fi indoor security camera helps you keep everything and everyone you love safe! This model is fully equipped with advanced features such as night vision and motion alerts. Using our proprietary app, you can receive mobile notifications whenever your camera detects motion, and can even link together with other cameras to create a security network around your home!*

The whole thing was ninety bucks out the door, which included a thirty-two-gig memory card. So it was definitely a piece of crap, designed to monitor a detached garage for break-ins, not to serve as the security system for a nightclub. But it obviously had, at least to some capacity.

The footage was likely stored in Shane Resznik's phone; it was a shame that the cards didn't appear to work.

But when I clicked back to my desktop, I saw that the second card had finally popped up. Maybe it just took a while? I opened it up and saw dozens of video files, all named with time stamps.

I clicked on the most recent one: Thursday morning, 4:06 a.m.

It showed the dirty floor in the hallway that ran from the dance floor to the restrooms, the office, and into the back area; the camera must have been mounted slightly crooked, because I also saw a section of baseboard on the opposite side of the wall.

I clicked play and watched a top-down view of a door opening, then closing, then opening again.

The top of a gelled blond head.

Shane, dragging something—which turned out to be the same chair I'd used to inspect the sticky area on the wall.

He set the chair directly below the camera, hopped up, and the last thing the video showed before he ripped the camera off the wall was his creepy goatee and scared eyes.

It wasn't a very good camera angle—all it would show was someone entering or exiting the office. Then again, if his main "security" concern was keeping people out of the room where he pulled his funny business with the books, cameras like these would do just fine.

I clicked down the list and saw the door open again, then close. Ditto for the third video.

I examined the time stamps and saw that there were thirty-nine videos of the office door opening and closing on Wednesday night/Thursday morning, whereas on a regular night, there were no more than ten.

I started at the earliest time stamp on Wednesday night and watched in order:

Shane walks in.

Shane walks out.

Shane walks in talking on his phone.

Shane walks out talking on his phone.

I skipped ahead a few hours.

Shane walks in with his hand clamped on the ass of a woman other than Lisette.

The woman exits, the visible part of her expression one of annoyance.

Then, Addison walks down the hall and into the back. I recognized her boots, the sopping-wet corduroy ones she'd left in her sunporch.

Shane walks out of the office.

A man walks down the hall toward the back.

I replayed it once, then a second time. Leather jacket, thick-soled shoes, pattern baldness in a buzz cut, a stiff, unsteady gait. He kept his head down, face tucked into his collar.

I couldn't say for sure without the face, but I was willing to guess that this was Mickey Dillman.

I moved onto the next clip: Dillman coming back the other way, being herded by an employee I didn't know.

Then: Addison coming back the other way. She ducked into the bathroom.

Then: Dillman came back into view, jiggled the office doorknob but didn't open it. He went back into the club.

Addison came out of the bathroom and went back into the club too. The camera caught a flash of the tattoo on her back as she walked away.

The next hour was nothing but increasingly drunk patrons accidentally bumping into the office door while feeling around in the semidarkness for the bathroom.

Finally, though, at one-thirty, I found something: Addison's corduroy boots and Dillman's thick-soled shoes, approaching the office together.

Addison punched the code into the keypad on the door and they both went inside, the door closing behind them.

Six minutes later, the door flew open and Addison bolted down the hall toward the back of the club. The door slammed closed, then popped open again, and the man who might've been Dillman staggered out, looked around, and followed the same path Addison had taken to the back door.

A short while after that, Shane entered the frame and pulled the office door shut, but didn't go in.

Neither Addison nor Mickey had reappeared.

I was approaching the end of the video clips.

In the third to last, Shane walked past the office door to the back room. Seconds later, same clip, he was backing slowly down the hall, toward the dance floor.

Second to last clip: Shane and Wyatt—I recognized him from his shoes, too—walking quickly down the hallway, then briefly reentering the frame and unlocking the office door.

Then I was back to the parting shot of him tearing the camera off the wall.

What the hell did I just watch?

I went through the section with Addison again. Her posture while walking with Dillman seemed more or less relaxed, but when she came running out of the office, her shoulders were around her ears, her hands balled into fists at her sides.

"That could literally be anyone," Detective Blair said on Monday morning, frowning thoroughly despite the fact that I'd brought coffee and bagels. "I mean, you don't see anybody's faces except for this club owner, who's exactly nobody to me."

"It could be anybody, but it's not," I said. "These are Addison's shoes. I'm willing to bet that somewhere on social media, you can find a picture of her wearing them. That and the tattoo? It's her. And this," I added, pointing at my screen at the form of Mickey Dillman, "is the guy who chased her out into the street and had her scared enough to run to my brother's place."

The rest of my audience—Mizuno, Tom, and the young Detective Clark—did not seem entirely convinced.

"So what you're telling us," Mizuno said, "is that for some reason, a well-respected cop came to a nightclub to harass a deejay, frightening her so much she ran to your brother's apartment for help, then left a terrified voice mail for her father, then shortly after, ran right back out into the street?"

I tapped the screen again. "We already know from Addison's roommate that he had come to their place, looking for her. We know he interacted with her second BusPass account. And this proves that he came to the club."

Blair blew a raspberry. "No, this proves that some guy came to the club. For all we know, this is your brother."

"Yeah, no," Tom said. "Andrew Weary's at least six inches taller than Mickey was, and he has a full head of hair."

"Do you want me to pass that compliment on to him?" I said, and Tom smirked. I nudged the bag of cameras that I'd brought. "I don't know if there is anything on these, or on the card I couldn't get to work. If only there was some bureaucracy around here that had access to digital forensics."

"She's pretty pleased with herself," Blair muttered.

"Not really. I just know that my brother is telling the truth."

"Sweetheart, no one can know that."

"*Sweetheart*. Did you really just say that?"

"Okay, let's keep it friendly here," Clark said, speaking for the first time since the meeting started; she'd been keeping busy taking notes. "So what are we supposed to think happened, after they went off the video here? How did Mickey—if this is him," she amended as Blair started to interrupt. "What happened between the club and the river?"

"These guys know something." I clicked on the file that showed Shane and Wyatt. "Owner, bouncer. They were holed up in a motel room together, refusing to talk, until a few days ago. Then Wyatt has his run-in with the SWAT team, and Shane suddenly feels chatty and bares his soul to Vincent Pomp, to whom he owes more than a little bit of cash."

"Bares his soul about what?"

"He claims that he was voiding transactions and skimming money."

"From himself?"

"From his business, which is in hock to Pomp up to its grimy ceilings."

Blair took off his glasses and polished them with a napkin from the bagel box, which appeared to make them dirtier. He was still frowning at me but I could tell he was getting interested. "So what's that have to do with Addison or Mickey?"

"Well, Shane told Pomp that all of this—meaning me being nosy—is because Addison discovered what he was doing with the voided transactions. She confronted him, he yelled at her, she got upset and left."

All four cops looked at me like that was the stupidest thing they'd ever heard, which it was.

"Maybe she told Mickey something about it?" Clark volunteered, a little hesitant. "And in the clip where she comes out of the office, she's scared of Shane?"

"Or," Tom said, "she's scared of Mickey because he's threatening to bust Shane if she doesn't, I don't know, cooperate or something?"

Clark shook her head. "But Mickey shouldn't be working a case. Shouldn't have been. He was on leave."

I said, "I have a whole list of bad theories that I can share if you want."

I played the video of Addison darting out of the office again and we all watched. It lasted twenty-five seconds, and it told us nothing.

"That should give them something to chew on for a while," Tom said as we rode down to the lobby in the elevator. "Props to you for bringing it forward, not just going it alone this time."

"Hey. I'm a paragon of professionalism."

The elevator stopped on the second floor and a half-dozen people pushed in. Tom bumped into me while trying to make room for them. "Sorry—"

"No, it's fine—"

He leaned close to my ear. "Are we back to things being awkward between us?"

"Why, because you co-opted my bed in the middle of the night?" I whispered back. "No, why ever would that make things awkward?"

He rolled his eyes, holding back a laugh until the elevator stopped on the ground level and the doors opened and our fellow passengers got out. Then he said, "I'm really sorry, about that. I keep thinking about it and cringing."

"I'm not sure if I should be offended by that."

"What—no, I'm saying I embarrassed myself."

We had paused just inside the doors to the street, which was the nothing color of the sky and vice versa. I looked at him. "Tom, we're past the trying to impress each other stage. At least I seriously hope we are, because if we aren't, I've really been fucking up."

She'd called me three times that morning, Catherine had. I still didn't want to talk to her. I knew I'd have to eventually, but now was not that time. Instead I went home and made tea and looked at Rose W's BusPass account.

Still no response from Rajit, but I had gotten a new message from Joseph last night:

> This is Joe's wife, you slut. HIS WIFE HE HAS A WIFE don't write him again.

I was, once again, worried about straight people.

I refrained from suggesting that she just delete his BusPass account rather than monitoring it and harassing the relatively innocent people who contacted him there, and instead sent her my phone number and said *we need to talk.*

BD E, meanwhile, had fallen silent yesterday after saying *brb.* I reminded him that I existed.

> ROSE W: Tired of me already?
> BD E: No sorry, got caught up. How's ur day going
> ROSE W: Not bad. Caffeine cures everything
> BD E: True dat. U at work

ROSE W: Sort of

ROSE W: I work from home

BD E: Doing what?

ROSE W: Social media

BD E: Rly?

ROSE W: Yeah

BD E: For what

ROSE W: A company that makes workout clothes

BD E: For men or women?

ROSE W: Women

BD E: U work out?

ROSE W: Duh

BD E: Want to show me what you wear to work out?

I typed *not really,* deleted it, then sent him a picture of my rack of leggings.

BD E: Are those all yours?

ROSE W: No, for work

BD E: That's the lady from cbus isn't it

BD E: Spinspo

ROSE W: You know your women's workout clothes

BD E: I just read a thing about her in the paper, that's all

ROSE W: Do YOU work out?

BD E: Every day

ROSE W: Match made in heaven

Too strong? He didn't respond to that. A few minutes later, my phone rang.

THIRTY-ONE

Joe and Cindy Javonovich lived on the northeast side of the city in one of those Gahanna subdivisions where the houses all had three-car garages that were at least one-third full of junk. Theirs was a vaguely mauve-ish stone affair with a two-story entry and a large wooden table that featured a bowl of blown-glass fruit just inside the door. I complimented the fruit as she invited me in, mostly because she seemed to expect a compliment of some kind.

She was tall and artificially blond and wearing a leather blazer and heeled ankle boots in her own home, so it was pretty clear that we were not going to be compatible as people. But she made a mean cup of Earl Grey and she had the air about her of someone who was very willing to dish.

"I thought about murdering him," she said. "I mean, not seriously? But sort of seriously. A little rat poison in his green smoothie? Ha!" She laughed. It was not apparent how serious she was, exactly. "But he never met her, never even talked to her on the phone. It was all just in the stupid app. The worst part? My brother-in-law works for that stupid start-up, too."

"Um," I said.

Addy Marie's profile was up on my phone, between us on the kitchen table. This one didn't have any blown glass on it.

"I found their little conversation by accident. The accident being that I thought it would be a good idea to snoop through his phone. My therapist told me to be honest about that. The accident part."

"That's healthy."

She sighed.

"So you accidentally thought that looking through Joe's phone would bring you peace."

"Yes! That's all I actually wanted. Peace. See, you understand. Why is it so hard for everyone else to understand?"

"What happened then?"

"Well, I read their whole dirty conversation and saw the pictures they were sending each other. And she's—okay, so she's young. But there is no way she's prettier than me. Hips like a crinoline. Joe never got to fuck a greaser in high school so all I can figure is that's what it's about."

She was a lovely, lovely person. "Okay, what then?"

"I told him what I saw, of course, and he swore up and down it was nothing, it was just the stupid app, that she contacted him and he was just playing a game and got caught up in it. But I called bullshit on that. He gave her money. And one thing you should know about my husband is that he doesn't part with his money over nothing. Throwing money around makes him feel better than everybody else," she said. I suspected the same could be said about her. But maybe that was why they were so perfectly miserable together.

I said, "What was the money for?"

Cindy waved a hand like a swarm of gnats had alighted from the table. "Her rent, is what she said. It's not like Joe would *actually* ever help someone *in need* but a pretty girl says she needs help with her rent and suddenly he's St. Francis?"

"Your metaphors are very creative."

"Thank you."

"But he never actually met her."

"No."

"Spoke on the phone?"

"No. Just chatting in the app."

"When was the last time?"

"The minute I found out, I made Joe swear he would *never* use the app again. I made him delete it off his phone. And I check it on the computer sometimes, just to make sure."

"And he didn't, I don't know, create another account without you knowing?"

"No," she said firmly. "Besides, even if he did? There's no way she'd ever talk to him again."

"Why's that?"

Cindy gave me a tense little smile.

I thought about the seemingly disparate clues I had so far, trying to find something that would fit. With Joe's name appearing on Addy Marie's list of recent connections, that meant that they'd talked as recently as two weeks ago. "Would you be willing to show me the conversations with her?"

Cindy was more than willing; she got out her iPad and gleefully logged into Joseph J's account. "I'm going to start dinner. Joe will be home soon."

"You still make this motherfucker dinner?" I said as I skimmed the messages from about three months ago, which was when the majority of them had been sent.

> Joseph J: I'm rock hard just imagining it
> Addy Marie S: Imagining what?
> Joseph J: You sitting on my face
> Addy Marie S: 😈 😜

Cindy said, "My marriage is not a failure."

That didn't answer the question, but at the same time, it did.

The mystery of the recent communication between Addy and Joe was solved with a series of messages from Cindy via Joe's account:

> Joseph J: Slut
> Joseph J: Slut
> Joseph J: Slut

It appeared she sent them once a week, and that Addison was smart enough not to respond. The point at which Cindy had wrested control of the account was obvious; at the beginning of January, I found this exchange:

> Joseph J: Hey where are you
> Addy Marie S: At home, why?
> Joseph J: Lying slut. I'm standing right behind you

I said, "You went to the nightclub, didn't you?"

The woman that Wyatt had poured into a cab after she lost her mind at Addison.

"Yes," Cindy said. "And you know what? I'm not sorry. She deserved it. I wasn't about to fall for her little *'I don't know what you're talking about'* act."

"That's what she said?"

"Isn't that what you'd say?"

If a drunk and angry stranger accosted me while I was at work? Probably. Cindy was chopping asparagus with violence in mind.

"But she never sent another message after that, so clearly she did know," she added.

An expensive engine pulled into the driveway—because the garage was full of crap, I assumed—and Joseph J himself entered through the front door, dropping his coat and briefcase on the table with the fake fruit. "Cindy, there's a car on the street—oh," he said when he saw me. His BusPass pictures were clearly of a younger Joseph J; in the present era, he was puffy and greying and wore a yellow-and-grey striped tie with a blob of mayo on it. He looked at me nervously. "Cindy?"

"This is Roxane, and she's a detective, and you're going to tell her all about the slut from the dating app," Cindy said. She kept her voice amazingly even.

Joe glanced at his wife, then at me, then back to Cindy. "A *police* detective?"

"Yes," she said.

Everyone was interested in making me seem more important than I was this week, but only to further their own agendas.

I nodded gravely.

Joe spluttered, "I haven't talked to her! Cindy, you know I haven't. I haven't! Did she say I talked to her?"

It was pretty clear to me that while the man had terrible judgment, he was being truthful now. So I left them to their dinner of root vegetables and marital discord and sat in the car on their dark suburban street, which felt like every other suburban street I'd ever sat in the car on. That was either what was wrong with suburbs, or it was what people liked so much about them.

I cranked the heat and thought about the days when I kept a flask in the glove box along with my gun. Not exactly a better time, but a shot of whiskey sounded good right about now. I was cold and discouraged. Addison Stowe didn't make any sense to me. From what her friends had told me, she wasn't the attention-seeking type. Intensely private, it was hard to imagine her sending the cat-face/tongue emoji combo to someone she hadn't met. And even if she had, would she really continue down this path of flirting with men online even after the spectacle at Nightshade when Cindy Javonovich showed up?

Anyone was capable of anything.

This was something I had to make a point of reminding myself on the regular.

I checked my phone to see if there were messages from Addy Marie's other chat mates.

> Rajit M: Hi, sorry, meant to change my relationship status! Seeing someone right now. Good luck!

A curiously polite response, given the general level of sleaze that seemed to abound in this app.

> BD E: What are u drinking tonight?

The message was accompanied by a picture of a bottle of Yakima Fresh gripped in a rough, blunt-fingered hand that floated above a granite countertop, grey, with a herringbone tile floor in the background.

I thought it looked familiar, in the anonymous suburban way I was just contemplating.

It could be anywhere.

Then I realized that it *was* familiar, actually. I'd spent quite a bit of time the other day at that counter, while Elise Hazlett folded laundry.

"Brock, you dirty dog," I said.

THIRTY-TWO

The Hazletts' street was quiet in the dark, lawns glowing faintly blue from the hard blanket of snow. Brock answered the door, the very same beer in his hand. "Elise isn't here," he said.

"Oh, that's okay," I said. "I wanted to talk to you, actually."

I remembered the brief darkness that flitted through his face when I mentioned Addison the other day. Now it made a lot more sense.

"Uh, okay." He stepped aside to let me into the house.

His hand grazed the small of my back, and I ducked away so that he didn't feel the revolver holstered at my hip.

I wasn't taking any chances.

"Do you, uh, want anything to drink?" Brock said.

We were standing around the kitchen island. He had on a Browns sweatshirt and tattered gym shorts and white socks pulled up to mid-calf. The house was quiet.

"Where's Elise?" I said.

"At Jordy's."

I wondered how big Jordy's place was; she was taking on a lot of refugees. "You have a fight?"

"Sort of, yeah."

"What about?"

"Just stuff. Married people stuff. What did you want to talk to me about?"

"Actually, a drink does sound good. Have any rosé?"

He blinked at me.

"Let's chat about BusPass, Brock," I said. I showed him the conversation he'd just been having with me on my phone.

"What the hell? Is this why Elise hired you? Because—"

"Calm down. Elise didn't hire me, though maybe she should have. How long have you been chatting with random ladies on BusPass?"

"I don't—"

"Can it. This is all the proof either of us needs to see."

I tapped the photo he'd sent me an hour earlier and held up the phone so the edges of the image lined up with the actual room.

"But—"

"Brock."

He sighed. His face was a hypertensive pink. Embarrassment, or anger? That remained to be seen. "You *entrapped* me into messaging you."

I shook my head. "That's not what entrapment is. And anyway, these messages are not my concern. Let's talk about Addison."

"Um, Addison? I don't really know her that well—"

"Brock. Sweetheart. I know you've been messaging her too. I guess the only question is, does she know that? Does she know that BD E is actually her childhood bestie's husband?"

The fight or flight went out of his posture and he slumped a little. "No. I mean, I don't think so."

"Were you careful enough not to send her pictures in your own kitchen?"

He nodded.

"I have a lot of questions, Brock. First of all, why?"

"She wrote to me! Like Rose did."

"Oh, okay, so you were powerless."

"Yeah!" Then he realized that I was being sarcastic and he added, "No, I guess not. I just thought it was funny at first, I mean, I only got the account because this buddy of mine from work was always wanting to send me stuff from the app and I couldn't see it so he's just like, 'Sign up for a fake account already.' So I did."

"So it's his fault too."

"No, I'm just saying."

I motioned for him to go on.

"So I got the account and then sometimes, I guess I'd just start flipping through, you know? For something to do. It was, you know, *there*. Then this one time, I saw Addison's profile."

"And you passed right on her?"

"I should've skipped her. But yeah, I passed right. I wasn't really thinking. But we kinda have a history."

My ears perked up at that. "Kinda?"

"Well," he said.

"Spill."

Brock rubbed his face. "Me and Elise have been together since high school, junior year," he said.

"Lovely."

"But before that, me and Addison kind of had something going on."

I stared at him.

"We were both on the swim team."

"What kind of something?"

"Just, you know. Fooling around. We were like fifteen. Riding to meets on the bus together out of town. But I mean, it was never serious. We weren't *going together* or anything."

It seemed that Brock thought that was a point in his favor. "Does Elise know about this?"

"She knew Addison and I hung out, before. But it wasn't a big deal."

"So when you saw Addison in the dating app, you just thought it might be fun to open up that Pandora's box again for no reason?"

"I don't—it's like—listen, I'm not proud of it. But Addy's just, damn, I mean, she's fine and she doesn't even care. She's fine *because* she doesn't care. She's just cool. And don't get me wrong, I love my wife, but Elise is not exactly cool."

"Perhaps because she is busy raising your children?"

That shut him up.

I added, "I thought you said you didn't know Addison that well?"

"Yeah, um. I don't anymore, I mean, I hardly ever see her."

"So you found her in the app and figured this was a great way to get some of that coolness into your life without hurting anyone?"

"Yeah, exactly."

"Brock, you need to work on your ability to detect sarcasm. I am not on your side here. What did you and Addison talk about?"

"Oh, just, you know, stuff."

"What stuff?"

"Like, music. She has badass taste in music, for a chick. And beer."

"Badass taste in beer for a chick too?"

Brock nodded.

"What exactly was she getting out of this interaction?"

"I don't know. Someone to talk to."

"About beer and music?"

He nodded again.

"Mind if I take a look at your messages?"

"What—no, that's private."

I drummed my fingertips on the counter and stared at him. He looked afraid of me. Finally, he said, "She sometimes sent pictures of herself. Like, sexy ones."

"Show me."

"I deleted the conversation. Yesterday, after Jordy was saying that Addison is missing or whatever. I didn't want anyone to get the wrong idea."

"No, of course not," I said. This time, he grasped that it was sarcasm. "So you never met up with her."

"No!"

"Talk on the phone?"

"No."

"Just beer, music, and sexy pictures?"

"And compliments. From me, to her. She always did like that. Validation."

I wanted my revelation about Brock to be worth more than this. I thought for a few beats and said, "Who's Corbin Janney?"

"Who?"

"Corbin Janney."

"I have no idea."

Brock wasn't a great liar, so I was inclined to believe him. But I didn't want to let him off the hook that easily. "So you didn't create another profile under that name to get even more sexy pictures from her?"

"No! Nothing like that. I wouldn't do that—" But he stopped, probably upon realizing that he already had.

"When was the last time you heard from her?"

"Not for like two weeks."

Roughly the amount of time she'd been gone. But she was still using the app—she'd talked to Wyatt that way.

Brock was fidgeting a bit in front of me.

"What aren't you telling me?" I said.

"I sent her money."

He leaned hard against the counter.

"Oh?"

"For the pictures."

I waited.

"She said she needed three hundred bucks or else she was going to lose her apartment. I told her that I might be able to help but I needed a little visual inspiration. I'd been, I don't know, trying to get her to send a pic or two and she wouldn't. But then I said that. I was gonna send her fifty bucks or something regardless."

"So what you said about her wanting validation?"

"I'm just embarrassed, okay? This is embarrassing. And isn't it, like, a crime?" he said, dropping his voice to a whisper on the last two words.

"I really don't care," I said. "I just want to find her. How much money did you send her?"

Brock muttered indistinctly.

"Come again?"

"A lot. I don't know. She sent me a lot of pictures. Are you going to tell my wife about this?"

"Right now I'm just trying to figure out what happened to Addison," I said. "Once I do that, then we'll see."

He looked at me for a while, clearly working out something else in his head. "So if you don't really do social media for SpinSpo, why do you have so many leggings in your house?"

"Brock," I said, "you'd be well-served by worrying less about women's pants, okay?"

I left feeling bad about the world, or at least the social media–era world. Would any of these problems have existed before? It was easy to blame technology, but really, people have always battled shitty impulses—BusPass just gave men like Brock a convenient way to act upon them without even leaving the house. I navigated the winding streets of Blacklick in the dark and tried to make sense of everything I'd learned so far. Corbin Janney—whoever he was—existed as an outlier on one end of the spectrum, and Mickey Dillman was on the opposite end. Both had interacted with Addison via the app through unusual but very different circumstances. Corbin was a made-up name that had carried on a relationship of some significance with Addison, while Mickey's contact with her was still a big old question mark. He'd showed up at her house, showed up at her job at least once, had some kind of tense interaction with her there, and then? Then Addison ran out into the street without a coat, and Mickey somehow got himself to the icy Scioto River.

Or someone wanted it to appear that way.

Everything here was different than it appeared.

I tried to imagine Mickey Dillman posing as an emo twenty-something to talk to Addison from his crummy little motel room. It could happen, but why? And if he had done so, why also interact with Addison's second account using his real name?

And while I was at it, why did Addison pack a bag and leave home but didn't take her recording equipment? She didn't plan to be gone that long, or she was done being DJ Raddish?

My thoughts skipped back to my suicide pact idea. It seemed insane, but was it crazier than any of the other prospects?

I found myself avoiding the freeway and driving straight down Main, past the East Side Motor Lodge and eventually into Bexley, toward Catherine's house.

There was a car in the driveway that I didn't recognize, something boxy and grey in the dark.

I slowed to a crawl and thought about driving past, just going home, but decided not to. Instead I parked and knocked on the door, my key to it burning hot against my palm. Through the tall windows that flanked the door I saw Catherine walk toward me, hesitate, then commit. "Hi," she said, holding the door open a few inches. "I thought you didn't want to come over."

"I didn't," I said, "not yesterday. But can we talk now?"

"You hung up on me."

"I was upset."

"Was?"

"Am? I don't know, Catherine, can I come in? It's cold."

"Wystan is here."

I stared at her.

"So this probably isn't a good time."

"What's he doing here?"

"Well, it's his house," she said. "Technically."

In the past eight months, her estranged ex-husband had been keeping a profile so low that I almost forgot he existed. He wasn't even living in Columbus, to hear her tell it, and as far as I knew, they hadn't been in contact at all. I supposed the operative words were *as far as I knew*. Maybe that wasn't really very far.

Some detective I was.

"Did you tell him about Rhode Island?" I said.

Catherine nodded.

"I mean before you told me."

She took a beat to answer that one. "I may have mentioned it. Because of the house."

I bit off a laugh. "No," I said.

"No what?"

"Do you really not see how unfair all of this is? To me?"

She made a face, the one that meant she was about to say something with the sole purpose of hurting me. "Has anyone ever told you that you're a narcissist?" she said. "Because I think you are. Even if most of your thoughts are about how you're garbage, that still means most of your thoughts are about you."

I felt my mouth hanging open. The cold air made my teeth ache. Catherine folded her arms over her chest and just blinked at me the way she always did in the aftermath of something like this, both bewildered and satisfied.

I held out the house key to her, but she didn't take it. She acted like she was just standing in an open doorway for no reason, like I wasn't there at all. I turned and dropped the key on the steps as I went back to my car.

It made a sound like glass breaking as it plinked down onto the concrete, almost musical.

THIRTY-THREE

I practically threw my driver's license at the clerk manning the visitation process at FCCC1. My head hurt and my chest hurt and I suspected that I might scream at anyone who looked at me funny, but no one did. When Andrew sat down across from me he said, "You look like a person with some bad news."

My hands were still shaking. "Not news, no."

"What's wrong?"

I studied my brother through the smeary glass. He looked like shit, with puffy dark circles under his eyes, a slick of perspiration across his forehead. "I don't want to talk about me. Are you doing okay in here?"

He closed his eyes. "Not really," he said. "Seven days without a drop of booze under these circumstances? It's bullshit."

"Seven days."

"But who's counting." He opened his eyes; they were bloodshot, shiny. "I've been thinking about Dad," he said. "The booze. I was thinking, no way he could've gone seven days without a drink. I'm nothing like him, that's what I'm telling myself. Look at me, I went seven days without drinking. Yeah, because I'm fucking in *jail*." He banged his hand on the metal ledge below the window. "Sorry."

"Hey, no."

"If I'm still in here on the eighth, promise me you won't let Matt—I don't know—be Matt."

"I promise. You won't be, though. Has Jules made any inroads on the search warrant?"

"Fuck if I know. Are you any closer to figuring out where Addison is?"

"Ditto," I said. "Listen, humor me a second, okay? Tell me exactly what happened the night Addison came over."

"I already told you everything."

"I know. But tell me again. Start before she got there. What were you doing?"

"Reading."

"Reading?"

"I do know how to read, Roxane."

"What were you reading? Come on, tell me a story here."

Andrew rested his elbows on the metal ledge. "Okay. I was reading *Slaughterhouse-Five*. Rereading."

I nodded for him to go on.

"I was like two-thirds of the way done with it. Debating whether I wanted to keep reading or go to bed. But then Addison showed up—"

I interrupted, "No, tell me exactly what happened. Did she ring the buzzer, did you talk to her through the little speaker, what?"

My brother sighed. "Okay, fine, I'll play this tedious little game with you."

"Thank you."

"The buzzer buzzed. I put my book down on the arm of the sofa. I stood up." He looked at me. "Is this minutiae minute enough?"

"It's perfect. Just talk."

"I said yeah or something. She said—she said, '*Andrew, please, this is an emergency, let me in, I need to use a phone.*' And I thought . . . I don't know what I thought. I didn't realize who it was, but she sounded scared. Actually, she sounded relieved, like relieved that I was home or something. But anyway, I said, 'Who is this?' She said, *'It's me from the Sheraton, please please open the door.'*"

"Two pleases?"

"Two pleases. I buzzed her in. Then I went out into the hall, like, to see if she was actually coming up, or if she just wanted to get into the building. But she came up. Stairs, not elevator. She didn't even really look at me, she just kind of bumped by me to get inside. Is this helping?"

"I don't know yet. Just keep going."

"She went into the kitchen. To the sink. She kind of leaned over the sink, almost hyperventilating. I said, 'What's wrong, what happened, what do I do?' She was trying to calm down, but she was also shivering. So I grabbed a sweatshirt from the closet and gave it to her. She put it on. The sleeves were crazy long. I asked if she was hurt, if someone had hurt her, I offered to call the police. She said, 'Please, no, I just need your phone.' I asked again, 'Are you okay? Please, let me help,' and she said, 'No, I'm fine, I need to make a phone call.' So I unlocked my phone and gave it to her. Then she made her call—"

"Where were you? Where was she?"

"God, you're annoying. She was still in the kitchen, at the sink. She kind of turned away and faced the refrigerator while she was talking. I was—I don't know where I was."

"Yes you do. I assume she put her back to you, when she turned towards the refrigerator?"

Andrew nodded.

"So you were somewhere between the sink and the hallway."

"I—yeah. I went over to the couch, I picked up my book again. She hung up the phone and kind of sighed and took a few deep breaths. So I thought, okay, she's calming down now—it was a really awkward situation. I wasn't sure what to do, I thought maybe I'd just sit there and read until she wants to talk or something. But I didn't sit down," he said, and paused. "Instead of sitting down I went over to the window, because I heard sirens. Shit, I totally forgot about that. I heard sirens."

"See, I wasn't just doing this for fun. What kind of sirens?"

"There was an ambulance going by, when I looked out. On Fourth." His blue-grey eyes widened. "That's what spooked her. The siren. When I turned back to her, she was fumbling with the dead bolt on the door, trying to leave. I ran over to the door to stop her, saying, *'Hey, no, you're not in good shape right now, let me drive you somewhere if you need to leave.'* I grabbed her elbow, or tried to, I just got a handful of sweatshirt and she kind of jerked away, but I was still holding the sweatshirt, so she was kind of stuck for a second, and she slapped at me with her other hand, I guess, and that was when she scratched me. And I let go. She left, I grabbed my shoes, and by the time I had them on and made it out the door, she was gone. Why would a siren have scared her like that?"

Because she'd just had an ugly altercation with a cop, that was why.

It made a lot of sense, actually. She didn't want Andrew to call the police in the first place, but then she heard the sirens and thought—what—that they were there for her?

Because Mickey needed backup?

Because Mickey needed medical attention?

I rubbed my forehead, wishing like hell the security cameras had been placed more strategically.

"Do you think I'm a narcissist?" I said after a minute.

"Um, where is this coming from?"

"It's just a question."

"No, Roxane, you aren't a narcissist. Do you even know what a narcissist is?"

"Of course I know."

"Then why are you asking? If there's anyone I know who is capable of empathy, it's you. Too much, even. And the last time I checked, you hate being the center of attention."

I kept quiet. I was picturing the flinty look in Catherine's eyes when she'd said it.

Andrew placed his palm against the glass. I guessed it wasn't too much like a Lifetime movie after all. I followed suit. "Do you need to talk?" he asked.

"No."

"Is that true?"

"Catherine," I said, but I wasn't sure what else to add to that. Apparently nothing was required. "Now there's a narcissist."

I sighed and stared at our hands lined up on the glass.

Andrew said, "Fucking February."

In the car, I pushed play on the stereo, hoping for something loud and ballsy. Instead I heard the strange music stylings of DJ Raddish. Anger stabbed at my brain and I turned it off. I had a piercing desire to break the CD in half, but couldn't figure out how to eject it.

"Jesus Christ," I said to the shadowy darkness of Mound Street.

But as I sat there, something was needling my psyche, hanging in the air like an unresolved chord. My entire relationship with Catherine was a bit of an unresolved chord, and it had been for almost twenty years. I didn't like thinking about it in those terms, in that amount of wasted time. But there it was. Andrew was stuck in limbo—that was a textbook definition of an unresolved chord. I turned the stereo back on in case the thing bothering me was an actual unresolved chord, but the meandering beat and layers of audio didn't have much in the way of an identifiable melody.

Just the crackling sound effect, and Billie Holiday's lonesome, broken-hearted voice.

I smacked the steering wheel.

Rick Dillman's big red headphones, the song I'd heard escaping from them while we were in line at the wings restaurant. Billie Holiday.

THIRTY-FOUR

A woman with dyed reddish-orange hair in rollers answered the door of Rick Dillman's house the next morning. The hosebeast, I presumed. "Hi there, is Rick at home?"

She gave me the eye. "And you are . . . ?"

I waggled a bottle of Shelby's hot sauce. "I just want to talk capsaicin. I'm a friend."

The hosebeast pursed her lips. "I'll let him know you're here."

She closed the door partway and yelled, "Richard, You Have A Visitor."

Rick appeared a moment later, pushing up his glasses.

"I come bearing gifts," I said as I handed him the bottle.

Rick was very into the hot sauce. We ate it on Saltine crackers while sitting in his basement, which had a separate bedroom, bathroom, and sitting room. Most of the sitting room was taken up by a wooden entertainment stand, a turntable, and a complex system of speakers.

I said, "It looks like you have a whole deejay setup here."

He shook his head rapidly. "It's for listening only. I built this whole thing around this one part—let me show you." He crawled over to the entertainment stand and opened the cabinet door on the bottom. Instead of concealing his record collection, it revealed a metal beam.

"What on earth is that?"

He pointed to the turntable in the center. "It's completely parallel to the foundation of the house. It's actually sitting on this thing that goes into the foundation. Because when there is play"—here he held up a hand and tipped it back and forth—"it can affect the audio. I wanted to create the optimal listening experience. It's so stable that nothing is going to mess up the sound. There could be a tornado and this thing isn't going anywhere."

"So you're a bit of an audiophile."

He nodded. "Well, expert. It's why I can sell so many sound systems even though people say I'm strange. I tell them, *neurodivergent,* that's the word. So I know you're here to put on the hard sell but I told you. The vault."

"I know. But I was hoping we could make a trade."

"A trade?"

"Hot sauce recipe for the whole story?"

"You *made* this?"

"A friend did."

Rick didn't say anything, just studied the hairs on his arm and smoothed them down.

"I want to talk about Addy Marie," I continued. I showed him her profile on my phone. "I know you know who this is. I know your cousin went to see her, didn't he? At the club where she worked? That night, after bowling?"

Rick leaned back against the couch and stared at the ceiling.

I added, "I know you promised not to tell anyone. But I think this woman might know something about what happened to him, and I really think Mickey would want the truth about what happened that night to come out."

"The truth."

We sat in silence for a long time. Finally, Rick dipped a fingertip into the hot sauce and smeared it around the plate a little.

"He said she was bad and he was gonna get the money back," he said eventually. "Even though I told him, it was okay, it wasn't about the money."

"What money?"

"That I sent her. It was for her car. Well, first it was for her car. Then she needed a new controller for her act and she asked me which one to get, and I told her the Pioneer DDJ-RX is without a doubt the best you can get, but it's like three grand, and she said she couldn't afford it, and that she was probably going to get this other one that was like ninety bucks, and I just—no, don't buy that piece of crap. I wanted to get it for her."

"When was this?"

"Right after New Year's."

So, well over a month ago.

"She said she didn't get anything good for Christmas. So I told her, no, you got the Pioneer controller for Christmas and I sent her the money on PayPal."

"Three thousand dollars."

"It's not that big of a deal."

"Actually, it is. That's a lot of money."

"I told you, I'm *really* good at selling sound systems. I just wanted to help her, to do something nice for my girlfriend. But Mickey said she wasn't my girlfriend. He said girlfriends don't take money from men they haven't even met and I said that I was the one who didn't want to meet."

"Why not?"

"I'm better online, is all."

"But she wanted to meet?"

"No. I said at the beginning, 'Addy, I like you a lot but we can't meet for a long time, because I have autism and meeting people is not so good for me, can we just get to know each other.' And she said of course, she said she got nervous meeting new people too, but that she liked me back because we could talk about anything."

"What kinds of things did you talk about?"

"Sound. Like what it means to actually listen to something. I told her about this, here," he said, pointing to the stereo stand. "And feeling different and how people have these ideas of what you are."

"Was it romantic?"

"Duh, she said she wanted to be my girlfriend. She sent me pictures. Sexy." He pulled his phone out of his pocket and scrolled through his photo album.

"Whoa," I said.

He wasn't kidding. The pictures Addison had sent went a bit beyond *sexy*.

Topless in the shower of her apartment.

A completely nude shot taken from behind, hands on her hips.

A selfie in bed, headphones over her ears, a sulky smile on her lips, the hand that wasn't holding the camera resting casually on her torso, fingertips just under the lace trim of her underwear.

"She's so pretty," Rick said mournfully.

"So tell me what happened when you told Mickey about her."

"It's the hosebeast's fault. She snooped in my email when she was cleaning down here, even though I told her not to clean down here because I have my own way of doing it. But she told my dad and he said she was making a fool out of me. It was right before bowling one week. So when Mickey got here, I was mad and I told him about why. And that was when he said my dad was right and that Addy wasn't my girlfriend and she was just taking advantage. But look." He flipped to another photo, this one of Addison clutching a box and beaming. The box said PIONEER on the side. "I wanted to get it for her, and she has it now, so how is anyone taking advantage? Mickey was so mad about everything though. Because of his surgery. He thought everyone was out to get everyone else. He said not to use the app anymore."

"And did you?"

"No, because the hosebeast changed my password on the app that night and now I can't access it anymore."

"That's totally fucked up."

"Yes! It is!"

"So you kind of ghosted Addy."

"I guess. But by accident. Default ghosting due to hosebeast."

"What did Mickey do?"

"He told me he found her address but she was never home."

"When was that?"

"Last month. Then on the last bowling night he said he figured out where she worked and he was gonna go there. I told him to just leave her alone but he said no, he was going to get my money back." Rick shrugged. "He said he felt so useless and worthless, because of his back. He wanted to do something good. I said the good thing he could do was buy me another game of bowling but he'd already had too many beers and was just not in a place to listen to me."

"Do you know how he figured out where she worked?"

"He said there were pictures on her profile and he figured out what bar they were in."

I remembered the image of Addison onstage. It didn't have a giant flashing sign that said THIS BAR IS CALLED NIGHTSHADE or anything, but it was distinctive enough. I pictured him visiting every bar in the Short North, trying to find the one from the picture.

Rick dipped another cracker in the hot sauce. "Pretty sure I got the better end of the deal here," he said.

"I don't know. This is very interesting, Rick."

He shook his head. "It's just stupid. I wish we'd stayed at the bowling alley longer that night instead."

"Yeah."

"Maybe he wouldn't have gotten so sad. Maybe he would still

be here. He would love this, you know." Rick pointed at the plate. There was only one cracker left.

I said, "All you."

Wyatt's mother was asleep in a chair in the corner of Wyatt's room, a blue blanket draped over her frame. Wyatt's eyes were closed as well, the room still and silent except for the beeping heart monitor. But he was no longer attached to the ventilator. As I stood there, he opened his eyes, closed them, opened them again, and focused on me. "Shh," he whispered. "She needs rest. I keep telling her to go home, that it's okay."

"Glad to see you awake," I whispered back. I quietly lifted a visitor's chair from its spot under the television on the wall and moved it next to his bed.

"I should have listened to you. I should have told you."

"I agree, but no judgment. Wyatt, why don't you tell me now?"

He lifted a hand to wipe his eyes, wincing slightly.

I said, "It's not too late to do the right thing. A guy came to the bar, looking for Addison. Right?"

He closed his eyes and nodded. Finally, he started chatting. "I thought he was just some drunk creep. And he was. I mean, drunk. But he kept grabbing her and saying, 'We need to talk, we need to talk.' I was going to throw him out after he tried to follow her into the back room. But then he left."

"Did she know who he was?"

"No."

"So what did he want to talk about?"

"I don't know."

"But he left?"

"I thought so. She thought so. I went on break. I was in the staff room and I heard shouting, like, from the dock. So I went back there and—Addison just goes flying past me, like to the back door of the building and then outside. And I looked around, like, to see who she was yelling at. Then I saw that the fence was open. By the loading dock. It's where trucks pull up to unload kegs or whatever. There's a garage door back there, then a big concrete ledge, so if you're standing there, the back of the truck, it's kind of even with the ledge, right?"

I nodded. My chest was tight.

"And the gate isn't supposed to be open, because the fence is, I don't know, it's what keeps the dock from just being a giant concrete ledge for people to fall off."

Here Wyatt shook his head. He glanced over at his mother; she was still asleep.

"So I went over to it, to close it. But I looked down, like over the ledge. And he—the guy—he was down there, just splayed out—and blood—and he was just gone. I jumped down there and checked but there was just nothing."

"He was dead."

Wyatt nodded.

That wasn't true, though, because Mickey Dillman's official cause of death was drowning.

"I was freaking out. I texted Shane, like, 'Yo, there's a problem back here.' And he came back and—" He stopped talking as Gwen stirred in the corner, shuffling the blanket off her lap.

"Oh, hi," she said. "Wyatt, hon, how long was I asleep?"

"Just a few minutes," her son said. "Hey, could you go see if they have mints in the vending machine? I just still have this nasty-ass taste in my mouth."

Gwen got stiffly to her feet. "Sure." She met my eye. "You want anything? Your choices are pretzels and pretzels. Well, and possibly mints."

"Thanks, but I'm fine."

Gwen squeezed Wyatt's ankle as she went by his bed. "I'll be right back."

Wyatt's eyes were on the ceiling.

Once his mother was out of earshot, he said, "Shane said we had to get the guy—his body—out of there. Because the guy was coming, from the bank."

"The guy from the bank?"

"He comes every night, to get the deposit."

Oh.

"Big guy, blond?"

Wyatt nodded.

I didn't bother correcting him about Bo's provenance or Shane's involvement with someone like Vincent Pomp. "What did you do?"

"Well, I was worried about Addison. I mean, she ran out of there like she was not okay. And I didn't know what he did to her or— but Shane said, if I didn't help him with this guy, he'd tell the police I had something to do with it. So we put the guy in my truck and dumped him in the river. That was Shane's idea. After that, well, I didn't want to face my mother. I just wanted to lie low for a day or two. I dropped off my truck to get a new liner put in the bed, in case, you know, there was some trace of him back there. But then we heard on the TV that the guy was a cop. So what was I supposed to do then?"

I had some ideas; *do nothing* was not among them. "Tell me about the night you messaged Addison. I read the messages. So I know she asked you to go over to her house. But what happened when you did?"

"I don't know. I don't even know. She wasn't home. No one was there. So I was just sitting in the dark in the little screened-in porch thing she has, and I heard a commotion but I had no idea—it all just happened so fast, then. I was scared. And I thought—that she set me up, that she told them what had happened. I wasn't thinking straight, and I couldn't see what was going on—" He stopped talking as Gwen walked back into the room clutching no fewer than five different types of mints.

"You take your pick, baby."

"Thanks."

Gwen sat down in her chair in the corner. "Don't let me interrupt you talking."

"No, we're done," Wyatt said.

"We are?"

He nodded, his eyes pleading with me.

I dropped my voice to a whisper. "You need to tell the police about this. If for no other reason than to get ahead of whatever Shane or Addison might say to them. I'll have a friend of mine stop by. It's not up for debate." Then I stepped away from the bed and said, at a regular volume, "I'll check in with you two soon."

THIRTY-FIVE

Rick had emailed me the photos of Addison that he had saved on his phone, and when I got home I fired up my computer and spent some time looking through them. Brock Hazlett had said sexy too, but somehow I hadn't imagined the photos being like this. From what I knew of Addison, this was very unlike her—and yet, here she was. Young, fearless, self-possessed.

I'd pitched my list of crappy theories, but I mentally added to it now.

6. Multiple personalities.
7. Secret twin.
8. Evil doppelganger.
9. Something else I still wasn't seeing.

I couldn't sit still. I kept coming back to the image of her with the Pioneer box. It stuck out from the rest of them. She was fully clothed, for one thing. There was nothing sulky or sexy about her expression in this one. Instead, she was beaming, a pure, effervescent joy. Her face was bare, her hair pulled up in a half-pony, bangs swept to the side. She wore a purple-and-blue-plaid flannel unbuttoned over a white V-neck tee and she held the box on her lap, her elbows balanced on the top of it, hands clasped with her chin resting on her knuckles in a classic picture-day type of pose. The other images were all artfully composed selfies or, in the case of the nude rear shot, relied on the auto-timer. But this one had the look of a snapshot, her posture as if someone had just said, *Hey, say cheese.*

I heard a knock on my door—faint, so not a cop knock. I parted the curtains and saw Shelby's friend Miriam out there, a heavy backpack throwing her posture off-balance. I opened the door quickly, afraid there was more bad news. "Miriam, hey," I said, "is Shelby all right?"

"Oh, yeah, she's fine, she's at work," Miriam said as she stepped into my apartment. "She told me I could stop by your place. Hope that's okay."

"Sure, what's up? Are *you* okay?"

"Yeah, yeah. Well, other than this," she said, pulling up the hem of her sweater to reveal a massive tear in the hip area of her Spin-Spo leggings. "I have class so I don't have time to go home and change."

"Oh," I said. "Um, that's unfortunate. I'm sure I have another pair in your size here." I flipped through the leggings hanging on my garment rack. "Wait. Did those just spontaneously rip like that?"

Miriam tossed her backpack onto my sofa and nodded. "When I put them on this morning I thought they seemed, like, not as thick as they usually do. But then after my photo class I—sorry, TMI here—I went to the ladies' and, you know," she said, pantomiming pulling the leggings down over her hips, "and my thumb just like went right through it. So I was like, shoot, that's bad, and I was super gentle with them when I pulled them back up, but it just kept ripping and now I'm afraid that by this afternoon . . ."

"Yeah, I totally get it." I handed her a hanger with a pair of stone-colored black leggings. "Better?"

She tugged at the waistband. "Oh yeah, this is the good shit. Can I use your bathroom to change?"

"End of the hall, just like upstairs."

While she was changing, I stared at my rack of leggings. The whole reason Gail had hired me in the first place was that someone was knocking off her brand, making subpar leggings and selling them under the SpinSpo name. But my investigation, such as it was, hadn't turned up any counterfeit tights; they all bore the signature metallic squiggle on the hip and the brand's special tag. Sure, someone could fake that too but it would require a lot more effort.

As Miriam walked back down the hall, she said, "Your place is trippy. The paint colors? Did you do that?"

"No," I said, "it was like that when I moved in. So these busted leggings, let's see them. Was this the first time you wore them?"

She nodded, holding out the anthracite pair. "They looked great and the fit was perfect, as usual, but the fabric is just flimsier or something."

"Could it be just that color?"

"I have another pair of anthracite ones that I got at Goodwill," Miriam said, "and they're amazing. Well, except for the part about how I ripped the knee open riding my sister's hoverboard. Roxane? What's wrong?"

"Yeah, it's just—" I was studying the squiggle on the busted leggings, trying to figure out if it was any different than the rest of the pairs. They looked the same, felt the same, until I tugged on the fabric and then I noticed it too, the extra give that made them seem structurally unsound. I looked at the inside of the waistband, where the so-called inspirational sayings were printed. This one said: *Do more than just be.*

"Well, I gotta get back to campus, though, hopefully that's not rude?"

"No, no, do what you need to do. May your leggings stay in one piece."

"You're the best."

Do more than just be.

It had been painted on the cinder block wall of Gail's warehouse, or used to be; the mural artist I'd encountered when I met with her the first time was putting bold flowers over it. I scanned through my collection of leggings. They all had some type of inspirational saying screen-printed in the back of the waistband.

Be yourself. Everyone else is taken.

Strength is beautiful.

You're tougher than you look.

I sat down at my desk and pulled up my research file, clicking through my screenshots of social media posts where people had complained about the sudden decrease in quality of SpinSpo garments.

Ninety bucks later and my thumb goes through the waistband like a pair of drugstore pantyhose? Trash!

The fit and length are right-on as always but wtf is this new fabric?

I was so excited to try these but they aren't well made at all. I love supporting local/women-owned businesses but come on. At least take returns!!!

Every post was accompanied by an image demonstrating the rips in the seams, which ranged from an inch or so to the entire thigh region. They appeared to be different colors—though the black vs. anthracite was still a mystery to me—but every single post had something in common.

They all had *Do more than just be* printed along the inside back of the waistband.

I remembered what Brock Hazlett had mentioned in passing the day before, about reading an article on SpinSpo in the paper. I found it on the Alive's website, Gail's perfect blond hair and brilliant white smile, beaming in front of her brand-new floral mural. The headline read: "From Rip-off to Right-on: The Amazing SpinSpo Comeback."

I skimmed the article, my eyes sliding past the buzzwords and platitudes that seemed to make up most of my client's lexicon. But in the fourth paragraph, two words caught my attention.

Detective agency

> *To get to the bottom of the fraud, Spinnaker even resorted to hiring a local detective agency to investigate the influx of imposter leggings. "They did really wonderful work," Spinnaker said, "and were able to find the source and put a stop to it. I just want customers to know that they really can feel empowered to buy the brand. If, somehow, anyone still winds up purchasing a knockoff pair, which definitely shouldn't happen, but if it does—just hit us up on social media and we'll take care of you."*

Aside from the fact that I was hardly an agency, the quote got something else wrong—as far as I could tell, there was no source. Until Miriam stopped by, I didn't even think I'd gotten *any* of the counterfeit leggings.

Gail was jumping the gun in saying the situation was resolved. Unless they were all counterfeit, or none of them were.

Maybe Gail was using me *not* to track down a source of knockoff merchandise, but to get old or subpar merchandise off the shelf, so to speak? That would explain why she was so liberal in authorizing ten grand in purchases.

"Damn it, Gail," I said.

It wasn't hard to picture, really. The age of social media meant that everyone had a platform from which to share their opinion. The brand had exploded in popularity and then, just as quickly, the poor-quality leggings had entered the marketplace and the social media verdict was swift and harsh. So maybe, instead of issuing a mea culpa and trying to make things right, Gail had cried knock-off, the retail equivalent of *my account got hacked,* in an effort to make it appear that she was blameless.

I slammed my laptop closed and stalked into my room and flopped on the bed. The pillow on the side next to the door still smelled faintly like Tom, like his cologne and Coast soap and a little like bourbon and I pressed my face into it for a second, breathing it in. I had half a mind to go over to the SpinSpo ware-house and confront my client, but I suspected the conversation might end up with me not getting paid. So it was probably best to save that for a moment when I was feeling a bit more clear-headed.

I wondered what had made her do it. Cheaper materials? Faster labor? She was obviously fine with those things until it changed how other people saw the brand.

Perception was everything.

Not just in social media marketing, but everywhere.

Dating profiles.

The way we present ourselves to the world.

I dragged myself out of bed and returned to my computer to look at the images that Rick Dillman had sent me.

Addison in the shower.

Addison in bed, her hand provocatively placed.

These images were the way she wanted someone to see her; her agency was evident in every aspect of the pictures. Her pose, her makeup, the lighting, the angle.

The picture with the Pioneer box was different. She wasn't in control of this photo. This wasn't the curated glimpse into a life the way the other ones were. So why would she send this to Rick? Proof that she'd spent his three grand on what she said she'd spent it on?

I thought about what Jordy and Elise had said about her father, how he'd bought her an expensive mixer. That's probably what this was—photographic evidence of a gift from her dad, and nothing to do with Rick at all.

She was already stringing at least three guys along, asking for money under the guise of who knew what. So did it matter if she used Rick's money to buy a mixer or not?

It was almost like there were two Addisons. Two profiles, two personas? There was the quirky, mysterious Addison with her note-book poetry and cryptic social accounts. Then there was Addy Marie, confident, forward, willing to send pictures of herself to strangers for money.

I didn't know how to reconcile the two. Human beings were complicated, of course. It was possible to send a sexy photo to some-body even if you weren't ordinarily the selfie type; I was willing to bet that a large number of the sexy photos in cyberspace were taken by someone stepping outside of their comfort zone. Maybe Addison just needed money—how lucrative could deejaying at a shitty nightclub be? The maxed-out Visa might be evidence of that. Or maybe she was bored, or wanted to punish the jerk men of the world, or was lonely, wanted attention, wanted someone to make her feel special, even if the version of herself she was present-ing was fake.

There was a part of this story that I still wasn't getting.

I thought about Brock again. Secretly talking to his wife's child-hood friend, unbeknownst to both his wife and her friend, claim-ing that Addison had contacted him first. Why? Similar to the first Addison profile I'd found, Brock's BD E clearly wasn't a real profile—he'd even admitted that it existed only because he wanted to use BusPass along with his work pals.

What were the odds that Addison just happened to randomly contact him?

Not great, I realized.

Not only was it a coincidence too extreme to be believed, his profile was basically empty.

Maybe he was lying, and he'd contacted her first. I figured the odds were about even that this was what had happened.

Maybe Addison knew exactly who he was and wanted to rekindle their ten-year-old swim meet romance.

Or maybe Addison knew exactly who he was and just wanted to fuck with him.

Or fuck with her friend.

Addison as a psycho? It would certainly explain the seemingly split personality. And I had to admit that my brother's taste in women tended toward the psycho; in fact, Addison had already demonstrated herself to be a bit of one when she got Andrew fired from the hotel. But that was impulsive, childish behavior, not a full-scale offensive.

Then we had Corbin Janney on the other end of the spectrum, catfishing Addison. The odds seemed pretty much zero that she was being fooled by one person at the same time she was doing the fooling on the other side.

Much more likely that there was someone playing both sides against the middle, I realized.

I opened a new browser tab and tried to pull up Corbin Janney's Facebook page, but it had been deactivated since I looked at it the other day. I started clicking backward through my dozens of open browser tabs, for once grateful that my lack of housekeeping skills applied to my digital life as well. Finally I found it, still up from the other day when I'd first looked at it—the day of the SWAT situation at Addison's place. Once I'd discovered that Addison was active in the dating app, I'd almost forgotten about this teensy bit of usable evidence. Then all hell broke loose. I saved his profile picture to my desktop, then opened a new tab to do an image search.

If the image of Corbin had been posted anywhere else, this would show me where. For all I knew the man in the picture was an underwear model, but maybe I could finally catch a break.

"Oh, shit," I said when the results loaded.

I was looking at the "About the Instructors" page of the Blacklick Community Center's swim lessons schedule.

THIRTY-SIX

His name really was Corbin—his last name. Jamie Corbin. He was twenty-five, six foot something, dressed in nothing but some very small swim briefs that didn't even try to cover the sharp V of his hipbones. Water poured off of him but he made no effort to wipe it off even though he was holding a fluffy white towel. "Sure," he was saying, "ask away."

"Perhaps we could go sit in the lobby or something," I said. The natatorium was hot and splashy and loud and smelled like chlorine and something sour.

"Oh. Uh, yeah," Jamie Corbin said. "Lemme just get changed."

I went back out to the lobby of the rec center and got a Coke from the vending machine and sat at a small table next to a foggy window that looked over the pool. Jamie Corbin came out of the locker room dressed in warm-up pants and a tight white T-shirt, his collar-length hair still wet. I'd learned through my research before I drove out here that he had gone to USC on a partial swimming scholarship. He was just the rec center's most popular teacher but he seemed happy enough about it. "So hey, what are we talking about? You looking to enroll your little ones, or . . . ?"

"Um," I said. "You ever use the BusPass app?"

"That dating thing?"

I nodded.

"No, ma'am," he said. "I don't do that. Online dating. Never felt the need. Never had trouble meeting people in person. Why?"

"I suppose it helps that you're shirtless for your job."

He grinned at me.

I showed him Addison's picture. "You know who this is?"

He took my phone and gave the photo a thorough look. "No. Should I?"

"She's been talking to somebody online, through the app, who looks an awful lot like you."

Corbin shrugged. His posture was easy, unconcerned. "Not me. I'm engaged."

"Congratulations. How about him?" Now I showed him a picture of Brock.

"Well, yeah, that's what's-his-name. Mr. H. He's the facilities manager or something here."

"So you do know him?"

"Well, I know he's the guy you call when there's, like, an incident," he said, lowering his voice, "of a bodily fluid–type nature. Extension nine-one-one."

I almost laughed. "Ew."

"Yes. Ew."

"Other than such incidents," I said, "you ever talk to him?"

Corbin shook his head. "Nope. He's always stomping around with his walkie-talkie, all busy. Now, his *wife* on the other hand."

"Oh?"

"I mean, I don't really know her either. But I don't know how she wound up with a guy like Mr. H."

"Because she's pretty?"

"Yeah, she's just—look, I really shouldn't talk about her like that. He could probably get me fired."

"I promise I won't say a word to him."

Corbin leaned back in his chair. He was long and lean and his limbs seemed to be everywhere. "Yeah, she's pretty. She's had kids, two, I think? But you wouldn't know it. Then again, she's always up there," he said, pointing up the steps to the level that housed the fitness equipment, "grinding away on that treadmill. So no wonder she still looks twenty."

"You seem to know an awful lot about her, given that you don't really know her."

Finally, his chill demeanor seemed to thaw a little. "I don't want to get in trouble. Or her to get in trouble."

"And why would she get in trouble?"

He sat up, elbows on the table. "Just the lowest of low-key flirting, is all."

It was entirely possible that this was just his ego talking, that he assumed any woman who spoke to him was flirting with him. He probably assumed that I was. But while I was interested in something now, it wasn't him. "Oh?"

He scooted his chair closer to me so he was practically inches away from my ear. "Upstairs, on the fitness floor? There's windows that look over the pool. She's always on the same treadmill, right above the shallow end, which is where I teach her son's class. And she's always up there, the whole hour, just cranking on that thing. Sometimes I'll look up, and she's looking right at me. Not just looking out at the pool. Looking at me. Eye contact is sexy, you know that? But nothing ever happened, obviously. When she gets her kid after class she acts like the rest of the moms."

"Which is?"

"Impatient and kinda mad."

Before I could ask him more about that, I heard someone say my name.

I glanced over my shoulder and saw Jordy in the atrium, expression confused. "What are you doing here?"

Jamie Corbin, sensing trouble, got up and disappeared into the men's locker room. "Just following up on a couple things," I said. I got to my feet and went over to her. She was dressed for work—grey suit, ankle boots—and snowflakes dusted her hair and shoulders. "What are *you* doing here?"

"I'm just getting really worried," she said. "I mean, I don't know why she'd tell him she was with me if she wasn't."

I stared at her. "Elise?"

"Yeah."

I remembered what Brock had told me last night—that he and his wife had argued, she'd taken the kids to go stay with Jordy for a few days. "She's not staying with you?"

"No! My stepsister is, but Elise isn't. What the fuck is going on? Come on, let's go talk to him."

"Jordy, wait," I said.

She'd gone a few steps down a hallway toward the administrative offices of the rec center but she paused, tapping the toe of her boot on the tiles. I thought about Elise, cranking away on the treadmill with the only hour she really got to herself every week. I thought about her throwing out the fish she'd made for dinner the night I brought over fried chicken and nibbling on a tiny portion of kale. I thought about the ways in which she and Addison were complete opposites, and how that must have been infuriating, that her idiot husband had a thing for her friend, her messy, breezy, eccentric friend who'd made all the mistakes that Elise tried so hard not to make. That Addison was *still* the one men looked at, not her.

Then I thought about how she was the only connection to both Addison and the tattooed hunk that Addison thought she'd been talking to on BusPass all this time.

About Brock's claim that Elise had failed to mention her old friend had been missing for two weeks.

I'd assumed that he was lying. Or was so tuned out to his wife that her words straight-up hadn't registered.

But what if she actually hadn't said anything?

Jordy was staring at me. "What?"

Worry squeezed my chest. I said, "I just got a theory, and I don't think you're going to like it."

THIRTY-SEVEN

Brock Hazlett turned white as a sheet when I explained. He said, "You mean that I was really talking to my wife? She was pretending to be Addy?"

"I think it's possible," I said. We were in his office with the lights off—either he was hungover from last night or hiding from someone—Brock behind the desk, Jordy in a chair opposite him, and me leaning against the credenza below the windows. Beyond them, the parking lot was turning white again; the snow was falling quickly now. "But look, never mind that. I think that if Elise lied about where she was going, and if neither of you can reach her right now, she might be in a bad place. Mentally. And Brock, she's got your kids. So it's really important that we figure out where she might be."

"Oh my god," her husband murmured into his hands.

Jordy said, "But she—why—" Then she gave up on verbalizing it, just sort of flapped her long arms.

"I think Elise was pretending to be Addison on the app. I think she talked to a lot of different men through there, using pictures of the real Addison, which she got from Addison herself—under the guise of the guy she called Corbin Janney, but who's really named Jamie Corbin and he's your son's swim teacher."

Brock slapped the desk so hard the cold coffee in his mug rippled.

"And one of those men happened to be related to a Columbus police officer, who took it very personally that his cousin was being jerked around this way. So he launched a bit of an investigation to figure out who she was, and because"—I paused to make air quotes—"'*Addy*' sent a picture of herself at the club, he succeeded. And he went there to confront her about it. Except he found the real Addison, who didn't know anything about it. And, by the way, he's dead."

"This is so messed up. It's just—but she—she wanted to help me pay you. Why would she do that?" Jordy's voice was tight.

For the same reason that Gail Spinnaker had paid me to prove something unprovable. "Because the only thing that matters is how it appears."

The three of us stared at each other.

"Addison took her suitcase when she left. But she didn't tell you guys, her best friends, where she was going. She didn't tell her dad. Or her roommate."

"But maybe she told the guy, this Corbin guy," Jordy said. "Which means she did tell Elise, right?"

I nodded. "Brock, did your wife take her computer?"

The traffic was heavy but the Hazletts lived just around the corner from the rec center. The three of us drove separately, a convoy of big, dark vehicles moving through the snow. Brock opened the front door and briefly paused to wipe his boots on the doormat. But then he looked down and seemed to realize that the status quo in his home had changed. He gave up and tracked the snow down the linoleum and Jordy and I did the same. "Computer's here," Brock said, pointing to the brand-new iMac in a corner of the living room. "But she doesn't use it much. She has an iPad she's always reading on."

Another dawning flickered through his face as he realized that his wife had probably not just been *reading* on her iPad.

I wondered how many times they'd sat in the same room, communicating through "Addy."

The thought gave me chills.

I said, "If she ever signed into it using the same log-in as her iPad, some of her history might be saved in the browser."

Jordy nodded and stabbed at the space bar to wake the computer up.

"Brock, you check Elise's things in her bedroom. I'll check the basement."

"What am I looking for?"

"I don't know," I admitted.

I ran down the basement steps and into Elise's "sanctuary." The mystery of how she'd managed to afford such a well-appointed yoga space in her house seemed to be solved. I wondered how much money in total she'd gotten on "Addy's" behalf. Five grand? Ten? I opened the desk's only drawer and found only a manila folder full of user guides and warranty info for various appliances in the house, with receipts stapled to each.

The fancy refrigerator had been three thousand alone.

The new Mac upstairs was twenty-one hundred.

The washer and dryer were nine hundred apiece.

I put the folder back and kept looking, but the room yielded no secrets.

Somewhere else in the house, I heard Brock yell, "Fucking *fuck*."

Jordy's long strides echoed on the floor above me. "Did you find something?"

I left Elise's sanctuary and took the steps two at a time. When I got to the kitchen, Brock and Jordy were both staring at a black case, open on the counter between them.

Brock said, "She took my gun."

His expression was deadly serious.

"I'm gonna kill her—"

"No, nobody's killing anyone—"

He shoved me out of the way as he headed toward the front door.

"Nope, no, Brock, back to the kitchen," I said. I squeezed by him to block his exit. "We need to take a minute and think about this, not just go out on a rampage, okay?"

My own handgun was holstered at the small of my back, and it dug into my spine as I leaned against the front door.

"Get out of the way."

I shook my head. "Where are you going to go?"

He was sweating, breathing hard. But he blinked and took a step back. "I don't know."

"Exactly. We need to think about this."

Brock hung his head.

"I know this is a lot. And hopefully, I'm just wrong, and you can go back to being pissed off at me. That's the best-case scenario. Worst case—well, where might she go?"

"Her sister?" Jordy said. "In Tampa?"

Brock shook his head. "No, I texted her this morning. To ask if Elise had talked to her since Sunday. I was just looking for a way to . . . I don't know . . . an idea to get back in her good graces. But anyway, Meg said she hadn't heard from her in a while."

"Other siblings?"

"No, just the one."

"Her parents?"

"They're on the great American road trip in that stupid fucking RV," Brock said.

I tapped the edge of the counter as a thought came into focus.

"Jordy, do you remember anything else Addison said about BusPass Guy? Where he lived, where he worked, anything?"

She scrubbed a hand over her face. "She said he traveled a lot. A photographer, or art director? Something like that. He was working in Detroit, temporarily, she said. But that was months ago."

"Detroit?" Brock paced the length of the room, his muddy boots still squeaking on the floor.

"Does Elise know anyone in Detroit?"

"I doubt it."

"Jordy, what else did Addison say about BusPass Guy?"

"He'd been in the Air Force? He hates cilantro?"

"This isn't helping," Brock snapped.

"Hey, let her talk. You don't know what's going to help."

"She's got my boys with her. She has my *gun*. What if there isn't time to talk about cilantro?"

Jordy grabbed my elbow. "She showed me this place on Airbnb. Like six months ago, maybe longer. I think she was saying that it's his. That he rents it out while he's gone."

I remembered her mentioning the tiny house thing when we first met. "Where?"

She shook her head. "It was outside the city. Like, somewhere rural, some random place. It was, like, a shipping container. This place had a huge window on one end and a yellow mural on one wall that you could see from the outside." Then her face fell. "But that could be just a picture. It doesn't mean anything."

"Didn't Elise spend summers in Hocking Hills when she was growing up?" Brock said.

The three of us stared at each other.

"How many yellow-muraled shipping container rentals could there be?" I said, already pulling up Airbnb on my phone.

As it turned out, only one. "But it doesn't give an address or anything," Jordy said. "Just a green dot over the general area."

She held up my phone and I glanced quickly at it as I backed out of the driveway. She was right; rather than a pinpoint location, it showed a mint-colored circle over an area to the south-southeast of Lake Logan in the Hocking Hills area.

"Is there a key? How big is the green area?"

She tapped and zoomed. "Okay, if this is five hundred meters," she said, holding her thumb and index fingers about an inch apart, "then that means the green part is, what, a thousand meters? Er, a kilometer?"

"Okay, so about a half a mile," I said. I gripped the steering wheel as I turned left out of the Hazletts' subdivision, the snow crunching under my tires.

From the backseat, Brock groaned. "A half a mile? That's—how many streets is that going to be? There could be hundreds of houses."

I shook my head. "Not out there. But you're right, a half-mile radius is less than ideal." I sped up a little to make it through a yellow light. "But, it's also a lot smaller than, well, however far Elise could get in two days."

Jordy was fidgeting beside me, irritated. "I can't believe you," she muttered. "Two days without hearing from her and you didn't even think it was weird."

"She was fucking *pissed* at me! She does this all the time, okay? I know you think that I'm a big dummy and Elise is Miss Perfect but you don't know the half of it."

That made her go quiet. "You're right."

I called Tom from the road. "Hi, you're on speakerphone."

"Uh, hi, I got your message about Wyatt—"

"Tom, sorry for interrupting you. But I'm here with Addison's friend Jordy, and another friend's husband, Brock. We have a bit of a situation."

I explained the situation as concisely as I could.

"We're on 33 now, leaving Blacklick," I said. "But a half-mile radius isn't great. Especially not in the snow, plus those hills. Do you know anyone in Logan? Or the Hocking County sheriff's department? Maybe someone would know exactly where this house is."

Tom was quiet for a bit. "Can you take me off speaker for a sec?"

"Not really," I said. "I don't know how to do that in here yet."

He sighed. "Well, you know what I'm going to say."

"I know. That I'm impulsive and reckless and should leave a rescue operation to the police entirely."

"Yes."

"Logan probably has all of six patrol cops working at any given time, and the roads are bad. They're going to be busy. And the sheriff's department is probably spread even thinner, given the size of Hocking County. And we don't know that she's there."

I gritted my teeth as I changed lanes and various lights in my dashboard flashed either outrage or encouragement, but the fishtail never came.

"You don't know, but obviously you think she is."

"She has their kids, Tom," I said. "It's not a wait-around-and-see type of thing. Would you rather her husband goes off half-cocked?" I met Brock's eyes in the rearview and winked. "Because he'll do it."

"Definitely," Brock added.

"Send me the link to this place," Tom said. "I'll see what I can find out."

"Thank you, Tom."

"Hey. Be careful."

"I will."

"I mean it."

"I know."

He sighed. "I'll call you back when I have something."

I punched the button on my steering wheel that I thought was supposed to end the call and said to Jordy, "Copy the link to the Airbnb and open my email."

"Okay."

"Start a new message and type T-H-E-I and it should come up."

"Theitker at columbuspolice dot org?"

"That's him. Send the link."

Jordy said, "Who is that?"

"Someone who always comes through," I said.

She curled up against the door frame and didn't say anything else.

By four o'clock, we'd gone twenty-six miles in an hour. The snow was still falling fluffy and thick, and what was left of the light was going now too. The sky was asphalt wrapped in gauze. We were one vehicle in a long string of blinking red brake lights; it got worse the farther south and east we went, both because of the weather and because Route 33 constricted to only two lanes and began to curve over and around the Hocking Hills area's namesake landscape. Brock kept calling Elise, over and over, the tinny sound of five rings then the start of her chipper voice mail intro drifting from the backseat to serve as the soundtrack for our trip. Jordy had her head tucked into her collarbone, her long ponytail partly covering her face. I might've thought she was asleep except for the anxious fidgeting of her hands in her lap.

When my phone rang—Tom's name filling the screen in my dash—all three of us jumped. I fumbled with the buttons on the steering wheel until I successfully answered his call.

"Roxane, hang on, I'm getting someone else on the line."

I waited through a series of beeps.

"Brian, Roxane, you both still there?"

"Yes," I said.

"Yes," a gruff male voice said.

"Great. Brian's with the Hocking County sheriff, okay? He knows the place you're talking about."

Brock grabbed the back of my seat.

"Yeah, it's on a property out Starr Route Road, right about half-way between 664 and 180," the deputy said. "Six or seven small cabins on the parcel, which is probably close to two hundred acres."

"Fuck," Jordy said.

"Pardon?" the deputy said through the line.

"Um, never mind," I said. "Okay, so can you give me the address?"

"There's nobody up there, ma'am, I promise you that."

I saw Brock's shoulders dip in the mirror.

"How do you know?"

"Road's damn near impassable in weather like this, and I actually just drove through there and I can tell you there aren't even tracks up the driveway."

That didn't exactly seem definitive. "Is there more than one way to get there? Another driveway?"

"Roxane," Tom said. "You said it was just a hunch."

I shook my head—at him, at the traffic, at everything. Beside me, Jordy had her own phone out and was comparing it to something on mine. Then she looked up, her eyes bright with something like excitement.

"Um, thanks anyway," I said, and hung up.

"Two hundred acres," Jordy said. "Sounds like a lot, but it's less than this stupid green circle. About half the size, okay?"

"How do you know that?"

"My job," she said. "Corporate real estate."

"Hey, look at you."

"So anyway, Starr Route Road, midway between 180 and 664—those are here and here," she said, pointing. "So midway between them is here, which is at the lower middle of this circle. So now I'm looking at the Hocking County property lines—Brock. Phone. Give it." Jordy held a hand into the backseat. "I need another screen."

He obliged.

Jordy leaned forward, all three of our phones spread out over the glove box. She tapped and pinched and typed for a few minutes and Brock and I stayed quiet.

Finally, she clapped her hands together.

"I found it," she said. "Right here. This is the only property that meets all the criteria. And besides the driveway off of Starr Route Road, there are at least two other ways in."

THIRTY-EIGHT

By the time we got to Starr Route Road, it was night. The road itself was barely visible under the white blanket that had fallen over the past few hours, so I had to rely on the curve of the trees to really see where it went. The ride had been white-knuckle to say the least. I was growing fonder of the Range Rover, though; its stupid-expensive tires held their own.

"Okay, we're almost there," Jordy said as we crept past a log cabin encircled by a sagging split-rail fence. "This is going to be the driveway that guy was talking about." She wiped the fog off her window with the sleeve of her coat. "It goes up through the middle, and there are cabins on each side. We could go up this way. But the place we're going is almost all the way up the hill. So we'd be visible the entire way."

"What are the other options?"

"There's another road up here. It's probably gravel, or dirt. Do you think we can make it up a hill on that?"

"To be honest, I don't know if that matters," I said, "because it's under at least eight inches of snow."

Jordy glanced into the backseat. "Brock?"

I looked at him in my mirror, but his face was shrouded in shadow.

"Go the back way."

Half a mile later, a small gap in the trees opened up to the right. "This it?" I said.

My navigator nodded. "It's going to cut sharply to the right, then start up the hill."

I eased into the turn. The road was claustrophobically narrow, barely wider than my vehicle. "I guess let's hope no one is coming down."

"I suspect that won't be an issue."

I killed the high-beams in favor of the running lights once I discovered just how steep the incline was. I'd long forgotten everything I learned in geometry but the angle was extreme enough for gravity to tug on the back end of the car—if I let off the gas, we began a downward slide—and the headlights pointed up at the blinding snow rather than at the road.

My palms were sweaty as we crested the hill. The top of it was ridged with trees so heavy with snow and ice that some of them drooped like willows. With the engine no longer straining, things were eerily quiet.

Jordy tapped her window. "I see it. The shipping container."

It was up ahead to the right, angled off the gravel road to face away from us. But the large window Jordy had mentioned cast a yellowish glow onto the snow out in front of it; the lights were on.

There was no sign that a vehicle had been up here today. The snow on the driveway was undisturbed.

Brock smacked the back of my seat. I jumped but didn't say anything; I figured he was entitled to be angry.

I closed my eyes and listened to a faint whining sound. We were idling in place, but the sound was getting louder. "Do you hear that?" I said.

Jordy wiped off her window again and peered out. "Are those headlights?"

I looked. Down through the trees, something was moving.

Behind me, Brock scooted over to the other side of the car and looked out.

Whatever the movement had been, it seemed to stop. Either that, or the headlights had dipped below our sightline. The whining sound got louder still.

None of us even took a breath for what felt like an eternity.

Then the movement started again as what was clearly a small SUV struggled up the driveway.

"That's her. That's Elise."

Before I could stop him, Brock dove out of the vehicle and stumbled through the deep snow. In his bright green and black coat, he stood out from the snow as if a spotlight were on him.

The SUV stopped.

Brock was still moving toward it, hobbling through the snow with exaggerated steps.

"She's going to turn back," I muttered.

Jordy opened her door and started out too.

"No," I said. "She can't see us back here."

I opened my door and stood halfway up, sticking my head outside. The air was wet and cold. "Brock," I whisper-shouted, "come back here."

He didn't seem to hear me, just continued galumphing through the snow.

All at once, the headlights of Elise's vehicle arced away from him as she spun awkwardly in reverse and started back down the driveway.

"Brock, get in," I shouted. He froze in place, his hands outstretched.

I sat back down in the driver's seat and closed the door and stomped on the gas.

Once Brock was back inside the Range Rover, I got us turned around and said, "Buckle up, guys. I don't think this is going to be fun."

"We could go down the main driveway this time," Jordy said.

I shook my head. "It's less steep, but it's longer. We can get down faster going back the way we came. Plus she won't know that we're behind her. For all she knows, Brock Ubered here."

He was brushing snow off his jeans in the backseat with his bare hands instead of buckling his seat belt.

"Brock."

"I'm fine."

Jordy turned around and punched him in the arm. "Buckle your damn belt."

"Was she by herself in the car?"

"It looked like the passenger seat was down," he said. "It just looked like an empty space. I don't know."

The gravel road seemed steeper and narrower and rockier on the way down. The ground disappeared into a murky black tunnel a few yards in front of us. Jaw clenched, I eased off the brake and down we went, bouncing off of ruts and branches on the ground as the Range Rover locked into the tracks we'd made in the snow on the way up. It had felt like we spent hours getting up to the top of the hill, but the reverse trip was over in a flash.

Jordy said, "Roxane, remember the hairpin—"

I saw it just as she said it, the sharp bend in the path that we'd made shortly after turning onto the gravel from Starr Route Road. I racked the wheel to the left—too far—and clipped some low-hanging tree branches with my side mirror, turned the other way, skidding back across the road and almost into the trees on the other side before I finally got a grip and eased us to a stop.

"—turn," Jordy finished.

I tried to laugh, blood pounding in my ears.

We sat quietly for a second, looking for signs of Elise's SUV coming down the main driveway. I rolled my window down and heard the whine of tires spinning against the ice. Brock reached for his door handle again and I employed the child locks. "I'm sorry," I said, "but you're not getting out of the car again."

"She's stuck. She isn't going anywhere."

But as he said it, the unseen SUV lurched its way out of the snow and continued down the hill, headlights dancing through the trees like the aurora borealis.

I crept the Range Rover forward until the nose was sticking out onto Starr Route Road. In the time since we'd turned up the gravel driveway, the snow had filled in the tracks we'd made.

It was almost peaceful out here. Almost.

Brock said, "What are we going to do?"

"Jordy, what happens if you go that way?" I pointed to the right from our position in the mouth of the gravel road.

"Nothing," she said as she thumbed the map on her phone. "Nothing for about twenty miles. So if I had to guess which way she was going to go, I'd pick left. Back to 33."

I thought about it. I had to agree. I didn't want either of our vehicles to careen through the snow anymore, which meant preventing Elise from turning. I drove back toward the main driveway, my window still down. The jerky whine of her vehicle told me it was still pretty far up the incline. As I pulled around the corner, I realized the dancing lights weren't just from Elise's vehicle, but from two Hocking County sheriff's patrol cars.

I braked gently and pulled to a stop alongside one.

"I hope you're Roxane and not the other one," the guy said. "Brian Mahaney. Heitker's buddy."

"Hi."

"I thought I told you the road was impassable."

"You also told me nobody's been up there," I said, "so I think we're even. She's coming down."

"I gathered. You keep moving, and we'll block the end of the driveway so she can't get out."

"She probably has kids with her," I said, gesturing to my backseat. "His kids, and possibly another woman. So just, I don't know, don't do anything permanent."

The deputy nodded and motioned me to move past the sheriff's cars.

Meanwhile, Elise's lights were getting closer.

The two deputies coasted forward. Mahaney stopped at a forty-five-degree angle on my side of the driveway, and the other went past, spun around, and parked opposite the first car so that they made a V pointing at the driveway.

A disembodied bullhorn intoned, "Begin braking now. Your speed is unsafe."

The bouncing headlights got closer and closer and it became pretty clear that she wasn't going to stop.

"Oh god," I said.

Elise was speeding up.

I laid on my horn and stuck my head out the window. "Get out of the way, guys, she's not stopping."

The passenger door of Mahaney's car opened and he dropped into the ditch just as Elise crashed into the noses of both cruisers, knocking them apart almost gently. Mahaney popped up but the deputy in the other car let out a wail in the dark. Elise shot across the road, through a rusting, snow-covered guardrail, and down a slight embankment. One of the headlights went dark but the car was still moving.

"Goddammit." I pulled a jerky turn and rolled down the passenger window. Mahaney was crouched over the other deputy, who was splayed in the snow, a misty red around his legs. Mahaney spoke urgently into the mic clipped to his lapel. "How can I help?" I called.

He stabbed the air in the direction of the crunched-up guardrail. "Someone needs to stop her."

Thusly deputized, I rammed the Range Rover through the opening in the guardrail. Its jagged edges squealed against the passenger side of the vehicle and Jordy clutched my arm as we slid down the embankment until it gave way to a snowy field fringed with more trees along an elevated ridge. Elise's SUV was still motoring away from us, but slower now.

"What is she doing?" Jordy said.

"Is there a road over there?"

"Um, yes, it looks like there's one on the other side of the—oh shit shit shit there's a pond or a lake or something right in front of her."

THIRTY-NINE

Elise's SUV stopped, skidded sideways. The snow under her tires seemed to dissolve as the ice below it cracked.

I punched the gas and we jetted toward it. There were signs, I could see now, cautioning about the pond. I stopped just shy of them and the three of us jumped out of the car in unison.

The back of the SUV was sinking.

Brock sprinted toward the car as two small faces appeared in the back window.

"What do we do? What do we do?" Jordy gasped, clutching my arm again.

"Rope," I said. "Blankets." I knew I'd seen both items recently. I threw open the back gate of the Range Rover and pawed through the crap I had back there. "Here." I seized the coil of nylon rope that definitely wasn't mine and thanked that sketchy individual who'd lost the vehicle to the impound lot.

The SUV driver's side door opened and Elise tumbled out, her boots skidding.

As Brock lay down on the ice and shouted for his small son to put his window down, Elise stared—at the car, at me, her features hard and still.

I leaned to the side to survey the situation. Brock was lying on the ice, lifting one of his sons out through the window. The other little boy was safely on solid ground, his face bright red and streaked with tears, his tiny, exposed hands balled into fists at his sides.

Elise turned and headed the opposite way toward the ridge.

"Jordy, get him. Put him in the car."

She nodded and ran over to the kid. I grabbed the pile of blankets and rope and went down closer to the car. The older of the two Hazlett kids was standing on the edge of the frozen pond and I scooped him up and handed him up to Jordy. I called, "Brock, what are you doing?"

"Addy's in the front. She doesn't look too good—shit," he said. The passenger side of the car plunged into the pond, taking Brock with it.

"Fuck fuck fuck," I heard myself mutter. I walked as close to the edge of the pond as I could without stepping on it and tossed the rope toward the car. "Brock?"

"Oh, Jesus," he said through chattering teeth. "I got it. I got it. But Addy. She's not opening the door—"

I heaved myself up the slight incline that ringed the pond and tied the opposite end of the rope around the base of a fir tree into what I remembered was a sturdy knot, something my father had taught me when I was a kid; I tested it by yanking on it as hard as I could and it held. From this vantage point I could see Elise's pink soft-shell jacket nearing the top of the ridge directly across from my vehicle. Brock was lying on top of the ice again, his clothes soaked through. Addison was in the front seat of the sinking SUV, reclined, still. The icy water was up to the bottom of her window now. But I saw a puff of air as she breathed through her mouth.

I unholstered my gun. "Brock, stay down, and cover your ears, okay?"

He looked at me. "Are you a good shot?"

"The car has three windows on this side. I just need to hit one of them. Can I do this?"

"Go. Go."

I dropped to one knee in the snow and aimed as steadily as I could and fired.

My shot sailed through the top third of Addison's window, leaving a small hole in its wake. Brock used his elbow to break the rest of the glass; as soon as he did, water began pouring into the car and Addison stirred.

"Come on, hon," Brock said. From his position on the ice, he slid his hands under her armpits and pulled just as the ice cracked under the driver's side and the entire vehicle began to sink in earnest now. Addison's hips cleared the window and she flopped onto the ice next to Brock, her head lolling. "What's wrong with her? I don't—"

"Brock, just grab the rope."

He patted the ice almost gently, like he didn't know what it was. Then he started to tie the end of it to Addison's belt.

"No, grab it—Brock—"

I climbed the bank again and waved in the direction of my car, hoping Jordy was watching. She flicked the headlights and started driving toward us. I could no longer see Elise's pink coat, but there wasn't time to worry about where she'd gone. Brock's teeth were chattering, his eyes slitted. Jordy stopped the Range Rover a few yards away and ran over to me.

"What do I do?"

"We have to pull them over. The ice will break if anyone stands on it. Brock," I called, "grab Addison's hand."

He patted the ice near her knee. "I miss you," he mumbled.

"Oh my god," Jordy whispered.

Brock and Addison were only four or five yards away from the edge of the pond, but there might as well have been an ocean between us.

Addison opened her eyes now. They were red and puffy, her eyelashes matted together. But she looked at me and seemed to understand something. She hooked one wrist through the loop on the shoulder of his coat.

"Jordy, you're probably stronger than me but I'm heavier, so get in front of me—"

We pulled on the rope in unison, the world's most dire game of tug-of-war.

Addison slid a few inches across the ice.

"Pull," I said.

We pulled.

"Pull," I said.

We pulled.

Addison's hips were almost to the edge of the pond.

"Pull," I said.

We pulled. Jordy burst into tears, spots of blood appearing on the snow before her as her palms tore against the rope. I scrambled down to the water and grabbed Addison by the collar of her coat and dragged her safely away from the water.

Brock was still lying there, arms stretched out, his feet kicking gently as if he was still in the water. "Brock. Come on. Come on."

I lay down on the snow. I was not entirely sure where the line between ground and water fell. But I grabbed his coat and pulled him toward me an inch at a time. Maybe less. Maybe I wasn't even pulling anymore. My eyes were streaming. I'd told Tom I'd be careful, and I didn't think this counted as careful.

"I'm sorry," I heard myself mumble.

The rope felt loose in my hands, slack and wet. And I was so cold. When had it gotten so cold?

Suddenly someone gripped my shoulders, jerking me back.

A child's voice: "Mommy—"

Then a flash of bright pink, the terrible cracking of the ice as the pond became a gaping mouth full of jagged, frozen teeth.

"Elise," Brock whispered. He was next to me on the ground now, reaching one trembling hand out to the water. "You came back."

But she was sinking, sinking slowly in a wash of white teeth and blue lips and pink, until there was nothing left except the cold.

FORTY

For a second I thought I was back in Wyatt Achebe's hospital room. But then I opened my eyes and realized I was in my own—I was horizontal, under what felt like ten pounds of blankets.

"Hey, you," Tom said.

His fingers laced through mine.

I cleared my throat but no sound came out when I tried to talk.

I closed my eyes again.

The next time I opened them, it appeared to be day and most of the blankets were gone and the visitor's chair was empty and I was desperately thirsty. I sat up on one elbow and looked around for my coat, my phone, anything.

Then the door swung open and Jordy came in, sipping from a paper cup of coffee.

"Hi," I croaked.

She almost spilled the coffee. "You," she said. But she didn't say anything else.

"What happened?"

"You don't remember?"

I thought about that. I remembered Brock paddling his feet against the ice. I remembered a piercing, startling cold. "I guess not."

I closed my eyes again.

The sun cast strips of light from the dusty mini blinds onto the foot of my bed when I opened my eyes for real. Jordy was beside me now, doing a crossword. She had white bandages wrapped around both palms. She glanced up at me, saw that I was awake, and broke into a big smile. "Good morning, badass," she said.

"Is Brock okay? And the boys?"

She nodded and set down her newspaper. "Hypothermia, same as you. But seeing as he kept his head above the water, he's fine. And the boys are perfect. Not a scratch."

I pointed at my bed. "Can this sit up or something?"

"Sure, sure."

Jordy pulled a beige remote out from a tangle of wires below my bed and fiddled with the buttons until I was halfway sitting.

"Addison?"

Another nod, this one a little more hesitant. "She has pneumonia. Which is why she was so out of it, I guess. But she's going to be okay too."

I had a flash of Elise's perfect white teeth, her pink coat, blue lips. I said, "Did she pull me out of the water?"

"Addison?"

"Elise."

Jordy's mouth flattened into a thin line. "What do you mean?"

"Someone grabbed my shoulders, and then I saw her—the coat."

She rubbed her eyes, which were already raw. "She was in the water. But, um, she was gone by the time they brought her here. The ice must have broken when she was running away. I can't—I just can't believe any of this."

I couldn't imagine what it must be like, being in Jordy's shoes. I said, "I saw her on the other side of the pond, but then she came back."

My memory was hazy but somehow firm, like a mountain shrouded in fog. I was certain that Elise had come back to the pond. I saw her sprinting toward the ridge, and then I'd lost sight of her.

Until I heard her small son's voice, clear and scared in the dark, and I saw her in the water, framed by the jagged ice in front of me.

Jordy's features pinched. "It was all happening so fast, and I was focused on Addy and the boys . . . look, I'm barely keeping it together right now."

"Of course. I thought—never mind."

We sat in silence for a while.

"There was a note," she said. "In the shipping container. It was— she was—something was very wrong. I think she was unhappy for a really long time. But none of this was supposed to happen."

"Where were they?" I said. "Where were they coming from when we saw her pull into the driveway?"

"She was trying to come here, to the hospital, for Addison," Jordy said. Her eyes got shiny. "She wrote that she was going to leave Addison and the boys here and then go—end things. But the hospital told us that 664 was shut down because of a wreck for most of the afternoon and evening. So it seems like she must have turned around to go back. I don't think she wanted anyone else to get hurt."

I didn't believe that. Not with what she'd done to Wyatt. We'd never know what she was thinking when she made that phone call as soon as Wyatt said he'd arrived at Addison's house. If she considered the implications of crying wolf from the comfort of her house in Blacklick, miles away, claiming that an armed black man was terrorizing someone. If her privilege led her to think that he'd just get in trouble, not get shot.

Or if she knew exactly what she was doing.

Either way, it was irredeemable.

But she'd pulled me out of the water. Why would she do that?

I closed my eyes, suddenly exhausted again.

———

When Brian Mahaney came by to see me in the hospital, he said that the other deputy had a broken leg but would be fine. "Damn lucky," he said. "Everyone, really."

I supposed that was true on some level. On another, Addison and Jordy, Brock and his kids—there was no coming back from this, not all the way. I said, "Was Elise still alive when they got her out of the water?"

"Barely. That ice cracked like a candy shell, the whole thing tore up. There wouldn't have been anything for her to hold onto."

"Where was she?"

"What do you mean?"

"How far out into the pond?"

He looked at me, quizzically. "Right by the car," he said. "Whole thing's no more than twenty feet across."

In my memory, the pond had been impossibly wide. But then again, it felt like we'd been pulling on that rope for hours when everything had really gone down in a matter of seconds. Time and distance had expanded, twisted, stretched, fell back on itself.

I was sure of what I saw, though. More sure than I'd ever been of anything.

Mahaney asked if he could do anything for me and I said he could get me a copy of Elise's note.

"Is that a good idea?" he said.

I said, "It's *an* idea."

Either he found this argument compelling, or I looked too pathetic to say no to. A while later, Tom came back in and sat down next to me and lay a manila envelope on my lap. "Brian asked me to give this to you."

"Thanks."

He was drinking bad hospital coffee and I was drinking bitter hospital tea. My body temperature was, allegedly, back to normal.

But I couldn't seem to feel warm. "He also asked if you'd mind if he gave you a call sometime."

"To reminisce about this horror show?"

"I think he had other ideas in mind. I told him you were attached."

I shook my head.

"Speaking of, I called Catherine but—"

"She said I'm a narcissist and she regrets I didn't narcissistically drown?"

Tom's eyebrows went up. "But she didn't answer. Has she been here?"

I shook my head.

"She's not going to come. So you can tell Brian I'm not attached, but I'm also never answering my phone again and fully intend to die alone, so."

Tom looked a little bewildered.

"Sorry. I'm still working through some things."

"Hey, I get it."

"Distract me. Give me some good news."

"Your pal Wyatt made a statement, about Mickey Dillman."

I sighed. "That's good. Unless it means he violated his parole."

"He did."

Maybe it wasn't so good, then.

"He's cooperating though. Against Shane Resznik, who's of major interest to the organized crime bureau."

"He turned up?"

Tom nodded. "He went home. His girlfriend finked on him."

I laughed. It hurt my ribs and my ears. "Good for her."

"Hopefully he'll cooperate re: Vincent Pomp. But that's going to take a bit longer to settle. That's confidential, by the way."

"Don't worry, my days of halfway trusting someone like Vincent Pomp are over."

I wondered if my days of trusting anyone were over. I hoped not, but at the moment it sure felt like it.

Tom glanced down at the envelope. "What's in there?"

"Oh," I said, my stomach twisting, "nothing, just some paperwork."

I waited until he was gone to read it.

> *Brock,*
>
> *I suppose you want to know why.*
>
> *I don't have to tell you, but I want you to know why too.*
>
> *Remember the first time we made love? We were sixteen, in my parents' waterbed. You said it wouldn't hurt but it did, a lot, and I thought there was something noble about not letting on. It was winter, like now. The snow outside made a sound like shhhhhhhhhhhhhh hhhhhhhh shhhhhhhhhhhhhhhhhhhhhhhhh.*
>
> *Then you told me about your first time, with her, and you ruined everything.*
>
> *Every time she opened her mouth all I could think about was her closing her lips around your cock. Then, and now. Knowing that she knows what I have, that she's had what I have. I thought it would go away if I got everything. Your babies, your name. You swore you never thought about her again, not after we got together. But I'm not an idiot. I have eyes. I see the way you look at her. Like she's still a mystery to you. Then how you look at me, like you've solved the mystery already and forgot you ever wondered at all.*
>
> *Meanwhile, I did everything for you. I became the*

*thing you needed. I stayed ninety-five pounds and
Brazilian waxed, tight pussy and polite, good cook,
hostess chauffeur, perfect mom, well-dressed and
WHY? So you can make me look like a fool? Sit across
the table from me chatting with her? Say, "Oh just
playing Words with Friends" when I ask you what
you're doing?*

You never ask me what I'm doing.

*God knows you don't notice anything, either. Oh,
the secrets I can keep! Meanwhile, you're so intrigued
by her. Your word. INTRIGUED. She's about as
mysterious as a world almanac, Brock. She thinks she
has secrets, but she's an open book, she just lays it out,
heart on sleeve, and that's supposed to be VULNER-
ABLE? It's fucking weak. She gives it all away, up
front, but pretends she's deep just because she got a
tattoo and is "in recovery" from some eating disorder
she invented to make herself sound special?*

*Being a woman is an eating disorder! Doesn't she
know that everyone is hungry?*

*It's snowing now like that day you screwed me for
the first time. It doesn't sound like shhhhhhhhhhhhh-
hhhhhh anymore. More like screaming.*

*I thought it was an old wives' tale, that you could
catch your death from being out in the cold. But
maybe it isn't. Her breathing sounds wet. Her car
wouldn't even make it up the hill. Stupid little red
car. Exactly the kind of car someone like that would
drive.*

Inconsequential.

*Why would you love someone inconsequential
instead of me?*

*I could lie down in the snow and just go to sleep. I
might. I thought I wanted to hurt her, but now I just
want to be free. Of her, of them, of you. I just want
quiet. I want to slip away into the quiet. I'm taking
her to the hospital. I can't listen to this death rattle
anymore. I'm leaving the boys there too. Then I'm
disappearing—so who's the mystery now?*

She'd left the note on her iPad in the tiny house, along with a
digital trail that confirmed everything I'd suspected. Thousands of
emails between Addison and "Corbin," including dozens in the aftermath of the incident at Nightshade. Addison's fear was obvious,
as was her desire for someone to tell her everything was going to
be okay. Which Corbin did. He told her how to get to his house,
promised to come down that weekend, ordered food to be delivered
to her. Elise, keeping Addison as something of a pet all that time we
were talking about what might have happened. Addison's messages
started to make less and less sense as she got sicker, delirious. It was
after Wyatt was shot—something Addison saw on the news—that
she wrote she finally wanted to go to the police.

That was something Elise couldn't stand for. Her efforts to contain the truth of what had gone on were successful up to that point,
more or less. Successful for her. Not so much for everyone else
involved. That was when Elise went out there.

Being right had never felt so bad.

Elise's iPad also revealed the extent of her deceit—almost a
dozen men taken in, sending her money via PayPal. Her beautifully
appointed home was the fruit of that tree, and another clue lying
in plain sight. But no one had wondered how the Hazletts afforded
all that on just Brock's modest salary.

When I'd lost sight of her that day, her pink coat against the
snow, she'd been almost to the top of the ridge. Far enough that she

might have managed to get away clean, or to lie down in the snow like she'd said, alone, at peace. But instead she came back. Not for me, but for someone. Brock? Addison? Her boys? Jordy? Just to cement her legacy as the most mysterious one?

I'd have to live with not knowing, and I hated it.

FORTY-ONE

Addison's father couldn't even look at me. But I was just there to make introductions, so I didn't especially care. "Julia is very smart about these things, so just follow her lead, okay?"

Addison nodded. She was still pale, still tired-looking, but moving on her own steam, at least. The conference room at Julia Raymund's office had been freshly dusted, I noticed, and I wondered who'd done it. "Do you want me to leave, or stay?"

"Stay," Addison said, as Julia said, "You can go."

Julia still hated me, but she'd grown on me a little: she'd managed to get my brother's remand lifted while I was in the hospital, so the gross little visitation booth was a thing of the past. The possession charges were still open-ended—the court system moved at a snail's pace for everyone—but Julia was talking to the prosecutor about a plea to a lesser charge, one that kept him out of jail.

Addison gave a small smile. "Please stay."

I took a seat in the corner and listened as she recounted her version of the events to her new lawyer. I knew most of it already, but hearing it again didn't make it any less shocking. Especially the part that took place in the office of Nightshade, the six minutes off-camera.

"I knew he was drunk," Addison was saying, "and it wasn't anything new, dealing with drunk jerks in there. He kept telling me,

'Hey, you look so familiar, don't I know you from somewhere?' But he wasn't the kind of guy who usually comes to the bar. When I took a break between sets, I thought he was gone—so I went over to get a drink but there he was. And he said he had to talk to me privately, that he was a cop, and if I didn't want to get in trouble I needed to cooperate. He said he'd been trying to find me for weeks. I just didn't know any better."

Julia nodded. "Did he threaten to arrest you?"

"It was, like, implied? He acted like Shane—my boss—he acted like Shane had already promised that I would. I don't know. It was confusing, and I'd had a few drinks already. So during my break we went into the office."

She wiped at her nose. "He said he knew who I was, and what I'd done, and that I had to pay him back. I legit had no idea what he was talking about. And that's what I told him, but it only made him angrier. He was so drunk—it was like, how with some people it's hard to tell, they seem sober one second, then totally out of it the next. Like that. He said I ought to be ashamed of myself, that he was going to make me pay. He lunged at me—tore my shirt, actually. That was when I ran out of the office. I should've gone into the bar, where there were people. But I went back to the dock, and he followed me. Grabbing at me, shouting. At one point he pulled me down. I told him to get off of me, but he just kept grabbing, his hands were all over my backside—he was saying, 'Where's your wallet? Give me your wallet.' It was terrifying."

Her father couldn't seem to look at her either; he just stared at the dusty calla lilies on the table, a silent ball of rage.

"I finally got up. I tried to get past him. But he grabbed me again. We were standing just above the loading dock, next to the fence. And this time, instead of trying to pull away, I pushed. I shoved him off of me as hard as I could, and he fell backward, the fence just kind of sagged in and he fell—and I looked down and saw him. He was clearly not—his head, there was so much blood. And I just panicked."

Addison paused here, breathing slowly. "In the morning, after I'd been at Andrew's, and I walked home, I called my voice mail—my phone was still in my locker at the club, but I thought maybe I could get Wyatt's phone number out of a message he'd left me or something." She rubbed her eyes. "And I had so many messages from him. He said the guy was dead, that Shane made him help—it was just awful. I wanted to get as far away from the whole thing as I could. I wasn't trying to kill the guy."

"No, of course not, honey."

"I just wanted him to stop grabbing me."

"Of course."

"Am I going to go to jail?"

"No," Julia said.

"Can you promise that I won't?"

"It's not ethical of me to promise, but you're not. You've been through something terrible. Anyone can see that."

Addison glanced over at me. "If it hadn't been for you—"

"Don't," I said. "Don't go down that path."

I'd been down my own version of it a lot lately. There wasn't anything good for anybody on it.

FORTY-TWO

On the anniversary of my father's death, I woke and stared at the ceiling for a long time. Over the past week it had warmed up, the snow that paralyzed most of Ohio melting and leaving everything a muddy grey. Then the rain started. It was still at it, big drops slanting sideways against my bedroom window. The day of his funeral had been like this, raw and damp. I'd read somewhere that Columbus had as many cloudy days as Seattle, and I believed it.

I didn't want to go to the cemetery. But no one ever wanted to go to a cemetery, and I'd probably gone to other places I wanted to go to even less. So I dressed in black cords and my new Sorel boots—the old ones weren't the same after a swim in a murky, frozen pond—and a black sweater under my raincoat.

I was still cold. There was nothing wrong with my body temperature. But there was a chill under my skin that I couldn't quite shake.

Reading Elise's note hadn't helped.

Neither had rereading it, which I did right now, then I crumpled up the note and threw it away, then fished it out of the trash. This was my morning ritual. The copy paper it was printed on had gone soft and worn from all the creasing and smoothing.

Eventually I'd throw it out for good.

But not yet. I felt like I owed her that much.

I made one stop before I headed over to Greenlawn. I'd decided a few days earlier that I should wait until I had a clear head before confronting Gail Spinnaker, and while I didn't exactly have that now, I did have a desire to rid my apartment of her thirty-odd pairs of leggings, and to yell at her a little.

"I was starting to get worried about you!" she said when she saw me, a false note of cheery concern in her voice. "I called you twice, and I didn't hear—"

I waved her away. "I just wanted to tell you that I'm taking some time off. A few weeks, maybe more. So I'm not going to be able to finish up the investigation before your big launch after all."

Gail's pink-glossed mouth was a flat line.

"I hope you didn't have anything riding on it," I went on. "For instance, I hope you didn't tell anyone it was already taken care of. Like a newspaper, for example."

Now her eyes narrowed. "That's—"

"Why couldn't you just have been honest?" I said. People elsewhere in the warehouse were beginning to notice our conversation, heads popping up to watch it unfold. "I don't know if you hired me just to give the illusion of being on top of it, or if you were just trying to get the faulty product off the shelves. But you should have told me. I still might've helped you. It kills me, that despite your whole women-supporting-women buzzword campaign, you still don't get that."

She put her hands on her hips. "I didn't do anything to you."

"You could have turned this into a real opportunity. So you made some styles with a material that's lower quality than the norm—why not notify your wholesalers, have them return it to you, and then donate it to a shelter? It might not be performance quality, but it would sure work for layers in this weather."

"What, and have a bunch of hobos as walking advertising? Do you know what that would do to brand perception? God," Gail said, almost laughing. "Do you not know anything about marketing?"

I'd been planning to dump the boxes of leggings on her doorstep on my way out, but I suddenly got a better idea of what to do with them. I turned and headed through the doors and said over my shoulder, "I'm happy to report that I don't."

There were six of us at Greenlawn, crowded under three umbrellas: my mother and Rafael under one, Tom and me under another, Andrew alone under the third, Matt standing half in the rain rather than cozy up to anyone else. My father's headstone was slick with rain. It said,

> *Detective Francis J. Weary*
> *Born December 11, 1957*
> *End of Watch February 8, 2015*
> *Blessed are the peacemakers, for they shall be called*
> *sons of God. Matthew 5:9.*

Generic and tacky at the same time; he would have hated it.

He would have hated the plastic American flag staked into the soft ground too, the silk tulip that had seen better days.

A bottle of whiskey would be more appropriate.

I made a mental note to come back with one at some point.

I made a mental note to come back.

My mother read a little bit from the Precious Moments bible and we said all the prayers we could remember and that was that.

"We ought to warm up with some coffee," my mother said, wiping her eyes. "Why don't we go to the old Clarmont. It's a Panera now. Get some coffee to warm right up. A little Weary family break-fast."

"Sure, yeah," Andrew said.

"I'm in," I said.

"I don't like their coffee," Matt said, but no one acknowledged him.

As we filed back to the five vehicles we'd arrived in, Tom said, "Maybe we can get together later on, for a drink?"

"Do you work today?"

He shook his head.

"You don't like Panera coffee either?"

"As you know, I like any and all coffee, even instant. But your mom said Weary family."

"Rafael's not family, but he's going, I mean, they drove together."

"Yeah, but he's, you know, they're together. A unit."

We looked at each other for a long time.

"Would you just come to breakfast already? The mini soufflés are going to be gone and I'm going to be mad, okay?"

Tom nodded, his warm brown eyes crinkling up into a smile. "I can do that."

"Good."

"Roxane."

"Yes?"

"Never mind."

"No, tell me."

He stood there for a moment, debating.

"Just tell me. I'm not up for deciphering any new mysteries just yet."

Tom smiled, lifted a hand to my shoulder, then to my cheek. "Eyelash," he said.

"Is that really what you were going to say?"

He shook his head, his fingers still brushing my face. "You said something the other day that I really didn't like. In the hospital."

I thought back to the hospital room. "What did I say?"

"Like hell you're dying alone," he whispered.

Then he pulled me into him, tight.

I'd forgotten what that was like, the solid safety of him.

No, I hadn't forgotten.

I leaned into his chest, a rush of relief in my blood. For the first time in a week, I wasn't shivering. Maybe longer. Maybe a lot longer.

"I know that later you're going to say this is just because today is a hard day, and it brings up a lot of memories. But Roxane, I've been thinking a lot about this, and not just lately. About how we never gave it a shot. You and me. Not really. You were always so quick to insist that it was just sex. But hey, we're pretty good together even aside from that, and I want to go on record as saying that I think we should try."

I didn't say anything.

"Of course, it might be the worst idea ever."

"It probably is."

"But isn't it worth finding out?"

My face was still pressed into his chest, my eyes closed. I said, "But all the reasons we never tried are still reasons. I don't want to get married or have kids and those things matter to you. That's what you said the other day. That you didn't want a relationship that wasn't going to go somewhere."

I felt him smile against my temple. "I know who you are. And maybe those things matter less than they used to."

"You'll change your mind."

"Why don't you let me worry about that?"

We stood in silence for a while that way. A car cruised past over the wet pavement and a voice said, "Get a room."

I pulled away and opened my eyes, saw my brother's Escape rolling past us. "Andrew, what are you doing?"

"I made a wrong turn, I'm still trying to get out of here."

He grinned at me and rolled up his window. The gloom of the last few weeks had disappeared from his eyes, which made me happy. Even though I was the one who'd absorbed some of the gloom on his behalf.

I said, "Hurry up before Matt gets the last of the soufflés."

"You're very concerned about these soufflés," Tom said.

"Hey, I like what I like."

I laced my fingers through his and we watched my brother's car disappear through the cemetery gates. "Is this all an elaborate way of saying you want me to be your emergency contact?"

Tom squeezed my hand. "That depends on how you answer."

I wasn't exactly in the frame of mind for making plans for the future, but when I'd been lying on that ice, it was Tom I thought about, and that had to count for something. Standing here now, I felt better. Not like everything was okay, but like maybe it would be. I leaned my head against his shoulder. "You know what my answer is."

ACKNOWLEDGMENTS

Thanks, as always, to my readers. You're why I do this. It means the world when someone tells me they love Roxane Weary, and I'm so fortunate that I get to keep telling her story. I'd especially like to mention my book club ladies—you're the best!

My writing career wouldn't be possible without my wonderful agent, Jill Marsal, who wasn't afraid to take me on as a client even though I'm really bad at phone calls. Huge thanks to her for all of her work on my behalf. I'd also like to thank Jerry Kalajian.

Daniela Rapp is my editor, and I can't thank her enough for believing in me as a writer and for always finding ways to make the story better. I'd also like to thank everyone at Minotaur Books, especially Sarah Schoof, Lauren Jablonski, and Alison Ziegler.

The team at Faber is wonderful as well—thanks to Angus Cargill, my editor for the UK edition of the book, who pointed out that two of the names I'd first chosen for characters herein were, respectively, the names of a prominent UK car service and a serial killer, and that I should probably change them. (I did.) I'd also like to thank Lauren Nicoll for her great work on publicity.

Thanks to Dana Kaye, Julia Borcherts, and Meredith Liepelt for their publicity efforts in the US.

I was lucky enough to be honored with a Shamus Award for Best First P.I. Novel in 2018 for my (and Roxane's) debut, *The Last Place*

You Look. Huge thanks to Private Eye Writers of America and everyone who makes the organization and the awards possible, especially Robert Randisi. So many thanks to the amazing crime fiction community for reading, reviewing, and recommending my work. I'd especially like to mention Eric Beetner, Matthew Turbeville, and Kristopher Zygorski for going out of their way to be supportive.

To the real Michael Dillman: thanks for letting me use your name, and I hope seeing it in print gives you a thrill.

To my Pitch Wars family: you set all of this in motion, and I can't thank you enough. Shout-out to Kellye Garrett, who's so talented and generous that it's not even fair.

Thanks to my dearest friends who put up with having a neurotic writer (and the related, even scarier creature, the neurotic writer on deadline) in their lives: Megan Brandstetter and Doreen Vanunu.

Thanks to Ernie Chiara for always being willing to read my work (and for acting like I'm way smarter than I am).

Thanks to my parents, Kevin and Eileen Lepionka, who have got to be seriously tired of hearing the "book talk" that I give at events by now, but who still come anyway. I love you.

Finally, thanks to my partner Joanna and our cats, Snapple and Spenser. The three of them are always here for me when I'm done writing about murder and need a dose of something sweet.

Turn the page for a sneak peek at
Kristen Lepionka's new novel

Once You Go This Far

Available July 2020

CHAPTER 1

I t happened on the first day that felt like autumn. Overnight the air turned crisp and the trees burnished into orange. It was a relief after another Midwestern summer that, emboldened by climate change, seemed determined to stick around until winter. The long, narrow parking lot behind the nature center at Highbanks was still mostly empty when I pulled in; there was a school bus at one end, a gaggle of kids in Catholic school uniforms in an unruly line beside it.

I was wearing a new jacket, a plum-colored canvas anorak that I'd been looking forward to wearing for weeks. If not for the coat, I probably would've been more pissed off that my brother was standing me up.

"Andrew Joseph Weary," I said into his voice mail. "It is nine forty-five in the morning and I am not in my bed right now, because of you. And yet, you're nowhere to be seen. Giving you five more minutes and then I'm leaving."

It wasn't like either of us to engage in traipsing about in nature. But Andrew was trying to turn over a new leaf. A week in jail will do that to a person, and his particular new leaf involved aspirations of hiking the Pacific Crest Trail. After he told me that, and after laughing my head off and asking who in the hell had left a copy of *Wild* in his apartment, I decided I should probably be supportive. Turning over a new leaf wasn't such a bad idea, not for anyone. So I'd agreed to join him in some practice hiking. Thus far, we'd actually managed to do it only once before.

Neither of us were morning people, new leaf or no.

I waited the five minutes and thought about leaving. But the crisp air convinced me otherwise. I was here already; why not take a walk anyway? I opened the car door just as a silver Chevrolet Equinox whipped into the spot next to me; I barely managed to close the door in time to avoid it getting ripped off.

The passenger window of the SUV went down. "Sorry, sorry," Rebecca Newsome said. I didn't know her as Rebecca Newsome at the time, just as a sixtyish woman with short, ashy-blond hair and a wide, thin-lipped smile. "I hate it when people do that." She got out of the car and I saw she wore dusty hiking boots and ripstop cargo pants. She opened the back door and a brown dog jumped out, small and fox-like with pointed ears that looked comically large for its head. "It's just so gosh darn beautiful out today that I couldn't wait!"

I waved her off. "No harm done," I said.

Still smiling, she tugged at an imaginary lapel. "Great coat. I like that color."

I wasn't prone to small talk with strangers either, but the weather had made me downright friendly.

I said, "I like the fact that it's cool enough out to wear it."

She grinned. The dog, antsy to get after something in the woods, strained at its woven leash. "Well, have a good one."

"You too." I gestured at my own car door. "And be careful."

Rebecca gave me a thumbs-up and set off briskly toward the woods.

That "be careful" came back to haunt me less than a half an hour later. After wandering through the shrieking middle schoolers in the nature center, I went out onto the observation platform and looked into the trees growing from the steep embankment. Somewhere out there, a shale bluff towered over the Olentangy.

But all I could see was sun-dappled gold and orange. The only sounds were foresty rustling noises and birds and the crunch of sneakers on the gravel trails and, somewhere far off, traffic.

Then I heard something that was distinctly unnatural.

A dusty scrambling, a startled gasp, followed by a series of snaps and the startled bark of a dog.

I pushed off the railing and started down the Ripple Rock Trail, calling out, "Hello? Everyone okay?"

I heard a voice but couldn't quite make it out.

I scanned the sloping path for the dog, the woman from the parking lot, or a sign of what had caused the noise.

"I don't think doggies are allowed on this trail," a voice said, lilting. I rounded a corner and finally saw someone, a woman in lime-green running gear farther down the path. She crouched before the fox-like dog, which hunkered just off the trail, tail swishing like a metronome. "What are you doing out here all by yourself?"

"It was with someone," I said.

The lady in green spun around to look at me, while the dog growled and let loose a tirade of barks that echoed through the trees around us.

"Did you see a woman? Silver hair, cargo pants?" I had to raise my voice to be heard over the dog's barking.

"No, I just came around the corner and saw this little dude. He seems terrified."

Over her shoulder, I saw a strange divot in the surface of the trail, an irregular-shaped hole where it looked like a rock had become dislodged.

"There," I said, pointing. I took a few steps closer while the dog continued to snarl.

The woman in green grabbed ahold of the leash, which had caught on a branch. I headed for the divot. Everything on either side of the path was orange and golden and brown. Off to the right, the ground sloped gently; to the left, a much sharper drop-off to a creek at least fifty feet below.

The left side was where I saw the bottom of a hiking boot, the hem of ripstop cargo pants, midway between the trail and the ravine below.

"Oh, shit," I said. "I see her down there." I stepped off the path and nearly slipped on a pile of dewy leaves.

"The rangers' station," the other woman said. "I'll go for help."

I gingerly stepped over a moss-covered log, bracing myself against a tree trunk studded with mushrooms. "Can you hear me?" I called.

The lady from the parking lot didn't make a sound. She didn't move, either. I picked my way down the steep embankment. Now I could see signs of her fall—a patch of earth freshly exposed when another log was bumped aside, a swatch of nylon caught on a sharp root.

I nearly lost my footing twice more before I reached her. She was on her stomach, neck twisted harshly, the side of her face planted in the soft ground. I felt for a pulse at her throat—faint. She was bleeding from a gash at the right temple and her palms were scratched up, mud caked under her fingernails. As I leaned over her, I saw that her eyes were open, staring into the dirt.

I didn't know what to do—she was at an angle, meaning the blood was rushing to her head, but I remembered something from a long-ago first-aid class about not moving someone with an injured neck. Fortunately, I heard shoes on the gravel above me. "Where are you?" the woman in green called.

"Down here. I'm down here. She's really hurt."

"Thank you, ma'am," a new voice said, "please stay on the trail." I looked up and saw a young woman in a park ranger's uniform coming down the steep hill. She spoke into a walkie-talkie in urgent tones. Her dark eyes swept across the scene and her expression hardened.

The beautiful quiet morning suddenly felt anything but.

They took her to St. Ann's. I followed in my car, unable to shake the sound of my own voice—*be careful*—from my head. Was I the last person who'd spoken to her before she fell? It seemed more than possible given how empty the trail had been, and it left me feeling responsible. If not for what had happened, then at least for making sure she wasn't alone now.

The woman in green had the same idea. She was waiting outside the emergency room doors, the dog's leash looped around a wrist while the creature on the other end backed itself into a bush and whined.

"I don't really know what I'm doing here," she said when she saw me. She held up the leash. "That ranger said something about calling animal control and, well, that would be terrible. You fall while hiking and your dog ends up in a shelter? But you can't take a dog into an emergency room, it turns out."

I scratched my wrist and nodded, thinking of Rebecca's open, blank eyes. I hoped the whereabouts of her dog were not beyond her concern.

"I'm Stacy," she added. She went to offer me a hand but found her right one wrapped in the leash. So she settled for a small wave.

I smiled, or tried to. My face felt weird. "Roxane."

"I can't believe a woman fell off a cliff right in front of me and all I noticed was her dog." Stacy shook her head. She had dark, ageless skin and hair pulled into a high, tight bun.

"I saw her in the parking lot earlier," I said. "That's the only reason I knew."

Before too long, a woman rushed in from the parking lot.

Pregnant—very—in a striped maxi dress and a denim jacket. Her face was pale and worried as she went through the sliding doors and up to the nurses' station.

Stacy and I stood outside in relative silence, neither of us sure what we were supposed to do next. Would anyone need to know what we hadn't seen and hadn't heard? The breeze, which had felt deliciously cool earlier, now just seemed damp and chilly.

Eventually, the pregnant woman came back out outside and walked over to Stacy and me as if seeing us for the first time. Her face was bloodless, a faint spray of freckles across her nose standing out like a splash of paint. Her hair was corn silk, damp and frizzy at the temples as if she'd just stepped out of a shower. She had a tiny golden cross on a whisper-thin chain around her neck. "They said you two were—oh, God," she muttered, noticing the cowering dog. She reached out for the leash; the dog yipped defensively and moved farther back into the bushes. The woman flinched. "What happened? Did you see what happened? Did she trip over him?"

"I heard it," I said, gently. "I heard her fall. But I didn't see anything. I'm sorry."

Stacy handed over the leash, which the pregnant woman then clutched so tightly her knuckles went white. "I'm Stacy, and this is Roxane."

"Maggie Holmer." She was looking at something behind us, or at nothing at all.

"Are you her daughter?"

A nod, curt.

"What's your mother's name?"

"Rebecca Newsome," Maggie said. "I can't believe this."

Stacy glanced at me, then tried a change of topic. "When are you due?"

Maggie didn't bite. "They took her for a, what's it called. A CT scan. I guess I'm just supposed to wait? How is a person just supposed to wait like this?"

I glanced down at her hands; her left sported a modest wedding set. "Is there someone we can call for you?" I said.

She pulled a phone out of her handbag and promptly dropped it on the concrete. Blotches of red had appeared now on her ashen cheeks. "My husband is on his way. He'll know what to do. I can't believe this."

After that, Stacy led her back inside the ER and I took a turn with the dog's leash. I was on the lookout for Maggie's husband, James, who was en route from Findlay, where he worked two days per week for some petroleum company. I hoped the dog would like him better than it seemed to like me. While it low-key growled from its place under the bushes, I scrolled through my phone and read a series of apology texts from Andrew about standing me up. It wasn't that big of a deal, but I wasn't in the mood to reassure him.

James Holmer was bookish and flushed, dressed in a brown Carhartt jacket over a burgundy polo shirt and khakis. I knew who he was from the way he rushed past me, then noticed the dog snarling from the bushes and turned back. I said, "James?"

He stopped and stared at me from behind his frameless glasses. "Where's Maggie?"

"She's inside."

He didn't ask me who I was, just proceeded into the emergency room.

I sat for a while on a concrete bench. Eventually a Delaware County sheriff's deputy approached the door and we had a rather perfunctory conversation about what had happened. Then he went inside, and a few beats later James Holmer came back out. "You're still here."

I held up the leash.

"Thanks for watching him." He tugged on the leash and the dog came forward skittishly, whining now. "Let me put him in the car. Sorry you got stuck here—hopefully you were on your way out of the hospital, not in."

"No worries. I was actually at the park. I talked to your mother-in-law, briefly."

"Oh." He looked up at the grey-white sky over the lenses of his glasses. The dog strained against the leash, trying to retreat to the safety of the bushes, but James ignored it. "Wow. Did she say what happened?"

"No, this was before."

James nodded, his eyes drifting down to the dog. "Did you see what happened?"

"I didn't."

"I hope she didn't trip over him," James said, nodding at the dog. "He's always underfoot. I've tripped over him already once this week—she's been staying with us. Maggie's due date is tomorrow." His expression hardened, probably as he realized how the birth of his child would be, one way or another, affected by what had happened this morning. He cleared his throat. "Okay, well, thanks again, for your help."

"Of course." I found a business card in my wallet and gave it to him. "If you need to reach me for anything."

"Great. That's very kind."

He went off to one side of the parking lot, and I headed to the other.

I didn't hear anything else about it. I called the deputy twice, hoping for an update, but he didn't answer and he didn't return my messages either. I thought about trying the hospital, but I knew they wouldn't tell me anything.

Not knowing was hard for me. It always was. This was part of why I'd bailed on my plan of becoming a psychologist—I was too nosy, too hungry for the why. You can't act on people's problems as a psychologist, just talk. And talking had its place, but so did doing.

This time around, there was nothing to do. Nothing except wait out the deeply unpleasant poison ivy that developed on my hands and arms and try to move on.

About the Author

Coley & Co Photography

KRISTEN LEPIONKA grew up mostly in her local public library, where she could be found with a big stack of adult mysteries before she was out of middle school. Her writing has been selected for *Shotgun Honey*, *McSweeney's Internet Tendency*, *Grift Magazine*, and *Black Elephant*. She is also the editor of *Betty Fedora*, a journal that publishes feminist crime fiction. Kristen lives in Columbus, Ohio, with her partner and two cats.